———— ❧ ————

Born in Cannock, Staffordshire, in 1964, the fifth of seven children, Paul Tonks grew up in a typical working-class environment under the guidance of loving parents. Following secondary school education, Paul joined the army in 1980 at the age of sixteen. In November 2004, Paul retired from the forces following 24 years' service in the Parachute Regiment. During this time he served operationally in Northern Ireland, Kosovo, Iraq, Kuwait and Sierra Leone. The army gave Paul the chance to visibly experience the diverse cultures of the world having left the UK over 65 times during his career. This exposure to the world's diversity has helped foster an already active imagination with The Mapping of Markesh, *mainly being scripted in a bamboo hut in Africa during the final year of his military service. He now lives in Kent with his wife Maria and assorted menagerie.*

———— ❧ ————

THE MAPPING OF
MARKESH

THE MAPPING OF MARKESH

Paul Tonks

ATHENA PRESS
LONDON

THE MAPPING OF MARKESH
Copyright © Paul Tonks 2005

ISBN 1 84401 314 6

First Published 2005 by
ATHENA PRESS
Queen's House, 2 Holly Road
Twickenham TW1 4EG
United Kingdom

Printed for Athena Press

Prologue

They say there's a bit of the Devil in all of us, I suppose it keeps the balance in our everyday actions, but from experience it is fair to say that some people hold far more of the horned fellow's attributes than could be considered healthy. The Ajya-Na-Ku, certainly consisted of individuals who where of the worst sort, their ranks were full to overflow with thieves and murderers, and they supported highwaymen and other such scoundrels. They where, by their own accounting, a Society of Owls, skilled practitioners in the black arts, being able to blend with the night; and as such they appeared, enforced their will and disappeared in the thick of the darkest nights. However, to others they were the scourge of the Earth, who harboured only death, destruction and disorder.

The Hidden Continent, Markesh, was the last area on Earth to feel the grasp of civilisation. Slavery was prominent. Females, in general were treated as skivvies and lowlife. Children starved whilst the corrupt filled their bellies. Here, family, tribe, or clan were held in the highest regard, and to be born on the wrong side of the lines drawn in ancient times meant your life had little hope and prospects were dim. Wars had ravaged these lands for centuries whilst outsiders looked on with shielded eyes.

The Twelfth Age had seen an increased interest from external nations, for two reasons: firstly the continent was rich in resources, and secondly the Ajya-Na-Ku had begun to expand their sphere of influence. By the beginning of the Thirteenth Age, Broderland, the largest and most influential of the outside nations had sent a large expeditionary force to the ports of the Green River. Their order to gain a foothold in the Provinces surrounded by the Dragon Mountains, which in turn provided a gateway to this mysterious continent.

The force despatched to enact the bidding of the western nations consisted of a mixture of Dwarves, human and Protalien soldiers. They were ferried to Markesh aboard Elvin ships, and after a difficult battle their foothold was secure; but following two years of struggle they had advanced no farther than three miles inland. With supply lines strained, all efforts were channelled toward the security of the port, and local ceasefires were sought. That was over a century ago, and today the Port is still the only area of Markesh influenced by the outer world.

The death of various Leaders and ever-changing attitudes brought about a status quo regarding international involvement in the affairs of Markesh. After all, the Ajya-Na-Ku were no longer spilling from its borders, and the only know entrance to the continent was securely in western hands. The ports of Green River were well garrisoned, and most people cared little for the plight of those oppressed in Markesh.

In the year 1023 of the Thirteenth Age, a Protalien chieftain name Izacon III sent out a call for volunteers to undertake an expedition deep into Markesh. It was an expedition of discovery, for little if anything was known of this 'hidden continent' or of the intent of its inhabitants. The Ajya-Na-Ku had disappeared from the port areas some twenty years earlier and few individuals strayed outside the boundaries laid down during those besieged years. Yet rumours lead to fears regarding a new menace and tension in all quarters was rife.

So it was on the twelfth day in June 1023/13 that a small band of unlikely characters set out into the unknown in search of adventure, unaware of what they might find, but all filled with personal ideas, hopes and dreams. This journey would change them forever and their world would no longer be the same.

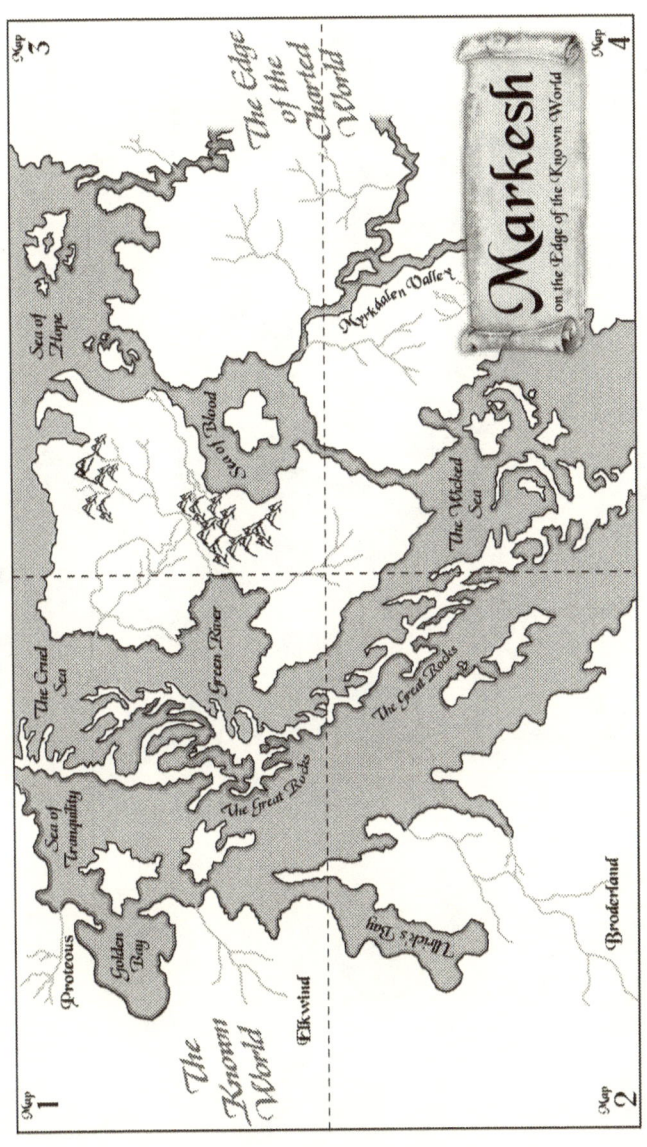

MAP OF MARKESH, AS DRAWN BY IDRON WILLOWSMATE, DURING
THE EXPEDITION. IT HAS HAD PLACE NAMES ADDED IN TYPE
SINCE IT WAS ORIGINALLY DRAFTED.

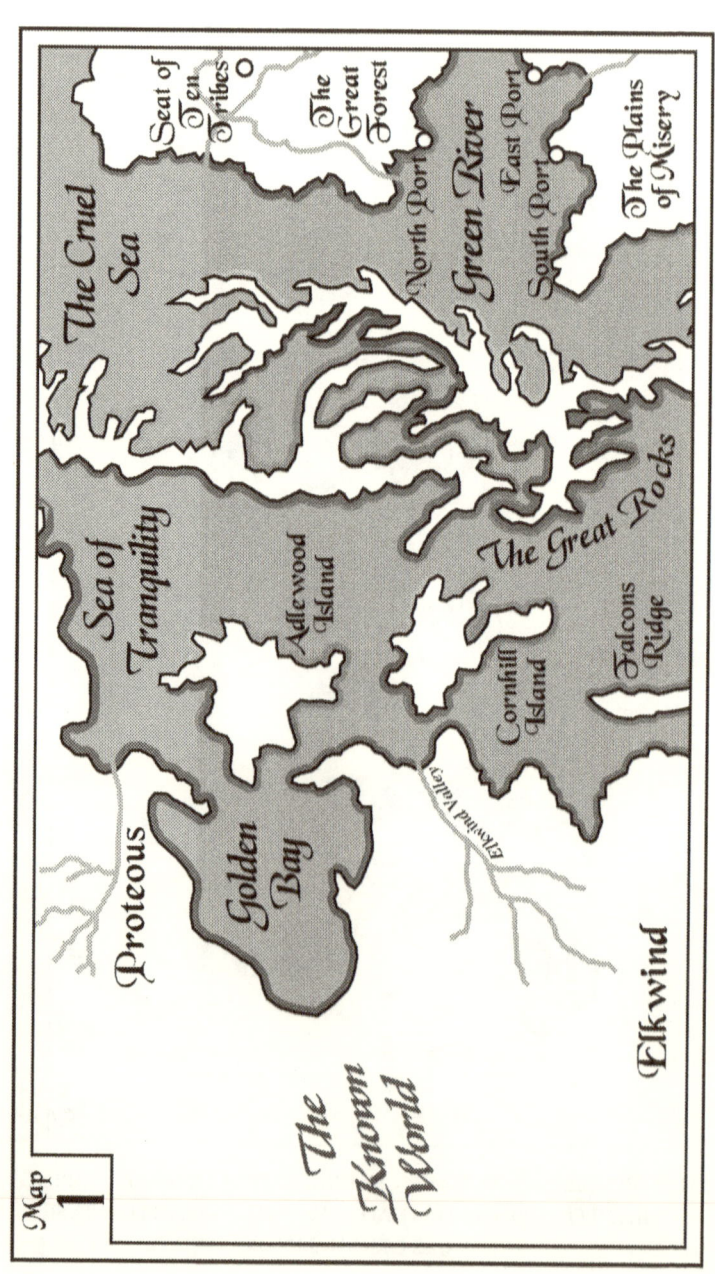

Map

1

The Known World

Proteous

Golden Bay

Sea of Tranquility

The Cruel Sea

Seat of Ten Tribes

The Great Forest

Green River

East Port

South Port

North Port

The Plains of Misery

The Great Rocks

Adlewood Island

Cornhill Island

Falcons Ridge

Elkwind Valley

Elkwind

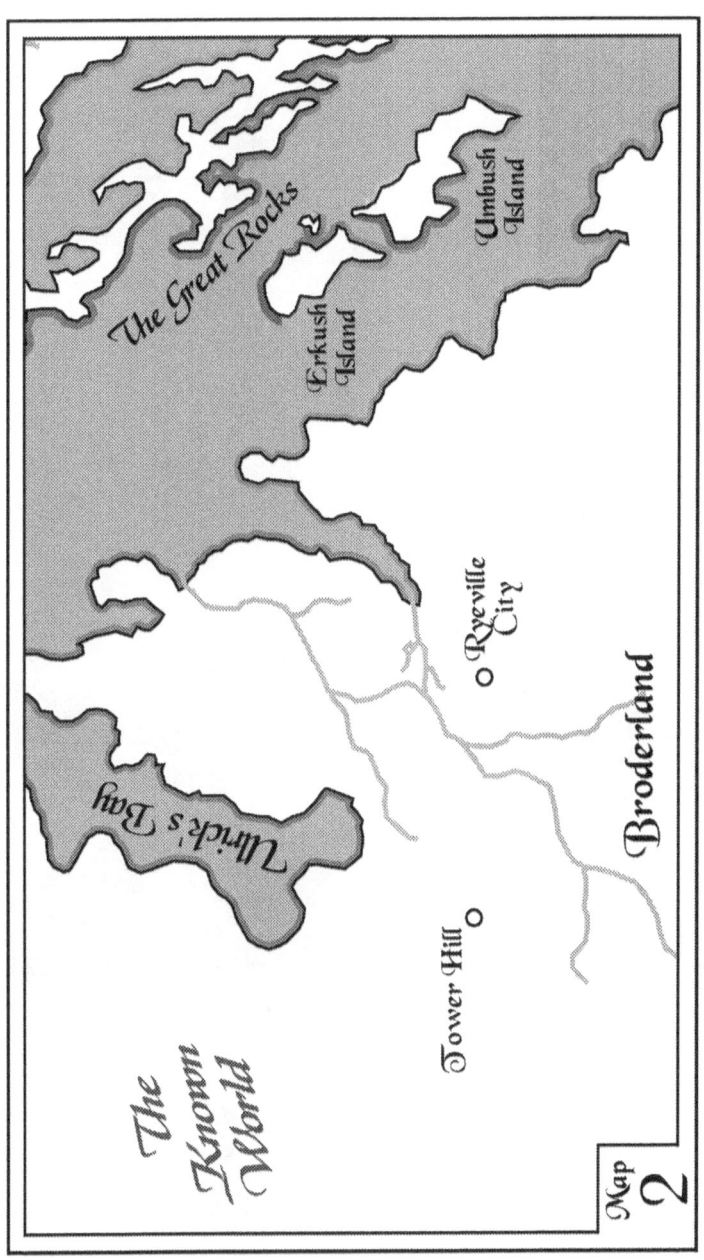

The Known World

Ulrick's Bay

The Great Rocks

Erkush Island

Umbush Island

Tower Hill

Ryeville City

Broderland

Map 2

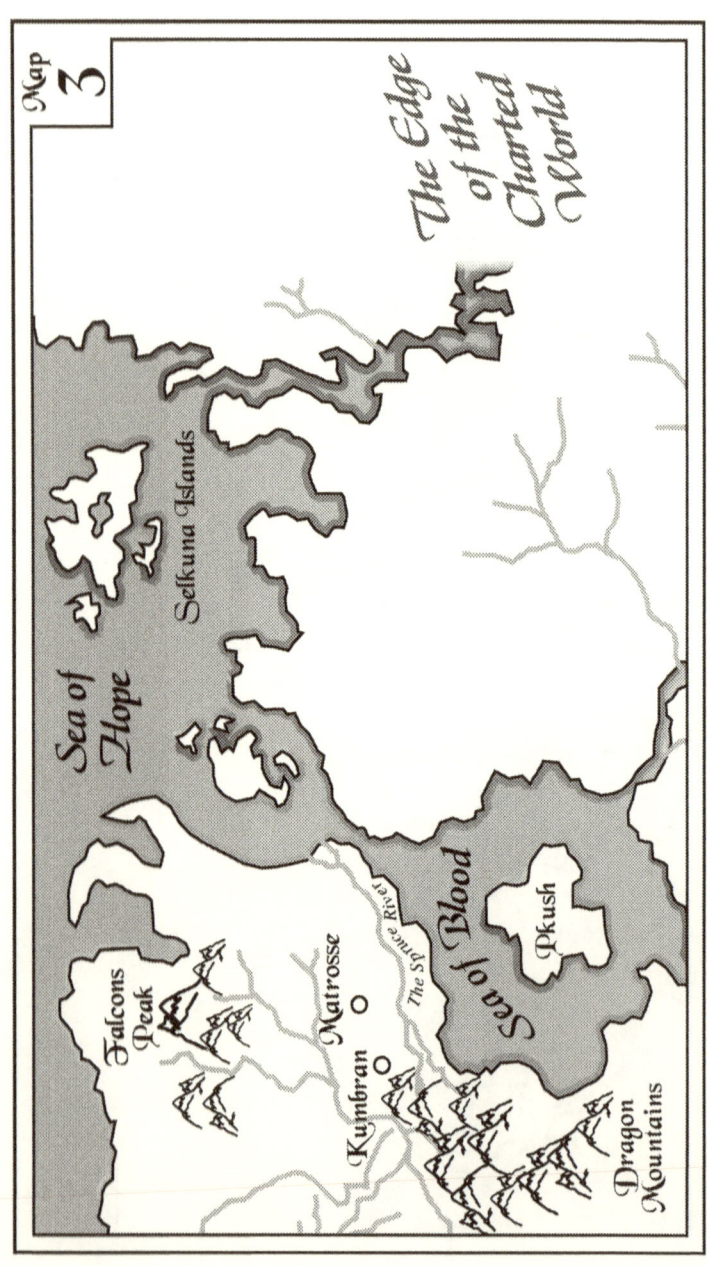

Map 3

The Edge of the Charted World

Sea of Hope

Selkuna Islands

Sea of Blood

Falcons Peak

Matrosse

Kymbran

The Spitice River

Pkush

Dragon Mountains

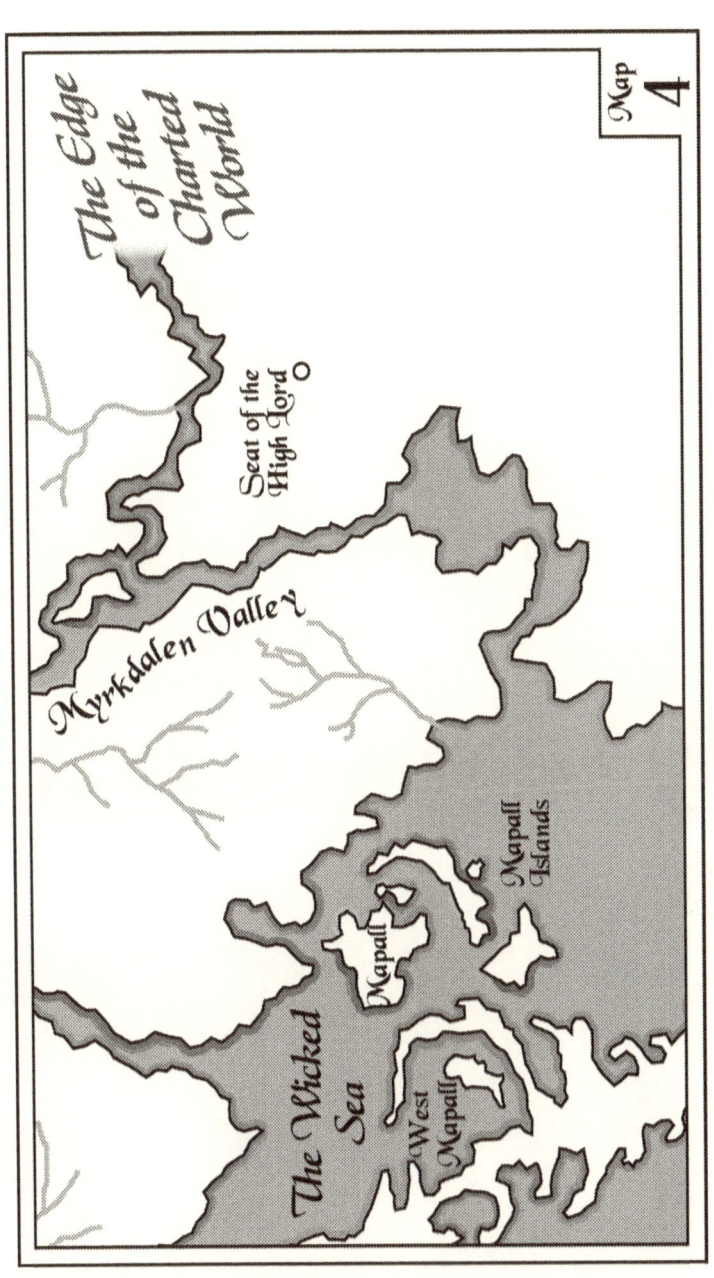

The Edge of the Charted World

Seat of the High Lord ○

Myrkdalen Valley

Mapall

Mapall Islands

West Mapall

The Wicked Sea

Map 4

Gathering Steam

Idron sat on his small pack awaiting the arrival of his new companions. His short dagger stuck uncomfortably in his side; this irritated him, for he was a stranger to the carriage of weaponry. He was of mixed blood – half elf, on his mother's side, and Protalien on his father's side. This uncommon mix had been shunned during the time of his conception, but times had changed – as had attitudes – and most, but not all, accepted love's ignorance to the boundaries made by men.

The Protaliens were a race not dissimilar to Elves, though they tended to be broader, slightly taller and less concerned with the enchantments of the Elvin folk. The Elves however found enchantment everywhere, especially in the very nature of things, and this made them at one with the Earth. Protaliens were a Warrior breed, skilled soldiers, trackers and woodsmen. They tended to be unsocial creatures, who kept their distance from one another, only coming together for important issues, such as fight days, mating and training. The most social of its institutions was its Army; a very large and very professional Army, the pride of its race and a dominating force in the wider world. Yet even its soldiers sought solitude outside their duties. They were a seemingly sad race if viewed from the outside, but still a proud people, who were loyal, brave and almost to a man, skilled soldiers.

Idron had had little contact with his father and had been nurtured by his Elvin mother. He had grown to love the finer things that life has to offer and loved all the fruits that nature provided. To the untrained eye, he appeared Protalien, slightly larger than an Elf, standing around five foot ten; he had broad shoulders on his lean body and wavy golden locks crowning his angular face, features that were recognisably quite different than those of the dark-haired Elves. These differences Had brought him unwanted attention as a child and he had been treated as an outcast by those of his own age group. However the elder Elves, loving all that lives, had treated him well and taught him all the Elvin ways and customs. Thanks to these teachings, Idron felt at one with nature, and seldom had call to use a weapon apart from the bow he had occasionally used to put food on his mother's table. The dagger, which now pained him so, was a gift from his uncle, Mithred, an experienced elder from his village, who was now in his 500th cycle and was rumoured to have been a combatant in the famed battle of Falcon Ridge during the Dwarf Wars. Idron had been only too pleased to accept this gift, but was still none too keen about its presence on his person.

He had been waiting all evening on the quayside of the Green River's Southern Port. Directed to meet his unknown companions there at midday sharp on the twelfth of June, he had not wished to be late. He was beginning to wish he'd caught an early morning ship and savoured the delights of his mother's home for a final night; his eagerness had, however, not been rewarded. The night was drawing in, and a fine drizzle was in the air. He had little in the way of shelter and knew nothing of the port's layout. He had hoped other travellers would have turned up early and that this night would be spent in the company of new friends; evidently this now seemed highly unlikely. The evening light faded fast, and with it came a drop in temperature accompanied by an unexpected sudden heavy downpour. The chain mail vest he wore now felt colder than ever and his thick woollen royal blue coat became his only comfort. He was just about to move when a voice cut through the blanket of rain.

"Ere, young sir! Are you completely daft, or what?'

He looked up to find a human soldier peering out from the parapet of a wooden weather-beaten lookout post on the quayside.

'Get yourself up the road, you silly sod! There's an inn not less than a quarter of a mile up yonder – it can be pricey, but not as costly as the doc's fee for a pneumonia cure.'

'Thank you, but I've been waiting for my friends,' Idron replied, feeling nothing short of stupid, for he knew the meet wasn't until tomorrow. But wanted to appear as though he had some purpose sitting in the cold and wet, which of course he did not.

'Well, fine friends you seem to keep! Company they certainly are not... However, should they appear I'll be certain to guide them in your direction, although we don't tend to get too many ships in after dark, so I think they've more than likely abandoned you!'

So replied the soldier, who had some experience in life and did not for one minute believe this young lad was waiting for anyone. He had seen many young adventurers in his time and knew the lonely, lost ones when he saw them.

Oblivious to the world, that one, he said to himself as Idron passed his post.

After a brisk walk, the din of the bawdy inn's occupants could be heard. The noise made Idron reluctant to enter, even though the warm yellow lights spilling from its coloured glass windows seemed so inviting. He stood at the door, rain dripping from his hood, his small but heavy pack weighing on his back. He had spent his days amid the Elves, and even there he had been an outsider. Now he became very hesitant. He was anxious to enter, but fearful of how he would be received halted his advance. He was young, knew nothing of the world, and although he wished to find his place in life he began to question whether he had made the right choice. 'He who hesitates is lost,' his uncle had told him, and these small words of wisdom rang true in Idron's mind as his decision to enter was unexpectedly made for him.

A jolt from behind suddenly thrust Idron through the inn's doors; losing his footing in the process, he arrived with a tumble in a most haphazardly fashion and found himself sprawled across the inn's entrance foyer under the watchful eye of the inn's patrons. There was a sudden silence as strange eyes took in the sight laid before them. The silence amplified Idron's embarrassment and was followed by an outburst of deep, roaring, belly-bursting laughter. He had indeed looked most comical, slipping and sliding through the door like some half-drowned calf. His attempts to find his footing were akin to the slapstick comedy found in the travelling fairs. The laughter continued and he felt blood rushing to his head as a veil of colour cloaked his cheeks.

'What the blasted! Oh, well, I never did see... Sorry there, my dear boy,' said a confused but apologetic voice from his rear.

'Mark you, what with the rain and the wind, I just didna see you lurkin' around the doorway. Not the best of places to hover, after all!'

The voice belonged to a burly Dwarf who was now peering down and dripping cold rain on the fallen lad. He was dressed in muddy well-worn boots that stopped short of his exposed knees; Close-fitting black woollen breeches could be seen below a brass breastplate that was only just visible under a long – for a Dwarf that is – distressed brown leather hooded coat.

'Come now, no hard feelings,' the Dwarf said as he aided the boy in regaining his composure. 'Now, let me buy you a drink, it's the least I can do! What do you say?' His rugged face was broken by a wide grin, showing that behind the weathered face and the long black, silver-tipped beard there dwelled an honest and compassionate soul.

Once the Dwarf had Idron back on his feet his face turned to thunder has he faced the laughing crowd, 'An' as for you miserable lot, you can just quit yer laughin, 'tis a fine way to treat strangers! You oughta be ashamed of yerselves... now get back to your own business, afore ye makes me angry!' He scowled angrily at the inn's chuckling customers, bringing a sudden solemn demeanour to his audience.

Compassionate maybe, but obviously no pushover; and apparently not a Dwarf to upset either, by the look of it, thought Idron.

'It's no problem, I shouldn't have stood there as long as I did. "He who hesitates..." my uncle says; but thanking you kindly, it would be a pleasure to keep your company on such a foul night, and a drink would be most welcome.' Idron thought one hesitation was enough for the night and could see that in this Dwarf's company he would at least be safe.

'Two large mugs of "Just one more" for this young fellow and me, my dear girl, and add it to my slate,' said the Dwarf. He had scrambled up on a large stool to gain the height required to peer over the bar. Once seated he turned to Idron and introduced himself.

'Benjamin's the name, Benjamin Brandsaw, although my friends call me Bsore, due, they say, to my short temper... and you'll be?'

'Idron. Pleased to meet you, I'm certain, and many thanks for the drink, but I'm not accustomed to "Just one more". Is that a Markesh drink?' Idron replied, trying to keep the rapport going.

'Certainly not!' Benjamin, snapped back. 'It's a Dwarven ale, so called because that's how the night progresses when you drink it. Very apt, I think.'

'Sorry, I didn't wish to offend, it's just that I've not ventured much out of Elkwind Valley, where red wine is the mainstay of those who drink,' replied a rather sheepish Idron; feeling as though he'd already turned sour a promising relationship.

'Take no heed of my manner, laddie, it's just my nature. I mean nothing by it, suppose that's why "Bsore" has stuck.' He muttered the last line as it was aimed more to himself than Idron. 'Elkwind Valley, hey? And I took you for a Protalien. What were you doing living amongst Elves?' The sour-faced Benjamin raised one of his wild bushy eyebrows.

Idron thought quickly and played safe, as he was uncertain of the expression crossing Benjamin's face. 'I was orphaned following a shipwreck on Elvin shores. The Elves kindly took me in and raised me as their own.' He remembered his uncle's stories of the Dwarf Wars, so he quickly added, 'Although I never really fitted in' – which in some sense was a truthful statement, even if the ship-wreck was a falsehood.

'Not surprised! I never did take to those damned Elves too kindly, don't trust them spiritual types, but Protaliens are a fine lot, if a little reserved. It's hard to believe they are akin to those Elves, though.' Benjamin shrugged as he finished his ale, 'Just one more – well no, another two, actually!' he called to the barmaid. 'Come on lad, drink up! Just one more, eh?'

So thus the night progressed. 'Just one more' continued in its normal vein and Idron and Benjamin drank long into the night. Many tales were told that night, mainly by Benjamin, who being the older, more experienced, traveller, had in all honesty more stories to tell. He told tales of unknown creatures, huge battles and treasures one could only dream of. Idron was fascinated and transfixed by every word; this pleased Benjamin and encouraged him to carry on with his elaborate story-telling. Idron, although enthusiastic, was unaccustomed to ale, and as the night turned to early morning he was more than worse for wear and his head had hit the bar long before Benjamin stopped his tale telling.

Idron was shaken at around 11 a.m. He felt sick, and the whole world spun violently around him. He had never experienced this before but did not like the feeling. Benjamin found the boy's predicament most amusing; he of course was a seasoned drinker and 'Just one more' ale had been his drink of choice for many a year. So last night's session had been merely an appetiser to him, which he thought made Idron's after-effects even funnier. Idron stood up gingerly, then staggered quickly to the window to despatch the contents of his stomach onto the unsuspecting street below.

'Careful, young fellow, you done want to upset them there soldiers down below, or they'll run you through before you get a chance to get to wherever it is your going to!'

Benjamin chuckled as Idron painfully deposited the unsettled ale.

'Mind you, Protaliens are not to be reckoned, with and it may be your saving grace, even if you've been softened by Elf folk; but looking at you won't show the truth, so people will more than like give you a wide berth – at first, anyways,' Benjamin continued, although in a somewhat sarcastic vein.

They were now in a two-bedded dormitory that Idron had no recollection of ever having set eyes on before. Benjamin had in fact only arrived in Green River the night before Idron and had only by chance managed to obtain a room in an ever increasingly busy inn, and as luck would have it for Idron, the only room available had been meant for two. Benjamin had carried his comatose companion there an hour or so before dawn and put him to bed. Although Dwarfs are relatively small in stature, they are in fact remarkably strong, hardy fellows, and would give most human-based races a run for their money. Benjamin was, above this one of the more exceptional Dwarfs and could give most of his own kind a hard time. He was an adventurer extraordinaire, a freebooter and a seasoned veteran. Idron had been fine company, a pleasing young fellow and a source of amusement, but Benjamin had more pressing engagements and time was running short.

'Well, my young fellow, dinna waste all that ale now, and take care, as I have to be getting on my way now; but the room's paid for and it's good until two, so no need to rush yourself. I'll bid you farewell now, it's been a pleasure!' With this Benjamin was out of the door and on his way.

Idron lay back on the bed, trying to collect his thoughts, when he suddenly remembered his engagement; he looked at his timepiece only to discover it was ten to twelve. He quickly grasped his belongings and found setting his uncoordinated feet in motion a great effort, but he was driven by an inner desire, a desire for adventure and to find his place in the world. He rushed down the cobbled streets, trying desperately to contain the contents of his stomach. His manner and rush drew many a strange glance, then his blurry eyes caught the outline of figures at the quayside in the place where they had been told to meet. He slid to a halt, dropped to his knees and was sick once again.

'Well, well, wasting more ale are ye?' came a familiar and welcome voice. 'So I take it you're the sixth man, then. Welcome aboard, Idron!'

Benjamin held out a hand. Idron was grateful that he'd made his first friend in this group of strangers, and the journey somehow now seemed less daunting than it had the day before.

Flanking Benjamin where four other adventurers, Idron quickly scanned their faces for their reaction to his graceless entrance, his second such first impression in less than a day. The gathering consisted of two Protaliens, whose expressions remained cold, as was to be expected of Protaliens. They were both very alike in appearance, standing around six foot in height, reasonable for there race; Idron's Elvin side belied his Protalien appearance, and although their faces neglected to show it, he immediately felt uncomfortable before them, as though he didn't quite measure up... in more ways than mere height.

The two were in fact brothers: Jethro and Tyler, of the Westerman Clan, both skilled in the art of tracking and of all issues military. They were dressed in typical Protalien combat gear, consisting of deeply reflective golden breastplates, with drab over capes gathered at the plates sides', these were used, when needed, to camouflage the splendour of their armour. They were crowned with ornate protective skullcaps, complete with nose and nape protectors. Jethro had a deep red short-cropped plume attached to the pinnacle of his cap, whilst Tyler sported a similar plume in royal blue. Both had neatly trimmed beards and golden plaited hair that protruded at the rear of their helmets. Their braids ended at around shoulder length and were held by a sharp metal comb, which in emergencies could be used as a weapon; and weaponry they had aplenty: traditional Jim-kas, mid-length double ended swords, with a pivotal handle joining the two blades, difficult to use yet deadly effective in the hands of a skilled practitioner. They sported a multitude of daggers about their person, and secured onto their small packs were small bows of Elvin design. Collapsible, three-bladed throwing spikes, called Shun-kus were stuffed into the right side of each man's calf-length boots. Traditionally, these Shun-kus were meant to dispatch a companion about to fall by the enemy's hand, as Protaliens, being such a proud military race believed that to fall to a less skilled opponent would be considered an insult.

To their right stood Torres Nearbrooke. Her sweet, playful grin immediately put Idron at ease, and he warmed to her thoroughly. Standing a little shorter than Idron, with jet black almost waist-length hair tied in a ponytail, she was crowned by an intricate headband made from silver coins that draped from the band. Her pale, almost angelic complexion contrasted with deep blue sparkling eyes that instantly captivated Idron's when they met with his own. He was instantly smitten by her enchanted presence. Deep red puckered lips framed perfectly shaped pure white teeth, she was indeed a beauty. Her enchantment was, however, only what should be expected of an Elvin maiden.

She was clad in suitable Elvin expeditionary clothing, flat-footed below knee-boots, black opaque body-hugging tights and a soft brown leather belt with small pouches attached, worn low in a way that accentuated her feminine hips, making her even more desirable. She also wore the finest, most intricate yet very feminine chain mail bodice. Tied about her shoulders a wild, lively green over cape fluttered in the light breeze. It had been made by finest tailors, and it seemed as though the leaves of trees had been woven into its fabric. She too only carried a dagger, although slightly longer and finer than Idron's own battle dagger.

'Glad tidings, oh Elf friend,' she sang out in pleasingly sweet tones, which only added to her appeal. 'I'm Torres, of the houses of River and Brooke.'

'Charmed, for sure,' returned Idron, for he truly had been. He could see the final party member behind Torres, another female, though of human origin, she was slightly shorter than Idron, dressed in a colourful patchwork tailed jacket that followed her contours well and covered her legs to mid-thigh, leaving only a small gap of flesh visible between the jacket and the top of her black boots. Her tanned face gave the impression of a seasoned traveller in her early thirties. Her hair was a shade of deep auburn and fairly short and was gathered at the rear; its length did not quite meet her shoulders, and a few stray locks fell along the right side of her elegant face as she nodded at Idron in acknowledgement of his glancing introduction. Benjamin introduced her as Erin. She seemed pleasant enough, but her light brown eyes hinted at a woman very much in control of her own destiny. The pommel of a slightly curved sabre protruded from her jacket – a fairly plain weapon made of men, and nowhere close to the craftsmanship observed in the Elvin lands.

To the rear of the party were three ornate bird cages, each housing a Pigeon Hawk, so called because they were used as messengers and observers working under the enchantment of Elves.

'Now then, we must be off,' said Torres. 'Oh! And Idron, would you kindly give me a hand with one of these cages?' she requested. 'They've had a long journey here and are keen to be free; I will let them loose once we exit the port.'

'No problem,' Idron replied, happy that he had been put straight to task by so beautiful a woman; and besides, it also aided the masking of his embarrassment over such an atrocious entrance.

'Fine birds... do they belong to you?' he inquired.

'Birds belong to no one, yet if asked nicely they are willing to work in unison with those who understand them,' she answered, and went on to explain how the Pigeon Hawks had always been inquisitive regarding the doings of the 'two-legged folk', as the birds referred to all those of the manlike races, and how long ago they had made friends with an Elvin maiden who had taken time to learn their tongue whilst helping an injured Hawk, but no ordinary Hawk, for he was King of Birds, and in his gratitude he vowed that the Hawks would follow the lead of the Pigeons and aid the two-legged folk whenever they were needed.

'These fine flighty characters are Stinger, Winger and Singer. Stinger works closely with myself, Winger works with Chantelle and Singer with Chevon.'

'Sorry, but who are Chantelle and Chevon?' Idron asked, with a somewhat puzzled expression on his face, having thought he had met everyone.

'Why, they're Elf maidens, of course. We will meet them anon,' came her answer.

Jethro then interrupted. 'Come quickly, the ferry will leave shortly and we shouldn't miss it; the others will be waiting and will no doubt be keen to get underway.'

'Where are we going?' Idron asked Torres.

'Have you been told naught?' she questioned, not waiting for an answer but continuing 'we have to reach the Northern Port by tomorrow's sunset, and it's a long journey for we have to go via the East Port due to the distance. The others came a week ago with the horses and provisions.'

'Others? Just how big is this expedition?' Idron further inquired.

'I'm not certain. I, like you, have yet to be fully put in the picture, but it is wise to send a reasonable sized force into Markesh, what with the Ajya-Na-Ku and all,' she replied as they made their way towards the ferry port.

The ferry was certainly a sight to see, it had none of the splendour of the Elvin ships that sailed in and out of the Green River ports. No, it was a mere platform of rough-cut planks, held together by twine and vine, although a song and a prayer might have been of more use. There were large gaps between the floorboards, and safety was obviously not of paramount importance. Around the wooden side rails were a motley crew of ferry workers, hired for brawn rather than brain. Most were naked from the waist up, and their lean bodies showed many cuts and scars gained during long hard days of labour.

The ferry was full to overflowing. Carts, horses, goats and people were huddled in close proximity, making the whole air stink in the most unpleasant of ways.

There was no seating, so everyone fought for floor space, with the centre of the ferry seeming the prime location, as it was farthest from the water. Once loading was complete, the makeshift wooden ramps were pulled aboard and the crew worked as one hauling on the short anchored rope; this aided the launch of the ferry into deeper waters. Once floating freely, it was guided by oar and rudder in the direction of the East Port.

It was shortly after one o'clock and it would be three hours at best before the first destination was reached. Idron once again sat on his pack. His dagger was still a discomfort, but now at least he had companions. His journey into the unknown had begun.

Horses and Riders

Bramley Barrowmaker was a master craftsman. He had made carts, carriages – and of course barrows – all his life. He was also a skilled horseman. He loved animals of every kind, no matter how large, small or insignificant they seemed to others; he actually preferred them to people and often commented that the people were the most destructive creatures on the planet. On his thirty-second birthday he had made his mind up to escape his craft for a more challenging lifestyle. He had read about Izacon the Third's call for volunteers willing to explore the hidden continent of Markesh, and immediately set off, on horseback, as was his wont, from his home town of Tower Hill, to Ryeville City 280 miles from his home. Broderland, the home of the human races, had become too stale for his liking and he wished to see more of the world before age overtook his ambitions.

On arriving in Ryeville he had sought out the Protalien Embassy and immediately applied to join the expedition. His mastery of horses secured his ticket, and within three months he found himself standing in the port of Caratush on Cornhill Island. Here he had been charged with the care of the animals that had been assigned to the expedition. Fine animals they were too, from the best stock that Proteous, the Protalien homeland, had to offer. The stock consisted mainly of horses although there were also two ponies, for the Dwarves, and four mules. He spent a month with the animals in the Caratush Garrison stables, and soon got to know each of the creatures quite well, noting all their little quirks and mood swings.

The horses were all named by letters as was the Protalien way, yet the letter had to be pronounced in the way that it made a quick name. The horses were Q (Que), a tall flamboyant and powerful chestnut mare. She had a heart of gold that was often overshadowed by her temperamental nature.

C (Cee), a dapple-grey gelding was a genuine character who

did everything to please, though Bramley considered him a novice ride, as he required little effort to back, hence he also lacked the thrill one gets from conquering a challenging mount.

P (Pee), was a pure white stallion who thought he ruled the roost and was so full of himself he often proved difficult to handle. A talented rider was needed to keep him in check hence Bramley took him as his own: the exact opposite to Cee so much more to Bramley's liking.

T (Tee) was a black mare who also loved herself, but was far easier to handle than Pee. B (Bee), a small horse just taller than a pony, was a palomino gelding, very talented and kindly.

D (Dee), was the dunce of the stable, not that she was bad, just a little slower and less talented in comparison to the other fine mounts. She was a dull brown colour and always looked as if she required grooming, being far too fond of rolling for her groom's liking, but a stalwart ride nonetheless, and a real genuine character.

G (Gee) was the youngest, probably the fastest and definitely the bravest amongst them, a young chestnut mare with a prominent blaze.

E (Eee) was the eldest, a dun-coloured horse with many scars from battles passed, a gelding and a warhorse.

V (Vee) had also been a warhorse, but being lighter had been a charger for a light cavalry unit. She was a grey mare who was both competent and reliable.

Finally there was U (Yew), a wild card, taken to escaping whenever possible, although not very far, and he always came back for lunch. Another chestnut, he was a gelding with comical white socks, 'for sneaking out in', as Bramley would say.

The horses had also quickly come to recognise Bramley, a man of average height with a lithe frame that hid his strength; his weathered and battered hands were strong and firm and the horses quickly gained respect for this fine man. They all sensed he was not someone to be crossed, but they could also see the great admiration he had for each and every one of them.

The ponies were both coloured ponies, strong and sturdy with a hardiness that came from years spent in the Tricon mountain ranges of Proteus. Grumpy was a stallion and always tried to live up to his name, often a little too well, whilst Stumpy was a little more carefree and kindly. The mules were called Hardfoot, Surefoot, Longfoot and Strongfoot. They all came from the same bloodline and all were dun-coloured and, well, mules – strong, temperamental and occasionally very stubborn; but they felt this to be their given right, so cared not what the horses, ponies or people thought.

Chantelle Levaux was another Elf half-breed, though unlike Idron she was half human, on her father's side. She was also an animal friend, chiefly a pigeon hawk handler, but also knowledgeable in all matters of an equine nature. She had been tasked to help Bramley with the control and delivery of the stock to the Northern Port of Green River. So she and Bramley had been working closely together for over a month and she had proved a superb stable hand. Her Elvin background meant she had knowledge of the animal tongues, so she was able to communicate with most of the known creatures of the world, this had been one of the key reasons she had been chosen along with Torres and Chevon, also Pigeon Hawk handlers. After all, the expedition had been organised and called for by Protaliens, who as you may recall are a proud military race; and they of course had planned the chemistry of the team that would venture into Markesh.

Their plan was to produce three teams of four. Each was to have a Protalien to act as tracker and double as leader, and fighter, should the need arise, or more likely, when the need arose. These Protaliens were Jethro, Tyler and Idron; they had failed to look into Idron's background, taking him at face value. Each team was also to have a communicator, hence the Pigeon Hawk handlers discussed earlier. The remaining six, two per team, were chosen for what they could offer the team as a whole. Bramley we have discussed already; a fine animal handler. Benjamin was chosen for his vast experience and ferocious fighting ability, which was legendary in certain parts of the world. The four other members we have yet to discuss, but their selection will become apparent as the story progresses.

The Protalien plan – and plan they did, and often – was to

have three self-reliant teams who could work independently from one another but come together to work as one when necessary. This way they could cover more ground and also avoid the possibility of any unforeseen event ending the expedition prematurely. This method of operating was typical Protalien doctrine, used by its military, a tried and tested formula; but tried and tested in Protalien formations. It had yet to be tried using a unit of mixed races, and with each race being prone to doing things their own way, this overlooked point would prove a tad interesting.

Their expedition brief was short and to the point. They were to enter Markesh, explore and map all the ground that they covered. No time limit was given, for Markesh's expanse was unknown. They would be provided with provisions but would be expected to find their own food and water once supplies became short, as re-supply would be nigh impossible. The hidden agenda behind this expedition was to gather information on the Ajya-Na-Ku, who had not been seen for some time, but information had slowly dripped through over the last year or so. Rumours were rife that some sinister plot was in the making and the Ajya-Na-Ku would suddenly resurface, deadlier than ever, although in reality no actual evidence was available. This unnerved the civilised nations, for knowledge is power, and their knowledge of the Ajya-Na-Ku was virtually non-existent. Most of the band of adventurers knew this was the real reason behind their task, yet their passion for adventure betrayed any fear of a group who had remained unseen for near on twenty years, a group that was fast becoming the bogeyman, and creeping into the realms of folklore and myth. Some of the group, however, were much older than others and knew only too well the reality of the Ajya-Na-Ku but they had their own reasons for wishing to find them.

It was now late afternoon on the thirteenth of June 1023/13, and Bramley's group were camped in a small glade just inside the boundary of the Northern Port's military sphere of influence. A small border post was just forward of their encampment and beyond it stretched the Great Forest, a sea of green that appeared to go on forever. The group had been here for a week now, preparing the livestock and gathering together their provisions. Today they were to be joined by the remainder of the team; this was good news for it indicated that they would soon be on their way.

Two members of the group had volunteered to greet the ferry and guide the new members to the encampment. Both were female, although exact opposites in appearance and manner. Elsbeth Gladron was a rounded and lively Dwarf, talented in the crafts; she was pleasant in nature and a motherly character. Her face was rounded and somewhat permanently flushed and bordered with brown hair that was pulled around to a tail that was plaited right down to her waistline, which incidentally, was rather generous. She wore simple clothes made of hardwearing drab materials. They consisted of an all-in-one gown that ended at the knee and was complemented by canvas, light-brown knee-length boots. Her weapon of choice was a small mallet-type mace with a head that was blunt at one end and pointed on the other; to look at her, you could imagine her beating a henpecked husband for falling under the influence of 'Just one more' and then nursing him back to health for the guilt she would undoubtedly feel from her actions.

The other woman was extremely fit in her appearance, pretty in face yet seemingly cold-hearted. She had perfect blonde hair that was just below shoulder length. Her face was chiselled with large pale almost aqua blue eyes and deep red lips set perfectly upon it. She was Protalien, and a warrior, hence she was clothed in scarlet with a golden breastplate and sandals. She also had a drab over-garment that could be used to conceal herself should the need arise. She was armed in the same fashion as Jethro and Tyler. She was also a skilled cartographer, and had been involved in the mapping of a large portion of Proteous.

Unexpectedly, the two women had built up an admiration for one another over this past week and were becoming close friends. They rode the 2 ¾ miles to the Ferry Port with Elsbeth riding Stumpy, and Meme, the Protalien, atop of Vee, the light charger. They took the horses and pony that had yet to be allocated riders with them, along with the mules, to help carry any belongings or supplies that the group may have brought.

As usual, or so a local told them, the ferry was not on time, so

Elsbeth and Meme sought temporary accommodation for the horses, sound preparation in the event the ferry failed to arrive. After a short enquiry they were directed to a local coach house that was able to provide an adequate pasture for all of the horses. With the animals secured, the two women decided to wander about the port until news of the ferry's approach was broadcast via the large brass bell in the watchtower. It was sounded out with three short rings each time a ferry came and four longer rings if a ship approached.

The port's streets were fairly narrow, as they had been built under siege and rather quickly. They were uneven and in ill repair due to the weight of traffic that crossed them on a daily basis. Many of the holes were filled with dark red water, so coloured by the soil of the area, which had a high bauxite content. People trod carefully as they moved through the streets, as one could never tell how deep the holes were. Passing carts brought verbal abuse to their drivers who were responsible for large splashes if they drove too fast. Life was hard enough and staying clean a difficult task, so careless drivers who cared for nothing but themselves were not at all popular.

The two friends found a large market place that sold many basic things such as fruit and vegetables but little of interest to such well-equipped travellers. They wondered how people managed to sell anything or make a profit, as virtually every stall sold the same selection of goods. Competition was obviously difficult and seemed to rely on stall positioning and luck more than anything else. These people, native to Markesh, were poor and struggling to survive; hence there were many beggars about the market area.

Some played of the sympathies of travellers by showing their crippled arms, legs or badly scarred skin. Others gave sob stories of how they could not work, or had a relative in dire need of medicine. It was hard to spot the genuine from the con men, and people either gave everything they possessed or became cold to their calling.

Elsbeth and Meme were approached by one such beggar. A large wiry man in his late fifties, he towered above the women, especially Elsbeth; after all, she was a Dwarf. The grime on his face and scraggly hair did little to conceal his wild staring eyes as he made his move.

'Give me something!' he demanded in a rather aggressive manner.

'We have naught to give,' replied Elsbeth.

'You must give me something!' he retorted, undeterred by Elsbeth's reply.

'Sorry, but we really have nothing we can spare,' Elsbeth answered, feeling somewhat guilty.

'No, you must give me – for God!' he shouted back.

'No!' butted in Meme.

'Give me for God, you must give me for God!' he continued, ignoring the refusals.

'No, we said we have nothing – now go away,' said an increasingly annoyed Meme.

The two women then turned and began to walk quickly in an attempt at defusing the situation. The beggar's ranting was beginning to draw the attention of others, and the two women were uncertain how the local populous would react.

'Give me for God, give me for God!' he pressed, following them and raising his voice even louder.

They increased their pace, yet he persisted: 'Give me, for God!' Then he aggressively grabbed Elsbeth's arm. 'You must give me, for God.'

Immediately Meme turned in an assertive manner, drawing her short dagger from her belt and pointing it at the towering figure's throat.

'All we have to give is the piercing comfort of cold steel, so unless you piss off, I'll gladly give it to you!'

Shocked, the man stepped back, but continued to blare out, 'You must give me for God!'

Meme had not expected this reaction, reckoning he would back off completely. She was now really contemplating running him through when suddenly Elsbeth started on her own offensive.

'Why don't you give *me* for God!' she shouted at the beggar, 'Go on – give me for God… I want something – what have you got? Give me for God!'

The beggar now looked really confused, she was using his lines, but he was the beggar and suddenly none of this made any sense to him. He began to freeze up and back away as the 4' 2" crazy Dwarf woman shouted, 'Give me for God, you piece of shit, you must give me!'

The beggar, now in a befuddled state, started to shy away. Seemingly from nowhere a small man with mangled legs supporting himself on crutches leaned towards Elsbeth and said, 'Don't you worry about him, he's quite crazy. Everyone around here knows it. We'll be certain to make sure he don't bother you no more.'

Elsbeth seemed fairly relieved, as a confrontation in a place like this could really turn nasty. Two women in an unknown land surrounded by so many locals... they had been lucky. Had it turned sour they could now be facing a mob, and no matter how capable they both might be as fighters, they would be no match for an angry crowd.

'Thanks,' she said to the small man, and really was grateful of his reassuring words.

'No problem,' he said. 'Now, if there's anything you need or wish me to do for you, be certain to ask. They call me "Sticks" on account of these here wooden things, but don't pay no pity towards me; I was born like this so have had to cope all my life. I know everyone and most there is to know, so just ask for me, okay?' With this he smiled and looked Elsbeth in the eye.

She was taken by his cheeky, confident manner; he was only the same height as her on account of his mangled legs, and appeared to be fairly young. But he was dreadfully skinny, and looking at him she felt instant pity.

'Again thanks, my poor lad, now take this for our trouble,' she said as she handed him two gold coins.

He grinned a cheeky grin, said 'Thanks,' and sped off at a remarkable speed for someone on crutches. It was hard to believe anyone could move two pieces of wood so fast.

'Well, you've just been had, my poor gullible Elsbeth,' Meme commented.

'What do you mean by that?' Elsbeth answered defensively.

'You see, the ranting guy only got our back up, put us on the defensive. Then along comes a poor soul with a few kind words playing the old "don't take pity on me" trick... add a smile and a grin... reaction, instant handout... many thanks... off like a highwayman before you can say Elsbeth! Mind you, you did look comical screaming at that huge man, he's probably never been bitten by someone so small.'

'Well, thank you! But I suppose the old charm did work, blast him, though he was a poor soul. I mean, those legs and all, you can't fake them... and better by guile, I suppose,' she answered with a knowing smile. 'Yep! And I suppose I must have looked quite comical.'

The two women looked at each other, a smile grew on each of their faces which quickly turned to chuckles and escalated to deep belly laughter.

'You know what?' asked Meme, still laughing in mid-sentence, 'they were probably together and have made fools of us both!' she concluded and laughed even louder.

'Would you really have given him your dagger?' Elsbeth inquired, still chuckling.

'No, but I would have loaned him the blade – if he was lucky, that is,' she replied, after which she continued to laugh.

The sound of three short bell rings sobered their mood, but only very slightly. The ferry was approaching so they departed the market area in a still jovial manner, laughing and chatting merrily about their close call, or close con, as Meme put it.

On reaching the dock Meme shouted out, 'Jethro, Tyler, over here!' for she knew them well, due to her having attended the same military academy as them both, although she had been a couple of years behind them and therefore their junior. She knew Tyler far better than Jethro and had long had a crush on him; Tyler felt the same passion in her presence, but their culture made any open display of affection difficult.

Jethro replied 'Ay,' in the military manner they were accustomed to using aboard ship. Benjamin found this a little weird, since he came from the 'every man for himself, be brave, do not falter and should one fall then so be it, it was meant to be' type of culture. The new arrivals grabbed their belongings and made their way toward Meme and Elsbeth.

'Come!' Meme ordered, although not so as to annoy. 'We need to be getting on, there is much to do and the ferry has made us all behind schedule.'

'Oh! There's a schedule, is there? So, someone is organising this little field trip after all!' Benjamin jested.

Meme offered no answer to his sarcastic question and simply made her way towards the enclosure where the horses were grazing. Jethro and Tyler looked at one another and shrugged their shoulders. They were used to a strict regime where you just did what you were told to, no questions asked, though you still carried those orders out honourably and to your best ability; they also said nothing.

Once at the field, Torres informed them that she would let the birds go, they could make their own way to the encampment, after all they had been cooped up too long and needed to spread their aching wings.

'Now, my fine flighty friends, Chevon and Chantelle are just under three and thirty soars from here, over by the north and short of the woods, make speed and light work of all distance; yet if it suits, gander at the woods as it may perhaps be of use in days to come; so fly without care and care take you well.' She spoke in the words of the birds and none but the birds understood the words she spoke, although the horses, the pony and mules understood enough to get the drift of the conversation.

So off they flew, first Stinger, then Winger and finally Singer. They moved with grace, speed and beauty and were certainly a magnificent sight, majestic raptors, masters of the sky, ever free in flight. All present were transfixed by their movements until they had climbed out of view, which for some came quicker than others, as human and Dwarf vision cannot compare to that of the Elves or the Protaliens.

With the birds out of view, the focus turned to the horses.

'Well,' declared Elsbeth, 'time to pick a ride, although Grumpy is obviously for you, my Dwarven friend; so apart from Stumpy and Vee, the rest are for the taking.'

'Well I never! Who does she think she is? Glad she's not on me!' said Que, although only Torres and Juran knew the true message behind her snorts.

'Pay no heed to the babblings of the misguided, they know no better; we work to one purpose, so let you and your friends decide who they wish to be with. However, I warn you now, not all can be pleased this day and we will ride,' Torres informed Que, although she did not use snorts but an ancient tongue, that was once common to all that lived within the Earth's influence. The horses understood its words but had forgotten how to form the words themselves, so had created their own tongue long ago.

So it was that Que chose Torres as her companion, and the others made their choices quick enough. Gee chose Tyler, as he seemed young and was Protalien, so probably brave, and they could no doubt charge, without fear, into the unknown together. Eee sided with Jethro; he was after all a warhorse, and he stuck with what he was comfortable a warrior of the race he had served all his life. Bee also wanted a Protalien, and being slightly smaller made for Idron. Erin was not Cee's type, she didn't seem warm enough; but as she was a kindly horse she accepted that choice was limited and was certain she could win the seemingly cold heart of this woman. She had considered Juran, who had arrived with Meme and Elsbeth; after all he was an Elf and would probably be able to converse with her, but there was something about him she was unsure of, she couldn't pinpoint the doubt she had, but she remained an animal of instinct and her instincts had always aided her in the past. Hence Yew was stuck with Juran; he didn't like him either, but he didn't really like anyone who climbed on his back, he only tolerated this lifestyle because it made for easy feeding and plenty of grooming; he did like that, and it was in all an easier life than living wild in the cold rugged hills or harsh windswept plains.

The pony, being Grumpy, wasn't interested in all the fuss; everything was a chore, so what did it matter what or who was on your back? 'Let's just get it over with' was his philosophy. The mules were all happy; this trip was easy, they could carry anything one cared to throw at them, so a few small packs and three empty cages were a doddle. Happy days... they all thought.

They travelled the short journey with ease and were soon around a table discussing the journey onward. They would head north, past the watchtower straight into the forest. They had considered leaving from the Eastern Port and heading up the Green River north but because this was an obvious route had decided against it. After all, from a military point of view it would no doubt be observed and considered a natural line of drift, the easiest way to move from A to B; so it was therefore the most likely place to encounter any hostiles. A move through the forest would be easier to conceal, and besides, they had to map the whole area, so it was logical to start at a cardinal point and work one's way round. North was as good a start as any, so north it was.

They were split into groups and decided to head out on diverging paths, using the Hawks to scout and pass messages. Just before the plans for the following day drew to a close, Stinger, Winger and Singer arrived; they spoke with Torres, after which she translated their findings to the others.

'They say the Forest is vast, none of its edges can be seen. It has dense foliage in its canopy, so will probably be quite dark at its floor. What's more, they spoke with the other birds; they say that the trees uproot themselves and move about, and that the ones that move have eyes – eyes that see all. They say it's quite unsafe in there. They warn that only Death will be there to greet us.'

All that is Green!

Following a hearty breakfast, the group packed their camp and made ready the animals. They moved as a complete group the short distance to the watchtower. They wished to speak with the soldiers on duty there before splitting into the three teams and heading off on separate routes.

The guards at the outpost were edgy but willing to speak.

'Not a good place, we've lost more men along this forest's edge than anywhere else in the Province,' reported the post's commander; the Province being the name the soldiers gave the foothold in Markesh.

'Lost to whom?' inquired Tyler. 'The Ajya-Na-Ku?' he added.

'No, we don't think it's them; at least not by any description I've ever been given of them. We aren't too certain who it is, I suppose they could be Ajya-Na-Ku, after all they do attack at night, and they steal off with the bodies; but by all I've heard from rumours, they say it seems as though the forest itself comes out at night, extending its border and causing chaos. It's a bad place to be, and all the soldiers are jittery. We can't wait to be relieved – this place belongs to the Devil. No one's safe!' it was obvious from the commander's nervousness that he believed each and every word he had said.

'Well, now what?' asked Chantelle. Being Elvin led her to the conclusion that the forest was indeed alive; enchantment, after all, came in many guises...

'We go in,' said Juran, rather businesslike in his manner, calm, focused and ready to meet whatever was ahead.

Juran was also an Elf. He had an extremely quiet manner and seemed very reserved yet strangely confident, as if he knew things others did not. He stood around five foot three and was of medium build; his hands were a notable feature, with his fingers being overly long for his frame. They were well manicured and looked as though they had never done a day's work in their owner's long life; as Elves tended to live for centuries. Some even seemed to be immortal, but mortal they indeed were, and could die or be killed as easily as you or I. Juran wore no armour and carried only a small knife, and one wondered how on earth he intended to defend himself, let alone engage in battle. However, he had managed to be selected for the journey so must have something to offer, although what none of the others yet knew. His obvious cool, collected manner showed the first glimmer they had seen of a capable individual. He wore a ragged cloak, which had seen much better days and obviously much wear, and its patched brown entirety reminded one of mud splashes. Beneath this in contrast he wore a crisp white blouse, a black silk cummerbund on which his knife was sheaved, and loose-fitting black trousers. The addition of his long black boots gave the impression of some swashbuckling freebooter, but how he kept these undergarments so clean puzzled everyone.

'So, in we go then!' exclaimed Benjamin. 'Fine by me.'

'Then so it is. It begins, and remember one and all we chose our own path, our fate cannot be blamed on anyone, so may the gods favour our plight and our cold steel serve us well,' commented Tyler, as though he had suddenly been elected the group's leader.

'Take care, one and all. We will meet soon, have faith that all will be well,' Elsbeth remarked in her usual motherly tones.

This is how the groups departed that historic day, the start of a task beyond the realms of what anyone expected when the decision had been made to mount such an expedition. No one really knew how big Markesh was, and most did not expect this said continent to be much more than a few small islands; after all they knew the boundaries of the earth, and the parts that were hidden couldn't be that big or they would already know about them. Ignorance and belief in a history that has been written and been taught for centuries make a difficult shell to break. History told of a small divide that had occurred during a gigantic earthquake, it had pushed great impassable rocks through the earth and divided the ocean, cutting off the tribe of Markesh, believed to be a small continent of three or four small islands making up the majority of the landmass and smaller islands dotted around. In a way they were quite right, but the scale was conservative to the extreme. The Ajya-Na-Ku were believed to be this lost tribe of Markesh, and most people believed all local peoples around Green River were related to them, so they would no doubt look virtually the same. Ignorance again assumed only one tribe or race had been cut off so long ago. An entrance to the continent had only appeared a few centuries ago when a section of the great rocks had collapsed due to erosion, though getting to this gap was still a difficult task and its shallow rock-filled waters had grounded many a ship. It seemed only the Elves now possessed the skill and knowledge of seamanship to successfully negotiate these waters. This problem had helped the world outside Markesh become a safer place, as the separate races began to need one another's aid if Markesh's resources were to be exploited.

Diplomatic efforts brought to a close the 200-year War between the Dwarves, humans and Elves with the final battle of Falcon Ridge ending in stalemate; and with the appearance of Ajya-Na-Ku raiding parties, diplomacy seemed the best option. In order to meet this new threat, nations formed alliances, much to the disgust of many of the combatants.

Now, centuries on, the western alliance was finally going to discover Markesh's true nature. It was an historic day indeed, though this day none of our travellers knew just how historic their efforts would become in the shaping of a new world order.

Tyler's group consisted of Meme, Juran and Chevon. They set off towards the north-east on their various mounts along with Hardfoot, the mule, and Chevon's Pigeon Hawk, Singer. The rest of the group had arrived earlier than Tyler, so they had already gotten to know each other well enough, and Meme had spoken very highly of Tyler. Tyler was also overjoyed to have Meme with him; at least he knew he could rely on another Protalien; and unbeknown to the others, Meme and himself had been something of an item for years. He also felt that he'd done fairly well with the other two team members, both being Elves. They, as mentioned earlier, are related to Protaliens, so he thought this far better than having to nursemaid humans or Dwarves. He, like everyone else, was uncertain about Juran's secretive manner but he couldn't have everything. Chevon, the chief communicator of the team, seemed reliable enough; she was a small, fragile-looking woman, but was every inch the tomboy. She held her own, worked hard and was very independent. She loved nature and bathed in all its glory and wonderment. Her boyish manner was betrayed by an extremely pretty face and dark silky hair that flowed gracefully about her shoulders. Her eyes stood out in the crowd: large, oriental and almost amber in colour making her quite stunning to behold. She preferred simple, no-fuss clothing, so her deep black, all-in-one trouser suit with sleeveless arms catered to her needs most adequately. Her small pack held a light leaf-green coat that could be donned during harsher weather, and her soft kidskin pixie-style boots completed her look. She was armed well, although she had shunned armour of any sort, but knives of all sizes and shapes she housed in some quite unexpected places; because 'you never could tell when you need one' – or so she often commented. Her backpack also had a small crossbow and bolts hung on the side, although her main weapon – pride and joy – was a light blue-bladed cutlass, with a slightly curved edge. Its length was engraved with ornate Elvin writing of ancient origin, a quite dead language now. It showed the blade had a deep-rooted history and had obviously been made by master craftsmen, the likes of whom had long since disappeared from the world. On her left arm was a thick leather gauntlet with open fingers, worn to allow Singer to perch and whisper in her ear when the need arose.

The two other teams, who we shall meet up with later, had headed due north and north-west. They had all agreed to ride out for three days with the Pigeon Hawks keeping an eye on each team's progress and relaying any important messages, such as a location where they would all meet up when the time arose. The birds were a key part of their plans, so were well looked after and admired by one and all. This made these special birds feel somewhat important and thus only too happy to serve.

The trek north-east began without hitch; the forest was initially quite sparse, so visibility and movement was good. The tales of walking trees preyed on their minds and they all felt as though they were being watched; this made them edgy and somewhat agitated. Thus from the outset tension was high. They were entering the unknown, armed with countless myth and legend and few facts about what they might encounter. Tyler always kept ahead of the team, using his skills as tracker, observer and general woodsman to his best ability; but even he had his limits, and to keep up sustained keenness of the senses was both stressful and tiring, no matter how proficient the individual. Chevon remained some distance behind Tyler, at his request, to prevent them both being caught by the unsuspected. Her Elvin eyesight aided her in keeping tabs on his location; she was also well positioned should any messages arrive or require sending, as she could stop the whole team's progress more easily than had she been at the rear. Behind Chevon rode Juran, with Hardfoot in tow, and Meme brought up the rear as only a soldier would, keeping an eye on the flanks and the way they had travelled in, just in case some mischievous character decided to follow them. The climate here was fairly temperate and at this time of year the air was fresh during daylight and chilled at night. Rain came often and mist formations crept in and out like prying fingers grasping the landscape from view.

It was late afternoon when the shape of the Forest began to change. They had made excellent progress by this time and had not yet taken a break, a point that was beginning to try Yew's patience. He had never liked anyone riding him, so he complained constantly. Vee had been on his back for some time, saying she'd marched for days without complaint and that a stint in the military would sort out his ill-disciplined attitude. This only made Yew complain further, saying she was weak in allowing any bi-pedal creature to control her to such a degree, and that they were meant to be free, not contained. Their argument continued for many miles. The two Elves in the party found it amusing and quite entertaining initially, but after a while it began to wear thin and tax their patience, so the only solution was to take a break. With a sudden change from open to dense forest, this seemed as good a time as any. Tyler agreed to a halt; he too was fatigued and needed to rest his eyes and ears, which had been overstrained and had brought about an aching throb in his head. The team halted and Meme brought forth a pot and small wood stove and began to boil water for a tea – a much-needed tea, I might add. Tyler, now on foot, although still very weary, wanted to check their position's security. So he and Juran decided to stretch their legs and take a look around, whilst Chevon brought water from the containers carried by Hardfoot, to water all the animals. She also used her silent horn to call Singer in for a chat and a rest.

Tyler and Juran found they were just short of a steep downward slope of thick undergrowth and both agreed it would be foolish to attempt its decent before the morning. They found a small brook to the east that cascaded refreshingly down the slope and would prove a good source for water replenishment before they continued north-east. They returned just in time for tea and broke the news of their plans to make camp for the night. No one voiced any objections, although Yew did sarcastically comment, 'Oh! And I was just getting into this lump-carrying exercise.'

A fire was lit, and the horses, (and of course the mule), were fed. The team set up their bedrolls around the fire and strung out a makeshift shelter that could be used should rain arrive. They then settled down to make the evening meal and jot down the details of the ground they had covered so as to aid the map-making they were tasked to complete. The light began to fade as though a shroud was being drawn above the canopy, and before long they were in complete darkness. They were lucky to have stopped were they had, for not less than two hundred metres onward the floor of the thicker undergrowth was as black and thick as oil; here they would have been unable to see their own hands even if poking themselves in the eye.

With night came noise, an almost deafening noise: screeches, clicks and croaks from all manner of creatures. It was akin to jungle noise, where every beast uses the night to go about its business, and for those who have not experienced the sound it could be most disconcerting. The noise was bad enough, but the bright eyes glowing all around really made the team nervous. It meant that rest came in fits and starts, and sleepers would quickly awaken to any sound, worried that their inability to remain awake would bring about some horrid event beyond their control.

The horses were also on edge, but not because of the noise; they were after all natural flight animals and they sensed something sinister in the air. The problem they had came from the fact this threat was all around, so no exit presented itself. Therefore they agreed to stay close and hold their ground, which for the time being was at least safe. Restless horses are unfortunately not rested horses, so a testing night would probably add to their fatigue and cause them problems in the morning.

Chevon decided to sit with her back to a tree looking outwards with her crossbow cocked and ready. She tried to sleep but was uncomfortable and on edge. The feeling became worse when she saw what appeared to be bushes rush through a gap, illuminated by the fire, to her left. She alerted the others who took her lead and sat up around the same trunk facing outwards and armed. Singer's keen eyes confirmed that trees and bushes with glowing eyes were indeed all about them. As yet they seemed to be making no effort to advance, but appeared content to observe the group. So they decided to bring the horses closer to the fire. This they did by call, as none of the horses was tethered; that was not their way. They then took it in turns to keep a vigilant watch throughout the night.

Jethro's group had had a more challenging first day, and with him were Benjamin, Erin and Torres. To begin with, he had only just met them all; he also had been given an old Dwarf on a small pony and a human woman who seemed full of her own importance. At least he had Torres, an Elf and a communicator, but he held little hope for his group. It must be said that this attitude was a fairly ignorant one and revealed the self-centred side of Protaliens, who if you remember are insular solitary creatures and thus have little in the way of people skills amongst their own breed, let alone others. This attitude would cause more problems than the fact they came from different races, and would prove the major flaw in Jethro's leadership ability and position.

The ground in their area became thicker much sooner than it had along Tyler's route. They were heading to the north-west and their progress had been slow. Jethro had blamed everything on his team, telling them what to do, how to do it and complaining every time things weren't done his way. This caused much unneeded friction, and Benjamin became very sore indeed. Erin became very defensive and Torres tried hard to bridge the expanding gap that was forming. In-house bickering only achieved one goal that day, it took their focus off the task in hand; hence tattered wits caused more mistakes to be made and they forgot the threat about them all too quickly. They too were being watched, but only the animals were aware of it, and although they tried to tell Torres, her mediating between argumentative companions shaded her vocational skills and she did not really get the message in the way she would have had she been focused on her skill.

The group were almost at blows when the darkness came, and it was upon them before they had a chance to prepare for it. This was their undoing. A mass of sudden unearthly screeches met them from the darkness, bushes rustled, mounts became scared, reared and bolted, branches struck bodies and a sudden thick mist enveloped them. They were caught with uncanny speed and had no time to even draw weapons. Each of them had been unhorsed in an instant, and the mist they now inhaled worked its poison on them with rapid efficiency. Only Que and Stinger escaped that night, Grumpy, Eee, Cee and Surefoot were lost along with their riders and Torres (Que having escaped).

Idron was also having a difficult day but for other reasons. His team – Bramley, Chantelle and Elsbeth – were all kind-hearted folk, so they all got on fine and there was much merriment in their group. Idron's problem was that he was by no means a tracker. He could head due north of course, but he could not easily choose the best route, so often had the team fighting through the undergrowth, which in this area of the forest was midway between the sparseness of the north-eastern area and the thickness of the north-west. This of course made the movement a chore, so breaks were frequent and their progression was much slower than that of the other teams. The horses could see Idron was no true Protalien, as they had spent their lives in their service and knew no Protalien would ever choose the routes Idron was now using. They were however grateful of the frequent breaks, and it was not until early afternoon when they had entered an area with thorny bushes. Bushes that did not take kindly to folk trying to walk through them, so in their defence delivered scratches and lashes to their assailants. At this point Idron's bad route selection became an issue.

The animals voiced their concerns to Chantelle, and suggested that she take the lead, as Tee had spent most of her days ridden by a tracker and could surely do a better job then Idron.

During their next break Chantelle had a quiet word with Idron, and they agreed that the suggestion was probably a good one. So from then on Chantelle, under Tee's guidance, took the lead and their passage became easier, even though the undergrowth had begun to close around them in an almost claustrophobic manner. They continued on for around another hour then came upon a large open area, an almost perfect circle that showed sign of fire damage but was beginning to be reclaimed by nature. Grasses and small shoots had begun to creep over the scorched earth, adding some rather pleasant patches to the glade. On closer investigation they found a ring of water about the opening: far too odd a shape to occur naturally, they thought, but maybe constructed in a hurry to lessen the spread of the fire. The water was stagnant and unfit for consumption, but they carried enough on the two mules, Longfoot and Strongfoot. Having no requirement to locate a suitable water source they decided that this would be an excellent location to set up camp for the night.

By the time the dark of night had encroached upon them they had settled in well. All had fed and they had built three fires in a triangular pattern to act as a perimeter for themselves and the animals. This had been Bramley's idea, as he reasoned it would help keep all that was wild away, as most wild things have a strong distaste for fire not fully understanding its make-up. They only knew that it burnt and destroyed what it touched, so was best avoided at all costs.

Their location also benefited them by way of natural light. There was no canopy, so the available ambient light illuminated them quite well and the fires showed a great deal of their surroundings. The noises – similar to those heard by Tyler's group – were also present, as were the glowing eyes. Yet the gap between them and the tree line made them seem all the less threatening, which in turn allowed a far more tranquil atmosphere about them, and their rest proved far more invigorating.

Idron had been sleeping for quite some time, though as sleep – good sleep – manages to speed up ones comprehension of time, he did not know it. However, with the progression of the night so too did his dreams progress, or digress if you wish, for the pleasant dreams of home and his valley faded and underwent a metamorphosis…

…only to be replaced by something far more sinister. A feeling of claustrophobia overtook him, as if unknown dark assailants were slowly crushing him. Panic, fear and dread surrounded him and he thought he could hear a woman scream in the distance. Sleep became uncomfortable and, wishing to escape its horror, his senses came to his rescue as he woke with a frightful start.

Focusing his eyes, with his heart pounding like some possessed drummer, he thought he could see bushes moving towards him. Then it dawned upon him that the perimeter of the opening was far closer than it had been when he had settled down to sleep. He sprung to his feet hollering, 'To arms, quickly, to arms! They are upon us, to arms!' At the same time he was kicking his companions to ensure his cries did not go unnoticed. To his right the horses were in one hell of a commotion, and he could see the two mules bucking and lashing out with their hooves at what appeared to be close undergrowth, but was undoubtedly the living trees they had heard tales of.

Idron had now found a bow and was despatching shaft after shaft toward the ring of trees and bushes. The others joined the fray, wielding swords and mallets. But the fight did not last, as the trees were surprised by their prey's sudden offensive. They had lost the element of surprise and were uncomfortable with no longer having the initiative; but what well and truly dislodged them was the surprising amount of fire that now rained down on them. Fireballs of all shapes and sizes joined with long flashing jets of flame. Leaves were burnt and the ground was once more scorched in that area.

Bramley, Chantelle and Elsbeth stood in their tracks, transfixed no longer by the trees but by a small Protalien named

Idron, who had discarded his bow and was now using his hands to draw flame from the three fires like a demon conductor controlling his fiery orchestra. He redirected these very flames in all directions, making the air a burning canvas, amid which he seemed most eerie, lit by flashes of orange flickering flames that illuminated his face then faded to black. Sparks and splintered wood were all around, zipping past at speed in reds, yellows and oranges – quite a firework display, yet a very effective one as the perimeter was quickly restored to its original boundary. Idron, it seemed, was full of surprises, not quite the defenceless kid they had spent the day with. Now they looked at him with different eyes, and with admiration, renewed respect and suspicion.

'Well, you kept that quiet,' remarked Bramley.

'Yes! A Protalien, harbouring Elvin secrets... Is there perhaps something you're not telling us, Idron?' asked an inquisitive Chantelle.

'No matter, you certainly saved our hides and we are eternally grateful, young sir,' butted in the ever-pleasant Elsbeth. She was grateful and cared not for an inquisition into Idron's obvious powers. After all they had all only just met and knew little of each other's strengths or weaknesses.

'Well, of course we're grateful, but Protaliens don't go in for that kind of thing. So what gives?' pressed Chantelle, eager to find out how he managed to perform Elvin magic.

'It's quite simple, really. I was raised in Elkwood valley by Elves and my mother happens to be an Elf, if you must know,' Idron replied.

'But you look...' Chantelle began, but was cut short mid-sentence by Idron.

'Like a Protalien? Well, yes, I suppose I get that from my father. You of all people should know all about half-breeds, Chantelle, after all...'

Chantelle continued, 'I am one, yes, but I make no secret of the fact. So why do you hide your heritage?'

'Merely for the expedition. I turned up to enlist and they seemed so happy to have found a Protalien tracker that I could not tell them the truth for fear of rejection,' Idron said defensively.

'But why tell us you were Protalien? You'd made it, you were on the expedition, you could've lead us into anything,' argued Chantelle. 'It's a good job Tee saw through your charade,' she added.

'I'm sorry, I'd told Benjamin I was Protalien because it was clear he thought that was what I was, and he didn't seem too fond of Elves having fought them in the Wars; so I decided to play along and stay on his good side… sorry,' said Idron, defending himself and sounding very apologetic with it.

'No harm done! We're all here, ain't we – thanks to Idron,' commented Elsbeth, in mediation.

'Yes, she's right. Early days, and no doubt we've all little secrets we'd rather not share, for our own good reasons,' said Bramley, wishing to calm the situation.

'Well, one lie leads to another and before you know it there's no trust, and deceit and betrayal follow,' concluded Chantelle. She was honest beyond belief and thought everyone should follow the same ethos. As far as she was concerned lies were what corrupted the world, and she would now keep a close eye on Idron, the Elf mage…

The welcome light of dawn broke through the gathering clouds and they decided to check the inside of their perimeter to see if any of their foes had been downed, for they wished to take a good look at these tree folk. However, as they moved about not a branch, splinter or leaf was evident – as if some ghostly form had been and gone. This thought did nothing to boost their confidence. Only Idron's magic gave them faith in their ability to deal with their foes, should they appear again, and they had no doubt that this would not be the last the saw of these strange creatures.

'Lookee here!' shouted Bramley. 'Drag marks, like spinney fingers have been scraped along the ground! It appears we may have hurt at least one of them, if this is anything to go by, and if they can be hurt…'

Chantelle completed the sentence before Bramley had a chance to.

'*They can be killed!*'

House of Elderwood

Chevon moved about her group, shaking them. She had taken the last watch and like the others was dreadfully tired. It had been a restless night but they had gotten through it unscathed. A light breakfast was prepared, though portions were fairly meagre to allow their rations to stretch as far as possible and thus conserve resources. A warm drink ignited their aching bodies and this helped bring about a renewed purpose in the preparations for the journey ahead. It was decided that they would press on at the hour's end. The forty or so minutes would allow the horses' stomachs to settle following their feed, making them easier to handle. In the meantime Tyler decided he would scout around and see if he could locate any tracks or note anything suspicious, following the night of tension.

Chevon spoke with Singer and they agreed the bird should, to air on the side of caution, act as an over watch for Tyler. Skyward she soared, circling the encampment; instantly she saw a sight which froze her heart. The dawn was new, and not more than a few leagues ahead she spotted a flock of maybe one hundred Owls heading east. These were no ordinary owls; no, they were Black Owls, the dread of the sky, evil birds in league with some demon king, or so it was said. Some believed they were not even real birds but evil souls, who took on this form to carry out the bidding of all the evil-doers that roam the earth. They had become renowned for spying and plotting and general connections to all that is ill in the world. The Ajya-Na-Ku, a Society of Owls, had obvious connections with them, as did a little known group, a group that no one was certain existed, the secretive Coeur-Vu-Do, said to be dealers in the black arts and protectors of the seat of the Demon King. These Owls had probably been responsible for some of the glowing eye's they had seen the previous night – but perhaps not all. Singer swooped back down with an increasing sense of urgency to inform Chantelle of her disturbing discovery. She would remain below the forest canopy and continue to look out for Tyler as he pressed forward. This would restrict her vision somewhat, but even so she could still see farther than her two-legged companions.

Tyler returned before the hour's end; he was far happier with the route that lay ahead, having discovered a narrow track leading toward a stream. The stream seemed to meander off in the direction they wished to travel, so would act as a good handrail to their journey. He was however disturbed by the news Singer had brought them regarding the Owls. Folklore held that the Ajya-Na-Ku and Coeur-Vu-Do had an all-seeing eye that held vigilance over the lands and coasts of Markesh, and if this were true, and these Owls did appear to be the mythical eye's true source, then, if spotted, the parties' encroachment into the forests of Markesh would soon become common knowledge and the undesirable keepers of the land would be upon them. This thought was far more daunting than trees with glowing eyes, no matter how eerie they might seem.

They set forth on their second leg unaware of the fate of the other teams, so could only assume all was well. The start of the day's journey was difficult, as they had to dismount often and lead the animals under the tangled overgrowth. It was hot, sweaty work, and after the little rest they had managed to grab the previous night their fatigue soon returned. Once at the stream's end they came upon a wide but fortunately shallow river. This they decided to cross, and once across they would take a break. The cold water felt good on the heated hooves of the animals, who were beginning to feel the strain of the close country; they preferred wide open spaces where they could see for miles, and gallop over soft meadows; this constant ducking and scratching from twig and vine was really not their idea of fun.

Once across the river, the Forest once again opened out, which would make movement both easier and faster. During their break, they had taken the opportunity to make some much welcomed coffee, and refilled their water containers. As soon these tasks had been completed and the coffee consumed they moved on. They were eager to try and spend as little time in the Forest as possible, and thus hopefully avoid the appearance of the Ajya-Na-Ku.

Mapping the land was now at the back of everyone's minds; they didn't take to this constant feeling of being watched, and they wished to make haste. Only a short distance had been travelled following their break when suddenly the knocking sound of hollow wooden pipes could be heard, manipulated into a rhythmic beat. Then out of nowhere sprang an unearthly group of moving trees and bushes. Instinctively, Gee charged forwards, meeting the ambushers in mid-flow. Now, a muscular horse, charging without fear towards you is a frightening sight. It will cause any man to falter, and fortunately the effect on the bushes was no different. Tyler, seated upon Gee, could do little but hold on and follow Gee's lead, and now firmly amongst the enemy he began slicing and slashing with all of his might. His anger was attuned with that of Gee's, and both seemed to have reached an almost berserk rage. Bushes and trees fell about them, although a few did manage to turn tail in a type of blustering panic that was most unfamiliar to them. The remainder of the team only caught up with Tyler as he put an end to the last living bush that lay beneath Gee's stomping frame.

'You okay?' asked Meme, annoyed that she had missed the sudden skirmish.

'They die like men, because they *are* men,' retorted Tyler, slightly out of breath. 'They're men – Green Men – the leaves, branches and all are merely used for camouflage, which seems to work far too well for my like.'

'Superstition, then,' Juran added. 'But look at them, green skin, large eyes not unlike those of cats… no wonder they prefer the night! But indeed they're men of a sort, but definitely not made of wood, eh!'

'That eases the mind. Nothing to fear from men! Those I can handle,' added Chevon.

'I bet you can, but I wouldn't spread it about if I were you,' joked Meme, a comment that gained her a knowing grin from Chevon, although she was somewhat flushed.

'What now then?' said Chevon.

'We follow them, right?' said Juran, expressing his view.

'Yes, we follow,' agreed Tyler. 'I'm certain one of those who escaped was badly wounded, and it shouldn't be difficult to pick up his trail, as long as we're quick.'

With this the group carried on immediately, but with an extra air of caution, stopping often to listen and look. Singer kept a keen eye on proceedings from above and spotted the movement of the wounded foe long before those below, and so guided them onto their target. Turning sharp right and crossing a small rise, a limping and slow-moving Green Man came into view just ahead of them. It was apparent he was loosing blood fast. A gaping wound was visible on his right thigh, and bright red oxygenated blood was spurting between the fingers he held over the wound in an attempt to stem the blood loss. It was clear that his efforts to move and to contain the bleeding would not work and he was in fact entering the last stages of his life. He knew they were upon him and that he had no hope of escape. He anticipated a sudden blow from his enemy so instantly dropped to the ground, his will to survive gone. Tyler reached him first and turned him over, then instinctively applied pressure to the wound.

'Why did you attack us?' he asked the Green Man, in a puzzled manner. 'What did we do to you?' he added.

'Youse, Ajya-Ku, youse burn our homes, youse kil we families, youse tack first,' replied the spluttering Green Man.

'What? We're not… They think we're Ajya-Na-Ku! We've got to put them right, or we'll have to fight our way right through the whole damn forest,' said Tyler, in a rather desperate and frustrated tone.

'We'll take him with us, find his village and explain who we are,' said an ever hopeful Chevon.

'He's not going to make it, he's already lost too much blood,' said Juran. 'But we must still go to his village, if we can find it, that is.'

'Oh! And you think they'll welcome us with open arms?' Meme answered in her normal sarcastic way.

'Of course not, we go in disguise, there's plenty of tree and bush garments back that way; I'm certain not all are drenched in blood. At least let me try alone, if it pleases you, but no matter what, we have to try,' came Juran's reply. He was confident in his own abilities, abilities the others knew nothing of, but now seemed as good a time as any to reveal himself to them.

There was and instant blinding flash of light whose brightness stunned the group. The light was quickly replaced by a cloud of purple and white dust that rose skyward as though some hidden spirit had been released. Now before them stood the figure of a Green Man, similar to those they had encountered earlier; complete with bushy clothing and wooden spear. It was of course Juran, though magically transformed.

'Hey, how'd you do that?' asked a baffled Meme.

'Sorcery, of course. I'm full of tricks, but only use them when the need is there, and it does seem the need as arrived, so stop gawking or I'll turn you into a ragwort!' Juran chuckled.

'So a wizard, is it?' said Tyler. 'I just knew something wasn't true with you! This explains a great deal, and may I add 'tis much more pleasing than what my mind's eye had envisioned.'

Wizards were few in the civilised world, but those conversant with such arts were respected by most folk. They were considered wise and all knowing, and if you failed to respect them they could always do you a nasty turn, so it was best to stay on their good side.

'Elves are not wizards, we're Mages. Human folk have wizards, different magic entirely... can often be black, you know, easily corrupted, not like Earth magic,' said Juran, suddenly transformed into a talkative soul, and not at all like the character he had been thus far. His secret was out so he felt this allowed him to relax his guard and become more himself.

'So,' he said 'I suppose I had better introduce myself properly this time. My name is Juran Garrand, born of the two ashes of Glade East and Pool West, long before the time of men, I was frozen as one with the craft of the Pristin Priests of old, I am knowledgeable in the incantations and charms of Belaphorus and keeper of the silver crest of Siselmere, here at your delight.'

They of course were flabbergasted and had no idea what he had just said, but a Mage amongst them could not be a bad thing; suddenly a renewed confidence came over them, and they agreed they should find the village of the Green Men.

In the middle of the forest Idron's group were also on the move; it was around midday when Stinger met up with Chantelle. She was initially pleased to see the bird heading toward her, but she in no way expected the news she received.

'Oh! God, no, no!' she squealed, and then suddenly, feeling faint, she tumbled from her mount like a cast stone.

The others rushed to her aid, unaware of the cause of her fall. She was out cold so they checked her over, and finding no evident injury sat her against a tree. A blanket was produced and wrapped around her whilst Elsbeth made a sweet hot drink, just in case she came around.

'I wonder what ever the matter could be,' stated Elsbeth. 'She's normally so bright and cheerful. Do you think she hit her head on one of them branches?'

'There don't seem to be any lumps or bumps,' said Idron in answer to Elsbeth's concern.

'I'd say that by the way Stinger's been flapping around he's brought news; and given both her reaction and his manner, it can only be assumed his messages are dire,' added Bramley. Although lacking the ability to speak with Stinger, he knew enough of various creatures to notice a distressed animal when he saw one.

After five minutes or so, Chantelle began to stir, and she merely kept repeating, 'Oh! Dear no, it can't be!' in an obvious state of shock. Try as they might, little more could be extracted from her for some time. She was obviously distraught and was having problems coming to terms with what she had heard. It wasn't because she was particularly close to any of Jethro's group, although she had known Torres for some time; it was mainly due to the fact they had only been on the road just over a day, and if this had happened to one of their teams already, what chance did any of them have...

'All gone, they're all gone, horses, pony, mule people, everyone!' she finally let out.

'Are you certain?' asked Idron.

'All gone,' she replied, still in shock.

'Yes, but did Stinger see them all? Were they dead, is he certain?' continued Idron, not wishing to believe that all had fallen.

'All gone, all fell, and only Stinger flew out... they poisoned them,' replied Chantelle.

'We must inform the others at once. Can Winger take the message onwards?' asked Elsbeth.

'Of course, we must inform everyone – if there's anyone else to inform. I mean, not everyone had magic as an ally, so what chance have they?' Chantelle's answer was gloomy, and she nodded to Stinger to speak to Winger, who in turn and once in the picture set off in search of Tyler's group.

Back with Tyler, Juran made certain all were dressed in an appropriate costume, complete with green skin, they looked every part the tree folk they had encountered; only their lack of knowledge would expose them now. They left Meme to guard the animals – much to her disgust; but she conceded that someone should stay back in case anything went wrong, and Chevon after all had a knowledge of communications which would probably be required when dealing with these odd green fellows.

The group made their way on foot in the direction their wounded foe had been travelling. He had, as Juran had foretold, not lasted long, but a quickly cast spell had helped ease his suffering and allowed his final thoughts to be of pleasant memories. It had been all they could do; not even Mages are allowed to mess with the nature of life and death, only the black arts dared delve into the type of shady practices required for such actions, and those practitioners who held council with the dark side suffered greatly for their use of such magic. The trio walked on for some time without a sign of anything that would help guide them to the village.

Juran even tried a slight magic spell: 'Oh! How hidden you are from our view, but all of a sudden we see you!' But this revealed naught, and he was most baffled. It was not until Chevon called Singer to her that once again the bird showed her worth. On re-entering the canopy, she had observed the result of Juran's spell. A ring of illuminated structures were housed below the canopy yet high amongst the tops of the great redwood trees. The village was now revealed, and Juran's magic had worked after all. The error had been with their failing to look more laterally and thus in the right direction. The spell had in fact illuminated the structures in bright reds and blues, and made what were normally drab houses glow brightly.

'Great, I hate heights,' said Chevon, 'I thought that's why we have Pigeon Hawks as friends. Too high is it not?'

'Then it looks as if it's time to experience the world as Singer sees it. But hey, it'll help you bond more, and that's bound to be a good thing, isn't it?' jested Juran.

'Really? I think not,' came Chantelle's crisp reply.

'Come, let us not fuss, let's just do it and put this problem to rest,' said Tyler, as he made his way past them to a vine and began to climb. The other two did not follow but looked at each other and giggled.

'Shall we?' asked Chevon.

'No, let him go for a while, it'll be entertaining and all, you'll see,' replied Juran.

Tyler had climbed around fifteen feet when he paused and looked back at his two companions below, who were chuckling at his efforts. 'Well, are you coming or just going to stay there enjoying yourselves?' he snapped, certain he was the butt of their joke.

'Well, of course we're going to join you!' laughed Juran.

'But we've decided to take the stairs over to the right, if that's okay by you,' added Chevon, trying not to laugh. The sight of a Protalien super-trooper, dressed as a bush, hugging a tree so close to the stairs was just too much for her to contain her amusement...

Tyler gazed over to the right, and glowing there was a flight of stairs that rose elegantly through the trees. He felt really stupid. How could such a well-trained observer miss a glowing staircase? It had to be fatigue, but he still felt damned stupid.

'Not too bright, are we?' taunted Chevon. 'All brawn, no brain? Like we should call you meathead from now on.'

'Okay, point taken, silly me,' Tyler replied, and he was actually grinning.

This threw Chevon. Protaliens were normally so serious. Tyler of course was mortified, but could see no point in trying to save his error, and to his own surprise he did feel as though it was a little funny. What most non-Protaliens failed to realise was that they only ever observed the military side of Proteus. Yes, the Protaliens were private and unsociable, but this did not mean they had no sense of humour, as Chevon and Juran should have already observed from Meme's mannerisms.

Juran and Chevon glanced at one another and smiled a knowing smile, but contained their laughs. 'I can see this magic of yours is going to be a blast,' said Chevon, prompted by the truth. For in all honesty the stairs had not been in view when Tyler began his ascent.

Juran had again used a spell, a whispered spell: 'Down below is all we know, but up above we have to go, so the route between you now must show.' These were his words and the concealed stairway was instantly set aglow for all to see.

The climb to the village was testing despite the stairs being well made, but the top was now in sight and they could clearly see a multitude of houses set amid the strong boughs of the thick redwood trees. The houses were a feat of engineering, wrapped closely to the trees, well concealed and practical. Walkways led from one structure to another, and at present the whole village appeared deserted. Upon gaining the landing, Tyler cautioned the small group.

'Something's afoot, it seems your lighted way has advertised our presence; perhaps the vines would have been more discrete, eh!'

'If we hadn't tumbled to our death first,' said Chevon, in Juran's defence.

'Stop, youse ther! Who is dis dat com ere?' shouted a hidden voice.

'You have naught to fear, we come as friends,' said Juran confidently.

'U, no fer Elderwood, were u fe?' said the voice.

'Underwood, we came from Underwood,' said Chevon, drawing looks from Juran and Tyler almost in unison, to which she shrugged her shoulders.

'Underwood, eh! Dat so? Wel, com in den, brothers,' said a more relaxed voice.

A small Green Man advanced toward them. He had the huge eyes they'd seen earlier, and they couldn't see how he differed from the others they had seen, apart from the fact he did not have his bushy garments on.

'Underwood, u say? No herd fe ther fer longer time. Wat brin u dis away?' said the man.

'We're looking for mercenaries that we hired, to fight the Ajya-Na-Ku. Have you seen them?' said Juran, trying to bluff to gain their confidence.

'Oh! Maybees. Wat dey look lik?' asked the man.

'Tall, short, fat, thin, pointed ears, rounded ears, bright clothes, dull clothes, males, females, horses, ponies, mules and Hawks. There, I think that about covers it. There's lots of them, you know,' came Juran's answer.

'Dem, yeh! Sin dem, taut dem Ajya-Ku,' said the man, looking as baffled as he possibly could, if a little confused at the same time.

'Are they okay, I mean, we need all the help we can gather against the Ajya-Na-Ku, after all,' added Juran.

'Wel don no, we din no, u see, tak em we did, sorries, sen call Ise wil, stop taks,' said the Green Man apologetically.

'Do no ting, tis trick, tis,' came another, more confident voice. 'Day twas sin, tak-in us, den chainin te look lik we, kil dem!'

A sudden rain of arrows flew towards them, accurate, poisoned-tipped and deadly; fortunately for Tyler and Chevon, they had a Mage in their midst.

'*Fear of flight, put you in plight!*' he shouted, and the shafts instantly dropped to the ground.

'We come in peace, do not anger us!' shouted Juran, looking rather dramatic and a little scary. The green folk were however none too bright, despite their building prowess, and sent forth more arrows, while foot soldiers lunged forward from all directions towards the trio. The arrows fell almost instantly as the spell was still cast:

'*From rock and stone, all things are thrown!*' screamed Juran, at which pieces of the houses began to rip from the very walls they formed, branches were torn from trees and rocks and stones scrambled from the earth to meet the glowing light of the houses. All these objects rained down on the Green Men as they attacked, sending them reeling. Some fell from the walkway to the forest floor, whilst others were crushed where they stood. A few managed to close with the group, and Tyler and Chevon were soon engaged in rather ferocious hand-to-hand fighting; no quarter was given on either side of the fight.

'For the last time, stand you down, we do not wish this fight!' yelled Juran, desperate not to unleash his powers any more than he had to on these simple but stubborn folk.

Again they ignored his warning, believing sheer numbers would pull them through. The Ajya-Na-Ku were not to be trusted, and trickery was in their nature after all. A fresh assault was mounted. Assailants swung forward on vines, while others rushed along walkways; there seemed no end to their number.

'So it is, then, I warned you!' squealed Juran. *'From cloud and water, to strike and slaughter!'*

With this the sky instantly turned black, hard torrents of rain fell about them – a powerful wind swayed the trees supporting the village. There was a sudden ear-piercing crack, followed by bright flashes as a melee of lightning bolts lashed out at every Green Man in view. Other bolts found rooftops, walls and branches; the more powerful ones toppled trees. It was an overwhelming onslaught. The Green Men were battered and torn, their assault faltered, surrender was their only course of action… but how do you surrender to lightning bolts? Juran had not wished it to come to this, and was quick to see the change in attitude of the enemy.

'Enough! *All that has been changed, let it not remain!*' he shouted in an authoritative voice, and with a flash the lightning was gone, the flying rocks and debris met with gravity and the blackened sky receded to allow light free passage once more.

'Fools, this did not have to be! We are not the Ajya-Na-Ku. Now send forth your messengers, so we may pass through this forest unhindered! Let what has occurred here be a warning to you all, and if peace must be fought for, then consider us the victors. Spread word where all you tree-folk dwell, and spread it fast; we have others in this forest, and if harm comes to them you shall all feel my wrath!' bellowed Juran. 'Let it end here, we only sought safe passage.'

With this the group departed the lofty quarter and returned to the forest floor, which was now littered with bodies, burnt tinder, rocks and fallen trees. They made their way back to where they had left Meme, but on arrival were dismayed by what they found.

'Quick! Heavens, no!' shouted Chevon, 'she's down.'

Before them lay Meme, an arrow shaft stuck in her left shoulder. She was conscious but in a bad way.

Chantelle had now fully recovered but was not her normal joyful self; she could not believe the news, and did not wish to continue onwards. The others tried to console her, but they too were shocked and felt pretty bad themselves. It was only mid-afternoon, and they could easily advance twenty or so miles before nightfall, so long as the route favoured them. They however agreed it would, given the circumstances, probably be best to find a place close by and settle down for the night. They wished to gather their thoughts and assess their options before committing to any hasty decisions. This was probably wise in the circumstances, so Bramley and Elsbeth left Idron to comfort Chantelle whilst they looked for a suitable and defendable position to set up camp.

'Idron, how did you know we were in danger last night?' enquired Chantelle, in a rather thoughtful voice.

'I didn't know, I was dreaming... I felt we were being closed in, then a woman screamed and I awoke, I seemed to know instantly that the trees were coming at us. Why?' responded Idron, not quite knowing why this topic was suddenly brought up.

'It was Torres,' said Chantelle.

'*What* was Torres?' replied a puzzled Idron.

'The woman who screamed – it was Torres. She was in danger from them also, she reached out to tell us only to discover we were with the same horror as they were. It was too late for her, but not for us,' Chantelle answered, looking somewhat distant, as if deep in her own world.

'The old Elvin way! I'd heard stories of some kind of remote viewing or projection, but thought they were mere myth,' continued Idron, hoping to bring her back from wherever she was drifting to.

'No, it is real, though uncommon. All handlers are taught its theory but few actually master it, Torres never had, until last night, when fear must have sparked her inner talents – but alas, only too late.' She paused. 'What is to become of us, Idron? This land feels so cruel. I sense it everywhere – the hatred, the oppression.'

'Hope, can you not feel hope? Not everything here can be evil, there must be hope!' exclaimed Idron, having some faith in the triumph of at least some little good.

'There's hope all right, but so little it saddens me. It's not natural, Idron, it's just not natural,' said Chantelle. She drew her knees to her chin, placed her arms around her legs and laid her head to rest in a self-comforting pose.

'Rest now, all will be well, you'll see!' Idron's voice was low, as he attempted to reassure Chantelle, though he too was uncertain of what lay ahead. He was however still determined to continue, and should the others wish to turn back he would find a way to carry on.

Elsbeth and Bramley had found a reasonable position for their night camp. It was not as splendid as the position the night before but it was well raised and could be easily defended. They were on their way back to Chantelle's position when out of the trees ahead of them came a small dark figure mounted on a chestnut mare.

'Que, it's Que!' shouted Bramley. 'But how, who?'

'Like I says, anytime you need something just call Sticks!' said the figure riding Que.

Elsbeth looked quite taken aback. What on earth was this crippled lad doing out in this forest? And how had he found Que – and come to think of it, them.

To Journey Onward

'Your friends should really be more careful,' said Sticks, as he drew nearer, bringing Que to a halt, 'Now, if you please, I could do with so help here.' He gestured that he wished to dismount his rather tall mare. Bramley moved to his support while Elsbeth collected the crutches that were secured to Que's saddle. Now firmly on the ground, Sticks began to tell his tale.

'I was at the Forest edge, not far from the Northern Port, when all of a sudden there's a crashing and stomping, quite a commotion, then out of the tree line bolts this fine mare – and quite relieved I was too! Such noises normally associate themselves with all manner of nasty thingy-jigs. So I sees her, and wondered where I recollected seeing her before. Then it came to me, and as you'd seen me right on our last meet I figured I'd return her to you. After all, to lose such a fine animal could cost you dearly. So here I is – and her she is!'

'But – the Forest and the folk that dwell here, did it not occur to you – the danger, alone and all?' queried Elsbeth, quite suspicious of such a simple story. She was aware that he may have conned her before, and was Jethro's group's demise maybe linked to this rogue in some way? She held many thoughts and questions that remained unanswered.

'Them tree fellows don't bother me. I mean, look at me, will you, they know I'm no threat. They have their own problems and fears, and they pass me by as though I'm not here. No, it's the Ajya-Na-Ku that they're afraid of, and each other too at times! Them tribes don't get on too well. You see, there's ten tribes, those to the north and those to the south; a fiery river divides them, as does ancestry. They have only one sacred place where all are equal, their seat between Oak and Birch beyond the river; though trouble is riding the coming rains, and will cause quarrels, I fear.' Sticks spoke intently, with a knowledge of things past and possibly ahead. He paused solemnly to consider his next words, then continued.

'This mare is brighter than most, she sees well and knows more than most. She probably holds the keys to questions, if one knows how to ask them.' He paused again, and sped off in the surprising manner mentioned much earlier to the flank of Que. 'She's a treasure, you should look after her.'

Both Elsbeth and Bramley found themselves transfixed by Que's frame as if some enchanting spell was holding them. Sticks was out of their sight but they could hear his low solemn words of warning: 'Do not hold about these lands, seek Oak and Birch as allies, Willow or Pine, beyond the fiery waters, and at its banks you must not linger, but make ye haste, take heed its waters. Now, journey on you must, but take care, take you care.'

His voice faded, and they broke from the captivation they had felt. They looked toward were Sticks stood, only to find him gone, vanished into the shadows of Maple and Ash; yet on the wind they heard a whispered farewell, 'Now journey on, journey on!'

'Who or what was that?' asked a rather dazed Bramley, trying to figure what had just happened.

'You know, I'm no longer certain. We thought him a beggar and a con man, yet he delivers, asking no reward, then disappears... weird! Come to think of it he's never seen Que before either, she was stabled when we met Sticks,' replied a bewildered Elsbeth. 'And did you feel unable to take your eyes off Que or was it just me? As if his words paralysed me far worse than his poor legs!'

'No, I felt it too, there's more to that fellow than meets the eye, I fear he's not quite what he seems; to move in such a style is unnatural for those who have legs, but he... well, I just don't know... though by his actions he proves himself a friend,' said Bramley, moving forward to pet Que. 'She's a beauty, and it's good to see someone else survived. Well done, girl. Now come, let's get back to the others. Perhaps Chantelle can shed some light.'

Meme's fate was discomforting; the wound, though small, was having an effect far exceeding its size. Time was running out for her; had they been a few minutes later she would surely have died. Juran cast a small spell to ease her pain, but as mentioned before he had no control or mastery over life or death. Indeed it was Chevon who stabilised the patient, although this was not achieved without a great deal of effort and discomfort for both of them. The arrow's shaft was deep and barbed, thus difficult to remove. Discovering the barbs had unfortunately not occurred before an initial extraction was attempted, and the excruciating pain sent Meme into deep shock even with Juran's comforting spell in action. Water had to be boiled and knives sterilised, this took time and Meme's condition was touch and go. Tyler was unable to watch; she was Protalien, a friend and his soulmate. He should do the right thing and send her to their gods with honour, not allow her to die here in this hopeless way... yet kill her he could not. Chevon gave them hope, and he just hoped it would be enough, for if he denied her an honourable death he would be unable to live with his conscience for as long as he lived.

Chevon was no surgeon, but he managed to cut cleanly around the wound. There would be a great deal of scarring, but better than death, she thought. Blood was everywhere and soon hands, wrists and clothes were as red as a butcher's coat, and the sight of such efforts was not a pleasant one. It was difficult to cut around the barbs, and each cut caused more problems to poor Meme's condition. After approximately twenty minutes – though it felt like hours – Chevon had managed to remove the vicious arrowhead. Then, using needle and sinew, she made her best effort at closing the wound. Meme was now unconscious due to the overwhelming pain; only the addition of a magic touch managed to prevent this agony from killing her. Chevon was exhausted, but was both stubborn and determined, and would not give up so long as a whisper of breath remained. She, like many of those skilled animal friends, knew many remedies and concoctions and there was enough at hand upon the forest floor to work its wonders. Using this Elvin medicine, she was able to quell the poison that had felled Meme.

'This will see you right, though I'm apprehensive as to whether this will completely cure whatever cocktail was used in the arrows tip,' Chevon cautioned, as she applied a poultice of herbs to the wound. 'I'll examine the head I removed and will find a remedy for whatever vile liquid was delivered to you. Don't worry, you'll be fine.'

She spoke to a completely comatose Meme, who was still hanging on to life, but barely. Chevon had done all she was able, but now time would be the only medicine at their disposal. She slumped to the ground and burst into tears. Emotion finally overcame her composure and now was her time for release. Tyler tried to comfort her but felt awkward doing so. He did not understand her anguish; she had after all battled on obstinately, a true warrior. He began to admire qualities he had failed to notice in her before; this too unsettled him, for after all she was an Elf.

'She's stable now, thanks to your effort, you've done us proud,' said Juran, also impressed by the perseverance Chevon had displayed. 'We will have to make camp for now, and see what the morning holds. But you need to rest. It's our time for work; you've done your bit and you should be proud. She'll pull through, you'll see.'

Que was a welcome sight to one and all, and her telling of events gave some relief to everyone. She told her version of events and Chantelle conveyed it to the others.

'Big stupid folk, they wouldn't listen! Argued all day, they did,' Que began.

Chantelle translated, 'The other group weren't getting on, arguing and all.'

'We kept telling them but wrapped up in themselves, they were,' continued Que.

'The horse tried to warn them, but without luck,' came Chantelle's interpretation.

'Then we were surrounded, but still they argued – dumb fools!' said Que.

'They were surrounded, but still missed the horses' warnings,' conveyed Chantelle, looking a little uncomfortable. She knew Que was agitated from the way she was relating the tale, but saw no reason to interpret word for word.

'Then, bam! On us quick smart they were. Riders fell instantly, it was everyone for themselves, I'd eyed an opening to the side and galloped as fast as I was able, and fortunately I was too fast for them and the mist. Oh! The mist, thick and heavy on the lungs, took my breath away, but thankfully I only inhaled a little, the others caught the brunt of it. Down they were, oh so quick, one and all! My heart was pounding and I was sweating profusely, so I hid amongst the shadows and watched. Those green folk came out and were prodding with sticks; most of those fallen reacted but seemed unable to move, paralysed by that terrible mist. Then they bound them and dragged them away, I tried to follow as best I could, but had to move slowly for fear of noise. My ears are keen, though, and I heard tell of them being taken to some "seat of the ten", but I did not know what they meant; but maybe it's the seat Sticks was talking of between Oak and Birch. I know they're alive, but not well, I'm certain, for mention was made of offerings and sacrifice, so we should prepare for the worst.' Que completed her version, showing how sharp she really was, a fine mare indeed, and with a tale that gave hope despite its sombre ending. Chantelle relayed to the others what Que had said almost word for word this time, so it need not be repeated here.

'Oh, my!' said Elsbeth. 'Winger's on route to Tyler, I fear she has the wrong message.'

'True, it may be too late to prevent that now, but Stinger's rested, so a new signal could quickly follow... but what to say?' Bramley said thoughtfully, as though some plan was being posed in his head. 'We should meet with them, and make for this seat, over the fiery river, between Oak and Birch, seems this Sticks fellow knows much more than we give him credit for.'

'The river,' said Idron, 'it's probably our best bet for meeting up with them; it'll also ease the Hawks' task, let's prey it's not too far.'

Winger had had great difficulty finding Tyler's group until the great flashes and bolts illuminated the previously calm atmosphere. Of course she was unaware that such a display could be conjured up by any of Tyler's company, so she flew with caution. Her vigilance was well rewarded, for the sudden outburst of magic had attracted prying eyes. Black Owls appeared in droves and were circling the light show, eager to catch a glimpse of whatever was causing such a ruckus; no doubt the Ajya-Na-Ku would be deeply concerned about such developments in their outer quarter. Winger remained concealed near the pinnacle of a giant redwood, watching and waiting for the Owls to depart.

She had a long wait. Even when the excitement was long past one or two of these savage birds remained watching and waiting. As darkness fell, she could see no way forward and knew that night would be on the side of these dreaded birds, so her only option was to sit it out and remain patient. Her message was filled with woe and she did not see how adding herself to the casualty list would aid their now dwindled number.

Under the towering redwoods, and still showing concern, Chevon waited beside Meme. The nursing had given her renewed focus and she had managed to subdue her emotions for now, though she desperately needed Meme to pull through, if for nothing more than her own peace of mind. Meme was now gripped by fever, which at least showed her body was fighting its invaders. The group were far more relaxed than they had been the previous night even given the poor condition of one of their members. The green folk were no longer a concern; after the licking they had received it seemed improbable that they would attempt to attack, but to err on the side of caution fires were lit at the camp's perimeter to illuminate the surrounding woodland. Eyes were still evident during the night, but they were few in number and they remained of little concern. The calming ambience around them led to a refreshing rest for the majority of the group, though Chevon could not bring herself to leave Meme's side, and fell in and out of desperately needed sleep throughout the night.

The morning brought about an improved diagnosis regarding Meme's condition. She had awoken but was still very weak. Chevon had also had chance to study the poison; she had a cure in mind, but needed apples to express the juice required to complete the medicine.

Singer was tasked to scout the forest in search of apples and if found and she was able, to bring some back. She took off, breaking the canopy with urgency; she knew the importance of her task but also the vast expanse of the forest. No sooner had she entered clear air than she was set upon by two of the devilishly wicked Black Owls. Her wings were cut by vicious talons as sharp as the finest blades; she was however faster and more agile than her muggers, and her ability to roll with the blows prevented serious damage from occurring. She dived back towards the tree line, knowing the confined spaces would give her a slight advantage against these much bigger birds. She dodged and ducked through branches and leaves, yet the two would not be shaken. Then suddenly she pirouetted in mid air and cut beneath them; they were slower to turn, but still pursued. Then a squawk sounded out from the rear and black feathers burst forth across the sky. A screaming Owl faltered and was seen careering to the floor, hitting limb and creeper as he fell.

Winger's patience had been rewarded; she had seen Singer's exit from the trees but was unable to warn her without fatal consequences. Yet the Owl's focus had given her an advantage, allowing a sneak attack with a sufficient delivery to turn the tables.

Singer turned rapidly to see what had happened and to confuse her pursuer, and was relieved by the sight of Winger closing with the Owl. The remaining Owl saw he was now outnumbered, so he tried to climb up and out of the forest; for once in the open he could soar higher than the two Hawks and call upon aid, as other Black Owls were bound to be in the neighbourhood. The Hawks could not allow his escape, so with wings beating for all their worth they closed the gap with a more determined purpose. Winger caught him first, grasping a foot. Scratching and kicking they began to tumble. Singer's talons caught the Owl at its nape, sinking in quickly and severing vital nerves: a perfect kill.

The Owl dropped, but Winger's foot was caught, and with wings flapping desperately made every effort to keep the two of them aloft. However, despite his courageous efforts the weight was too much to hold and they were soon plummeting to the ground with increasing speed. Singer noticing the problem and adopted a state of free fall in an effort to grasp the limp Owl and share the weight of Winger's burden. Not a moment too soon, Winger's struggling paid off. She was free of the icy grasp and managed to swoop upward as the carcass crashed against a rocky outcrop.

The birds returned to Tyler's company to inform them of

what had happened, and for Winger to deliver the terrible news of the attack, (although it was now much outdated). The group received the message rather grimly, as was to be expected. What with Meme's condition and an entire team dead, their prospects were looking dire. After a short respite both birds set off in search of apples.

Idron's party were now advancing north with increased vigour and purpose. They knew not how far ahead the river lay, nor even how many rivers lay in front of them. Stinger had been given clear orders to find Tyler's band; tell them to go north to the fiery or flaming river in order to link up with Idron; then move to free his brother's group, who were alive but under threat of sacrifice. Both those on foot and Stinger had set off at the same time and none of them knew the distances that would need covering before they once again joined company.

The trees about them were mainly maple, although oak, birch, willow and ash also dotted the area. The Great Forest had been in control of this area of Markesh for immeasurable years. It had started with the area know now as Elderwood over in the east, near the Green River, north. It had a wide variety of trees but was predominantly redwood, elm, apple and pear. Upon the arrival of man, the Forest began to, well, branch out, as it were. It grew to almost three times its original size, but each region favoured one type of tree over another, not by design but due to various reasons such as soil types and other such causes as nature chose to have. These areas grew, and with them their own tribes of man; and man being a simple creature, as he tends to be, he named his tribe after the most successful tree in his area, thus the tribes of the ten trees were born. There were of course more than ten types of tree in the Great Forest, but only ten that were found in vast numbers. The tribes thus became Ash to the south-west near the Northern Port; Elm to the south-east as far as the Green River, north, with Pear being on the east of the river. Apple was to the north of them dominating both banks in that area; Redwood bordered Apple, with Elm to its south and east but met with Maple on its west; Maple was surrounded by Redwood to its east, Elm to its south and Ash to its south and west. Its northern boundary met with the river of fire. Now across the river were Oak on the west, with Willow beyond its borders and Birch holding the east, with Pine beyond its northern border.

The men south of the river were the true woodsmen, born of the Elderwood. They were nocturnal and had green flesh and worshipped the great redwoods. North of the river were white folk, whose origins were with the plains that had once swept over the land. They lived by the day and had adapted to the forest through necessity; they worshipped the Mountain gods of Falcon's Peak over to the north-east of the forest.

The tribes had struggled against one another for as long as anyone could recall. After years of conflict alliances were formed many times, and they were often broken, but one alliance remained sacred. This alliance was centred on an area straddling the Oak and Birch border area, and it was known as the Seat of the Ten Tribes. A most magical place, where the differences between tribes meant nothing and were put aside; this was a place for sacrifice, worship and consultation. It was said to be the place where the first seed fell to the earth, and from it sprung life.

A ring of ten trees, one from each tribe, encircled an area on top of a great mound, with their branches joining and intertwining to form the roof of the great hall of the ten tribes. This was where the one seat was housed, the seat that would one day be held by the great leader who would unite the ten tribes; although the day when this would happen seemed far from reach at this time.

Idron's party pressed on to exhaustion that day, but the river did not reveal itself. No camp was made that night. They stopped amid an area covered with heather where they sprawled for a short break – or so was their intention; nevertheless, no sooner had they sat down than the power of the sandman set to rest any ambitions of continuing into the night, and each and every one of them slept like a newborn.

On hour before last light, Winger and Singer returned bearing two apples each, more than enough for Chevon's needs. They told of how they had found a whole area of apple trees straddling the Green River, north, and that from there the end of the forest could be seen, although still some way off. The river's flanks were fairly open and would make for a good route to the north-east. All agreed that the following day they would head towards the river, which was due east from their location, and then follow its course north. The loss of their companions had come as a blow, but it wasn't something they could do anything about, so they decided they had to continue. A cart had been acquired, salvaged from the area of their short battle at Elderwood, and it was prepared to transport the still injured Meme. She had improved as the day had progressed and her temperature was now only a little above what was considered normal. They prepared to spend their second night in this location – not something Tyler was comfortable with, but he checked his yearning to move and kept a watchful eye on their perimeter.

That night Tyler's keenness paid its dividends. He heard a twig crack just outside the perimeter's edge; it was only a small crack but to Tyler it may as well have been a tumbling tree. He took leave of his position and crept between the pillars of trees in search of their visitor. He stopped in his tracks as just ahead he caught sight of two small sharp eyes gazing at him. A low growl began to emanate from the direction of these eyes, and white pearly fangs were caught by the flickering light from the campfires. They seemed to drip with foaming saliva. The beast rose from the ground in a way that belied its form. It towered over Tyler and let out a rancid roar that sent a deathly chill through Tyler's entire body. He had never seen a beast of such magnitude; it was both wolf-like and somewhat bear-like, but had a strong hint of something far more sinister. He quickly threw his Shun-ku at the beast's frame, which caused it to let out a deafening bark unlike any noise he had heard previously. He stood his ground, spinning his weapon of choice, his Jim-ka. Its razor-sharp blades met with the beast's thick, leathery hide, causing it to cry out in further pain, and in retaliation it lashed out with its huge clawed paws – a powerful blow that sent Tyler reeling into the undergrowth.

The beast rushed toward him but he knew he was in no position to defend himself. Horror engulfed his body; he was helpless. Then, to his surprise, the beast leapt over him and disappeared into the undergrowth. He lay there winded for some time, thanking his gods that he had been spared. He knew not what he had just encountered and did not wish to see it again, but deep down he felt that he most probably would. It was dawn before he regained his senses completely and only then did he manage to pick himself up from where he had fallen; he felt a pain in his chest and was aware that he had most likely cracked a few ribs. He rejoined his sleeping companions and moved to Meme's side. Reaching out, he placed his hand upon hers. She stirred, and a smile drew over her face: a good sign, he thought, it more than made up for the pain his own body was feeling. Cheered, he sat at her feet and drifted into a deep sleep.

The pit-pat of rain woke Juran from a pleasant dream filled with fine red wine and succulent food, the dripping red refreshment held aloft by a beautiful handmaiden. This was transformed into a large redwood leaf, dripping heavy drops of a bitter rain into his waiting mouth thus destroying his image.

'Drat! I'm still here,' he grumbled. 'Well, not to worry,' he said, cheering himself almost instantly; for Mages are realists – if a magic-wielder can be such a thing! They tend to accept their lot quite easily and just get on with whatever the day holds in store.

'I wonder how our patient is this morning?' he whispered to himself, as though he was expecting an answer. 'Well, I hope,' he continued, as he meandered through the trees to Meme's position. He was quite pleased, although surprised to see Tyler at her feet like some obedient hound, looking out for his mistress, but became concerned when he observed a small pool of blood about his midriff. He shook Tyler to be certain the wound was not life-threatening. Tyler stirred and took some time to focus before he could speak to Juran. While he was collecting himself Juran woke the other members of the group and asked Chevon to take a look at Tyler's wound.

Now awake, Tyler told the tale of his strange encounter with the unknown beast – a story that unsettled them, for they had just overcome one bogeyman only to have it replaced by another. Juran said from the description it sounded as though Tyler had come across a were-creature of some sort, but like none he had ever seen himself. He thought it strange how the creature had not finished him off, and that perhaps fear had made Tyler too hasty to attack the creature, which unfortunately is a quite natural reaction. He added, 'You know the old saying – what is it? "Don't know, it's dead now, whatever it was."'

This was of course a predictable by-product of an all too healthy fear of the unknown, but of course not the best way to explore the world. He had been fortunate not to have been killed during the incident; Juran said that this might mean the beast was in fact not as great a threat as it had initially seemed, so not to worry.

Meme was in much better form but would still have to be moved by cart, so after a long and rather cheery breakfast preparations were made for the move east, where they would meet with the Green River, north. Their plans were disrupted when the third and final bird of the whole party, Stinger, arrived with a message.

Captive Heart and Fire

Blistered and torn, battered and beaten Jethro, Benjamin, Erin and Torres were dragged along like dangerous animals on a long leash. They were bound in cold hard heavy chains whose bite was unforgiving as it gnawed into their wrists. They had walked for days, uncertain where they were being lead. Although the tongue of the Green Men was alien to them, it did seem to be a basic variant on the common speech used between nations, so a general idea of what was being discussed could be gleaned. Mention had been made of a sacrifice to some Tree god, and it did not take much fathoming to work out who would become the offering. The effects of the mist used during their capture still subdued them, and even the animals were having difficulty bearing their own weight as they pressed on through an unrelenting forest. This weakened state greatly reduced any prospect of escape and all seemed quite dire. Over the first few nights they walked hard at an impossible pace for their numbed state. The march continued, and it seemed they would never stop, for they only rested a short while with the coming of each new dawn. This was to enable the Green Men to pray to their gods.

Their captors proved cruel and provided a huge quota of harsh treatment. They frequently taunted their prisoners and struck them often with long, thin but very hard, sticks that produced an excruciating sting and cut deep into the flesh. Jethro's defiant attitude managed to draw attention away from the other members of the group, but it merely meant he received the full brunt of their callous aggression. The second and third day of captivity brought them through areas thick with widespread thorny bushes amid maple trees. These bushes made progress far more torturous, as the thorns were only too happy to embed themselves into the flesh and deliver cuts and scratches to whosoever passed, even when only just within the reach of their splayed branches.

They stopped at around eleven in the morning, on what must

have been the four or fifth day, though by then they had lost all track of time. They sat upon the crest of a wide valley that opened up before them; it was still forested though thankfully more sparsely than the area they had just traversed. The vantage point allowed a clear view above the roof of the trees below, and a fiery red haze could be seen amid the line of trees in the distance, towering upward as though some wall of magical flame was splitting the land. It looked out of place and rather eerie, as the reds contrasted with the greenery all around. The midday sun was due and the Green Folk, who had no love of travelling during daylight hours, in no way wanted to be caught out in the hottest part of the day. Not that it was unduly warm; it was in fact rather cold and drizzly, but to them it was still hideously hot, and although similar such stops had not been conducted on previous days, the eroded forest canopy in this area gave much less shade. They sought cover in the darkest areas beneath bushes, where the shadows seem eternally trapped, unable to escape the rooted grasp of such plants, thus providing ideal locations for those seeking to avoid the sun. The prisoners were left crumpled on the ground, where they had been halted. Thankful for the break and beginning to feel more attuned with the surroundings they began to enquire after each other.

'Erin – you okay, my dear?' said Benjamin, who had a habit of calling everyone 'my dear this', or 'my dear that' and so on.

'No, my feet hurt, I'm scratched to buggery and I want to go home!' replied Erin in a slightly sarcastic voice, which showed she was indeed okay.

'Well a fine mess, eh!' said Torres. 'We've really gotten off on the wrong foot, and it looks as if our quarrels will now be the death of us.'

'Well, I promise, if we get out of here there'll be no more arguing,' Jethro spluttered, with a voice that showed evidence of the beatings he had endured these past days.

The conversation they had sparked did not go unnoticed by their captors and two rushed out of their hollows to quickly quash such behaviour.

'Shad u up, critchers!' they bellowed as their feet met with the sides of their captives' crumpled bodies.

'Stud dem up!' shouted one of the Green Men who was still under shade.

With this, the two delivering the blows forced the prisoners onto their feet and lined them up on the hill crest, facing outward across the valley. They felt awfully vulnerable as they now peered over the sudden decline that lay before them.

'Do hit, den!' ordered the seated controller, after which the two lackeys pushed each of the prisoners sharply down the slope. With hands bound they could do little to stop or slow their fall, so one by one they began to tumble. Down they went, rolling and bumping, yelling and cursing. They were greeted by soil, rock, grass, twig and leaf, none of which lessened their plight. Eventually, and after much discomfort, they slowed and then came to rest at the base of the slope. Breathless, they lay still for some time. Their bodies were tired and the strain of this recent journey had definitely taken its toll. Their captors had returned to the sanctuary of the shade and there was now by all evidence some distance separating them. As noted before, the animals were unbound, a grave lapse on the Green Men's part. The animals, incidentally, had been treated remarkably well, as such beasts were a rare commodity and therefore prized. Torres, the animals' friend, had also noted the error; and knowing the creatures as she did, had faith in their speed, strength and bravery. The effects of the mist, having subsided in her present company, drew her to conclude that the same could be said for the animals. So it was that she began to sing, in a voice so pure, so honest and so captivating, that time itself was unable to escape its tranquil snare; and thus she sang, in the pure and mystical Elvin tongue:

> 'Aqnor arum teh blosmere sue saramayer asli so the mariees,
> Puquar arum teh bliyeema supra geyong saloong.'

The chant, so beautiful when heard in Elvin verse, did however have meaning, and important it was to their present dilemma. So its translation must now here be told in full:

> Sweet are the flowers in summertime,
> Soft is the breeze.

Gentle are the folk under bell chime,
Grand are the seas.
Happy are the creatures that rhyme,
Heedless are the trees.
To ride oh, such a fine a friend,
Is really bound to please!

So take me on your shoulder,
So take me far beyond.
To ride with you is but a charm,
We're humbled so, yet fond.
So take me far away from here,
To safer pastures clear.
Then I will be forever true,
And love you through the years.

Upon hearing these emotive words the animals began to stir. Then suddenly, as if they had become one, they lunged forward over the hill crest and down the steep slope toward their fallen comrades. Their purpose was unswerving and there was nothing the Green Men were able to do in time to check their move. Screaming and shouting, they leapt up from their seated position, and faltering, they made a poor attempt to gain the ground now covered by these super-swift animals. No, the horses, pony and mule were upon their companions in record time, and soon by hold of saddle, mane or neck the captives managed to make sound their escape and were in a flash carried forward and away from the thraldom that had held them these past days.

Though all seemed well, all was not. When their halt was finally made they discovered to their horror that not all the company had made good their escape. Jethro, in his poor condition and still restricted by his chains, had been unable to keep his grasp and fallen shortly after rescue. Surefoot confirmed that he was once more in the enemies' grasp; Surefoot had attempted to return to his fallen rider but was surprised how quickly the magical mist of the tree folk was spreading its paralysing fingers. He could take no other action, so fled from the deadly noose this vicious vapour held.

Still, most had made good their escape, and what had once appeared as a grim doom was now reversed, and a glimmer of hope had aligned itself with them once more. Only Jethro's lot was now of concern, and they had no intention of giving him up without a contest. The short halt allowed much needed adjustments to the awkward and somewhat fumbled holds that had been made under dire circumstances to be corrected. They were of course still in chains and bound at the hands, so they needed a way to break the bonds; but for now they settled with the urgency needed to place a healthy distance between themselves and their recent masters. They were also well aware that other tree folk could be in the region, so they tried as well as they could, given their position, to remain wary. Hearts raced and nerves strained as they picked their way through the forest, they were not in the clear yet, and needed help if they had any chance of assisting Jethro.

They rode on amid sparse maples set on fairly flat ground, which was now turning damp underfoot and proving tiring for the brave steeds. They stopped once more to assess their progress and Grumpy, under much duress, was selected to move back and keep an eye on the rear, on account of his being the smallest and therefore, the others argued, the easiest to conceal. Benjamin, of course, went with him, though mainly because mounting and dismounting under present conditions was such a chore and would undoubtedly slow them down if they had cause to move quickly once more. The others drew close to each other and plotted their next move; they knew nothing of the advice given to Elsbeth, so were unaware of likely allies in Oak and Birch, or of the fiery river ahead; though they had seen its towering flames. Luck, fortune and maybe that which is preordained allowed the correct decision to be made, and on toward the flaming wall they would go, for unbeknown to them all other directions would have taken them into the thick of territories held by Green Men.

They were about to move when a cry was heard from Grumpy's direction. Then, bolting forth from the bush, came the pony – and to the alarm of the others he was without rider.

'Go, go, go! They're upon us, we must go now!' snorted Grumpy to all the other equine escapees.

No time was wasted and they turned tail and charged headlong through the trees, downcast at losing another friend. It appeared as though their fortune was starting its decline, and to lose another of their company was a great blow.

Benjamin however had not fallen into the hands of the enemy; Grumpy's flap had been caused by a couple of small children moving in his direction; granted, they were children with green skin and large eyes, but unconnected to the men who had captured our party. In his haste he had reared, turned and bolted quicker than Benjamin could keep up with, and this sudden change in direction had dispatched him to the ground in an ungainly manner. These children did, however, pose a threat, for if they saw the Dwarf they were most likely to run off and alert their parents, and thus bring fresh adversaries into the arena. So Benjamin, although pained, crawled off under a bush and hid until the children had past, by which time his associates had long since gone.

These events had occurred over the course of the afternoon, and time once again had run on with itself, quicker than one would have believed; and before they realised it darkness overshadowed the land once more. Darkness gave the advantage back to the tree folk, whose large nocturnal eyes fared better in darkness than those of the men and Dwarves, and even Elves were no match for them. Benjamin knew that under such circumstances it would be foolish to move. Now, although Dwarfs are of course used to working in dark, dull and dim lighting conditions, due to the excavations and mining activities they frequently conducted in search of gems, ore and treasure, as was their wont, they were not nocturnal by design. So Benjamin rightly decided to sit out the night and remain in hiding. His body ached, he was still tethered in hideous chains, and a feeling of terrible hunger overtook him, adding to his discomfort. He now longed for a hearty meal and a few flagons of 'Just one more'; but of course his dreams were not to be and he remained a lonely fugitive in a strange land. Benjamin 'Bsore' Brandsaw had gotten out of many a pickle in his day, and he was certain this minor discomfort would not get the better of him, even if it meant starving. After all, he had scores to settle, and settle them he would.

Following the Elvin Dwarf Wars, he had fought for the

alliance of western states in the Green River ports. Here he had encountered the Ajya-Na-Ku at close hand, they had killed many of his brothers and scorched many villages and camps, they brought torture and terrorism to everyone, and for these reasons alone Benjamin hated them deeply. However, they had also taken the Horn of Ristador, a prized Dwarf artefact that had been crafted, or so the stories went, at the dawn of time; and had been held as a symbol of Dwarven perseverance through the ages. It had accompanied Dwarf armies through centuries of battles, and some said that without it the Dwarf nations would crumble and Dwarves would become fewer in number, a dead race, and that their crafts would disappear, as would their homelands, and they would eventually become mere freaks and outcasts. He wanted revenge, he was determined to seize the Horn for his people and return it to its rightful place amid the centre of the Dwarven armies. A long shot, maybe, in such an unknown land; but he was old, experienced and stubborn, and if he did not try to do something, then who would?

The remainder of the group broke through the clearing of the maple forest's boundary and met with a small open plain, beyond which there was a remarkable sight. Shimmering and dancing as it lit the night, a wall of flames in blazing colours stood before them. Scorching reds, sizzling oranges, whites as white as the foam upon a wave, blistering blues and searing yellows, the flames ran as far east and west as the eye could see, and rose high into the blackness of the heavens. Yet remarkably no heat radiated from their direction, and it was clear to all that such a sight could not be an act of nature. No, this had to be the creation of some unknown mystical charm or powerful sorcerer, though its purpose was unknown to them. Perhaps it was a warning, maybe a barrier, or some sort of demarcation line; whatever the reason, it still remained a magnificent vision to behold. The problem now was would it allow their passage? If they came too close would it lose its apparent chill and burn them? If they entered its flames, would they be engulfed? If the flames were, as they seemed, without heat, would some other trickery reveal itself once inside? Fear ran circles through their minds. Discomfort at this unknown entity causing countless questions that none of them could answer, and their only chance seemed to lie in following the river bank east or west. The other option was of course to take the plunge into the unknown. The decision could not be take lightly, so they decided to follow the river bank to the east for a mile or so, and then, once this dog-leg was done, to rest for the night and to see what perchance the daylight would reveal. They were of course also still suffering from the restrictions placed upon them by the burden of their bondage and did not savour yet another night of restricted movement. But little else could be done at present to relieve the pickle they were in.

'Hold in there, Torres, you've done us proud, girl,' said Erin in a surprisingly endearing tone. Perhaps she was not the cold bitch they had taken her for; no, there was sincerity in her voice and her positive attitude gave Torres' psyche a much needed boost.

'Sure,' she replied, 'but less of the "girl" – I'm a good deal older than you are, believe me.' She paused and thoughts of her youth and days gone by troubled her heart once again, then she continued. 'I remember the days before Markesh had even been heard of, when the great rocks marked the end of the world. Beyond them was said to be the resting place of those since passed. Oh! But how one's perceptions change with the passage of time, and the teachings of old fade to myth. Though I suppose in the oddest of ways the opening of Markesh did bring luck to our people; I mean, both of our people not just Elves. After all, the scourge it unleashed on our folk ended the wars that had rumbled on for centuries; it unified our peoples and at last peace came to the west. Elf, man, Protalien and Dwarf were able to see eye to eye for the first time in near on three hundred years. I was but a child, fresh of the world when the wars began; I have treated many of the fallen and each time I fear it takes away another piece of me. Will I never know a time where no one has to fall victim to another's desires? Now, what with Benjamin and Jethro captive once more, and our still being bound...' she paused, deep in thought and obviously disheartened by the situation, then continued... 'and the other two groups' locations or fate – well, truly the gods only know.' She paused once more and looked up, pained by her thoughts, and said, 'Erin, what is to become of us?'

'We're going to pull through; we will break these bonds and find the others. Have faith! After all, are not the Elves the enchanted folk, and do you really think your enchantments will be disgraced so easily? A few slimy men with saucepan eyes should not cause us to falter! No, we must think only positive thoughts, and positive results will follow. You make your own luck; I don't believe we are in the hands of the fates. We will pull through. I always do – and you're right, you are older than me, but Elves take longer to age, so relatively I'm older than you. So behave yourself and buck up, or I'll just have to save the day on my own,' said Erin, being distinctly jovial in an attempt to help calm Torres' worries.

'Now, can we please get some rest? All your blabbing will even keep the maples on edge, though you may scare the flames away… but eh, that would be good!' she joked, with a foolish grin.

Torres couldn't help but grin back at her – such a serious woman, all tied up cracking fun at her, how could anyone remain so serious? After all, it was just too much to believe, so surreal; nothing she had seen in her many years compared to the threat of the Ajya-Na-Ku, and to add other threatening and strange races to the challenge almost seemed as though some great dream had taken hold of her; but she knew that unlike a dream she would not wake in the morning in the safety of her own home.

So it was that they drifted into sleep that night with Surefoot keeping guard over his resting companions. Mules do tend to have remarkable stamina, and Surefoot did not tire as easily as most of those present. He was proud of his abilities and as stubborn as they come when the fancy took him. A few hard nights were of little consequence, and he was in fact enjoying the variety this journey was giving him. He had worked in the mountains lugging boulders and rocks all his life; this was far easier and much more exciting, a real adventure to tell his children of in his later years. This made him feel rather special and greatly needed on this unpredictable expedition.

So on that night and many subsequent nights to follow, he kept an eye on proceedings, ready to alert everyone to any danger that may arise during their rest. He hoped deep down that his efforts would make up for his being unable to save Jethro – even though of course it was not his fault. He had done all he was able; any more and he would have undoubtedly met with the same fate. But he was proud, and despite the facts he felt as if he had let the side down.

All our travellers were woken prior to dawn by driving rain, so heavy and thick that it reduced visibility to nought. Raindrops smashed through leaf and branch and nowhere escaped the blitz it delivered. Holes quickly filled to the brim, and tracks quickly formed streams and then rivers. It was accompanied by a chilling wind, and only the strong trunks of the maple trees managed to resist its might.

Benjamin cursed the weather and the ill luck that had befallen him; he tried as hard as he was able to find cover in his hiding place. He waited, watching each hammering drop drive into the ground around him, praying for daylight to reveal his way and thus allow his advance. Cold ships and heavy storms came to mind, memories of journeys between Umkush Island and Ulrick's Bay – a harsh voyage he had taken on the way to the battle of Falcon's Ridge; a journey taken amid a hurricane to help reinforce human allies pitted against Elvin foes. That too had seemed an impossible situation, and many ships in the fleet were lost, along with the cream of the Dwarf navy, skilled practitioners who could not be replaced; and it sparked the demise of a once fine fleet.

He had survived then under far direr circumstances, and the memory strengthened his resolve; his sodden body would dry eventually; it had back then, and on reflection the situation then had been much worse. The coming of first light did nothing to stem the flow of rain. The visibility improved but only because the dark veil of night was dissolved by the rays of a radiant sun fighting to break through the clouds. With this new light the advantage that had been held by Benjamin's foes was now transferred to him, so he clambered out of his hiding place and headed in the direction he had last seen the other members of his party.

The rain helped wash away any sign that may have been left by his equine allies, which deprived him of a guide but also meant the green tribe would have nothing to follow. So his loss, although he thought it a little annoying, would aid his friends – a thought that gave him some comfort. He walked on and on. His legs were stiff and weary and his chains became colder with each splash of rain. Soon his hands were numb and his feet were chafing from their soggy footwear, yet he did not yield. Eventually he came to the wall of flames set below and above the banks of what appeared to be a river; he too had no desire to try his luck in the flames, so he turned west and continued to plod on.

Erin and Torres, along with Cee, Surefoot, Grumpy and Eee, faired little better than Benjamin. They were now soaked to the core, and had began to continue east in the hope that they would find a crossing somewhere in that direction. They came upon a narrow track that meandered down along the river bank; a clear path, and not under the control of the mighty flaming wall. They decided to drop down and follow this track; it was the best hope they had encountered so far, and might even show them a way across the barrier. The track continued for mile after mile, and persevering they stayed on its course as it weaved its winding route. Their choice paid dividends when late in the day they spotted an opening that tunnelled straight through the flamed wall. A broad felled maple served as an overpass – or underpass, if you wish, as it formed the floor of a tunnel whose fiery arch seemed to be held by magic; for no structure was visible, and the flames were contained mysteriously above its passage. It was just high enough for dismounted travel. Above the shoulders of the highest horse the flames could be seen dancing erratically as though trying to break through this invisible barrier that contained them. The small party made its way over the log with many of them stooped in fear of the flames above. During the crossing they maintained good spacing between each other, just in case. Erin's confidence came to the fore, and showing no fear she boldly led the way, standing fully erect, taunting the flames about her. Next went Cee then Eee, followed by Torres, who led Grumpy, with Surefoot as brave as ever bringing up the rear, with ears and eyes strained in the event their progress was followed by more evil-doers.

Below the log they could see a violent river crashing past, with its blackened oil-skimmed waters cascading down from the east, carrying what appeared to be large carcasses with it. The bridge was quite solid and safe underfoot, and within a short time they had all crossed the expanse and found themselves in an area similar to the one they had left on the other side. They were below the bank of the river and the path continued along the bank, breaking its crown a short distance off. Here it gave way to a small area of open land, beyond which they could see the tops of trees. They had not escaped the forest, but the trees were distinctly different, and were a mixture of oak and birch.

They sat on the bank to take a short rest in the continuing rain. However, the rain on this side of the river was much lighter and proved a great relief from the torrents they had been subjected to. The horses were thirsty, and although the water in the river did not seem fit for consumption, Eee and Cee decided to go down and check it out. Grumpy and Surefoot, being of a hardier stock, suppressed their desire in the hope of meeting a better source further on. The flames near the water's edge were only a little warm and gave no indication of any threat. Cee bowed her head to sniff the water, a sensible thing to do when uncertain of its quality; but this sense did not pay off, as suddenly there came an enormous wave of black liquid spraying in every direction. There was also a sudden flash of movement from an unknown source, so fast it just caught the eye, and Cee was grabbed at the throat by huge merciless jaws from a nameless assassin. Both predator and prey were gone in an instant, disappearing into the depths of the murky water below, causing a second splash that rained down on the banks of the river.

Eee shrieked with the shock of what had happened and tried desperately to ascend the muddy bank, flustered and flapping with each pace as his hooves sank into the ensnaring quagmire below. He was drenched again when a third pouring of water descended on him. He knew this was a bad sign, but his speed was hampered by shrinking clay banks that acted as if they were in league with these watery snatchers. Instantaneously, sharp fangs bit into his right rear hock and claws as hot as pokers dug into his hind quarters; the pain was inescapable. The others could do little but look on in horror as Eee struggled to stay out of the river.

He was in the grasp of a frightening twenty-foot beast, whose green and brown scales looked as hard as diamonds – not that they had any weapons with which to pierce its hide, for these had been taken from them during their capture; and even if they had some arrows, they would probably just smash on such scales, and the beast would merely mock them. Its salivating jaws were almost as long as its body and the shrilling noise it made was like nothing any of them had ever heard in their lives. They wished it was all over, and a quick death was the only hope Eee now had. The beast's eyes looked full of evil, slitted and slimy with inner lids of shining black that allowed the flames around them to reflect onto its surface. An extremely powerful tail lashed from side to side, beating at the ground, while its muscular hind legs anchored deeply and helped the beast pull the horse rearward. Eee had no chance of escaping such a creature; it was similar to the descriptions they had heard of dragons but its size and slightly webbed feet prevented a precise match. Before long came the inevitable conclusion and both creatures crashed backwards into the sombre depths of the river. The desperate cries Eee had made in his efforts to escape had pained the group deeply. They all felt so helpless, and with eyes welling with tears they withdrew from the bank's dangerous edge and found sanctuary in the wood line.

Once there they dropped hopelessly to the ground, and wept like most had never wept before. They had all been traumatised by the grim spectacle, and the words 'expedition' and 'adventure' were now replaced with one word – *survival*.

Oak and Birch

The birds now flew in unison over the leaf green sea of the forest canopy. It stretched for miles below them and had become a familiar view during the past few days. They had set off in search of what they knew only as the flaming or fiery river, and now at long last after days of searching they beheld the awesome image it bestowed on the surrounding greenery. It danced before them in captivating and almost entrancing manner and it would prove only too easy to succumb to its majestic allure. The Hawks were, however, all too familiar with the threat of the ever present Black Owls, and this aided them in avoiding any mesmerised state. The three birds had continued to accompany Tyler's group, and once the river had been found they were intent on scouting its banks in an attempt to locate the other group. Once a link had been made with Idron's party, both teams would proceed to the seat of the ten tribes in an effort to intercept the tree folk and free their captured comrades.

Meme was still fighting with her wounds; after a promising initial improvement, she was now starting to deteriorate. Despite all their efforts, especially Chevon's, she was just not responding to the treatment. Tyler had cried for Meme many times, yet she, surprisingly, seemed to be nursing his concern and had managed each time to wipe away his tears, as though her problems were naught compared to his sober state. Her condition suddenly made Tyler realise how much they depended on each other. They had known each other for years, and although it had been difficult at the Academy to show their feelings toward one another, they had both always known their relationship went beyond that of mere friends. But because it was considered a sign of weakness to show one's feelings in public and was definitely not the soldier's way, they had had to sneak visits to one another and keep a facade over their emotional involvement. Meme had, since her wounding, travelled at Tyler's side, and they openly showed their bonding for the first time. They had been captivated by each other's presence since their first meet, but only here amongst aliens could they escape the scrutiny of a harsh and dispassionate society. He now hoped and prayed she would pull through; he needed her to, for without her by his side he would be inconsolable.

Tyler's group now knew that the river was close, and they were certainly in no doubt that this was indeed the river of fire from the amazing description Chevon had conveyed to them all after consultation with Singer, Winger and Stinger. The Hawks had been so curious about its the magnificence that they had flown along its shores and had also attempted to fly over it. Nevertheless the shear height of the vibrant inferno looked as if it continued upwards beyond the heavens and into eternity. Such a boundless barrier was way outside the limits of their powers of flight. All present were in complete awe at whatever magic had constructed this unearthly obstacle.

To reach the river they had trudged through the boggy, tree-filled landscape, and were now quite weary and much in need of a break. It had rained hard for days, thus making movement increasingly strenuous and most unpleasant, as the mud clogged boots and hooves. The transport of the casualty added to their difficulties, and it had been a testing journey to reach the river in so little a number of days. The rain had nevertheless appeared to have kept the Green Men at bay, although Juran believed it was his threat that had done the trick. As we already know, there were ten tribes in the forest; frayed alliances held, but only due to two reasons: firstly, the threat that the Ajya-Na-Ku presented to all tribes; and secondly, because of information – information that could only come from other tribes. This was complicated by the reality of the situation, in that the Green Men hated the white men, who incidentally felt the same about the Green Men. This hatred was deep but not as deep-rooted as their fear of the Ajya-Na-Ku. Hence the tribes tolerated each other in order to gain much needed warnings of their mortal enemies. Any appearance of the Ajya-Na-Ku in a neighbouring tribe's area would be passed via a network of villages and lookouts to each of the bordering tribes, thus creating strength in numbers. This mutual support had preserved many a village from total destruction, and had no doubt saved numerous lives. The Ajya-Na-Ku had however begun to withdraw some years previously and now rarely entered the Great Forest. Of course they still had spies in many forms but some unknown event or design meant the Forest had become unimportant to them, at least for the time being. This only led the tribes of the Forest to adopt a lax and increasingly complacent lifestyle, and the alliances were deteriorating with each passing sunset. It was only the path of time that waited for the inevitable tide of conflict to pass amongst the trees. The Seat of the Ten Tribes was arguably not about to fulfil its prophecy, and the tribes looked more and more likely to split than to unify.

The rains had made the more sensible tree folk seek the shelter of their homes. Few ventured out in such weather; they knew its effects well, and didn't need to stand in it to realise it would do little for their comfort and well-being. No, the only green folk who ventured out were those on key points of observation, keeping a watch for the Ajya-Na-Ku; but even they had become bored with looking for something that was no longer there, so they tended to sit in their lookout posts, snoozing, keeping warm, chatting with one another or conducting similar such boredom-breaking activities. This downpour differed from the normal with the addition of a small party of rather embarrassed green chaps who had mislaid some prisoners and were none to happy about it. After all, it meant they were still out in the elements when they should be rejoicing in the great hall of the ten tribes, having made sacrifice to the tree gods. They had spent days trying to find their missing quarry, and the one captive who remained suffered for his companions' successful escape. Now a shell of his former self, Jethro was waning, and death's release held a peculiar charm that he wished to savour.

Settled with the fact their search was now in vain, the Green Men made their way to the Seat of the Ten Tribes, disappointed but determined to complete their ritual and please the gods, though not quite as extravagantly as they had hoped. They crossed the flaming river by the same tunnelled bridge their escaped prisoners had, but remained unaware of the fact, and continued onwards toward the seat. They did in fact pass the sleeping fugitives by no farther than one hundred paces, and only Surefoot noted their passing, though fortunately not vice versa. At the great hall they placed thorny crowns on their heads and removed their footwear. They bowed and chanted before entry, leaving Jethro outside in a heap.

The hall was simple yet splendid; it was carpeted in close, well-maintained clover and grass, which had the most beautiful displays of wild flowers forming patterns amid its well-groomed surface. Ten small mounds were set in a circle, and the pinnacle of each had a wooden seat; each was fashioned from a different wood representing the tribe whose seat it was, and each chair had elaborate carvings over its surface. A much larger mound was set back from this circle; it had a dominating position looking down on the smaller mounds and seemed somewhat menacing. It too had a chair, but it was larger and more elaborate than the others, and was made of the smooth form of wonderfully patterned amber. Its base was rooted to the mound, as though the amber was a living tree still finding nourishment from the depths of the earth below. This was the one chair, the chair meant for the seating of the Great Woodsman, the one who would bring the tribes together to form a harmonious and prosperous society. The walls of the hall were provided by a series of interwoven creepers, vines and other such climbing plants, and were covered in blossoms of white, red, blue and yellow. The roof was, as already mentioned, provided by the various trees in a similar interwoven fashion observed in the walls. The plants were the only real group that held no quarrel, and happily formed alliances in the forming of the hall; they could undoubtedly teach the men a great deal, if only the men took the time to look around; for the Forest's message was plain to see.

At the far end of the hall lay four altars. Each altar faced a cardinal point, and so formed a square cross. The altars were ancient, made of black fossilised tree trunks, and had rough bark-like sides and smooth surfaces. Many were covered in stale dried blood, and the smell about them was somewhat fetid. At the base of each altar was a large metal ring for securing whom or whatever was to be sacrificed. Hence, once formalities were done with, Jethro was dragged in and secured to one of the rings. His keepers retired, seeking warmth, some food and rest. They had sent messages forth to the tribes of Maple, who would join them soon in a spiritual event, the likes of which had not been seen for many a days. Their sacrifice would please the gods and bring fortune, thus favouring Maple's position in the great forest; they would be rewarded well for their find and the effort made to deliver such an awkward quarry to the Seat.

Upon reaching the river following days of trekking, Idron's party set up base camp in an open area between the tree line and the wall of fire. They had stumbled across the perfect location in the form of a hollow in the ground that was concealed by fallen trees and scattered bushes. It was fairly large and deep, big enough for the whole party. On either side of the hole there were open caves that were raised from the sloping floor of the hollow. These provided shelter and the angled floor meant the rain drained quickly to a pool that formed in the centre. From ground level the hollow was quite invisible, although they were aware that the locals probably knew of its existence; but even so it provided shelter and would be easy to defend if the need arose. They posted a sentry to keep an eye on the sky, for they now had to sit it out and wait for the arrival of Stinger, Winger or Singer.

They stayed in the hollow for a day or so and were welcome of the relative comfort it provided but they were beginning to grow impatient. After all, time was pressing and they knew nothing of the fate of Tyler's party. It was decided that they had to move and if necessary attempt a rescue without Tyler's group. Luck once again dealt them a fine hand, as they were spotted from above just as they had started preparations for the move.

It was Stinger who noticed Idron's party; Chantelle was pleased to see him and enquired after Singer's – and most importantly her familiar, Winger's – whereabouts and well-being. She was content when she learnt they were also scouring the line of the river in search of their team.

So it was that Idron's party was found, and the link-up with Tyler's group was made.

Although most had not known each other long, the reunion

raised all of their spirits, even given the concerns over their captive friends and Meme's poor condition.

Chantelle and Chevon embraced each other affectionately, both fair maidens in love with life and happy to once again speak with one of their own race and occupation.

'We have much to contemplate, and work to do, I see,' said Chantelle, gesturing in Meme's direction. 'Come, we should see if both our efforts may stem the tide of the Reaper.'

Idron spoke with Tyler about the journey thus far and Idron explained what had been said to them by Que and Sticks.

Elsbeth, Bramley, and Juran sat down together and spoke of the things that had passed. The animals also happy to be reunited underwent their own quiet gathering.

On route to Tyler's party Idron had moved adjacent to the tunnelled bridge that crossed the river, so once their informal meeting was over they made their way through the tunnel of fire. Once across, Tyler, a keen tracker and woodsman, noted an area of crumbled bank to the left; it looked to him as though some struggle had occurred and on pointing this out to the others Bramley said, 'At its banks you must not linger, but make ye haste, take heed of its waters.' So, reminded of this sound warning, they made a beeline for the trees without delay.

'Chantelle, Chevon, over hear! Over hear,' called Surefoot, although the non-animal linguists only heard the sounds an excited mule makes.

'Thank the stars! Now, can someone please get these off of me?' said Erin, as the group approached, holding up her shackles for all to see. 'So, where have you lot been, then? Taking a vacation, no doubt, while me and poor old Torres here have been working in the dungeon display team!'

Erin made light of their misfortune, but at least it kept the mood on the same high that the reunion had established. Juran stepped forward, intent on the release of the two women's bindings, and said, '*Manacle and shackle, chain and bolt, be you now mist and paper, vapour and crumb and release these poor souls from all you have done!*'

At these simple words, the heavy chains dissolved first to a substance that shattered and broke, moving away from the flesh in a slow animated manner suspended in the air around them; then the fragments turned to a blue mist and were carried off on the afternoon breeze. A great burden had been lifted from Torres and Erin, and their arms felt as though they had been replaced with the lightest of feathers: a great relief.

'We're lucky you arrived when you did,' said Torres. 'They are not long in passing our position... sometime this morning it was; Surefoot spotted them. They followed the path ahead until they disappeared from sight. We were going to see if we could find some way of removing the chains before we attempted to follow. And mighty grateful we are that you turned up when you did, as it looked as though our only hope was with Grumpy and Surefoot pulling in opposite directions in an effort to break the weakest link – not something I was relishing, I can tell you!'

Just then Que spoke with Torres. She had taken a look around and noticed others were missing, 'Are Eee and Cee captive too? No one has made mention of them.'

Torres' grieving heart let out a burst of emotion as she told of the events that had occurred. She was of course speaking in a tongue only the beasts and animal friends understood, so the non-linguists looked on wondering what had caused such distress.

'It's the horses, Eee and Cee, both taken by some kind of small dragon-like creature. It came out of the water so fast, there's nothing any of us could have done,' explained a sullen Erin.

The mood amongst them was sobered by such bad news, but it increased their determination, Benjamin and Jethro would not meet the same fate if any of them had a say in the events to follow. The group moved on, following the path ahead, it continued on winding through the mixed towers of oak and birch.

After an hour's travel there was a shout from the rear of the column they had formed. 'Stop, we have to get off the path!' said Chantelle, 'Winger has spotted a large procession of the green folk. They're coming this way, and will be on us in around ten minutes.'

'How many?' asked Tyler, with the glint of impending conflict in his eye.

'Too many for us to handle, I fear, so we have little option but to break track,' answered Chantelle, pointing into the trees to her left as she spoke.

'Nonsense! Juran has vast power, and even Idron has some mighty magic within him,' said Tyler, keen for battle. He wanted to hurt these green folk for the pain they had brought, what with Meme's poisoned state and Jethro's imminent sacrifice.

'Maybe,' replied Juran, 'but if we stand here, what of Jethro? Do you think a slaughter here will save him? Or just speed his execution?' He looked Tyler deep in the eye and continued, 'Now look, I know you have been pained far beyond any of us can even begin to understand, but this isn't the way, not yet.' He paused, placing his left thumb and forefinger across his chin as if in thought. 'We have to bide our time a little longer, discover the location of the hall and, more importantly, Jethro and Benjamin. When the time is right we will act; for now, it is best we take Chantelle's advise.'

He placed his right hand on Tyler's shoulder and said, 'Worry you not, good friend, we will have our revenge!' With this he gestured to the left, indicating that they should move.

They continued down the track for a short distance then cut left, placing between one hundred to two hundred horse strides between them and the path. They then looped back parallel to the path in order to observe the track they had just taken. This way they would be able to tell if any of the green folk noticed any sign they may have left. After a brief wait they heard thunderous beats, as if the ground was being churned up in the wake of the mass of feet that marched forth. The sheer number of folk that now lay before them came as a shock to everyone. They thanked the gods that Tyler's wish to stay and fight had been averted, for the parade streamed back along the path as far as the eye could see. This was no mere celebration party, a sacrifice may have been the guise to set them over the bridge, but there was no hiding the fact that this was an army. It was also evident that this army was a coalition and not purely Maple, but most probably formed with representatives from all of the tribes south of the river. They trudged past for an eternity and all the expedition could do was observe; fortunately, the lead group had failed to notice the footprints in the mud and their own movement hid the marks from any more alert members of this procession.

The movement continued late into the night.

The Hall of the Ten Tribes soon had a representative in each of the seats of the southern tribes. Ash, Maple, Elm, Redwood, Apple and Pear all took their place, and a company of guards from each tribe surrounded their own mound. The remainder of the hall was empty apart from the altar party. The altar party consisted of the folk who had captured Jethro along with a cleric from each of the tribes of the south. Jethro was the only reluctant guest, and was chained to one of the altar rings despite his obvious shattered state. Outside the huge army was establishing a perimeter ringing the banks of the mighty mound that supported the great hall. Soldiers were cutting logs and sticks and a whole hive of industry was preparing for an impending siege.

Singer reported back all her observations to Chevon, who relayed the message to the others. They decided that Tyler, Idron, Erin and Juran would move to a vantage point to assess the situation, which now looked dire; hopes of their mounting a rescue attempt were diminishing by the second. They would move soon after dawn, which now beckoned on the horizon. They knew daylight disadvantaged the green fellows, and given the sheer number sprawled across the mound, they would need every ally available.

The move to their position of observation was uneventful, and as the day progressed the mound took on the form of a fortress. By midday work had stopped and most of the Green Men were under makeshift shelters on the slopes of the hill. It was at this point that the distinctive stomping of horses' hooves was heard. Approaching from the north, a party of around fifty riders each on dapple grey mounts came to an abrupt halt short of the great mound's base. The riders were unlike the Green Men and looked more like the humans of Broderland. All were white-skinned, with a variety of hair colourings and body shapes. They were dressed in wooden breastplates made from hardened oak. Each plate had a small oak leaf carved on the left breast. Forest green cloaks flew from their shoulders, and each rider was crowned with a rounded copper helmet. A giant of a man sprung forth on his mount, it reared up as he waved his short golden bow in an outstretched right arm shouting, 'Hear this, oh vile tribes of the south! What happened here this past night is against the words of

Arastoth. You prepare as for battle… Ignore you the sanctity of this great hall? The storm this brings is of your own design and will not pass unchecked. The hall sits amid our lands, yet we allow you access… The passage of flame is open as a sign of peace, though peace it appears did not pass this day! Abandon your grasp on the seat and return you from whence you came. Resolved this stand can still be, for blood that flows from mounds on high will not this land nourish.' He paused awhile gazing at his brethren, then looked up and continued.

'Take note to those who led this, the prophecy will never come to fruition through such acts. Until dawn we give. Now go as free spirits, or as spirits you will go!' With this he turned his steed and led the riders back in the direction from which he had come.

'I have a grave fear that what we've landed in is of greater consequence than I realised. We have to attempt to get Jethro and Benjamin tonight,' said Juran. 'For it is clear the words spoken are words of war, and those riders know the hall will not be abandoned. Daylight will bring destruction, by which time we should be far from here.'

'So what do you suggest?' asked Idron. 'We just going to walk in, release them and walk out?'

'How'd you guess?' Juran jested, although that was basically the general plan.

Returning to the group, the game plan was laid out in full. Juran spoke with ease and clarity describing what was basically a simple plan and required that small touch of magic to aid its success. 'Torres, Erin, Idron and I,' he began, 'will, dressed as clerics, make our way past the soldiers on the mound. Once in the hall we will find Jethro, unshackle him then leave: simple.'

'Simple, hey? How do we get past the soldiers?' inquired Erin.

'A blinding spell should work quite well, though it will only last a few moments, so we need to move quickly,' came Juran's answer, at which he looked quite smug, and appeared rather childish. He obviously revelled in his magical abilities and loved a chance to flaunt them.

'Fine, but once inside… remember the village? Our disguise didn't fool them then, what if the same happens here?' asked Chevon.

'We will just have to cross that path when we come to it; we got out of the village, didn't we? I'm certain we can get out of the hall in much the same way,' said Juran, but without the smug attitude he had shown with the last answer, for even he knew the risks involved, and they had been fortunate in the village; but even then Meme had gone down as an indirect result of the event.

'How do we get Benjamin and Jethro out if they're unable to walk?' asked Idron, knowing full well the two would by now probably be in a much weakened state.

'Good point! We may have to take one of the horses with us,' Juran said, looking in their direction. At this Tyler's steed, Gee, stepped forward, neighing.

'Well, I don't need to speak with an equine tongue to know a volunteer when I see one.'

'All well and good,' said Chevon, 'but aren't you forgetting something? The Green Men have no horses. It'll kind of give the game away, don't you think?'

'Have some faith, my dear, Gee doesn't have to enter the mound as a horse. Faith… you'll see,' Juran replied, already with a disguise in mind for Gee.

'What of the rest of us?' asked Tyler, a little distraught, that he had no part in the rescue party.

'We need someone reliable on the outside. You'll keep your distance, but maintain a close eye on events, and we may need your help at a crucial stage – maybe a diversion or a path-clearing. Besides, it's good practice to keep a reserve. You're a military man, you should be well aware of that,' was Juran's reply, knowing a promise of offensive action would be to Tyler's pleasing. 'I'll signal when I need you. You'll know my sign when it comes, as we cannot afford to use the birds; there are too many archers up there, and flight, though useful to us, would be far too risky.'

'How's Meme?' Juran asked, concerned for her health and how her safety may affect the plan.

'She's…' Elsbeth started, but she was interrupted by a groggy sounding voice.

'I'll be fine, set me back here.' There was a break in her speech while she coughed and spluttered before continuing. 'Do what is needed, I'll manage… best speed and good luck to one and all, only wish I could be with you.'

She was obviously in a bad state, and needed some antidote to the poison that held her. Chevon and Chantelle could do no more for her, and her fate lay in the hands of the gods. She was after all a warrior, brave and proud, who knew the risks that lay ahead of them. She did not wish to be the reason any of them could not be party to the rescue of their comrades.

'So, that's it, then. We move soon, so make preparations,' concluded Juran. The task was afoot, and a great deal of luck would be required to carry it off.

Short of the great mound Juran halted his small band, then turned towards them and said, 'Now we must prepare ourselves.' He looked at them and they nodded in acknowledgement. Juran then turned first to Gee and said, 'Don't take this personally!' Then he began to chant: '*A rat is but a rodent free, so a rat you'll be, for it pleaseth me.*'

Gee underwent an instant metamorphosis and shrunk to the size and shape of a rat. She wasn't too happy about it either, but she understood the need so put up with the discomfort and humiliation. Horse to rat... unheard of!

'Well done, my beauty,' said Juran, as he stooped down and picked up Gee. 'Now it is you who shall be carried for a change,' he said, as he placed Gee in a hidden pocket inside his ragged cloak. He then looked at the party and said, 'Well, I suppose it's our turn... *The ten tree tribes have many a god, to some this may seem rather odd; but if the ten tree tribes have men of god, then garb us so with robe and rod.*'

At this the ground below sprung to life, creepers grew quickly up their legs and covered their bodies, it was instantaneous and all were frozen with sudden dread. Had Juran's spell gone wrong? Just as quickly the link to the ground vanished, along with the feeling of entrapment. They looked at one another and realised the spell had worked, as each gazed upon an unfamiliar cleric positioned where Idron, Erin, Torres and Juran had stood.

'Well, that was different, I'll have to take note of that one,' said Juran, whilst checking his pocket to see if Gee was still there, half expecting to see a rat in some type of religious attire, which incidentally he was not.

'Good! So we now look like preachers from the backwoods. The rest is simple: walk up the hill, knock on the door, ask for their prisoners back and go home. Great! Well, best get on with it then, eh, boys!' said a somewhat sarcastic Erin, although she may not have looked herself at the time.

So they set off toward the mound, all heads bowed except for Erin's. She said, 'Now then, you lot, heads up, be confident, as though we belong! Look down or uncomfortable and the game will be lost before we start – got that?'

They all lifted their heads immediately like scolded children.

'Good,' said Erin.

'Right we're ten paces out. Time for a sudden daze to aid our passage,' said Juran, just prior to casting his spell. '*Let no sight or sound show them around,*' he intoned as he pointed his hands toward the mound and then waved them left and right in large sweeping motions.

With this, the troops lining the mound were suddenly dazed by a bright flash and were incapacitated, having no sense of sight or sound. Taking advantage of the sudden chaotic state, the raiding party strode up the hill at a brisk pace, dodging and ducking and in some cases tripping over the soldiers, who were stumbling around cursing and complaining, although they of course could not hear each other.

Juran's band reached the summit and entered the door of the great hall. Silence and a sudden gaze from those present met them. They froze, not having anticipated that everyone in the hall would stop what they were doing as soon as they entered.

'We bin spectin u,' said a Chieftain from the seat of Ash. This made them gasp, as if the game was up already.

'Ye, u prists, dat sacfis id oder der, goes deel wit im,' said the Chieftain from the seat of Apple.

'Prists, ha! ha! ha!' said the Chieftain of Maple, and all those seated laughed.

Juran's party thought this a little odd and it did nothing to comfort them. As they walked the long walk through the hall towards the altar where Jethro was tied, they could not see Benjamin and this troubled them. Had he been killed already?

They reached Jethro and could see straight away what a poor

condition he was in. He had been beaten far worse than they could have imagined, and his face was so swollen he was hardly recognisable. There were six other clerics near the altar, who looked up and smiled at the approaching clergymen.

'So, you have come for your friend,' said the tallest of the clerics. His face was thin and bony and thin grey hair barely covered his scalp. His speech was not that of the Green Men, and he looked through the disguise of those before him with icy grey eyes. 'Well, like my friends at the seat said, we've been expecting you. So if you want your friend, try and take him,' he said, pointing towards Jethro's inert frame.

Juran stepped forward and shouted, *'Tinder and match, flint and stone, let forth your sparks and torch this throne!'*

At this sparks burst forth from nowhere and danced and darted amongst the trees, feasting on creeper and vine. Flames grew quickly, catching bark and tinder. The sudden panic it caused among the seated tribe members was amazing. However, the victory was short-lived, as a devilishly quick pure ice blue bolt flew at Juran, knocking him stunned to the floor. The same bolt then burst, sending smaller rays everywhere; their aim to find, intercept and extinguish all flames. Idron and Torres looked on in horror as the bony cleric holding forth a staff controlled the bolts. Erin was not so mesmerised, and dropped to Jethro's side, checking he was alive. Then, using a small dagger, she pried open the lock on the chain that held him. Idron released his powers, drawing on the flames that had been ignited by Juran before the icy blue rays could get to them. These he fashioned into fireballs, and sent them careering into the cleric.

The other five clerics were chanting in the background in some uncommon tongue. Torres felt this had to be a bad sign, so grasping a sword she called on Erin to aid her and charged forward, slicing and stabbing at the clergymen. Juran was up once more, screaming, *'Oh! Silver crest of Siselmere, bring forth your beam of power and fear, and bless me with the ancient spears, let us defeat these foes with ice, flame and fear.'*

A radiant light grew instantly from Juran's neck as his pendant began to glow. Then in his hands appeared an icy blue short sword and a fiery red mace. He swung them alternately in the air and each move threw either jets of flame or frozen shards about the hall. The tribal guards had by now begun to advance in the direction of our group, but were suddenly met by streams of burning flame and frozen bolts that instantly diminished the enemy's effectiveness. Idron continued to send forth fireballs, but the cleric checked them in mid-flight. The fireballs burst in a frozen mist before any more could connect with the cleric's body. The chanting clerics were cut to ribbons by the two warrior women, but the intensity of the fight distracted them all from the area of the altar, here two unseen priests had drawn Jethro upon the slab, and just as Torres caught sight of them they had began their prayer:

'Oh ere meh, grit root o lif, a gi dis sol ad sacrifis, t'bing we luk an Vicoree.'

Torres sprang toward them as they raised their sacrificial daggers. She caught the first, slicing through his wrists with a powerful blow made thrice as effective by the pure blade she was wielding. She pushed aside the cleric she had assaulted in an effort to reach the second, but his dagger thrust down sharply, piercing Jethro's chest and causing him to let out a painful shriek. Torres thrust her blade into the throat of the cleric, blood began to spurt and he dropped to his knees, grasping his neck. In seconds he was dead. The sacrificial dagger was still embedded in Jethro's chest and was beginning to glow in a bright translucent yellow. Torres attempted to remove it but it would not budge.

'Farewell, my brave warrior,' she whispered to Jethro. 'You shall have your seat in the afterlife.' Then with flooded eyes she brought her own sword down sharply across his throat.

He died instantly and he was at peace long before the glowing dagger was able to devour his soul. Torres was livid; she had come to save a friend, a friend who had prevented the remainder of the group from suffering during their captivity; for he had taunted his captors to attract the brunt of their anger. The pain she felt was overwhelming, and she hurtled her body at the Chieftains' guards' lashing out without mercy at these terrible people. Erin, seeing her actions, moved to support her. She too was full of natural rage and was familiar with battle; they both fought well.

The mages were still locking horns with the wizard – and a

powerful wizard he was, Juran was no match for him, and he was grateful for the support of Idron's powers, however basic. Their combined efforts were just managing to force a stalemate, and the stray bolts of flame and ice were being deflected by Idron in the direction they were most needed – toward the guards.

Juran felt a stirring in his pocket and remembered Gee, who by now was eager to get out. Using his sword and mace to form a barrier, Juran manage to set Gee down, and muttered a quick undoing spell: *A rat of course is not a horse, so a horse must force the rat away, if she's to gallop and stride this day!*

Gee was soon her normal self and dashed to Erin's side, urging her to mount. Once Erin was seated they both forced the now rapidly diminishing number of guards to withdraw. Bodies now lay all around and the hall became emptier with each passing second. The Chieftains, seeing little hope, bolted for the door; they did not wish to be caught in the fray. Erin noticed their attempted escape, so still astride Gee, she moved to cut off their retreat. The Chieftains were flummoxed, and so Erin was quickly able to secure their surrender.

The wizard could see the situation had gotten out of hand, and knew he would soon have four angry combatants to deal with unless he acted quickly. A blinding flash of purple and white vapour froze all movement for what seemed only a second, though it may have been longer, and once the vapour had disappeared it was obvious that so too had the wizard.

'What now, then?' asked Idron, looking at his fellow Mage.

'Why, we leave, of course. There is nothing for us here, not now, we have failed,' was Juran's reply.

'We can't leave,' said Erin, in a demanding voice.

'Why ever not?' asked Juran, somewhat puzzled and annoyed, not to mention disappointed by their failed rescue attempt.

'They're not going to let us,' answered Erin, as she gestured toward the door.

They all moved to look and could see the massed army outside trying to force the huge door. 'We can't get through them, there's too many,' added Erin.

'You're right, we will have to hold here. Tyler's party is our only hope,' said Juran. 'The battle of the tribes is but a few hours away, we need a binding spell to strengthen the door, after which we'll send a signal, and maybe that diversion will help us sneak out.'

'Let's hope so, for all our sakes,' said Idron. 'We've lost too much already.'

'I'll keep an eye on this lot,' said Erin, pointing at the Chieftains. 'Perhaps we can use them for bargaining later on?'

Juran rose with a daunting expression. He seemed much taller and far more menacing than he had before, and turning to face the Chieftains he said, '*Hopping mad you maketh me, so hopping frogs I now make ye!*'

He motioned his hands towards the Chieftains as he said this and each of them was suddenly transformed into a frog. 'There! They should be easier to control now. Put them in a box or something… any problems, squash them.' He then turned to the near buckled doors and said: '*Stand ye firm, and stand your ground, harden your front and let no key be found, let you by, none but me, until I say, don't let us free.*'

The great doors straightened, taller and firmer than ever any door had been, and no rock or blade that was sent could breach its front. Dawn was nearing, and the tribes of the north would soon be here. The raiding party was now besieged, and had no solid plan that would allow their safe escape. Something drastic had to be done… but what? And by who?

Battle of the Ten Trees

Juran had never imagined the rescue attempt could be so disastrous, yet here they were trapped inside the hall surrounded by an angry hoard. On top of this, a battle for the hall and its surrounding mound was imminent. He had told Tyler he would give a sign if he needed a diversion or a path clearing, but he had not expected it to come to this, so he'd given little thought to just what this sign would be. His overconfidence had cost them dearly; he really had believed his sorcery would be the answer to all their problems, yet he had not counted on a wizard's presence, and in this his inexperience became clear for all to see. He contemplated the situation for quite some time. This made Erin and Torres a little agitated; they were still hyped up from their part in the battle for the hall, so their blood was close to boiling. Idron, however, was too concerned with what was going on outside to let anything else worry him.

'We need to get Tyler on the move, Juran, now,' ordered Erin. 'All your thinking hasn't bode well thus far, it's action we need – and now.'

'She's right, send that damned signal, will you?' said Torres, backing up Erin's order.

'Yes, of course, but this fix may not be resolved by direct action. And you know Tyler – he's likely to take the direct approach, and that could make things worse,' Juran said, voicing his concerns as well as defending his failure thus far.

'Well, time is running short, you said it yourself. We have to act before the battle begins,' said Erin, growing more irate by the second.

'Okay, okay, I'll do it now,' Juran replied, thinking quickly what type of signal to send. Then it came to him as he chanted, *'Show clear to all that need to see, a bright bird in flight trying to flee, but ensure to show its hopeless case, and send an arrow to it erase.'*

With these words, a shimmering bright golden mist flowed

from Juran's mouth. It floated in a prominent trail to the leafed roof of the hall, and its dimensions grew rapidly as it climbed skyward, passing through the great roof and disappearing from Juran's party's view. Entering the night sky it shone like a million candles, yet none of the Green Men saw it, for it was not for their eyes. Tyler's company, however, could not miss it, the mist formed the shape of an enormous Hawk that began to fly away from the hall; then, just as it began to escape to the heavens a second mist in the shape of a fiery arrow passed through the misty Hawk, causing it to burst and scatter like some spectacular firework. It was a clear message to see, but as with most of these types of things, they tend to be open to the interpretation of those who view them and the message received was not perhaps the message intended.

'Look – a sign! We must attack the flank,' said Tyler to his small band.

'Are you certain that's what they want?' asked Elsbeth, believing this to be a warning against direct action, or that those inside couldn't escape.

'Yes, it is as we discussed. He would send a sign that we would instantly recognise, after which we were to clear a path or cause a distraction. It was quite clear,' said Tyler, certain he was right.

'Maybe so, but things have a tendency to change, and it just looks more like a warning to me,' continued a rather concerned Elsbeth. 'But it's your call, and you can count on me.'

'And you two? Chantelle, Chevon, what do you think?' asked Tyler, although his manner showed he was being portentous and was attempting to pressure their hand.

'Yeh! I'm with you,' said a rather uncomfortable Chevon.

'Sure, but I think Elsbeth has a point, so a diversion would probably be our best course of action for the moment,' answered a more cautious Chantelle. 'At least that'll allow us to test the water. After all, we are few and they are many.'

'Fine, then we'll mount a swift assault on horseback, to the eastern flank. We'll keep our distance and try to draw them out,' said Tyler. 'Let's mount and make haste.'

So they took to their mounts, Chantelle on Tee, Chevon on Dee; Elsbeth took Bee, as Stumpy was a little slower, and speed would be required here. Tyler, in the absence of Gee, his brave mount, decided to ride another fine intelligent steed, Que.

To reach the eastern side they had to circumvent the mound screened by the lush foliage of the oak and birch trees of that area. Once in position they waited, nervous apprehension shook their bodies, heartbeats became increasingly faster as they slowly walked forward in an attempt to surprise the enemy, leaving action until the last safe moment. Sweat began to mix with the ever-present drizzle as the horses moved in line abreast and broke into a canter. Leaving the tree line, they began to gallop. A sudden rush of adrenalin now controlled their movement. Instantly, they were spotted breaking through the tree line. From the mound they were met by the odd shaft from enemy bows, but there came nothing effective enough at this time to cause them to falter. The Green Men were in a strong position, and under orders to let the enemy bring the battle to them. So the stayed their ground and were not tempted by these four lone riders.

Chantelle moved to a flank and began to direct arrows at the soldiers at the base of the mound, who simply made use of the wooden barriers they had constructed to avoid injury. After a short time Tyler called for a withdrawal; the green soldiers weren't as green as their skin, and had presented themselves as quite a well-disciplined force.

Moving deep into the trees, he halted, turned and then spoke to his companions, 'So much for that! They're not about to take the bait, we have to clear a path.'

'You've got to be joking! Did you see how many of them were up there? We'd be cut to shreds before we got a foot on that mound,' argued Chantelle.

'I didn't say we were going to attempt a full-on assault, now did I? I said we need to clear a path,' stated Tyler in his own defence.

'So how do you propose to do that, then?' asked an increasingly cynical Chantelle.

'I don't know, yet,' said Tyler in a softer voice. 'But we can't give up, can we?'

'No, we can't,' added Elsbeth. She was probably the most concerned of them all, due to her habitual motherly nature. 'I suggest we go back to where we left Meme and see if we can't come up with something. It'll also give us chance to check on the girl.'

'Good call, there's not much more we can do here at present,' agreed Chevon, who was also keen to check on Meme.

'Okay then, we go,' said Tyler, who also was swung by the thought of seeing how his love was.

As they rode away, their trapped colleagues breathed a sigh of relief.

'Well, that was a close call, and damned foolhardy! They're lucky they weren't all killed,' said Erin, peering through a small opening between the wall creepers, 'What message did you send them to make them attempt such an assault?'

'I warned them in the same way I warned not to use the birds,' said Juran.

'Like how?' pressed Erin, rather curiously.

'I showed a bird in flight being shot down by an arrow,' Juran said in answer to her question.

'Well, yes, I can see that, but what if you took the message as "we are trying to escape but there is too much firepower aimed at us"?' enquired Erin.

'But who the heck would think like that?' Juran answered with his own question.

'Duh! Tyler – remember, a Protalien, a warrior, a fighter! You saw how eager he was to do battle,' came Erin's sarcastic reply, not quite believing this Mage could be so dumb.

'Well, pardon me, but was it not you and Torres who wanted immediate action? "Too much thought", you said, so don't blame me for the results of your eagerness,' snapped Juran, rather angry that things were not going well.

'No harm done, it was quite entertaining there for a moment,' jested Idron. 'At least no one's hurt, and we now know were not likely to be released by Tyler's band of misfits, so here we stay.' He knew nerves were strained and wished to calm the flaring situation. The last thing needed now was in-house fighting; from Que's tale that was how Erin and Torres' group had been taken captive in the first place, and this predicament was where those quarrels had led them.

'Yes, here we stay, if not alive, then we'll bloody well stay here dead, and I certainly intend to show no quarter, so if this is how it ends then that's fine with me,' said Torres, with a uncharacteristic look of hatred over her face that chilled her cornered companions. She really hated these Green Men, and it was turning her into something far more sinister than the gentle maiden who had left the Elvin lands some weeks ago.

Back with Meme, it was evident that she would not pull through, she was near death, and the absence of her companions had only worsened her condition. The realisation that she was close to dying weighed heavy on them all, the whole journey now seemed to be one disaster followed by another. None felt pained more than Tyler and on Meme's request the others departed leaving the two to say their farewells.

'Tyler, I'm close, don't let me die like this,' Meme pleaded.

'I'm not certain I can do it, there has to be hope, there has to be,' Tyler said with saddened ache in his heart and heavy tears in his eyes.

'But my love, you know as plain as I, I won't pull through, I've needed you for such a long time, now it seems we we're not meant to feel the warmth of one another, I've often pondered over what it would be like – you know, without the restrictions, I yearned for you so much but they always got in the way. So don't fret, my love, and if you couldn't love me in life, then love me enough to give me death, I don't want to die, there's so much we could have seen, but if I'm to die don't deny me, don't let it end like this.' Her voice was weak and gentle like a whispering breeze that has reached its journey's end. She could hardly keep her eyes open as her cold hand struggled to grasp Tyler's. She was trying to say so much more, but her fatal condition gave her so little time to convey what a lifetime had not allowed.

Tyler was fraught with overwhelming emotion. Tears poured down his face, his hands shook and his face grew pale and hard. It just wasn't fair: they had only just been given the freedom to love, and in a mere whisper their chance was stolen. He did not wish to carry out this mercy killing, but he knew the traditions and her wishes and did not wish her to suffer another minute. He held his

Shun-ku above her and, trembling, pushed them down into her bosom, piercing her heart. Meme suddenly bucked and writhed in his arms; as he tried to contain her movements, he felt the life drain from her body, and soon she lay limp in his arms. Weeping with painful cascading tears he completed the ceremony with these words of farewell:

'To the gates of Nabreskum,
From Proteous' proud lands,
Protect her passage as she leaves my loving hands,
Pray, Godspeed her brave spirit, while her body here stands,
Proud, her soul is undone; let her heart remain with me,
Take care, my heavenly body, for I know that you will be,
Waiting in Nabreskum until my soul is free,
Godspeed, my love, Godspeed,
Rest you well, rest you well.'

Tyler remained holding her lifeless body for an age, her blood was on his hands; he was heartbroken and deeply disappointed that they had wasted so much of their time together. More than this he was angry, angry at everyone and everything, especially the Green Men.

He buried Meme's body in a small glade, marking her grave with the hilt of her sword and placing her helmet at the base. The mud from his digging mixed with the blood in his hands; he was sopping wet and had a face so thunderous the very sun would have shied from its glance. He went back to the others but spoke no words; he moved towards Que but she backed away, she wished no part of whatever design he now intended to field. He did not force the issue but took Vee, a trusted and faithful warhorse, who had not the sense to question the actions of a Protalien soldier. He was mounted and off before the others realised what was going on.

'No, Tyler! Don't be a fool, you'll be killed – stop!' shouted Elsbeth, fearing the worst.

'He's going to assault alone, the idiot! That won't help Meme's condition,' said Chevon, not seeing the obvious.

'She's dead, he killed her. Did you not see the blood upon

him? It's their way, and what she would have wished,' said Chantelle. 'We could try and stop him but he'd probably cut us down as well, there's great frenzy in his heart, and no talk will calm it; let's hope he doesn't suffer.'

'We can't just leave it at that,' argued Elsbeth, not wishing to believe he couldn't be reasoned with. 'Come on, mount up, we are not giving up so easily.'

Tyler became a madman, screaming like a banshee and wildly spinning his Jim-ka as he rode toward the mound. Vee was steadfast and met the front rank of the enemy with pounding hooves; Tyler's double blades made light work of those in the vicinity of the two assailants. They rode upward, trampling, cutting, stabbing and slashing all who dared to confront them. They were an awesome sight to see, like a possessed amalgamation of beast and humanoid. Arrows now rained down on them, many hitting Vee's side and rear, causing the horse instant pain. Tyler had an arrow lodged in his left shoulder, but still he fought on. The ranks of the Green Men tightened the further up the slope they travelled. Now a third of the way up the slope they met pike and spear amid a wall of pointed logs, all designed to pierce the hide of horse or man. They would be unable to get much further now without the hand of death taking them, but they strove on. Then suddenly they were unexpectedly flung rearward by an almighty force. Back down the mound they tumbled, rolling over the soldiers below. Legs and arms flailed but they did not stop at the base of the mound. This strange unearthly force had them and was pushing them backward; they continued to be thrust rearward until they were far back amid the depths of the forest, away from arrow, sword, pike and axe. They came to an abrupt halt and found themselves unable to move, gripped by powerful magic.

This had happened following the murmured chant spoken from upon the hill '*Aside you are thrust, with safety I trust, and hold you there I must*' – spoken by a desperately concerned Juran, who had observed Tyler's charge from within the hall, but thought it to be another misinterpretation of his sign; for he knew naught of what had occurred to make Tyler so bent on revenge.

The three women en route to Tyler were relieved at whatever

had saved his skin, for it was obvious that both rider and horse would have been killed on the course they had chosen.

No sooner had this event been abruptly ended then a rumble of hooves could be heard, thunderous beats with an increasingly deafening tone as the grey riders returned. They were in far greater force than they had been seen the previous day. Hordes of these mounted fighters now burst forth from the tree line; they had employed a similar tactic to Tyler's earlier probe and had moved into formation silently. Tyler's suicidal assault had worked in their favour, distracting the mounds' defenders long enough to bring the heavy weaponry close. Now large splintered logs were fired from heavy trebuchets and began to smash into the mound's defenders. A high angled volley of flaming arrows rained down on the green defenders as mounted troops charged forward below the arrows' trajectory.

Horses now galloped up the slopes on the northern and western sides, destroying all in their path. The barrier that had stopped Tyler now became a problem for these massed forces. The horses could not leap over the obstacles and many fell under the blows dealt from a determined defensive line. Cries rent the air, pain spread quickly as wounded troops on both sides lay screaming in agony. They called for loved ones, and suddenly wished they'd had no part of this barbarous act. The mounted troops were now losing men and horses at a rate that would soon leave them wanting; then a horn call was made, sounding the retreat and planned regrouping. The riders moved back, as fresh foot soldiers moved forward to take their place, in an attempt to hold the ground that had already been seized at heavy cost. Pressure on the defending Green Men was increased by the use of small bows at short range; small groups of raiding parties then used the arrow barrage as cover whilst they scrambled over the log obstacles to close with the enemy. Pioneer troops busied themselves at the base of the obstacles with some magical concoction, whilst the assault troops' distractions allowed them to work on unhindered. Once done, these elite soldiers ordered a fall back; a well-disciplined move was made by the troops below the obstacle while those above thrust further forward, maintaining the pressure on the defending troops.

There was a huge explosion in the area where the pioneer had been working. A dark black cloud quickly formed above the seat of the blast, and splinters burst forth piercing flesh and bone of all who were within a fifty-pace radius. Before the cloud had time to disperse, fresh cavalry units mounted on lean powerful dun-coloured horses charged through the narrow gaps the blasts had formed, and began to fight upwards, capturing more ground.

Green troops from the southern side of the mound had been repositioned on the brim; they added a heavy rate of arrow fire to the battle, which met the riders full on. Troops from the eastern side were sweeping around the side of the hill, adding more muscle to those defenders now locked with the enemy. The assault was checked once more, and the surviving troops had to once again pull back; but this time they needed to lick their wounds. They pulled back to the trees but maintained the pressure with long-range heavy weaponry; the battle wasn't over yet.

Soldiers from this tribe of Oak had been sent to discover who the brave souls were who had acted like a smokescreen for their approach. These soldiers had intercepted Chevon, Chantelle and Elsbeth, who had failed in their attempt to remain hidden from view. They were welcomed as allies and the hand of friendship was extended. The women were taken to the Chieftain, who was then told of how they had come to blows with the tribes of the south, and how their companions were trapped in the Great Hall. The Chieftain explained that his tribe, Oak, had taken the initial assault and that Birch would follow shortly, and that the siege would be broken with ease once Pine and Willow arrived. Already a company of Oak had moved to the river and sealed the flaming tunnel, thus cutting off the green army's method of reinforcement.

War cries rang out from the south as masses of small, stocky soldiers charged out of the wood line. They were brandishing mainly axe and mace, and had scars cut purposely onto their cheeks. Three lines were ranged on each side, stained with blue dye added to ensure they stood out, a mark of their tribe. No horses were in sight, but from the tree line, company upon company of longbows were trained onto the mound, sending forth accurate heavy arrow fire that cut down those troops on the southern slope. These small screaming footmen quickly closed with their enemy, and powerful little fighters they were. They went berserk, maiming and smashing everything before them and making a large dent in the enemy's defences. Groups of torch-bearers could be seen running among them. They acted like crazy psychotic arsonists, burning everything that could burn as they moved through the enemy positions.

Unexpectedly from the south-east came swarms of fresh troops, green army troops; it seemed the war had been planned better than anyone in the north had known. These troops moved quickly, some taking pre-planned routes onto the mound to strengthen its battlements, while others struck into the flank of the assaulting Birch soldiers. Now the fight was extended to the plain below the great mound and had also entered the woods to the south. Confusion reigned as lines were broken and the enemy seemed to come from each and every direction. The fight was costly and Birch barely managed to keep a hold of their position, though they had fought with dignity and valour.

From the top of the hill came sprays of molten lava; it came from no natural source but had been fashioned by the wizard who sided with the green army. It struck soldier and earth, destroying everything in its path, and on entering the tree line it demolished the line of the mighty forest. Panic suddenly struck, spreading through Oak and Birch as a battle for self-preservation took over; troops now scrambled in every direction, horns were sounded to indicate rallying points deep in the forest. The tribes of the north now needed to count their losses; this came as a deep blow to the attacking armies.

'We have to do something! He's far too powerful and it seems no others present can conjure any kind of defence,' said Idron to Juran, seeing that the attack on the mound was now is disarray.

'Indeed, but not yet. We wait for a renewed offensive; he now has nothing to distract him and remains too strong for us to dislodge,' came Juran's answer. He knew the turn of events only proved that the sorcerer was well skilled in the dark arts.

Night drew in and remained fairly uneventful. Small raids were carried out by Oak and Birch, though nothing significant.

New heavy weapons, with greater range and firepower, arrived along with news of Pine's approach from the Northeast. Good news, as Pine had a strong army with heavy cavalry, and a few skilled practitioners in elemental earth magic.

Daybreak brought a fresh offensive initiated by explosions on the mound as pieces of earth burst forth, escaping their confinement. Soil and stone showered the defenders; this was the dramatic entrance Pine added to the struggle. Their earth magic dealt with quakes and landslides, or other soil or rock-based incantations. This barrage was backed by a thrust of around two hundred mounted riders, coming from the north like a swarm of locusts.

Their powerful heavy horses tore the ground up as they dashed forward, and an extremely frightening sight they presented to the defending soldiers. Some of the defenders faltered and they rushed back in a bid to escape the power unleashed upon them. The soldiers of Pine where huge, burly men, heavily armoured in silver and gold, sporting sharp scimitars and angular shields. Their foot soldiers had small rounded shields and spears, and marched in line behind the cavalry. Battalions of archers with crossbows moved to the flanks to support this rush. Simultaneously the heavy weapons of Oak sent missiles crashing into the sides of the mound, whilst the remnants of their light horsemen, reinforced by freshly arrived medium cavalry, assaulted the western flank of the mound. Birch moved in from the east, sending wave after wave of troops across the small plain to charge up the hillside.

The green troops had little choice but to fight for the ground on which they stood, their numbers were still strong and the mound was well prepared. Spiked pits had been dug to ensnare the horses and huge log falls were used to great effect. The wizard now sent his own bolts and missiles booming and rolling into his foes' ranks. Idron and Juran felt this a time to act; the forces were many and the wizard's intervention would be a battle-winning factor that had to be eliminated. At the very least the wizard's powers had to be suppressed if the siege had any hope of being broken. They sent a combination of fireballs and lighting bolts to strike the wizard; these did not destroy him but distracted him sufficiently to ease the pressure on the tribes of the north. A separate battle now began between wizard and Mage, magic pitted against magic. Blinding flashes, ear piercing bangs and explosions rocked the area around the great hall, and a stalemate similar to their previous encounter now ensued.

The battle below was bitter and bloody, a terrible scene of death and destruction, the type that no living being should be witness to. The attack by the tribes of the north was unrelenting but the pressure was still unable to break the lines of the determined defenders. The battle raged for days, with few lulls. Many casualties resulted on both sides, with little ground being taken or given. The magical exchange continued throughout, with Idron and Juran relieving each other, but their opponent took no rest and began to grow weary.

Then, on the morning of the fifth day a mighty howl was heard from the south, causing many soldiers to hold fast and look in the direction of its source. Although their focus had thus far been unbroken by assault after assault, they felt a compulsion to stop their actions and concentrate on this sudden howl. Then, out of the concealment offered by the wood line, a huge beast that seemed half-wolf, half-bear appeared. The beast bounded towards the slopes on the southern side of the great mound; all were in awe at its size. Stranger still, seated astride its mighty neck a small Dwarf could be seen. Close behind the beast and his tiny rider followed a column of troops – soldiers from the tribe of Willow. The green soldiers were ordered to defend by the wizard, who still fought off Juran's and Idron concentrated attacks. Undeterred the beast tore into the troops holding the southern flank, disseminating their ranks, many ran scared by the power unleashed upon them. The beast continued upwards, carving a channel through the rapidly collapsing pocket of enemy. The vacuum he caused to appear in the enemy's lines was quickly filled by the troops of Willow, who then secured this access channel by placing line upon line of spearmen right up to the summit of the mound. When the order was given they began to sweep around the mound's circumference, clearing through the bewildered and beaten enemy's positions. The fight was over, and little resistance was met as the Green Men now surrendered in droves.

The beast, now at the top, stood on its hind legs, roaring loudly; he was easily twelve foot in height; extremely broad, heavy and powerful. Soldiers on both sides shook in fear and stood still, transfixed by his chilling roar too scared to move. The beast then bellowed in an echoing tone that hinted a human origin, 'Wizard, enough of your trickery! Your time is up – did you learn nothing in my service?'

The wizard faltered, his magic spent. Juran and Idron also slumped exhausted to the floor, welcoming the respite the beast's intervention offered. The wizard drew back, cowering behind a wooden barrier. He seemed shocked and terrified by the towering beast above him. 'No, it can't be! No you're dead! No, you died – I saw it for myself!' squealed the sorcerer, truly horrified by the creature looming over him.

'And how was it I died then, Ghimane, you snivelling wretch?' yelled the beast, shaking his clawed paw at the wizard. 'Come now, tell me, tell *them* you sad sorry fool!'

The wizard cringed and uttered a whispered word, 'I…'

'I, I?' screamed the beast, 'I *what*?'

'I killed you,' whispered the wizard, shrinking deeper behind the barrier.

'Louder, damn you, louder!' hollered the frenzied beast, 'so all present can hear.'

'*I killed you, okay, I killed you!*' shouted the wizard.

'Yes, you killed me, trickster! But I did not stay dead, and your treachery must be dealt with,' said the beast, lowering his tone to a calming state, though those present could still sense his words. 'Now lift yourself from your miserable posture. You are not a frail child. Stand before me like the man of strength you thought you were,' he ordered.

'Basterdor, have mercy! I knew not what I was doing, I beg you…' pleaded the wizard has he rose from behind the barrier.

'What say you, Master Dwarf? Is this a man of honour who stands before me?' asked the beast.

'Apparently not, or so I would deem,' said the Dwarf sitting astride the beast – a Dwarf named Benjamin.

'Agreed,' said Basterdor, the beast. Then, without delay the beast struck the wizard's face with his huge paw. However, the wizard did not move, although the blow was mighty. Instead he stood firm and began to glow with an unearthly aura; his skin reddened and his veins began to bulge and looked as though they would burst from his flesh. Then his skin grew darker and darker and was accompanied by a low shrill as pain surged through his body. Now he solidified like a brittle earthen pot which held for a moment, then – with a sudden sharp *crack*! – the wizard's body shattered into a million fragments and fell to the floor. In a trice he was gone.

The beast stood astride the mound, commanding the scene as he spoke to those present. 'Tribes of the south, you insult this place of tranquillity, your greed for power sickens me – and for what? Only shame has it brought your kind. Now, fools, lay down your arms and go back to your homes. This land is not for the taking! Take note of Ghimane's fate, and be mindful of whom you take as an ally. Remember, most sorcerers in these lands answer to me. Take heed, for Basterdor has spoken!'

All present apart from our adventurers instantly recognised the name of the Sorcerer Supreme, a sorcerer so in tune with the land he was said to be everywhere; hidden in every fold, behind every tree and friend to every beast.

The clash had finished, and the littered battlefield was slowly cleared of the dead and dying from both sides of the conflict. A mass burial trench was prepared to put to rest those poor souls whose lives were abruptly shortened by the expansive desire of others. A beaten and demoralised green army was escorted through the flaming tunnel, back to their southern lands, and the tunnel was sealed. Stinger, Winger and Singer, had been sat high in a tree watching the events unfold before them, uncertain of the final outcome of the battle. At this safe distance they had a grandstand view of events and had noted the odd Black Owl moving between the treetops. Now the battle was over, a flight of seven birds were seen departing the shadows and heading east. They were spies of the Ajya-Na-Ku, eager to pass news of their observations, no doubt; a point that would concern everyone.

Tyler had calmed down considerably, and was released from Juran's spell, allowing the whole expedition to be reunited in the great hall. The mighty Basterdor and the Chieftains of Oak, Birch, Pine and Willow also gathered in the hall. Benjamin was a most welcome sight, and he told how after finding the flaming river he had turned west and walked for many miles. He said that five hunters from the tribe of Ash had disturbed his sleep on the third night. They teased and kicked him, laughing at the chained Dwarf, for such a creature they had rarely seen. Then from their rear could be heard a low growling noise. This was instantly followed by a volley of fast powerful blows that instantly brought Benjamin's tormentors down. Then in their place the Dwarf could see a huge beast peering down on him, and he thought he would surely die. He said he had squealed like a girl as heavy paws came sharply down toward him, but the strike was intended to break his bonds and not slay him. He had been saved by the sorcerer, Basterdor, who many centuries ago had been transformed into a creature that was half man, half beast. He had since cursed many a man into taking the form of a beast whenever one of the three moons was in full illumination. This he used as a punishment for their ill-treatment of the animals in the forest. This created the werewolf and werebear legends that were told in the western states of the world.

Basterdor had been keeping an eye on the expedition's progress, although he'd had an unfortunate encounter with Tyler a few nights back. He admitted he had not expected anyone's senses to be so sharp, but his wounds had been slight and helped remind him that he too could still be humbled – although it had been a long time since anyone had managed to strike him. He had taken Benjamin south, beyond the Forest's edge to speed their movement. They had then headed north towards the land of the Willow tribes. Basterdor knew of the coming battle and Ghimane's involvement. He also knew of Benjamin's friends, so he considered Benjamin to be a part of the proceedings and brought him along. They linked with the armies of Willow, and Basterdor helped guide them south-east to the Hall of the Ten Tribes. En route they had encountered a company of Oak, who briefed them on the dire situation at the hall. They explained their plan of attack, and Basterdor and the Chieftain of Willow agreed to manoeuvre to where it was felt they were most needed. Hence their force mounted an assault from the south.

Basterdor then told how the wizard, Ghimane, had been his apprentice back deep in the depths of time, when the Forest was still young. The wizard had been called Mane back then, but he chose to follow a darkened path in pursuit of an accelerated mastery of his craft. This choice allowed his growing powers to corrupt him, as the dark path tended to do. Believing his master stood in his way, he had then attempted to kill Basterdor as he slept. Fortunately, Basterdor suspected that Ghimane's intentions had turned to another path so he created an illusion which managed to trick Ghimane (as he was now called) into believing he had succeeded. Basterdor was however badly wounded during the assault, and the injuries inflicted on him took many years to heal. Basterdor remained patient and bided his time, for he knew Ghimane would do no good in this world and that one day they would again clash.

Basterdor had taken animal form at this time and drifted into folklore as the Sorcerer Supreme who was part of the Forest. Ghimane had sided with the southern tribes; simple folk who were easily controlled and open to suggestion. Using them, he hoped to advance his influence in Markesh and intended to find the lost masters of the Coeur-Vu-Do and after releasing them into the world do their bidding. It was well known amongst wizards, mages and sorcerers that the dark path of the magical arts was controlled by the Coeur-Vu-Do, ancient lost masters who could not die. It was said they had been entombed and secured during an ancient war and that these tombs were guarded closely by the keepers. However, it had long been accepted that despite their incarceration they still controlled the black arts, and those who chose this path would eventually be led to the Coeur-Vu-Do.

With the battle ended, a time for reflection and mourning was upon them. The group had been on the road but a short time, and already four of their number were gone. Chantelle headed a small ceremony to honour the fallen. She began with an Elvin song, sung so soft and subtly that it sounded as though it had arrived laid upon the breeze that now passed through the great hall. Its

Elvin harmony cannot be captured in words, but the words went like this:

Cumjarrow, Cumjaylo, anor teh Dimnakor,
FetUl Terum, Nabrudor anie Gador.

Which to our understanding means:

Rejoice, Repent, before the Lord,
Ripened land, deliverance and Life.

The song and the service continued into the night, after which preparations for a large banquet the following day were made; a banquet where by request of the four Chieftains our party would be the guests of honour. The banquet passed without incident, but was a very welcome break from the events that preceded them; Benjamin again got Idron extremely drunk, whilst Chantelle, Elsbeth and Chevon consoled Tyler, who was still upset having lost the two people most close to him: Jethro, his brother, and his beloved Meme. Torres and Bramley danced the night away and a blossoming relationship was here born. Erin and Juran spoke with the Chieftains and Basterdor throughout the night, talking of the Forest and its history, and of how Basterdor had created the flaming barrier centuries ago to reduce the chance of war. They also learnt that the creatures that prowled the rivers shores had entered from the north-east and were indeed related to dragons, though everyone called them River Snappers. (It is believed these are the great lost ancestors of the crocodiles and alligators we see today.)

It was also agreed here that the expedition would be escorted through the Forest the next day, leaving via Willow's northern border. Beyond which there were open rolling hills and fields with many tracks that would eventually lead them to Kondama – a city of man, where once, it was said, a man could get anything he wanted – at a price, of course.

Night Owl

Their journey northwards began two days after the banquet; thus all were well rested. The relative safety they gained from the company of the escorting tribesmen allowed them to relax for the first time since they had left the Northern Port on the Green River. These escorts were knowledgeable in the ways of the Forest and pointed out much of the wildlife that dwelled there, along with the many edible plants. The trek north became both interesting and enjoyable; they even took time out to hunt Mustak, a small deer indigenous to the Great Forest. In addition much information was gained during this journey north that would aid their mapping of this part of Markesh.

They were told tales of the Spirits of Sycamore, ethereal creatures that were said to haunt the plains between the Forest and the Silver Birch; woods that lay below the mountains in the north-east. A deceitful alliance offering riches beyond belief had brought about a great fire that had been lit and fuelled by evil witches. This had destroyed the Sycamore portion of the Forest, along with its tribe, thus breaking the Forest's mighty reach and isolating the tribe of Silver Birch who still lived in the foothills below the mountains of Falcon's Nest.

Kondama came up in conversation often. A boom town, it was rich from the natural resources in that area. Gold, silver, diamonds and fossil fuels could all be found within a day's journey of this great town. Surrounding the town, three rivers created a large natural obstacle. They were wide, deep and fast-flowing, and helped to secure the town. These rivers formed the sides of the town's triangular layout, and each river had only one bridge, bridges that could be raised or lowered to isolate the community during times of siege. The town also had one of the finest armouries in Markesh, or so the forest tribes boasted, and the Chieftains had given Juran a seal that was to be presented to the armourer. The armourer would then supply them with anything they desired, courtesy of the tribes of the Northern Forest. This would help replace the weapons lost when Jethro's team had been captured. The armourer was also said to have some special weapons that had a hint of magic in their forging, but they would need to bargain in order to obtain such items. This was an intriguing proposition and something that sparked a curious interest in most of the party.

On the fourth night they were close to the day's halt and setting up camp was in everyone's mind; the mood was relaxed and jovial when the lead horseman in the party suddenly dropped from his horse in a lifeless manner. This brought a sudden panic amongst the ranks. Then disaster struck as the two rear riders struck the ground in much the same manner and now lay immobile on the forest floor. Their flustered, riderless horses instantly reared and bolted into the trees, quickly disappearing from view. Idron caught fleeting glimpses of dark figures moving through the trees but could not make out much detail.

The two fallen rear bodies disappeared before the group had a chance to reach them, but the front rider had been closed with almost immediately. Stuck in his throat was a small flechette, sharp, deadly and decisive, a weapon typically used by the Ajya-Na-Ku. The Pigeon Hawks were dispatched and stayed together for fear of Black Owls, but no sign was discovered and the Ajya-Na-Ku disappeared as easily as they had arrived. This incident quickly changed the mood from the carefree to the sombre, and the complacency that had accompanied them these past days was replaced by incredible tension and apprehension. The Ajya-Na-Ku's spies had indeed noticed the events of the battle of the Ten Tribes, and this had rekindled their interest in the Great Forest. A reminder of just who commanded the continent was required, so their sphere of influence had again been extended, signalling to all that they had not disappeared and were, as ever, firmly in control. This small incident was a mere sample of what was now occurring throughout the Great Forest, striking fear and despondency among the forest tribes, showing that their mortal enemy was as real as ever and not about to allow others to force their dominance in any part of Markesh, no matter how slight.

That night, Black Owls were observed wherever one cared to

look. Menacing and unnerving, their presence kept everyone on edge. All anticipated an imminent strike. Terrible screams of pain, fear and horror echoed through the forest that night – an effective reminder of who controlled these lands.

The following morning saw a break in the rain and the temperature dropped significantly. All day they caught glimpses of movement. Dark shadows and overactive imaginations may have been the root of some sightings, but certainly not all. Idron and Tyler, who probably had the keenest eyesight amongst the group, knew that some of the movement observed came from the same creatures they had spotted when they had been ambushed the previous day.

The tension was broken when finally they reached the end of the Forest and the group rode forth upon the open plains. The horses were happy to move into the open space the plains provided. After being confined for so long with such limited visibility, in a place where each crack, thud or bump could indicate danger, they took great pleasure in departing the Great Forest. At least in open country sound didn't bounce around as much, and a speedy escape was far easier than when struggling through the undergrowth.

Now the Forest was behind them they parted company with their escorts. They thanked the northern tribes for their guidance and wished them luck in their return journey home. The day was only a few hours old as they rode on across the open fields on route to Kondama. The sunlight troubled their eyes for some time; it had been fairly dim amid the forest undergrowth, and they had spent over a month beneath its shadow. The cold air was fresh and pure and a refreshing change from the soggy conditions they had suffered. Their clothes were damp and uncomfortable and in dire need of washing. Movement in such garments brought rashes and sores to most of the party; so all now relished the thought of entering a decent town, eating a rounded meal and sleeping in clean sheets; not something they had expected to be able to do when they entered Markesh, which only made the possibility of such things more appealing.

The ride north lasted another three days and the weather grew increasingly harsher as they progressed, as did the altitude. The grassy tussocks of the plains gave way to peat and heather along with the odd rocky outcrop. Rodents, wolves and buffalo were in abundance, but few people were seen, and those they spotted were some way off. The nights were freezing, though the peat provided fuel for the fires that quickly became their main source of heat. The Black Owls were ever present, monitoring their progress. Juran tried various spells to disperse them but the dark power that sided with them proved far stronger than the power he wielded. Wolves shadowed their route, and it was suspected that these too were in league with the Ajya-Na-Ku. Their constant howling only gave sustenance to the chills that everyone experienced and added vigilance to their routine. The sight of the distant river-bound city was most welcome, and without conscious decision the pace was increased. They joined the east-west road that led up to the bridge crossing the river to their front.

The road was well used and in a sound state, showing the wealth that this town generated. The bridge had a strong solid stone construction built on each bank, made from quarried stones of all shapes and sizes that were fashioned into a rather ornate finish and acted as the bridge's support. A thick wooden walkway spanned the river, held in position by huge iron chains that were secured to enormous pulleys mounted high on the town walls. The walkway was down as they approached, and many people were transiting the road and moving freely in and out of the city limits.

The hooves of the animals clip-clopped over the bridge and they all peered down at the crashing torrent of white foam that lay below; it was indeed a formidable obstacle.

At the bridge's end was a large square open wrought-iron gate. It led into a short entrance that was dominated by archers' slits high on its walls. A second gate made of wood lay at the entrance's far end; it too was open, and they passed through into a bustling street. Stalls lined either side as far as the eye could see and various characters carrying their wares moved up and down in a most annoying manner as they pushed their goods, determined to make a sale. Tools, food, cloth, clothing and all manner of hardware were on display, and competition between the vendors was high. Set slightly back from the stalls more secure buildings were positioned. These sold jewels, gold, silver and arms and armour of all sorts, and seemed free of the hustle and bustle of the market stalls. It was difficult riding through the street with people pushing and pulling in every direction, and often spilling onto the road and thus obstructing movement. Everyone seemed to have something to offer, apart from those who formed an even more irritating group: a troupe of semi-professional beggars, quite similar to the ones Elsbeth and Meme had encountered in the Northern Port on the Green River.

Soldiers and lawmen were dotted around, some shopping others relaxing, whilst some were manning lookout posts and checkpoints. Erin suggested they ask one of the lawmen how to get to the boarding house that had been recommended to them by the Willow Tribe's Chieftain. So, approaching one of them, she enquired, 'Hello there, I don't suppose you could be so kind, but we're looking for the Drowning Pool – a boarding house. Have you heard of it?' She gazed down on the lawman, smiling and flaunting all her womanly wiles.

'No problem, I've heard of it... but pray tell, if I aid your party, what do I get in return?' asked the lawman.

'I'm not certain I follow,' said a puzzled Erin, not sure or comfortable with exactly where this was leading.

'You know... let's not play games. After all, such a fine woman as yourself... I saw your come on plain as day, it's clear what you want,' replied a cheerful but quite serious officer.

'Sorry, but I don't know what you mean. I've done nothing, I merely sought direction, and any other offer was indeed unintentional,' answered Erin, feeling increasingly uncomfortable.

'Now look, you made the advance, it was quite clear and it would be against protocol to not honour what was offered. So let nothing more be said: you had best be ready by eight sharp, we can settle this then,' answered a now somewhat domineering lawman, whose face seemed dark and somewhat sinister as he ordered the meet.

'But I really don't know what you mean, and truly I offered naught,' pleaded Erin, only guessing the half of what she had let herself in for.

'Not another word! The Boarding House is straight on, taking the third on the right, followed by the second on the left. Then you'll see it pure as day, a bright yellow five-storey building. Sign's over the door. Now what's your name, my lady?' said the lawman.

'Erin, my name's Erin,' answered Erin, feeling the misunderstanding had been resolved.

'Fine, Erin, but Erin who? You surely have a second name don't you?' pressed the lawman.

'Er, well of course: Hathershaw, Erin Hathershaw,' answered Erin as though she had been chastised by her father.

'Fine, so Miss Hathershaw it is. Just you be more careful in future,' said the lawman, grinning from ear to ear. 'Now be on your way then.'

They rode on a short distance before they initiated a conversation. 'What was that all about?' said Chevon, looking sideways at Erin.

'I'm not too certain, but I didn't like it,' replied Erin.

'I thought he was probably after a tip or a bribe, or something?' said Elsbeth.

'No, I believe he was after our Erin,' said Juran, 'though he obviously couldn't smell you from down there, so looks like he had a lucky escape.'

'Ha, bloody ha!' said Erin.

The others laughed and they continued through the town following the directions the lawman had given them. Stinger, alert as ever, warned the others to look around the rooftops of the town, and sure enough they could see, peering down on them, more of the dreaded Black Owls.

The boarding house was a fine establishment with many rooms and a large stable yard that was more then adequate for the animals. The birds decided to stay in the stables with Que and Gee; that way they could come and go as they pleased and also keep an eye on any sinister goings-on. The animals had bonded really well and had much by way of reflection to discuss out of earshot of the human types. The stables were fairly big and fresh water and feed was plentiful. A young girl called Jarrow maintained the stables. She was very kind but did not understand the equine languages, so what they said to one another whilst there remains their secret.

Each member of the party had their own room and these were to be paid for using a portion of the rather large kitty of silver and gold that they had been given as funding for their journey. It was a generous amount and weighed heavy – as Surefoot, Longfoot, Strongfoot and Hardfoot could no doubt confirm, having laboured with it for most of the journey. The rooms were spacious with a huge soft bed and crisp linen; a large iron bath was situated in the corner of each room surrounded by a decorative screen and water jugs. The windows had shutters on the outside and all of the party's rooms overlooked a busy square.

Erin had finished a long relaxing bath when a knock came at her door. 'Just a minute!' she shouted as she donned one of the silk robes provided and moved towards the door.

'Hello, Miss Hathershaw – or should I call you Erin?' said the lawman who now stood before her, 'I see you are ready. I knew you'd honour the arrangement,' he continued in a smarmy manner.

'Look, I made no arrangements with you, I simply asked directions, that's all,' Erin said in a defensive and uncomfortable voice. 'So whatever you may think, we have no business together, and I think it would be best if you leave,' she continued, closing the door.

Pushing his foot in its path, the lawman said, 'Erin, you have no choice. I am the Law, and you have to obey the Law.' With this he forced the door, throwing Erin backwards and entered the room slamming it shut behind him.

'Now come here, you little slut! Leading me on with your smiles and looks, you will take me this night or you'll live to regret it,' he snarled, a look of wickedness crossing his face. He moved toward her, grabbing her arms.

'Get the hell off of me, you self-centred pig! Who on earth do you think you are, you jumped-up shit?' screamed a furious Erin, not believing this man's actions. She tried to break his grasp but he was far too strong for her. Then, without warning, he struck her hard in the face. Dazed, she fell backwards onto the bed and he quickly followed. Kicking and shouting, she began to scream in an attempt at alerting others in the house. She was a warrior and knew how to fight but this was no ordinary man. He had the very Devil in him. He fought back, hitting her numerous times until her screams subsided.

She now lay limp and submissive in a battered heap on the bed, whimpering and helpless. Then, just when all seemed lost, the shutters of the window crashed open as a hurricane entered, striking the lawman around the face in a flurry of claws and feathers. Stinger and Winger pressed their attack with such ferocious intensity that the lawman could not defend himself; they tore his face and plucked at his eyes. All he was able to do was flee. He ran through the corridors with Stinger in pursuit, but Idron, who had been alerted by Singer, blocked his path.

'Hold there, or I'll run you through!' squealed Idron, brandishing the dagger his uncle had given him. The lawman stood still and Stinger hovered close behind, allowing Idron to play his part. Then suddenly a great darkness came over the corridor and all visibility was lost. A sudden shattering of glass could be heard at the end of the corridor followed by an eerie gust of wind which passed Stinger. Its draught was so forceful Stinger was unable to remain aloft, and hitting the floor, was blown to the corridor's end. Instantly, great numbers of Black Owls entered the corridor, causing a powerful downdraught as they rode on the veil of shadows wedging a gap between the lawman and Idron.

'Ha! The boy,' said a voice. It sound sharp guttural and evil. 'That feeble filly of yours,' it continued arrogantly, 'has been most fortunate. She's lucky… our ranks are many, we are everywhere!' He suddenly wheezed and fiery lights lit darkened eyes, though nothing more could be seen. 'Our servants do our bidding, wherever and whenever we choose.' Then a dim glow illuminated the blackened corridor. A large dark figure came to view in the low light, eyes still fiery as it spoke. Standing in front of the lawman, most of its face shrouded by a broad dark nose protector attached to a dark hood, it spoke.

'This fool has served his purpose but has exceeded his station.' The figure raised the lawman from the floor by the nape of his neck, sniffing him. 'Utterly useless now, except…' he paused as a bright blood red forked tongue savoured the lawman's neck and face… 'maybe, but then again…' he continued, as if talking to himself; then suddenly a shower of blood burst forth from the lawman's chest as talons were thrust through, bringing instantaneous death… '*maybe not!*'

By way of conclusion, the figure, discarded the lifeless body. The fresh corpse hit the wooden floor with a crumpled thud. The figure took a laborious pace forward then, looking towards Idron, spoke again.

'This land is ours, and will remain ours. You will grow to embrace this fact; an understanding far better than your comrades you shall have. After this day, have no doubt, you will understand.' His tone was authoritative. Then he made a slight gesture that was difficult to see in the dull corridor. A sudden hot burning sensation struck Idron's right thigh; pain came instantly as he fell to the floor. A shrilling cry escaped his lungs that echoed through the house. He looked up towards the dark figure above him and through blurry eyes he observed a confusing sight. The human form began to expand beyond the boundaries of its natural body. He found the image before him difficult to comprehend as he began to slip into unconsciousness. He vaguely saw the body break into dark pieces; pieces that formed a flight of Black Owls.

They disappeared as quickly as they had arrived, and the shadow that enveloped the house was instantly lifted. Idron passed out, grasping his leg. He was splattered in the blood of the lawman, whose inert body lay before him; Stinger was perched in a corner beyond the limp bodies that lay in the corridor; the bird was still dazed and confused; Erin lay sobbing on her bed, trying to come to terms with what had occurred this night.

The Ajya-Na-Ku had been met at first hand, the evil they nurtured amongst their ranks manifesting itself in the horror and power they wielded. Even in a seemingly secure town such as Kondama their influence held no bounds. Idron's party had been followed by Black Owls for some time and they had become a familiar threat. Never before had they metamorphosed into human form, and it looked as though their presence was far deadlier than anyone had imagined. It became quite apparent that the expedition had definitely caught the Ajya-Na-Ku's attention.

But why didn't they just eliminate its members and be done with it? The group pondered over this question for many days. What unknown scheme was keeping them alive and in what direction would it lead them?

The expedition remained in Kondama for a further three months, waiting for Erin and Idron to recover. Erin was mentally scarred and no longer her normal confident self. She had felt utterly helpless for the first time in her life and she now had doubts about continuing with the expedition. Chevon was also having second thoughts, and the prospect of returning home had much more appeal than heading into the land of the Ajya-Na-Ku. Idron's wound had been a strange one; a flechette had pierced his skin and was deeply embedded. The hole it made was tiny, and as it seemed to be healing well it was decided to leave it in place and no attempt at surgery was made. The wound had initially hurt like crazy; he had felt as though his whole body were on fire. He had been immobile for five weeks, after which he seemed as right as rain.

One day towards the end of the second month's stay in Kondama, Elsbeth, Chantelle and Torres were sitting on the terrace of the boarding house and whilst waiting for their lunch to arrive they spoke with Erin and Chevon about their misgivings regarding the journey. They discussed Erin and Chevon's thoughts of turning back. The three women felt it would be just as dangerous, if not more so, for Chevon and Erin to journey back alone. They urged them to stay the course and continue ahead. After all, with strength in numbers they would fare far better. It was common knowledge that the Ajya-Na-Ku were now back in the Great Forest, so it would be difficult for them to travel unnoticed. During the thick of the discussion their lunch arrived. It was delivered upon a small trolley; a trolley that was guided by a poor crippled soul.

'Your lunch is served, I bid you all well, and drink to your good health,' said Sticks, bowing before them.

'By the gods – is there nowhere you are not?' exclaimed Elsbeth, far more surprised than the others, having encountered this strange fellow on more than one occasion.

'Fate knows no bounds. If I'm meant to be here, then here I shall be, and I see your journey joins our paths once more,' answered Sticks, smiling cheekily.

'So, what brings you here this time?' asked Elsbeth. She was actually quite pleased to see him; after all, he had so far only brought them luck.

'Your food... I began work today, and when I noticed your party I requested to serve you,' replied Sticks, knowing full well that was not what she meant.

'So you just happened to be heading through the woods on your crutches and thought, Oh! I'll head up to Kondama today a mere four hundred or so miles from where we last met!' Elsbeth said, in a somewhat cynical but light-hearted manner.

'That's about the gist of it, but I'm here now, and serve you I will. Just ask if there's anything you need,' stated the boy, giving the impression that it was not the food he was talking about.

'Well yes, I'd like to be able to persuade these two to stay with our party. Can you help with that?' asked Elsbeth, although she did not know why the words she had spoken had been said aloud.

'Now, let me see,' said Sticks. 'Thus far the trip has been challenging – adventurous, yes, but fun, no. Pain and fear grips you now, but friends have fallen, and to give up now lessens their sacrifice. What happens to us all during our days helps mould our future, the reason why these things are so ordained is beyond our comprehension, so try not to analyse their significance. The way back may be shorter in distance but perhaps not time; forward unifies one and all. With hope, necessity and friendship must you forward move. So with friends remain, for now better friends you'll not find.'

Stick's answer seemed deep and meaningful, and while he spoke all sensed the passion in his voice. His speech was remarkably eloquent and his audience was baited by his words. There was a silent pause and the women glanced at one another as a warm glow encompassed their bodies.

'Amazing! You definitely stirred me. Just how do you do that, and how is it you know so much?' asked Elsbeth, stunned by his knowledge of events.

'I was born lucky. Now enjoy your repast, and if I don't see you before your departure, safe journey… But remember this: beware, there is dark one close to you all, his influence is everywhere, above us, below us and within us. Much hatred is brewing inside, and he will bring misfortune,' said Sticks. Once again he handed out advise of a cryptic nature and suddenly disappeared. Elsbeth thought she saw him pass through the doors of the lobby.

'Yet again he comes, and I don't believe for a moment that coincidence has anything to do with his appearances. Just who is he?' said Elsbeth, deeply curious as to Stick's true nature. 'So did his words change your minds?' she asked Erin and Chevon.

'If onward is the only way, I suppose we have little choice, and as he said, we owe it to Jethro and Meme. So onward it is,' Erin replied, looking serious and a little more confident than she had done for days.

'And you?' said Elsbeth to Chevon.

'Well, I'm not going back all that way on my own, so I guess I'll be tagging along,' answered Chevon with a slight grin. It seemed Stick's words had worked their magic.

Elsbeth stood up and made her way to the lobby; she wished to thank Sticks for again aiding their cause but also wanted to try and fathom just who or what he was. However, once she reached the lobby he was nowhere to been seen. She spotted another staff member and asked where Sticks had gone. The house hand had no idea who she was talking about and pointed out that the very idea of a man on crutches being employed as a waiter was absurd. The mystery deepened. Why did Sticks seem to pop up when least expected? Just what was he?

Elsbeth returned to the others, who were now in an exceptionally cheery mood as though all their fears had been brushed aside. It may not have been what Sticks said that lifted them, but more the feeling he left every time he spoke with them; a peculiar yet useful ally.

Their stay in Kondama was fairly uneventful following the initial drama, and most of the expedition's time was spent relaxing and getting to know the town whilst the injured convalesced. Towards the end of the third month the weather started to take a turn for the worse, and soon winter's icy grasp would grip the land. The only way forward now lay in the direction of the mountains of Falcon's Nest, and if they wished to cross them before the onset of the frozen season they would have to move soon.

Before the journey to the mountains began they paid a final visit to the armoury that had been recommended to them. They had been there many times these past weeks, fascinated by the special weapons on offer. Idron had his eye on a long sword that was extremely light and decorated with engravings of dragons along the blade, and what a blade! Razor sharp on one side, and bearing long serrated flame-like edges on its spine. The sword was called 'Charlock', which meant 'Dragon's breath' in one of the local dialects of the area, for it wielded an intense fire that burnt as it cut a most magical and remarkable piece. Idron had of course to pay heavily for it but was determined to have it.

Erin obtained a simpler weapon, a short bow which looked quite plain to the eye but had a powerful delivery system and was both easy to use and accurate. She brought a selection of arrows with it; some could pierce armour whilst others exploded on impact, and she called the bow 'Mankil'.

Most of the others settled for more conventional weapons but Tyler picked a sabre of the finest quality called 'Cleaver'. It too had a magical power and was said to harness the wind in its blade, although the armourer had not seen its effects; but even without this its solid red blade was a masterpiece that could slice through almost anything.

Juran also visited a small curiosity shop whose proprietor was an old wizard called Krultch. Juran had spent most of his time in Kondama at the shop, though he never spoke with the others about what was discussed there or what items he had purchased. The only notable item that did not evade the prying eyes of the others was a short bronze baton that had an icy gem mounted at one end and runes written on the side. It also had a hook and wire attached at one end and hung from the Mage's belt. What it did, or was for, none of them knew, but since Juran was a dealer in magic they guessed it would probably be a welcome addition to their journey.

Winter clothes, consisting of furs, hoods and blankets, were purchased, along with heavier rugs for the animals. Supplies were secured to the mules and they set off at mid-morning almost 4 ½ months from the day they had set off from Green River. They were to head across the Plains of Sycamore until they reached the Silver Birch Wood and from there cross the mountains of Falcon's Nest, an ambitious journey that they needed to complete in two months, after which the onset of winter and the worst of the snows would arrive. The distance and the task were daunting enough, but the addition of a solitary Black Owl flying high in the sky gave them far greater concerns than the journey ahead.

Spectral Plains and Silver

The expedition headed north-east from Kondama across an open plain that stretched out as far as could be seen. Tyler led the way on Gee, with Chevon and Dee close behind. Bramley and Torres were next riding Pee and Que with the mules in tow; the two had become increasingly close over the past month and now seemed inseparable. Idron rode alone close behind on Bee and found Bramley and Torres' fascination with each other most irritating. Stumpy and Grumpy carried Elsbeth and Benjamin respectively, the two Dwarves chatted about the strange fellow, Sticks, pondering over who he could be, Benjamin of course lost his temper often that day, due to discomfort, the weather, the distance and the speed – but generally just because that's how he was. Elsbeth knew him well enough not to take offence, but did find herself having to bite her lip quite a few times. Juran on the ever-reluctant Yew rode, together with Chantelle who sat upon Tee; and Erin, now riding Vee due to Cee's demise, was at the rear of the group. The pace was steady and the good visibility allowed a less cautious advance than they had been accustomed to in the Great Forest. Stinger, Winger and Singer soared overhead keeping an eye on the distant but ever watchful Black Owls.

A cold wind blew from the north-west, its cruel chilliness cutting through the party's clothing. They knew things would become much worse with the influx of the winter's snow, so they decided to keep their winter clothing until they really needed it; although Elsbeth really did not see the point in freezing from the start of the journey. It was however soon pointed out to her that washing facilities were virtually non-existent, and if they were to get the full benefit of the clothing it had to be clean, thus allowing the fibres to work properly.

The first day went well, as did the following three; then on the evening of the fifth day the land began to change. The plain still appeared as the dominant feature, but now the ground had remnants of tree stumps scattered over it. The stumps were either rotten or fossilised, almost like stone in appearance, with a rough texture; they guessed they were now amid the ruins of the mythical Sycamore Forest. The area had a character of its own and emitted a tense, unfriendly atmosphere, as though some evil entity held its dreadful memoirs for all to see. They had only moved a mile or so through it when Chantelle began to sense an impending evil.

'We must stop, here, now,' she announced, 'there's danger ahead. I fear no good will meet us if we continue this way tonight.'

'She's right – I sense it too,' Torres said, backing her friend's concerns.

'What's the problem? We still have two hours of daylight, we will waste good ground if we do not continue,' said Tyler, eager to go on.

'No Tyler, I concur with the girls,' added Juran, 'I too can feel a presence. I'm not certain what it is but I dread to think what unknown power is at work here; and I do know this, it is not worth our passage to attempt to meet with it tonight.'

'So, we make camp then, is it?' said Tyler. 'If that's what you all agree, I'll not argue. Caution can often prove a successful tactic; but take note, we'll have to press harder tomorrow if we're to make the mountains on schedule.'

'Good, then I'll put a pot on,' said Elsbeth, glad the day's journey was done and keen to feel the warmth of a good fire. 'Ben, can you lend a hand and get some wood?' she added, which brought a strange look from the others who never referred to Benjamin as Ben. So eyebrows were raised at what was in fact an innocent remark. Benjamin huffed and puffed but said nothing audible and trotted off to find wood.

Bramley and Chantelle tended to the animals allowing them to cool down before rugs were secured and feed was given. It had been one of the easiest days so far for the animals, especially the mules, whose load had been drastically reduced due to a significant portion of the bounty having been spent. It took a great deal of time before the animals were sufficiently cared for and Bramley and Chantelle could themselves relax. By this time the tea was ready and food was being prepared for the nightly meal. The birds scoured the surrounding area, checking for spies, but also hunting. Their dietary needs could be met almost everywhere in the form of rodents or small insects.

Night drew on fast, and with it another drop in temperature. The group had brought sheets of canvas along, and whilst dinner was finalised, Tyler, Juran and Erin made improvised shelters to keep the wind at bay. Idron was not his normal self and seemed increasingly insular. He did little to help but sat to a flank staring off into the distance. Torres and Chevon checked and secured the supplies, ensuring the elements would not affect them should the weather take a turn for the worse.

That night, flickering lights could be seen dancing over the plain to the north-east, in the direction they had been heading. Juran watched, absorbed by the unearthly display.

With the dawn came a realisation that Idron was missing, he was nowhere to be seen, but had taken neither his steed nor provisions. They shouted and searched for him but he was nowhere to be found. Eventually Tyler pointed out that they had to press on or they would have no chance of making the mountains and would have to sit the winter out in Kondama.

Onwards they went, watchful for any sign of their lost comrade. The day's travel was harder due to the pace set by Gee and Tyler, who knew the importance of missing the worst of the weather. They had both spent many winters in the Tricon Mountains of Proteous, and knew only too well how unforgiving the elements could be. The plain was increasingly lifeless; even the small animals that scurried through the grasses and stumps were notable by their absence. This combined with the remoteness of the plain only added to the feeling of isolation. The ill feeling from the previous night did not leave them but intensified throughout the day as time progressed. Still they pushed onwards, hoping to escape its influence before the onset of another night. Towards the end of the day the ground began to rise sharply and on the horizon, but still some way off, they thought they could make out the edge of a wood. It seemed that another day of travel would be needed before they could exit the 'Sycamore cemetery', as they had nicknamed it; for it indeed was a lifeless and eerie place.

Once more they set up camp, and again distant lights hopped about the landscape. This time strange sounds accompanied them and figures could be seen dashing around in the dark. The whole camp was on alert, and so frightening was the feeling that they decided to strike camp and press on in darkness. They rode on, close to each other. The figures came nearer as they progressed, causing an increased pace. Then as anticipated, the figures came into contact with the party. Cleaver worked its magic, slicing easily through the dark attackers. Tyler worked like the professional, rallying the team and striking the assailants with shameless ferocity. In the darkness a fiery blade could be seen, blazing through the dark as though the Devil himself controlled its blade. It was Charlock, the Dragon's breath, Idron's sword. They pushed on, fighting short skirmishes as they rode. Each time, Charlock could be seen as though Idron was shadowing their move. The wispy lights always accompanied the dark figures but their shape or character could not be determined. The feeling of dread remained but they could do nothing but fight and move.

The night dragged on and the group were exhausted. Then, with the first rays of a new day, the struggle was over and both the figures and the lights were gone. They had travelled only a short distance in their plight, and the edge of the wood they had seen the night before seemed no closer. After a short but much needed break, they rode back in search of a body, in an effort to put a name to the countless assailants they had killed. Their quest for an enemy whose face they would recognise failed, as no sign of the battle remained; not a drop of blood, nor sign of fallen body was found. If this alone wasn't mystery enough there was still no sign of Idron.

"Tis an enigma that we may never fully understand, though it appears our attackers were perhaps wraithlike and therefore already slain before they met with our blades. Most likely not belonging to this plain of existence, but dragged back by some unseen force pent no doubt on evil undertakings,' commented Juran.

'Whoever, the feeling of ill remains and we need to flee or face another night of similar or far worse consequences,' said Chantelle, still uncomfortable with the aura that emanated from the land.

'But what of Idron?' inquired Torres, who despite her passion for Bramley still had a soft spot for the half-breed.

'If he made it this far he's probably fine, but as you well know, he does not come when called or reveal when approached. So what are we to do – remain in hope that he will come to his senses?' queried Tyler, who had been pleased to see Charlock's immense power on their side, but felt waiting on the plain to be foolhardy.

'Well, wherever he is, I hope he's not suffering or in trouble. I'd hate to think we had abandoned the poor boy,' said Elsbeth, concerned for the youngest member of their party and showing again her motherly manner.

'Don't fret, woman, our Idron's made of sturdier stuff than you give him credit for. You saw his blade – wherever he is you can bet he's fighting on,' added Benjamin, who had a growing admiration for Idron and had more faith in him than most.

'Come, let's make these parts history, for another night here would be way too testing,' said Erin, who during the night had also handled Mankil with great skill and an added rage born of the assault on her by the lawman in Kondama.

They rode on with added haste, none of them wishing to fight through the next night; the Spirits of Sycamore had again defended their domain, expelling all who dared venture onto their plain.

They now entered a lightly wooded area of silver birch trees, and after negotiating a rather steep rock-strewn projection they came upon a shelf of sheltered land. The shelf dominated the surrounding area and gave excellent views across the Sycamore Plains as well as the wood they had entered. It was close to dusk so once more they settled down for the night. The warmth this place radiated was a welcome change from the bitter cold of the plains and it gave them a chance to rest their bodies well. Whilst on watch they could all see the ghostly lights on the plain, and occasionally Charlock was noted in the thick of them. This made some of the company feel as though they had deserted their companion and guilt crept over them. Tyler decided after his duty that he was going back in search of Idron.

He did not tell the others, and leading Gee off on foot made his way out of the wood. Mounting the brave steed he made for the thick of the lights, which were only a short way off, and almost immediately he saw Charlock. The flaming blade once again locked with these spectres in a seemingly tireless battle. Tyler drew close to Charlock and joined the fray. From his mount he struck at the heart of the apparitions, screaming Idron's name as he fought. He thought he could hear a faint but seemingly distant reply, which puzzled him, for Charlock was now just ahead.

On reaching the blade he could not make out Idron but saw only a darkened figure brandishing the sword. He feared it had been taken by one of these wraiths and that Idron was forever lost. He moved closer still and heard a weak voice.

'Kill me! For the love of the gods, kill me Tyler!'

It was Idron's voice. Tyler paused, uncertain what to do, but the words came again.

'Strike now, before all is lost, you fool! Tyler, kill me!' came the desperate voice.

Not knowing what to do, Tyler lashed out and Cleaver cut through the dark figure that held Charlock. There was a burst of blinding light followed by a rush from the spectres. Charlock was down, and Tyler struggled alone with his honourable mount, Gee. They both made a frenzied effort, hooves stomping and blade cleaving; on they went through the remainder of the night. Again it was only the arrival of the light that brought the battle to a close. With the onslaught over only Tyler and Gee remained, but close by sprawled on the grass lay Idron, still clutching Charlock in his right hand.

A weary horse carrying Tyler and Idron's lifeless body struggled back up toward the plateau where the others were resting. Idron was laid upon a rug of animal hide and covered with fur. He was not dead, and no wound was visible, but he appeared to be merely in a deep slumber. Too fatigued to continue, the position they had adopted was maintained throughout the day. Most were grateful for the rest, but Tyler was annoyed that his condition was losing them valuable time, and he worried that they would not beat the coming winter.

Idron awoke around mid-afternoon. He remained groggy but was fine. He said that he had taken a stroll around the perimeter of the camp on the first night; he had felt uneasy all day and was unable to settle. It was then that he had encountered the strange astral figures; they had lured him towards them and a struggle followed that was to continue until Tyler arrived and cut him down. He had seen the wraiths plainly; they were once men not dissimilar to the northern tribes who dwelled in the Great Forest. They had ferried him into their plane of existence for reasons as yet unknown to him. With Charlock's help he had managed to anchor himself in reality, but the battle that raged had become wearisome and he was almost lost.

Fortunately, the cutting down of his astral figure had released him from the terrible nightmare, and his cries to Tyler had been designed to achieve what had come to pass. He was mighty relieved that he was now free from the disturbing clutches of the spirits. He also stated that no matter what lay ahead he would not go back through those plains. He was grateful of Tyler's efforts but made it clear for all to see that he was none too happy about his abandonment. His face was thunderous, and he knew he would never trust many of them again.

At dawn Chevon took her turn to prepare the horses for the move and discovered Yew was missing. The other animals said he had just walked off a few hours ago, heading east. They had attempted to discourage him but he was just too stubborn. This news could mean another delay, so she dispatched Singer eastward to find the wandering fool and bring him back. Yew's absence did not delay the move and Juran merely rode Surefoot after a quick distribution of loads. Surefoot was happy enough with this arrangement, as Juran was far lighter than the load he had been carrying, and he suggested to Chevon that if or when Yew returned he should be punished and made to carry a mule's load. This was a reasonable suggestion, and one they agreed might curb Yew's tendency to stray; he had been too scared to wander off in the Great Forest and happy to stay close on the plains, as he too could sense danger. Now, however, these woods felt good, normal and with little danger, so he decided to do his own thing. He had unbeknown to the expedition's human types, escaped quite regularly in Kondama but the stable maid, Jarrow, had always found him come dinner time.

Singer didn't take long to spot Yew, who was sipping water at a small brook without a care in the world. But instead of speaking with him the Hawk flew back and spoke with Chevon. A plan was hatched that would perhaps scare Yew into thinking twice about disappearing in future. With Juran's help, they planned to create a beast that would jump out and scare Yew, causing him to bolt and rush back to the encampment, which would of course be empty. They would then use Singer to meet with Yew and guide him to the group, tail between his legs and ready to carry Surefoot's load.

Juran decided to conjure up a small silver dragon, that would swoop down from the tree tops, roaring and breathing fire, then barely missing Yew ascend quickly to the heavens and disappear. So Juran began his spell, and said:

'Silver tree with silver bark,
Give silver free to frightful bark,
And rise above the trees so proud,
To breathe your flame and roar so loud,
Then swoop you down to fear the horse,
But do no harm to him, of course;
And when he does begin to run,
End your plight, for 'tis but fun,
And let the steed be on his way,
Then rise you high but do not stray,
For once up there your job is through,
And wanderlust will part from Yew.'

At this, a large silver birch tree to their front began to shake. The ground beneath it began to rumble and the roots sprang upwards. Its branches began to spread and fuse together, forming large silver wings. The pinnacle of the tree transformed into a long pointed tail and the roots closed together forming huge jaws that joined with the strong base of the trunk, which now became the neck and head of a rapidly changing beast. Some of the lower, thicker branches formed powerful back legs and the newborn dragon rose on its hind legs before their eyes – and right formidable he was too. A powerful downdraught from its wings blew across the party's faces as the silver dragon flew upwards and then headed off in Yew's direction.

Yew had just begun to leave the area of the brook when an almighty roar made his heart skip a beat. The huge beast closed with the poor fellow, who thought his days were numbered; and with his life passing before his eyes, he wished he hadn't been so self-centred and had remained with the group. Fire singed the hairs on his back as the dragon narrowly missed him. Then with great relief the dragon flitted skywards and was gone.

Yew galloped off as quickly as he was able and made the plateau in record time, only to find it deserted. Panic struck him and he did not know which way to turn, although he knew the group were headed north-east; but he just was not thinking clearly… The dragon might come back but this time it might not miss. Then Singer caught his attention and, calming him, guided him back to the main group. Yew was pleased to see them all but not too pleased at being relegated to mule's work; yet he would think twice about wandering off on his own again.

They journeyed on, and had only continued a short while when the sky above them suddenly turned black. A sudden powerful wind threw up the floor of the woods. Dust was everywhere and they had difficulty remaining on their feet. Looking up they saw to their horror three large sets of peering eyes looking down on them. A warm wind came upon them as the real dragon above exhaled. The dragons were looking for something, and fortunately it was not our travellers. They had seen another unfamiliar dragon in their territory, and the hunt was on to find out where he had come from and why he was there. For the moment these worthless animals below were of no concern, but were noted none the less, as they might provide a snack or two if their hunt kept them busy for longer than they reckoned. One of the dragons spat out a small fireball that smashed into the ground close to the mules, causing them to stumble and make for safety as the scorched earth around them flared up into a steady blaze. The dragons then sped off in the direction of the plateau, looking for their quarry. Breathing a sigh of relief, the expedition made the most of their near miss and pressed onward.

'Looks as though your little trick backfired big style, eh, Juran!' said Benjamin, none too happy that dragons now knew of their presence.

Juran shrugged his shoulders and said, 'It was only a matter of time, for if dragons are present then not much comes and goes without them knowing.'

'Ay, too true; but it still does not warm my frozen feet to know I may end up on some dragon's table this night,' said Benjamin in his normal grouchy tone.

'Well, at least we know they're here! We could have run into them blindly – at least we can prepare and make an effort to avoid their flight,' said Tyler, showing his positive military way of thinking.

'We could speak with them. After all, not all dragons are bad; alliances have been made in the past and could be struck again,' said Torres optimistically.

'Maybe, but those alliances were fostered during times of great need. We cannot assume an alliance would be easy,' added the more cautious Chevon.

'Indeed we can speak, if and when another encounter occurs; but I side with Tyler's view. For now, avoid them at all costs; we cannot gauge their intentions from the unpleasant meet they just gave us,' said Chantelle, not wishing to seek an alliance unless it became their only option.

'Well, I suppose I'm to be held to account for this problem, so I'll place my nose in my book of incantations and see if I can't come up with something that may help. But dragons are a difficult lot to bewitch, so I can promise little,' said Juran, whilst feeling for his book.

They moved onwards through the birch trees, weary of the sky. All the Hawks were on full alert and they made good ground before the day's end. During the night, flashes of flaming streams could be seen in the distance. The dragons were obviously giving someone a hard time. They did not build a fire that night and ate only cold food, not wishing to draw attention to themselves. Just prior to dawn Cleaver swung rapidly through the air to meet a sudden unwelcome visitor. Its blade stopped at the neck of the intruder and Tyler sang out a challenge. 'Hold you there, afore your head departs your body!' he yelled.

'That wouldn't be pleasant, now would it!' said the intruder. 'But you have nothing to fear from me, friend, for it is I – Sticks – at your service.'

Yet again this strange fellow had appeared in the middle of nowhere, seemingly from nowhere.

'Elsbeth, my good lady, it's good to see you are well and that your company are intact; but darkness is still threatening your core, and you need to look where you would perhaps not see it.' Sticks spoke in a concerned voice that warned of dangers that were hidden.

'Well, Sticks, I've given up asking how you do it, but you appear in the most far-off places, places we have had difficulty arriving at, and yet each time you follow close behind,' answered Elsbeth. She was happy to see him because no matter what he was he had thus far only aided their journey.

'My purpose is to serve, this I have told you on each meet. I ask nothing of you, for the deal was struck; then I aid when aid is due, and such a time is here. The winter is closing fast and it will not let you pass. The flighty fire-breathers will do you harm unless you meet with the Caverns of Martel. They will cover your move, as the fiery ones cannot enter their narrow pathways. Once through them you will be high in the mountains of Falcon's Nest. Avoid the Peak, for it hides that which should remain concealed. Yet on its slopes is a solid cabin, built centuries ago by the Elves that once lived in these lands. There you shall find shelter and provisions aplenty; its keeper is kindly and will secure your stay, for there you should remain until the thaw begins,' said Sticks in an informative and deliberate voice, as though he were guiding this expedition.

'So pray tell, how does one with such apparently broken legs get around as fast as the horses, and then happen to dictate our moves?' snapped Idron, in a hateful voice. He did not like this fellow and could see no reason to live by his word.

'Idron,' pleaded Elsbeth, disappointed by his attitude, 'this poor soul has brought naught but fortune to our party. If he were the Devil himself he would be welcome.'

'Please – anything but that name!' said Sticks. 'I have no pact with that fellow, and do not require association even by word to link my doings with his.'

'She's right. I too am bewildered by this man but he as yet to lead us astray. We should heed his words; after all anything that keeps us from the dragons' reach has to be good,' said Bramley, backing Elsbeth's thoughts on the matter. This only brought a distasteful glance from Idron, who was really beginning to dislike her new favourites.

'What say you, Juran?' asked Tyler, who respected the Mage although he had made some monumental errors.

'We have little to lose. The caverns sound as though they would lessen the threat posed by the dragons, and the cabin seems an interesting alternative to ice and snow,' answered Juran. He too had a good feeling about Sticks, although it was as clear as day that he was not, and never had been, a chance encounter.

'So, how do we find these caverns, then?' inquired Erin, keen to get away from the threat of dragons.

'Simple, I will be your guide,' said Sticks.

'So you're coming with us? Great,' said Elsbeth, gleaming with joy. She felt really comfortable when Sticks was around – at ease with the world.

'Not entirely, I will show you the entrance to the caverns, then we must again part company,' replied Sticks, smiling at Elsbeth, giving her a warm glow that felt as though it was running through her entire body.

'Now come, before the fiery ones return; it is not far,' continued Sticks.

He mounted no steed, but moved with incredible speed. Through the trees he sped, and led them higher and higher for some thirty minutes or so. He did not seem to tire and his pace never slackened. They came to a rocky gorge that cut the slope high above them. Its entrance was narrow, but had just enough room to allow the largest of the horses through.

'Here we must now part. Journey on, the gorge twists and turns for some way, but you cannot stray. It will lead you to the cavern's mouth. From there, heed my advise, it will see you well,' said Sticks, without a hint of effort in his voice; the fast pace they had just made would have any normal man labouring for air.

He stood at the entrance of the gorge and saw them through; they all bid him well as they passed, except Idron, who stared forward with a cold expression on his face.

'Until the spring, until spring,' whispered Sticks, though all heard his words, and a glance rearwards from Elsbeth confirmed he had again vanished.

Mountain Hop

The cavern's entrance was reached after a few hours travel; its dark interior did not appear inviting, but even so it was still more appealing than facing three or maybe more fiery dragons. Torches were made and lit to make their passage a little easier and they cautiously entered its gloomy interior. The birds, who preferred space and daylight, did not wish to fly among the darkened passages as they would more than likely run into bats or other such cave-dwelling creatures, whose eyesight was better suited to the darkened places of the Earth; so instead they safely sat in their cages, which had been secured to three mules – Hardfoot, Longfoot and Strongfoot. Though the entrance was tight the expanse of the cavern was huge, and many stalactites and stalagmites protruded from the floors and ceiling. Water dripped from the roof and the whole place had a damp, musty stench. The ground was slippery underfoot and made progress slow.

All day they plodded on, but the darkness betrayed time, and nightfall came and went before they decided to rest. Many tunnels linked the caverns and one could easily become disorientated amid such a maze, but Juran held devices that indicated direction with immense accuracy, so their route was fairly safe. It was difficult to find somewhere dry to rest, and this had been one of the reasons they had plodded on for so long. But eventually they found a chamber that had shafts breaking through the roof that allowed light to illuminate the interior. Although this unexpected light troubled their eyes the warmth it carried was most welcome as was the dry platform that lay at chest height. This shelf of rock captured the full rays of the sun on its surface and the wide ramps leading up to it made access easy. The platform, though plain, was large and there was enough space for all the party to relax in a relatively comfortable fashion.

The shafts above were many and some were big enough for a man to climb through, so they admitted a good deal of light and warmth, and this is probably the reason the platform remained dry. This platform had obviously been made, carved from the stone by fine artisans whose work would have made the skilled Dwarf races proud. Benjamin even commented that it must surely have been Dwarves who had constructed this resting place; for a resting place it had to be, there was no other purpose it could have served, and if this route was known to Sticks then it was probably known to many.

Elsbeth made dinner as usual, and mothered the party as only she could. Her maternal instincts were due to her having nurtured many children, some her own, some belonging to others. She had worked in an orphanage during the Wars and many children suffering from the effects of conflict had passed through her care. The loss of her own ten-year-old child had proved too much for her and she decided to leave her work to others and take a much needed break. That was twelve years ago, and when the appeal for volunteers to explore Markesh had been made she had to try a new adventure. Despite the ups and down so far it had done her a world of good, and now she felt as though she had a new family. Cooking and caring for them pleased her, and the satisfaction it brought her was the greatest therapy in the world.

The pots were on the fire for quite some time and the smoke and steam rose upwards, caught on the draught in a perfect natural chimney, and this kept the air fairly fresh on the platform. They maintained the fire long after they had finished the fine meal Elsbeth had prepared for them. The fire's heat helped warm their dampened clothes and they hung them out to dry. Bedrolls were laid out and they decided to get some rest. Surefoot relaxed, but was still on a self-appointed vigil, keeping a keen eye on the tunnels that led off from the chamber.

They had not been sleeping long when – Kaboom – there was a deafening explosive crash; rocks fell from above, smashing against the caverns walls as they tumbled down towards the shelf of the platform. Surefoot did not need to alert any of the group as the loud boom had stirred everyone. They scrambled to their feet and ran in all directions to gain the sanctuary of the tunnels. Heat scorched through the cavern as a huge flame of ashen fire was directed through the shafts of the cavern's roof. Scaly talons clawed at the holes trying to force an opening as a large amber dragon scavenged the area where plumes of smoke and steam had been spotted, a sure indication that the human races were again in the region. The beast struggled with the rock for some time, causing much damage to the cavern below, but was unable to force an entrance through which he could pass, so with a loud frustrating roar he zoomed off into the sky and away.

Below there was pandemonium. Rocks were strewn everywhere and clouds of dust filled the air making it impossible to breath or see. The group were well spread and many of their belongings lay beneath large boulders. Benjamin, Chevon and Chantelle found that the entrance to their tunnel was blocked and they had no way of getting through. Bramley, Torres and Idron had managed to move off with the animals into the tunnel that led onwards towards the mountains, and had fared better than most of the group.

Tyler, Elsbeth, Erin and Juran were still in the cavern and only a quick spell from Juran had managed to deflect the rocks from their huddled-up position, and now they had to attempt to scramble out of the tomb that surrounded them. The rumbling stopped as the last of the rocks stood fast, and whilst the dust settled all concerns in the group were for the condition of the party.

'Chantelle, Juran… anyone!' cried Bramley from the safety of the tunnel he had the fortune to choose. 'Can anybody hear me? It's safe this way, follow my voice!' He continued yelling, acting as a beacon for any survivors.

'Bramley,' answered Juran, 'Elsbeth, Erin and Tyler are with me, we're okay! It may take some time to reach you, though. It's quite tight in here, but whistle or something… we still need direction and I fear my instruments are lost.'

''Tis bad news, but at least you live! What of Chantelle and the others?' shouted Bramley. He had worked closely with Chantelle and was fond of her in a brotherly sort of way, 'Any sign of them?'

'No, and I hear no calls either. Let's pray they have not fallen,' came Juran's concerned reply.

Benjamin and the two women were unable to hear the shouting due to the thickness of the boulders blocking their path. They tried pushing, pulling, hammering and every method that sprang to mind to shift the rocks, but they would not budge. They yelled and screamed, struck sword against sword and knocked as loud as they were able, but their efforts passed unheard.

''Tis no good! Bloody dragons – what now? We could be wandering for an eternity in this maze,' said a disgruntled Chevon.

'Aye! Dragons are the worst pests I've ever come across, and if I meet with this one he'll wish he'd let us be, I can tell you,' said an angry Benjamin, full of bravado, though clearly no match for a dragon.

'We'll have to find another route. We have no provisions aside from a little water, and only the fates can say what has become of the others,' said a rather serious but positive Chantelle. She was concerned about the condition of the others, especially the animals.

'Fear you not! I was born in a cave, tunnels are like the womb to me, I'll have us out of here before you can say "Markesh sucks",' said Benjamin, who indeed was born in a cave and had mined many a tunnel in his time. Moreover, being a Dwarf he was accustomed to the dark damp arteries that cut through the rocks and earth to form the underworld.

So off he led them through the labyrinthine ways in search of their companions. However, they had only travelled a short distance when Chantelle heard a voice. 'Chan, Chan, can your hear me?' The voice was unheard by the others, but continued, 'Chan, Chan, are you alive? Please answer me, please!'

It was now clear – it was Torres. She had shown this ability once before after her capture in the Great Forest, and now it seemed a time of need had again allowed her skill to develop. 'Chan, Chan – answer me, Chan,' she continued.

'Yes, yes! I'm here with Chevon and Ben!' shouted Chantelle. This stopped Benjamin and Chevon in their tracks, for they thought the strain had suddenly hit Chantelle and sent her ballooning into the beyond.

'They couldn't hear us way back; I don't think shouting from here will work, my dear; but don't worry, we'll find them,' said Benjamin, attempting to reassure the poor girl.

'No, you don't understand! It's Torres, she's speaking in my head,' said Chantelle excitedly.

'Yes, my dear, but not to worry, eh! We'll catch her before long, you'll see,' said an increasingly concerned Benjamin, who thought she really had gone bonkers.

'It's okay, Ben, she's not flipped... It's called remote messaging, an Elvin skill that some are blessed with. Torres has it – it's a good sign, it means they're alive,' said Chevon, putting Benjamin's fears to rest.

'Torres, we're fine, but for how long I can't say. We were blocked off, but Ben's leading us and I'm certain he'll do us proud!' Chantelle shouted to Torres, though thinking the words would have sufficed. Her words cheered Benjamin, making him feel of great importance, Chantelle had just become his favourite Elf, though seeing as how he disliked Elves this perhaps wasn't too hard; but it was a start none the less.

'That's good, Chan. We will push on to the cavern's end and wait there. We still have to wait for Juran and the other survivors to reach us, but when they arrive we'll set off,' said Torres.

'Survivors?' questioned a shocked Chantelle.

'Sorry, I didn't mean... Sure, everyone's okay, we were lucky but a lot of provisions were lost, so we'll be on that crash diet we spoke of in Kondama,' answered Torres, trying to lift spirits while imparting the bad news.

'And if we get there before you?' asked Chantelle.

'Then you wait for us, of course. What else?' answered Torres.

'How long should we wait? I mean we have nothing, we cannot wait forever, we'd more than likely freeze to death,' said Chantelle, knowing these simple plans had a way of becoming complicated all on their own.

'Then go to the cabin. Wait a day if you can; if not, then we meet at the cabin,' came Torres' answer.

'Fine, so until we meet,' said Chantelle, hoping it would be soon.

'Take care and good luck, and may fate feel guilt for what it has brought upon you this day! Until we meet, my friend, until we meet,' said Torres, also in hope of a speedy reunion.

It was some time before Juran and company managed to reach Torres' position; in the interim Bramley and Torres spoke as only those in a close relationship can do: nothing bawdy, mind you, but still close and personal. This made Idron feel awkward and out of place. He'd longed to be with Torres, ever since he first laid eyes on her at the port. He had fancied his chances, and thought they had a special something, more so after she cried out for him when she was in need. He had thought that significant, until Bramley – that sly, smooth snake in the grass – had charmed her away from him. He resented Bramley's time with Torres; he was meant to be with her, and seeing them together boiled his blood and inside him the seeds of jealousy propagated.

Juran reached the tunnel with the others, tired and bruised; they had salvaged what little they could from the cavern, but a great deal had been lost. The winter clothing was gone, most of the food, the pots and pans along with the shelter pieces and the bedrolls. They had their weapons, most of their normal clothing, some water and a few rations. However, considering the downpour of rock they were lucky no one had been hurt.

Yes, their group was again split and this complicated matters, as did the loss of the direction-finding instruments. Under the circumstances they were still much better off than they had been at times in the Great Forest. A short rest had to suffice and before long they climbed upward through the blackened tortuous tunnels towards the mountains.

Benjamin set a steady pace and found tunnels that seemed to head uphill, so they were most likely climbing towards the mountains, hence he remained fairly confident. The two women followed and were amazed by the Dwarf's sense of direction and keen eyesight. They had travelled for around six hours and were in dire need of a break and some water when Benjamin found a bubbling spring that produced the purest, sweetest and freshest water they had ever tasted. This quenched their thirst and ensured their bottles were full to overspill before continuing; but they did not continue. One minute they were speaking with each other, the next they were propped up against one another snoring to their hearts' content. They slept for hours, unaware of the exhaustion that had hit them, and were only awakened by the disturbing sound of heavy feet coming toward them. Opening his eyes Benjamin, could make out the shape of two massive figures coming down the tunnel and instantly recognised them.

'*Trolls*,' he whispered, in a somewhat hasty voice, 'hide!'

So they quickly dispersed, finding tiny nooks in the darkest places they could find.

The Trolls stopped at the spring and began to drink from its waters.

"Ere, Cosh, can you smells somting funnies?' said the first Troll.

'Yeh! I thinks it's you Bosh,' said the second Troll, laughing as he punched the first Troll's arm.

'No, I is serious, funnies smell there is, like small folk – you knows, them Dwarts,' said Cosh, the first Troll.

'Nope, nothin', you must've had too much of that wine, me-thinks,' said Bosh, the second Troll.

'Huh! Well, funnies smells are 'ere, somwhere, an I'm gonna find ums,' said Cosh.

With this he began poking around the cave, turning rock and boulder, poking here and prodding there. Suddenly he gave out a painful yell, and pulled his arm back sharply. There, on the end of his finger, biting down was Benjamin.

"Ee's bities me, 'orrid creature!' cried Cosh.

'So it is a Dwart, you were right, Cosh! But look what it brung ya,' said Bosh laughing.

Benjamin by now had drawn his double-headed axe and swung it hard, severing the Troll's wrist. 'Run, Run now!' screamed Benjamin, as he jumped to the floor and quickly sank his axe into Cosh's foot, causing terrible shrieks to sound from Cosh's mouth.

Chantelle and Chevon wasted no time and sprinted past Bosh, whose laughter had subsided due to his friend's screams. Benjamin showed his skill in battle, and before Bosh had time to react he too was struck, having the Achilles tendon on his right leg sliced in two as Benjamin darted through his legs. The two Trolls lay yelping in the dark, and due to Benjamin's quick actions were in no fit state to pursue their attackers.

'See what happens, when you cross ole Benjamin! *Bsore* they calls me – and that's why,' said Benjamin, rather smugly, pleased with the result of the chance encounter.

'Ben,' said Chevon, 'do you think there'll be any more?'

'Possibly, but doubtful, they tend to pair up and stay with friends for life. Only at breeding time do they congregate, and that ain't till the spring,' said Benjamin, confident he was right. He knew of Trolls and their behaviour and surmised they would be no different in Markesh.

'Funny how they knew what Dwarts smelt like, don't you think?' asked Chantelle, adding a touch of sarcasm.

'Yeh! Whatever Dwarts are... but it may mean there are Dwarves that live in Markesh. See, I told you the shelf in the cavern had to be the work of Dwarves,' said a rather excited Benjamin.

'Yes, well, you know the little fellows, they do seem to get everywhere,' answered Chantelle. The mood was good and she felt Benjamin's actions meant they were definitely in safe hands.

Juran, Tyler and company came to the mouth of the cavern after a further four days of an uneventful but extremely tiring trek. The thought of adventure and exploring an unknown continent had excited them all, but they never even thought of the amount of walking it would involve. The caverns and tunnels were too varied in height to make any progress on horseback, so everyone had sore feet and was very happy to leave the caverns.

The view that met them was stunning: dramatic towering rock faces, winding paths and slopes covered in silver birch. Waterfalls cascaded from overhanging stream beds and falcons darted across the clear sky. One mountain stood prouder than the others; it already had a cap of snow securing its summit, and its size and beauty beckoned them to come and essay its slopes. This had to be Falcon's Peak, the place Sticks had warned them of; yet such a captivating place could easily push aside mere words of warning, and its magnetic lure the strongest of wills. All well and good, but it was still a long way off and a great deal of walking would have to be done before its foothills were gained.

They rested for a while then set up a base camp with what little supplies were left and waited for the other group to arrive.

The birds were released, but they did not fly far, as the falcons dominated these peaks and they did not wish to tussle with territorial birds who undoubtedly outnumbered them. It was not thought, or evident, as far as they could tell, that the Black Owls had any footing in this area. Juran's party waited and waited; four more days passed by and there was still no sign of Benjamin's group.

Torres spoke with Chantelle on occasion but without the fear and apprehension that came with dire situations her remote messaging did not come so easily. All she managed to confirm was they were still moving; they were hungry but fine and the cabin would now be their meeting place.

Juran's group were well rested but very hungry due to their meagre rations. They headed along the rocky paths towards Falcon's Peak. Their journey was long; days turned to weeks and still the mountain was not reached. They hunted deer and trapped rabbit and ate the plants that grew amid the outcrops. The temperature grew colder with each passing day; the rain came and was replaced by sleet then hail, and still they went on. The road was hard on their feet and treacherous in places, but still they pushed on. They met no one, and remained under the watchful eye of the Falcons. Occasionally, dragons could be seen in the distance but none ever flew overhead – much to their relief. Then on the third day of the fourth week they stood beneath the great mountain. Its sides were steep, and snow now drifted lower with each dawn. Soon the whole land would be carpeted in a pure white that would be accompanied by a deadly freeze.

A day of rest was declared. The journey had been longer than expected and everyone was undernourished and needed to sleep. Juran, using magic, heated some turfs of grass to act as warmed beds and they were a delight to sleep upon. The animals took time to graze stocking up for the inevitable climb that lay ahead. They could see the snows and knew their only hope was to reach the cabin as soon as possible – if it did indeed exist.

The morning brought a fresh assault on the mountains' slopes and everyone made their best efforts. They reached the snow in no time and wished they hadn't, for it was deep and difficult. Their pace was slowed as each leg had to be lifted high to clear the sinking depths of the last step made. Everyone had to walk, as the horses would have been unable to move with extra weight upon them. The snow was not yet as crisp as it would become in the heart of winter's freeze, so it melted quickly on legs and boots, making everyone uncomfortable and cold. They slipped often and knew not where to look for the cabin. By nightfall they had conquered half the mountain and were reluctant to stop, as they knew the night would bring a bitter cold; but to continue would be suicide in such treacherous conditions. They huddled together for warmth, animal and human types together. Juran tried to conjure up a fire but it just sank through the snow and was extinguished as quickly as it was lit. He even tried a floating fireball, but the wind caught it and sent sparks spitting at the surrounding company; so the idea, though good, was abandoned. No one slept that night, as they had to keep their feet, fingers and face moving to prevent the effects of a cold injury. Here Tyler's experience was of great help and his advice that night probably prevented anyone from falling victim to the bitter chill that enveloped the mountain side.

The arrival of the sun the next morning revealed a snow-covered group who had barely survived the night. Shaking and shivering, they tried to move, but lack of circulation and frozen limbs made movement a chore. They set off with a lethargic and painfully slow step and it was some time before life came back to them and a normal pace was managed.

At around midday, they heard a cry, 'Over here, over here!' an unknown voice was calling them. They looked up and could see a small figure up ahead. It was a Dwarf, but not Benjamin. This Dwarf wore a cap of white fur that had long pointed earflaps.

His face was red and plump and he had a thick dark handlebar moustache underlining his bulbous nose. He was clothed in a thick overcoat of bear fur and had heavy boots that were attached by bindings to short skis. 'Over here, this way!' he continued, happy that he had caught their attention.

He ploughed down to meet them and introduced himself, 'Greetings to you all! I am Cedric Clethrop, keeper of the Cabins of the Mountain Clan, a welcome stop to all travellers, and sanctuary from the evil that clouds these lands. I've been on the lookout for you. He said you would come, and I was beginning to lose hope. I thought you'd surely died, but here you are, and to safety you shall follow.'

'Pleased to meet you, good sir, and a welcome sight you are – and should your words be true, then doubly welcome you are,' answered Juran, certain this fellow was onside.

'Well, no time to waste, your friends are waiting,' said Cedric, with a sense of urgency.

'Friends?' inquired Tyler.

'Well, yes, Mr Brandsaw and his two female friends. They arrived over a week ago,' said Cedric, turning to lead the way.

'By the gods, some people have all the luck, and I thought they would meet far worse a journey than ours,' said Tyler, pleased to hear his companions were well and secure.

They followed Cedric, for few other options were left to them. They could trust him or remain in the snow, looking blindly for an unknown cabin. The group of cabins was still a fair climb away, but being led to a definite location added a renewed spring to their step and they reached the cabins before night once more shrouded the land. The cabins were set in a horseshoe-shaped ledge set in a re-entrant. There were six cabins in total each identical and capable of housing twenty people each. The beds were double bunked and gave little privacy, but with only ten people in the one allocated to them they had room to spread out. Each also had a small washing area and lavatory, a well-stocked pantry and a stove. A log burner was in the middle of the room, and four tables with lanterns set upon them surrounded the burner.

Outside was a bunker of wood and a water tank, though the water in it was now frozen. To the rear of each cabin was a large barn. This could house many animals, and the one they were given for their animals was already home to a couple of pigs, three goats, six chickens, two geese and a large dog called Woofer. The barn was protected from the elements and well stocked with feed for most animal types. The birds found a large empty nesting box mounted in the rafters, and after the addition of some stolen chicken feathers and straw this quickly became their home.

The expedition settled in and discovered that Benjamin's group had run into a party of Dwarves who were also of the Mountain Clan. They had guided them through the tunnels and caverns to an entrance at the base of Falcon's Peak and sent message to Cedric to collect them. The Dwarves explained the tribes, or Clans, as they called them in this area of Markesh. The Hill Clan lived at the foothills below the mountain range and was in fact the clan that the tribes in the Great Forest referred to as the 'lost tribe of Silver Birch'. The Mountain Clan lived amongst the mountains surrounding Falcon's Peak. Under the mountains lived the Cave Clan, who mined the area and built many of the tunnels and passages; and to the south were the Dragon Clan, those who lived under the shadow of the dragons and were not to be trusted, for they were servants of the fiery beasts. Apart from them, all the other clans lived peacefully and aided one another wherever possible. Benjamin had asked about Falcon's Peak and why they had been warned to keep clear. All they said was that a great evil had been entombed there long ago, and to venture up there would release those imprisoned; so its heights were forbidden and had been for as long as any of them could remember, even old father Finigal, who was said to be six centuries old.

It was clear they could go no farther until the winter's end, but they had found sanctuary and were all at last together again. All they could do now was sit and wait in the confines of their cabin.

The Long Winter

A daily routine established itself. Elsbeth would prepare the food for the day, often aided by Benjamin and Chevon; Bramley, Chantelle and Torres would tend to the animals, whilst Erin and Tyler, sometimes with Idron's help, would collect firewood and hunt. I say sometimes with Idron's help because he was increasingly acting odd and spent much time alone. Juran planned the next leg of the journey with Cedric's aid, and even managed to coax Idron into producing the first map of Markesh. It was fairly basic and many place names and rivers were missed off, but it was a start and better than the nothing they had travelled on thus far. Idron carried out the work on one of the few chests that remained from their tunnel encounter with the Amber Dragon and actually spent a good deal of time ensuring it was true to what Cedric told him.

The map, on completion, showed Markesh to be split into three main land segments, with great rivers separating them; in fact the rivers were so wide it was debated whether or not they should actually be called seas or in the least channels. Many smaller islands were noted on the map, and in particular an island set in the middle of the channels that separated the three landmasses. This island was called Pkush and was believed to be the stronghold of the Ajya-Na-Ku. The area beyond was fairly unknown to Cedric; he knew of the famous valley of Myrkdalen (The Dark Valley), for it was said to be the ancient home of those who had formed the Ajya-Na-Ku, and some reasoned that they might even still inhabit this secret area. Great swamps, jungles and plains flanked Myrkdalen, and few ventured through them. The landmass beyond these plains was unknown to Cedric, so they drew up to the paper's edge, leaving anything beyond in question. From this first mapping it was clear they had covered only a small portion of Markesh, and many months – nay, years – would probably be required to explore its entirety; and with the possibility of there being more land to the east, the expedition seemed nigh impossible. Juran would ponder over this for most of their stay in the cabins.

The cabin routine became monotonous and all of the party grew agitated by the confinement, but the heavy snows and harsh wind only helped confirm that they would never have made the other side of the vast mountain range before the winter had arrived. So despite the boredom they were grateful for Cedric's hospitality, and he enjoyed the company. Occasionally, during the first month, parties of Dwarves from most of the clans came from time to time and would use the other cabins – except of course for the Dragon Clan, who were not at all welcome. With the second month came the worst of the weather. The storms that travelled over the mountains took few breaks during that month. Cedric taught most of the expedition how to ski during the clearer days, though they did not stray too far from the cabins. With the third month everyone became tense, and small squabbles flared easily, showing that everyone needed to escape the confines of the cabin. Eventually, seeing the stress that was brewing, Cedric offered up more cabins to allow the party breathing space. It was a simple solution and gave great relief all round.

Elsbeth, Benjamin and Idron stayed in the original cabin, whilst Bramley and Torres took the second. In the third, Tyler and Juran stayed with Cedric; this allowed much work to be done, as Cedric had a wealth of knowledge regarding the western parts of Markesh. Here they learnt of the Plains of Misery, a barren desert without water that was inhabited by a few hardy nomadic tribes and was also said to be home to some strange beasts. They also learnt of the Dragon Mountains to the east of Green River's eastern port, and how it was teaming with dragons, some dark and evil and others honest and chivalrous. Erin, Chantelle and Chevon inhabited the final cabin they were given; this left two further cabins if any new travellers arrived. Despite the split they still continued with the daily chores and ate together, for it was not that they had grown to hate each other; they merely needed their own space.

One day the subject was raised of Falcon's Peak and the absence of the Ajya-Na-Ku in the mountain area. Juran was quite inquisitive regarding these matters, so he asked Cedric, 'One issue that puzzles me is why the Ajya-Na-Ku stay away from the mountains.' He slipped the question tactfully into a conversation after the many glasses of wine that followed a hearty meal cooked by Elsbeth.

'They're scared, that's why,' answered Cedric, with conviction.

'What, of the Dwarves? No offence, but I find that difficult to swallow,' Juran said, pressing for a more informative answer.

'Of course not! No, they're scared of their own history. This place cost them badly,' Cedric said, leaning over the table; the others drew closer eager to hear more.

'Long ago, it is said, the fathers of the Ajya-Na-Ku – those who came from Myrkdalen, that is – were locked in a mighty battle on these very peaks. They were said to be powerful necromancers who controlled the dragons of those times. But a clash occurred, a struggle for dominance, one house trying to overthrow another. The battles raged for years with little gain on both sides, and then new blood entered the arena: three wizards who had trained in Myrkdalen whilst the war was fought abroad. They were not linked to the Ajya-Na-Ku or their fathers, but were born of another race that for centuries had clashed with their evil neighbours. They schemed and plotted, vowing to put an end to the forefathers of the Ajya-Na-Ku, and entering these mountains lured them to the very slopes on which we are now sat. They tricked the necromancers and entombed them for eternity in the peak of this mountain. That is why these cabins are here, and why my people were entrusted with the security of these slopes.' Cedric related the story in a rather theatrical manner, playing fully to the audience.

'But that still doesn't explain why the Ajya-Na-Ku don't come here,' pressed Juran, wishing as much information as possible; for if the Ajya-Na-Ku had a weak spot he wished to exploit it.

'Superstition, curse or whatever you wish to believe, but they believe that if they enter this domain they too will become entombed. It's real enough for them. After all, their forefathers were necromancers, not mere thieves and crooks, and if they could be imprisoned here what chance do the Ajya-Na-Ku have?'

replied Cedric, believing his story done.

'They're not merely crooks and thieves!' snarled Idron, 'How would a crook form a man from a flight of Owls, attack and then burst back to Owls again? It sure looked like magic to me,' he continued, annoyed that the Ajya-Na-Ku were so underestimated. After all, they held most of the world in a constant state of fear.

'Magic, yes, but simple tricks do not compare to the forces controlled by the necromancer, and their forefathers, whether you choose to believe it or not, were far more dangerous than the Ajya-Na-Ku; so imprisoned is where they should remain,' said Cedric, determined to say no more on the matter.

This ended the conversation, and other more mundane subjects were discussed in idle chatter until everyone turned in for the night. Idron was for some reason furious. He had to constantly watch Bramley and Torres together and now they had their own cabin. This was way too much – and now the Ajya-Na-Ku were a second-rate enemy! Try telling that to the spook that attacked him. His frustrations were growing to a head and he just had to get out.

He had felt strangely drawn to this forbidden peak ever since he had entered the mountain's caverns. It had been an effort up until now to stay away from them, but his building dissatisfaction with the expedition fuelled his fascination, and in the night he slipped from the cabin, took some skis and made his way up the slopes towards the peak. The night was wicked, bitterly cold with a strong icy wind sending the falling snow sideways, and drifts formed in every sheltered spot. His focus on reaching the peak disregarded the elements and he strove hard as though possessed by some hidden entity. As dawn broke the darkness, he found himself on the summit of the mountain but he could see no chamber, tomb or prison. The morning sun dispersed the clouds and he sat down, allowing the warmth to work on his now aching body, though this was his first noting of the pains.

Idron drifted into a deep sleep and dreamt of long sinewy fingers grasping his arms and legs and pulling him down into the earth. He felt powerless and was unable to struggle as the fingers took him deeper and deeper. He was led into a fiery hall where five flames of intense heat were laid in a triangular formation.

Behind the flames were ice crystal walls, though they did not melt or even drip. He was flung into the centre of the triangle whilst four sets of hands from unseen darkened figures held him spreadeagled, allowing a fifth pair of hands to prod and pull at his skin. Long needles were pushed into his veins and leeches and maggots placed onto incisions the fingers had made. He remembered screaming and struggling as he was operated on by these eerie faceless monsters, and then suddenly he sat upright with a start.

It was dark and he was still on the summit of the peak, alone; his pains were gone and a full moon illuminated the fresh blanket of snow. He felt good and, having visited the peak and found nothing, felt he had put the myths to rest. There were no mysteries on this mountain and no secret chambers holding necromancers. The Dwarves were simply fortunate that the Ajya-Na-Ku believed the tales enough to stay away. This small trek had done Idron a world of good, he felt refreshed and at ease with himself. It was a different man who descended the mountain that night, and the skis meant it was not long after he had left the peak that he found himself back at his cabin, to be greeted by a surprised audience.

'By the gods, Idron, you'll be the death of me!' exclaimed an anxious Elsbeth. 'We didn't know what to think!'

'Indeed, and if you decide to take off again you could at least let us know,' added Chevon, 'we were worried sick.'

'Sure, like you were on the plains when you left me to the wraiths… only Tyler cared enough to bother looking for me, so why the heck should I inform the likes of you of my every move?' snapped Idron in his own defence.

'Don't take that tone, she was only concerned…' said Bramley, but Idron cut him short.

'Don't you start, you slimy cretin! I'd rather spend eternity alone than sit with you as a friend!'

Bramley was taken aback by this remark, and shocked, but he had noticed that Idron had been shunning him of late.

'Idron, *please*, Bramley's never done any harm to you, why do you have to be so cruel?' asked Torres in a low voice that showed how upset she was by the whole affair.

'Never done me harm? That's rich – and from you of all people! If it wasn't for him we'd—' He stopped before completing the sentence, but she quickly figured the meaning.

'No, it was never like that, I thought you were sweet, a friend,' said Torres emotionally, for she now felt his jealousy was all her fault, and she hadn't even thought that this could possibly be the reason he'd acted so strange since they left Kondama.

'*Enough*! This is pointless, and will lead to nowhere any of us wish to go, Idron's back and unharmed, and that's good enough for me,' said Tyler. 'Wherever he's been I'm sure he has his own reasons for going there.' He paused, glancing at Idron as a cue to tell them where he had been, but Idron said nothing so Tyler continued. 'And if he wishes to share it with us, all well and good!' He paused again, then added, 'but if not, then it remains his business.'

Tyler had tried to calm the situation and also coax Idron into enlightening them about his eighteen-hour absence, but Idron had not taken advantage of his friend's opening, so Tyler stared at him in disbelief, wondering what he had been up to that kept him so quiet.

'So silence it is, but remember tracks in the snow seldom aid the wanderer,' said Juran, raising an eyebrow and giving Idron a stern look, 'Let's pray nothing was unleashed that we cannot control,' he whispered to himself, though Idron knew from Juran's expression that the Mage knew only too well where he had been.

'Worry you not, Juran. There was nothing of concern that crossed my path, nothing can be told about that which is not there. Call it what you will, but I call it a stroll – an escape from the confinement of these walls and relief from you all,' said Idron, disturbed by the Mage's knowing look. 'Now, if you'll leave me be I'll take my bunk for the night. It's over there, third from the right. I'll be there till around eight in the morning… if that's okay by everyone,' he added sarcastically, but with no trace of humour.

Idron was better mannered in the morning, his excursion had changed him, and he now knew his purpose in life and was content with himself. The argument the previous night had been in defence of his feelings, but now they were out in the open he felt as if a weight was lifted from his shoulders. It was obvious Torres felt guilty and this made Idron happy. She deserved it, or so he thought. Now his change was noted by all, he was more confident, far more active and had finally matured.

The fourth month of their stay brought the start of the thaw, and soon they would be able to continue on through the mountains and down to the first of the channels that flanked Pkush. Excitement filled the air as preparations to leave the snow-locked cabins where made. Everyone wished to depart this place. They had a fine host in Cedric and he had catered for their needs admirably but they had still grown to hate the confinement associated with these cabins. Even the animals, who missed the exercise they were accustomed to, were chomping at the bit, literally. With the end in sight, everyone's attitudes changed, they no longer snapped at one another and the light-hearted banter they had previously enjoyed returned.

All seemed well until a few nights before they were due to depart. Everyone was sleeping in their bunks when the ground began to shake, pots and pans fell from shelves, walls shook and chunks of ice crashed through the windows. Then the door to Bramley and Torres' cabin exploded into a million splinters, dark figures poured in and a fight ensued. Similar occurrences took place in Tyler's and Erin's cabins; only Benjamin's was left unscathed.

Juran brought his power to bear on the assailants, sending blue balls of energy pulsating from his short baton. These energy balls would strike an opponent and disintegrate him instantly, a formidable weapon. Tyler was covering Juran's back, swinging Cleaver wildly as more dark figures poured through the windows. They seemed to come from nowhere, and from the description Idron had given of his confrontation in the boarding house in Kondama, it was clear that the attackers were the Ajya-Na-Ku. Thus it seemed the mountains of Falcon's Nest and even Falcon's Peak no longer held any fear for them. Cedric, also in this cabin, grabbed a short broadsword and handled it with great strength and uncanny skill. Erin battled at the doorway. Standing to its side, she could not be seen from the outside, and was piercing the assaulting troops as they entered the room with arrows from the powerful Mankil. Chantelle and Chevon covered the windows, firing their bows through the openings with great accuracy. Benjamin was eager to join the battle, but Idron held him back, arguing that they would soon have to defend their own ground and the enemy would be weaker when spread. This argument stood for some time, but eventually Benjamin could be held back no longer; it just seemed as though the enemy had no intention of assaulting their cabin.

'It's no good, waiting here is doing naught, we have to go! Come on, Elsbeth, Idron – with me!' shouted Benjamin.

'Okay, okay, I'll help Torres in the next cabin. You go to the fourth cabin, Erin will probably be faring less ably than Juran and Tyler,' reasoned Idron as they darted through the doorway.

'To victory!' shouted Benjamin, as he and Elsbeth charged off as fast as they were able to the rear of the cabins en route to Erin's aid. They met the Ajya-Na-Ku at the rear of the third cabin and axe and mallet met flesh and bone as they hacked their way through the dark figures blocking their way. Outside the fourth cabin bodies inundated the ground and flight upon flight of Black Owls could be seen circling the area. Some landed and merged into fighters of the sort Idron had encountered; but not all of the troops were of the same mystical composition. Some were made of normal matter, as human-like in their make-up as any of the other races of the world. The normal members were bad enough but the mystical troops were far darker and deadlier. Flechettes cut through walls blindly, passing with ease in an attempt to use firepower to dislodge the defenders, but the cabins provided a good makeshift defensive position and the Ajya-Na-Ku had to enter either through the door or the windows.

Erin used Mankil to fire the explosive arrows at the mystical fighters who lay in her field of view. The explosive worked well, forcing them to break up and scatter, killing some of the Owls in the process and preventing these fearsome fighters from inflicting too much damage. Juran spotted figures on the roof of number two cabin and shouted a quick spell to clear them off: '*I see you now up on high, but through the air you now must fly,*' he called and instantly the figures were snatched from the roof and deposited down the mountain side.

Idron, flashing Charlock in the dark, entered Torres' cabin to find Bramley struggling at the doorway. He bypassed the Ajya-Na-Ku and left Bramley to continue the fight. Torres was battling by the window with two darkened troops when Idron approached, and with a mere flash of Charlock the two fighters retreated. Torres looked around and was pleased to see that a friendly face had come to her aid, but was amazed how quickly the opposition had backed off considering how tenacious they where reputed to be, and she had indeed found it quite difficult to hold them back.

Idron looked her in the eyes and said, 'Come with me, Torres, it's not too late… we can make amends.' He held out his hand gesturing her to grab it, but she hesitated. His statement was not right, what did he mean? Again he pressed, 'My hand, take my hand, Torres, we can leave this place, it's hopeless, come with me!'

She still did not take his hand. She heard his words but they made no sense. 'The others, what of the others?' she said, 'don't you care about them?'

He looked at her coldly? 'What others? There's only you, or so I thought, but it seems as though it was really only ever me.'

He turned, his head lowered and moved towards Bramley, who was still fighting in the doorway. Idron then swung Charlock above his head, its flaming blade burst with shimmering sparks that showered down around him and in a commanding voice he shouted, 'So it is, then! Hold back and pull back, the night is through, let them have their moment.' He paused and the Ajya-Na-Ku assault paused with him.

'What magic is this?' exclaimed Juran, sensing Idron's words, 'he has more talent than I could have possibly imagined.'

'I fear it is not magic, my friend,' said Tyler. 'That was no spell, more like an order – an order from a general.'

'Idron, what have you done?' Torres pleaded, afraid of what she had heard.

'What have I done?' yelled Idron. 'Neither right nor wrong! I've done what I was designed to do. You believe in the fates, and so should not criticise the moves they make. Do you not see how feeble this expedition has been, a poor attempt at gaining power over those to whom the power rightly belongs? I was a fool, I fought against it too long, but it was there, beckoning me all along – the hall, the plains and finally the mountain. I was meant to be with them, and you, you could've been by my side. I see it only too clearly now – the power they're offering, it's overwhelming! They tried to wake me, when we were on the plains, but I was scared, blinded by the lies of the west. They needed me to break the curse, the curse of these mountains. I struggled with it all those painful months, but you helped me see the truth, with your deceit and betrayal, and I had to help them. I was drawn, nay destined to go to the mountain and free their incarcerated souls. They embraced my coming, it seemed like a dream and they, through me, were joined as one ultimate essence.

'If only you could see the power at their disposal you'd understand how hopeless your quest is! Take your map, go back and tell them to prepare. Prepare to be vanquished, prepare to be enslaved, prepare for defeat, for that is all they will achieve if they enter these lands. Tell them their time is short and not to waste it, because one day we will come, and when we do the very earth beneath them will tremble for fear of what is approaching. Consider this a token of goodwill for times past; we leave now a friendship destroyed. Never again will I be so lenient.'

He approached Bramley, who was still near the door and looked at him with sheer hatred, saying, 'You, however, I have no compassion for! You took her from me, but now seeing what I have gained, I suppose I should thank you, for had it not been for you, I probably would have resisted their call indefinitely, but isolated and shut out I embraced them. So here's my thanks!'

He screamed as he grabbed Bramley by the throat, and with a flash of flame Charlock was thrust into Bramley's midriff, burning upward into his chest cavity until it escaped between his shoulder blades. Torres screamed, 'No!' but it was too late. Bramley slumped to the floor as Idron casually left the cabin and was instantly transformed into a flight of the dreaded Black Owls, and flew off into the night.

The others rushed to the screaming Torres as flights of Owls departed the scene. The battle was over, but it seemed a war had begun. Idron had told them to leave, to take their map and warn the world not to interfere with the politics of Markesh or they would be enslaved. They had not seen the warning signs; Sticks had hinted that there was a dark one amongst them. It always seemed to be Idron who went missing or had encounters with unearthly creatures. He had been struck by a flechette, which they stupidly had left in him; this could have been the poison that guided his journey to the side of the Ajya-Na-Ku. It had all been there, though they had failed to notice even his attitude after his journey to the mountain top. Juran knew where he had been, and also knew of the myths surrounding the peak, yet he had allowed the incident to fade without further investigation. He felt foolish as did the others, but most of all they felt as though their poor decisions had allowed what Idron was suffering to manifest itself, and if he had felt abandoned after the plains incident he was most probably right; but now he was truly abandoned. He was one of the enemy – a member of the Ajya-Na-Ku; the whole group had failed him, and he was lost forever.

Torres poured endless tears over her lover and there was little any of them could do to comfort her. Worse still, she felt this could have all been avoided if only she had taken time to notice Idron's feelings from the beginning. Had she led him on? She was confused and heartbroken, and none of this made any sense. She wanted to turn back the clock and make it all change, make the pain go away; but the pain was now firmly anchored. Bramley had died instantly, and a quick death was the only mercy Idron had shown him. The remaining group now had to collect their thoughts, bury their dead and decide what to do next.

They had started with twelve and were now down to eight. To push on would be suicide, but to go back would also mean an uncertain journey. They knew dragons prowled the area, and that the Ajya-Na-Ku had re-entered the Great Forest; and then there was the Sycamore Spirits to pass through. Weighing up the options open to them and consulting with Cedric, they decided to push on to the Channel and attempt to find a boat; from there they would take to the seas and sail back around the north west of Markesh and to the Green River ports. The plan contained quite a few ifs, buts and maybes… but that was life. However, one thing was certain: they had no intention of attempting to explore the remainder of Markesh. Idron was right; they had a map, so why not take it back and let the ruling powers decide what action to take.

Benjamin was disappointed, he really had hoped he could've found the Horn, but he saw the reasoning, and the Horn had always been a long shot. So with their decision made and Bramley buried they set off for the water's edge in search of a seaworthy boat to take them home.

To the Sea Maybe

With the spring thaw, the surviving members of the expedition rode down off the mountain and headed east. They noticed a change in the sky above them, as falcons strove to fight back incursions made into their territory by the Black Owls of the Ajya-Na-Ku. Only the sheer number of falcons in the area swung the balance in their favour. The falcons held their ground but were unaware of the aid that would soon benefit them. The Dwarves had spread the word, and it was travelling fast. Already plans for an alliance with the Dragon Clan were being prepared, and with this clan would also come the dragons, for they too hated the Ajya-Na-Ku, but mainly because dragons are old creatures that live for a millennium, and they remembered only too well the forces that forefathers controlled, and would do whatever was needed to prevent such power resurfacing.

The mountain paths were much better on this side of Falcon's Peak and this, combined with the improving weather, made progress much easier. Still they were being watched, and the Ajya-Na-Ku, having gained one of their party knew everything about the expedition; but did not know of their plans to move back to Green River by boat. This meant the party's progress through the mountains was interpreted as being in direct defiance of the warning they had been given. The Ajya-Na-Ku also knew that the direction the party were travelling in would also bring them into areas that were completely in their grasp, so they bided their time, eyeing their progress, but in no rush to confront them. After all, there were only eight of them, and what possible threat could so small a number bring the mighty Ajya-Na-Ku?

The party now had extra carrying capacity, for Pee and Bee no longer had riders. This allowed them to spread the loads and carry more provisions, which had been supplied by Cedric courtesy of the Dwarf Clans. The route they had been advised to take took them through a small pass that was home to the city of Matrosse, a Dwarf city built into the solid rock flanking the pass. It was also a strong fortress and the capital of the Cave Clan. They had many skilled craftsmen and had promised to help restock provisions and provide any arms or armour the expedition required. Hatred of the Ajya-Na-Ku was strong, and it was worth equipping any ally well if they brought more muscle to the battle. A strong mining community born of their clan meant that they were the wealthiest of the Dwarves, and this allowed Matrosse to prosper, attracting many other races to the city. To the surprise of Torres, Juran, Chantelle and Chevon there was an Elvin embassy in the city, and a request had been made for them to visit the Ambassador there.

The journey to the city took five weeks, during which time the group had a fairly peaceful trip with few mishaps and no confrontations. They knew they were constantly under observation, being watched by spies, but they kept their distance, and this suited the party for now. Torres grieved for Bramley during the major part of the trip, and the lack of events made it even harder for her to come to terms with the loss. She consoled herself in the company of the animals, especially Que, whom she rode, and they were now very close companions. Juran tended to read as he rode, no doubt honing his skills and preparing for the unknown.

Tyler was as keen as ever. He still hungered for battle, the loss of his brother and lover had hardened him. He was now one hundred per cent warrior and had no intention of joining the group's boat trip to Green River; he had other plans but kept them to himself for the time being. At night during halts he practised with Cleaver trying to unlock the power it was said to have. He also brushed up on his use of his Jim-ka and Shun-kus. Benjamin and Elsbeth spoke often and with excitement, about the discovering of the colonies of Dwarves in Markesh and wondered if they would know anything about the Horn of Ristador. They also talked of poor Idron and how they should have spotted his problems earlier; but now he was possessed and there was no way to bring him back. Erin was also far more determined than she had been at the beginning of the journey, and like Tyler had no desire to give up yet, but she too said nothing about the expedition's plans.

Chevon spent the journey on the lookout for herbs and other items that could be used for medicinal purposes; this allowed her to keep her mind of Meme's death and Idron's transformation. Chantelle was finding it difficult to focus; she had been a great friend of Bramley's and had grown to like Idron too; and now they were both gone, along with Cee and Eee, fine horses and friends. Her only escape came from the pleasure the animals provided, especially the Pigeon Hawks, whom she considered the most regal of birds, due to their honour and service.

Grey granite columns protruded from the valley floor like sturdy sentinels of a great fortress fit for the hugest of giants. They marked the entrance to the pass and the western gateway of the city of Matrosse. There were no gates or barriers, just free access to the pass, for if people wished to enter then the Dwarves had no quarrel with them. Their defence lay in the very construction of the city. On either side of the pass long ramps and stairs were carved out of the rock and wound upwards like a dormant python. These met with walkways protected by rails of ivory coloured masonry which gave the impression of teeth, teeth that had been pulled from some mighty dragon's jaws. These teeth provided safety whilst walking but also acted as battlements and the city's first line of defence. Any attackers would be caught in a natural ambush with the pass as its killing ground.

Set back in the rock were long tunnels that zigzagged into the depths of the mountainside. They were fairly narrow but wide enough for a cart to travel down, and passing places were set at regular intervals. The roof of the tunnels looked like the inside of a flute, as evenly spaced circular skylights were set along its entirety to allow daylight to illuminate the city. Each skylight had solid bars of steel preventing access from above. Along the length of all the tunnels were shops and houses, together with inns and all manner of commercial and administrative establishments. The warren was deep, colourful and seemingly never ending, and each side held, at its farthest depths, their treasuries and their governing bodies. Each side had mirror image facilities, just in case one side should fall to attackers. Some of the cave houses had two, three, four and in some cases five levels, and those fortunate enough to own a wall that looked into the pass also had the privilege of providing part of the city's defence. Set outside their windows were fixed cauldrons of oil, that could be heated and poured onto any would-be raiders should the need arise.

Between the two halves of the city were strung many walkways constructed of wood and rope, and again if besieged these could be cut, isolating one side from the other, but only after evacuating as many people as possible. There were also two underground tunnels, but they were not common knowledge and were hidden using Elvin magic, courtesy of the Ambassador; only key personnel knew how to access these routes. The whole city was well constructed, well thought out and designed to utilise barriers that the natural landscape provided. It had been built during the rise of the Ajya-Na-Ku after the demise of their forefathers, but mainly as a result of conflict with the Dragon Clan, and the deep tunnels and caverns were designed to lessen the advantages a dragon possesses. This meant the city had long been looked at with envious eyes by the Ajya-Na-Ku, as their most fearful enemy were the dragons that dwelled in the Dragon Mountains. With the curse that had kept the Ajya-Na-Ku away from the mountains now lifted, Matrosse faced a new threat.

Taking one of the ramps on the left or northern side of the city, the group was met by a stout young Dwarf dressed in white flowing robes. He sported a small brown spiky beard on his chin and had long sideburns and his tight-knit dull brown hair stopped below his ears. He held a scroll in his left hand that had ornate gold filigree decorating its ends.

'Hello, I am Lotus… Cedric warned us of your coming, and our lookouts informed me as soon as they saw you. You are welcome, and Matrosse is your city for as long as you wish,' said this rather friendly fellow as he bowed before them.

'Your gesture is well received and we thank you! And, my friend, we will cherish the hospitality the city provides,' said Benjamin, shaking Lotus's hand in appreciation.

'Are there any inns you would recommend?' inquired Juran, eager to settle in and explore Matrosse.

'Why, you have rooms provided at the Drop Inn, 'tis the finest inn in Matrosse, and just a little way from here. It overlooks the pass and has a fine stable complex. The Hawks can stay in your rooms and will be able to come and go as they please via the window cages provided. Your other companion is already there, he arrived earlier today,' said Lotus. He gestured to them to follow him and began walking in the direction of the Drop Inn.

'Companion? Who?' asked Tyler, fearing Idron was lying in wait.

'I have no idea, I did not meet with him, but he said he was with your party and the innkeeper, Mrs Southhall, said he seemed genuine enough,' answered Lotus, as he continued walking.

Soon they reached two large circular doors set in solid stone, Lotus rapped the wood making a loud hollow but deep sound that indicated quality hardwood. An eyehole was pushed to one side and a large bloodshot eye peered through.

'Oh! It's you, then, and I see you have the party, I'll be with you in a tick, so I will,' said the owner of the eye.

Shortly afterwards the doors rolled to the left and right of the frame simultaneously revealing a surprisingly large courtyard with stables set on three sides. On the opposite wall a short flight of marble steps led up to a fabulous reception area. The animals were dealt with immediately as a melee of porters and stable hands appeared, all in bright tailed crimson jackets. Bags and chests were hurriedly grabbed and carried into the foyer, while each animal was led off by its own stable hand to be groomed, fed and watered. Horses like to be pampered, so this treatment was met without argument and a mint, carrot or sugar lump – depending on their preference – was only the start of what would be star treatment for the animals for the duration of their stay.

The reception area was amazing and no hint of being in a cave was noticeable. The floor was of a crisp aquamarine and was lit from below, making the whole area look clean, bright and airy. Distressed leather burgundy sofas of the softest of hides were set around unique oak coffee tables. That were merely segments from old tree trunks that had been treated, varnished and polished to perfection, and each one coming from a different tree meant that each was a different shape and size. Many of the clientele had succumbed to the luxury the sofas provided and were sleeping as though cradled in their mother's arms and each one had a pleasant smile across their face. The reception area's counter had been chiselled out of natural rock and was smooth and cold and had the most wonderful patterns running through it as veins of blues, reds and black meandered between the grey granite. All the books and stationary on display were finished in gold and oozed wealth.

They bypassed check-in, but were led by porters to the rooms that had already been prepared for them. All eight travellers were taken to the first floor, and each one had a room that faced the pass. Peering out helped confirm just how formidable a city this truly was. They had been told that their companion had wished to speak with them soon after their arrival and that a porter would lead them to his room. The group declined the invitation and sent message of a meeting on their terms: eight o'clock sharp in the foyer. This gave them an hour, and the venue prevented them from walking into a trap.

By eight, the eight of them were sitting around one of the coffee tables, trying not to give in to the slumber-inducing sofas, when their companion arrived. He scuttled across to join them, 'You are short two... I gather the dark one emerged,' said Sticks, 'I sensed trouble but was uncertain of who, but I knew not that the flechette was still embedded, or point a finger I would have. The poison held within their heads corrupts the mind and before you know it right is wrong and wrong is right, once transformed there is no way back. I'm so sorry, it seems I failed you,' he said, sitting down beside Elsbeth and looking disappointed with himself.

'You're not to blame,' said Elsbeth, trying to cheer him, 'you've done more than enough for us, and without your aid it is doubtful this many would sit here this day.'

'And you again appear, as you yourself predicted, in the spring,' said Chevon, still baffled by the composition of this fellow.

'Guidance will lead only where you wish to go, so the wise guide goes only with those who wish to be guided,' answered Sticks, not giving any hint of how, who, where or what brought him to be once more among them.

'So, what puzzle do you bring this day?' asked a cynical Erin, who found all the mystery a little too odd, and thought a true friend would reveal why he was helping them.

'No puzzles can I give, but advice I have an abundance of,' smiled Sticks in reply to Erin's comment. Then he continued, 'Stay you here and make use of the hospitality this city offers; for no hospitality will be found beyond its limits; only in the far islands would a welcome be made, and there is much between.'

'Are you saying we should stay here indefinitely?' asked Juran, none to happy at the advice's implications.

'Not indefinitely, but seek whatever aid you can muster in this city. Strong allies are needed if you are to venture outside; I would not move forward without an army, but I of course am not you,' answered Sticks, leaning forward towards Juran, and speaking with a lowered voice.

'And what of you? Are you simply to disappear as normal?' asked Erin, though she was happier than most about the advice he had given, for it could indicate a change in their plan.

'Oh! I'll be in the city, and like I've said on many of our meetings, if there is anything you need just call me... I serve to please and am pleased to serve,' he said, labouring the issue that he was always accessible should they need him, even if they did not believe he would just appear if they called his name. Then he stood ready to depart and added, 'So again I bid you farewell, but present I remain should you find need, and may I recommend the Victory Vault. It has many items that may be of assistance and is the finest armoury in Matrosse.'

He turned around and began to pull away from the group, speaking as he went. 'We will talk before you leave, if your call does not join us beforehand. Farewell, my friends, farewell!' thus he finished, and, waiting for no more questions, was gone.

His advice brought a frenzy of discussion regarding what to do next, whether to follow their original plan or to take Sticks' advice and bide in Matrosse for the time being.

'Stay, we should stay, it is sound advice, and I for one had no intention of returning to Green River; I had hoped to continue to Pkush at the very least and see if some damage could be inflicted on the Ajya-Na-Ku. I had pondered over how to go about getting that far, but our friend's suggestion of an army... now that would be something!' said Tyler, expressing his opinion on their planned escape for the first time.

'You made no mention of this before,' remarked Juran, surprised by Tyler's admission, and staring at him with dubious eyes.

'I made no mention of it because I had not yet confirmed my course of action, and whatever my decision, I had always intended on remaining with you until the boat was found,' answered Tyler, defending his loyalties in an attempt to quash Juran's unfriendly glare.

'I too had planned to remain,' said Erin, giving Tyler some back-up.

'So – another conspirator! Did anyone intend on using the boat, or was our agreement a mere folly?' asked Juran of his whole audience.

'I for one would be only too happy to go home,' said Chantelle, who was still upset by previous events.

'I too wished to leave,' said Torres, 'but if the advice is to remain I'm certain it has good reason, so I say stay.' Due to her religious beliefs she had trust in the fates and her gods.

'Ben and I are happy to be amongst folk of our own, so stay we will, but when the time is right we opt to find that boat,' said Elsbeth, speaking for both of them without first consulting Benjamin.

'I said nothing of the sort. Yes I will stay, but the boat bit can go to blazes, if Tyler and Erin wish to continue I'm with them, and in future I'd be only too pleased if you didn't assume I thought as you do woman!' snapped a grumpy Benjamin. Then he muttered something inaudible and probably unrepeatable under his breath. This instant flare-up brought a smirk to most of the party's faces, as Benjamin was once more living up to his nickname.

'So over half wish to stay and half wish to go on... but what of Chevon, what do you wish?' asked Juran, turning in her direction.

'I wish we had never come, but beggars would ride and here we are, and I suppose I owe it to Meme. Besides, who would pick you up when you fall? Stay it is, though not for love of what we do,' said Chevon, in a sombre manner, but with her mind truly made up.

'Stay then, how long only time will reveal. So Matrosse awaits your pleasure; there is much to do and it would seem there's now time to do it, I still think the boat would be our best option, but if onward we travel when the time comes then onward I must go, if I am needed try the libraries,' said Juran, ending the conversation. His tone of voice concealed his opinion, so none of them knew if he approved or disapproved of the decision to stay. He then stood up and left the inn.

'Hey, Tyler,' said Erin, 'you fancy taking a look for this Victory Vault or whatever it's called?' She knew Tyler and she too had a liking for the tools of the trade, and she also wished to purchase more arrows for Mankil.

'Sure, why not, and they said they'd give us what we wanted, so cost shouldn't be an issue,' he replied with enthusiasm, eager to see what was on offer.

'Mind if we tag along?' said Chevon, gesturing that she Torres and Chantelle wished to come too.

'Hey! We're a team, right? What about you two?' said Erin, to Benjamin and Elsbeth, answering Chevon's question and asking one of her own.

'Not at the moment; we wish to speak with the Dwarves and see if there is any link between our clans and theirs. We intend to walk around the town for a while,' said Elsbeth, again speaking for them both.

'Blast it, woman! What did I say about speaking for me?' said Benjamin, angrily.

'So now you want to go and look at weapons? Fine,' snapped back Elsbeth.

'Well, no, I'm going with you, but that's not the point,' said Benjamin in a quieter tone, realising how silly this could look.

'Damn you, you old fool! You just have to argue, don't you,' said Elsbeth, half laughing.

'No, I don't,' said Benjamin, at once realising he'd started again.

The others left them to it but were indeed chortling as they departed the building in search of the Victory Vault.

The vault was easy to find as everyone they met in the city was friendly and very helpful, and one chap even led them all the way to its doors. Once inside they found themselves in a pure white cylindrical room with doors around its entirety. A Dwarf garbed in brown leather trousers and waistcoat stood in the centre and welcomed them to the Victory Vault.

'Greetings, a visit to the vault will vanquish your enemies and lead you to victory,' he said. Then he continued, 'The following departments are currently available: armour and protective clothing, through door one.' He paused, indicating door one. 'Close-quarter weapons, through door two.' Again he pointed. 'Through door three–' he pointed – 'for long-range weapons and projectiles.' He paused and then said, 'Door four is closed today for stocktaking – sorry, and through door five, specialist weapons.' He indicated door five. 'Please look around and take your time. There are many assistants available, so just call if you need help.' He then stood silent and lifeless like some shop mannequin.

Chevon, Torres and Chantelle went into door one whilst Erin and Tyler went into door two. The armour and protective clothing room spanned an unbelievable amount of floor space, and all manner of protective clothing was on display. There was an Elf and a Dwarf assistant on hand and both had tape measures draped around their necks, as though they were tailors.

'Hello,' said the Elvin assistant, 'it's a great pleasure to meet new Elves in Matrosse, is there anything I can help you with?'

'We were just looking,' said Chevon, not sure what she needed exactly.

'Well, we would like chest-plates that are strong, hard to pierce and heat resistant – oh! And light and easy to move in,' said Torres, not expecting to find armour with all these qualities.

'Then come this way.' He lead them to a large glass display cabinet and unlocked the door, then he picked out a dull coal-black breastplate. Made for the female form, it had shoulder protectors of overlapping metal strips of gold in a glistening yellow, that contrasted with the coal black; gold also ran around the wide armholes and around the base of the piece, making the whole plate look quite special. The breast cups and abdomen area were moulded to represent a muscular form, but it looked heavy.

'This is an example of Isadle's work, a fine craftsman of the Dragon Clan. It was forged using dragon's fire to such an intense heat that it is virtually impervious to fire. The metal is an unknown alloy that fell from the heavens and is in short supply, but no arrowhead can penetrate it. It is also featherweight and you wont find lighter armour to wear,' said the salesman.

'If it's so light why do you struggle with it?' asked Chantelle, believing he was just trying to sell the product.

'It is heavy, but only in the hand, the metal is enchanted and once on you won't know its there. Here, try it,' answered the salesman, gesturing Chantelle to try the piece.

She turned around and the assistant helped place the chestplate over her head. As soon as the side clamps were sealed there was a sudden jolt as the plate contracted and expanded, shaping perfectly to Chantelle's contours. 'Wow!' she exclaimed, 'you're right – it doesn't even feel as though I'm wearing it. Brilliant!'

'So, you like it, then? There are only six such pieces in existence, we have five here, each one has different highlights; this one in gold, the others are in silver, fiery red, vibrant yellow, royal blue – and the other was in pure white,' said the Elvin salesman.

'We'll take them,' said Chantelle making an instant decision.

'What, all of them?' said a shocked salesman, taken aback by her instant purchase of all of these rare breastplates.

'No, just three – that is if you two want one too?' said Chantelle, looking towards her companions. 'You've just got to try one – amazing!'

They did try them, and decided on fiery red for Torres and vibrant yellow for Chevon. Chantelle stuck with the gold one she had tried and didn't bother to take it off.

'Fine! Now, ladies, I understand the treasury is footing the bill, so may I suggest the matching chin and wrist protectors?' said the Elf, who was probably in for a good commission on a pricey sale.

'Why not? If they fit like the breastplates I'm sold already,' said Torres. She then had a thought. 'Will the wrist protectors allow hawks to perch, or will they have difficultly grasping?'

'Ah! No, you'd have to have covers made, or the bird would probably slip off. But have no fear, our tailors can make hardwearing cloth that will match the metal's colour and leave the piping exposed so you shouldn't even notice a difference, we'll get them straight onto it, and they'll be ready by tomorrow,' answered the salesman, presenting an honest answer and an instant solution.

'Great, then we'll collect them tomorrow,' said Chevon. 'Now do you mind if we take a browse through your other items?'

'But of course… take your time, and if you can't decide today we'll still be here tomorrow,' replied the Elvin salesman.

The three women continued to look through the department before moving on, but there was just so much to choose from and they could see themselves spending many hours in the Victory Vault.

In the close-quarter weapons department, Erin and Tyler had been shown various weapons, all quite original and impressive in their own right. Erin had purchased a remarkably light sabre called Quicksilver. Its blade was wafer thin and razor sharp, and extremely strong for its thickness. It too had a hint of magic about it, and when used it moved quicker than the eye and exaggerated the speed of the arm, almost reading the owner's mind and reacting as fast as one's thoughts: an impressive sword indeed.

The department supervisor noticed Tyler's sword, Cleaver, and exclaimed, 'Cleaver, by the gods! That weapon is legendary – how did you come by it?'

'I brought it in Kondama,' answered Tyler, wondering what was known about his sword.

'May I be so bold as to inquire how much you paid for it, if you don't mind be asking that is?' asked the supervisor.

'Not at all. Two hundred gold pieces, I think, but we did buy other items with it,' said Tyler.

'A bargain! It's worth twenty times that… have you used its power often?' said the supervisor.

'I've used it often, and it certainly cleaves, but I've not been able to discover the wind it's meant to yield,' answer Tyler, sounding somewhat disappointed.

'So the switch is broken, then. Such a shame,' said the supervisor, also showing disappointment.

'What switch?' asked Tyler, his ears pricking up.

'You mean you weren't told? Seems whoever sold it did not know its history,' said the supervisor, holding his hand out for the sword. 'Here, on the handle: twist its tip, then press in the end, simple – ah! It's a little stiff. But—' he grimaced as he struggled with the handle and then, 'there you go, it seems it has not been used for an age. A little oil may help, but may I suggest we move into the battle room as unleashing it in here would not bode well.'

He indicated the door to the rear of the department. They moved through the doorway and found a large quarry was on the other side; around it were various targets and mannequins to test weaponry on.

'The lady and I will stay back here. If you wish to move to the far end, I'll send up an assault on your position… just use the blade as normal,' the supervisor said, pointing towards the other side of the quarry.

Once there, Tyler signalled he was ready. The supervisor then popped a switch and eight mannequins popped up, encircling Tyler, and simultaneously a large mock dragon appeared above his head.

Tyler swung the blade to cleave the first mannequin's head and he did so a whirlwind of power was unleashed. It thrust the blade and Tyler in a speedy pirouette that cut not only through the first mannequin but all eight; at the same time a powerful blast of air was sent skyward breaking the wooden dragon into a million splinters that rained down on the quarry's floor.

'Awesome!' shouted Tyler, 'that was bloody awesome!'

'Quite, but that's not all. The blade becomes a part of you and like you can differentiate between friend or foe. It will not harm those who fight with you, and its wind will pass through them like a gentle breeze, but your enemies will be powerless,' added the supervisor. 'I can't believe the fool who sold it to you. The sword is quite precious, and a treasure to hold, you have been so fortunate in finding it. The blade was said to have been owned by Blastair, the ancient King of Pkush, from the days before the Ajya-Na-Ku held a seat there. It was a gift from the Storm God himself, and helped protect Pkush until Blastair died of old age and the blade was lost. It even kept the forefathers of the Ajya-Na-Ku at bay; there are many pictures of it but they obviously did not consult their history books in Kondama or it would have never been sold.' He smiled at Tyler and added, 'It will see you well on your journey forward, so maybe fate has placed it in your hands. Use it well.'

The first visit to the vault had been well worth the effort, Sticks had again supplied a useful tip, and they had not even looked at the other departments, so a return visit was definitely on the cards. They returned to the Drop Inn for supper and beverages. All were present but Juran, and the night brought some much needed light entertainment along with a chance to unwind and let their hair down. Benjamin got as drunk as ever, and sore heads would greet the new day, along with a visit to the Elvin Ambassador.

Alliances

Sitting on a desk in the middle of the Grand Grateshaw library was a large and very old Owl; he had mottled grey wings with streaks of white on the tips of each. Cataracts obscured his left pupil but his right was still bright, large and sharp. His beak had seen better days and was scraped and scratched and chipped in many places. The ends of his claws were broken but he stood as proud as an old general who had won many battles and had passed gracefully into retirement. Juran had been in the aisles for some time and the bird caught his attention, so he decided out of intrigue and curiosity to ask one of the librarians why he was perched centre stage.

'Oh! Soothsayer,' said the librarian, 'he's older than the city and is a storehouse of knowledge; but you'd have to speak to him through Chloe, our Elvin linguist, and she's currently over the other side of the city, but will be back later.'

'I have companions who speak the animal tongues, perhaps one of them could,' said Juran, before he was cut short in mid-sentence.

'Afraid not... Chloe is rather particular about who speaks to the old bird. He's quite temperamental, you know, and she'd never forgive me if I were to agree to such a thing. I'm sorry, but she should be back before the new hour's ready,' said the librarian, answering the question before it was fully asked.

So Juran continued to consult the books in the magic section of the library whilst he awaited Chloe's return. Although Juran had made quite a dramatic introduction, of himself as a powerful Mage he was in fact quite inexperienced having only been a fully-fledged mage for five years. There were far more powerful wizards, warlocks and Mages out there, and they had been practising the arts for centuries. This meant Juran needed all the help he could muster in case he ran into another practitioner such as the one he'd encountered at the seat of the Ten Tribes; and of course he could no longer depend on Idron's aid, given such a scenario.

Juran had spent twenty-five years on Umkush Island, the southernmost island of the known world. It was a sorcerer's island and everyone there had some business with the arts. Many sorcerers took in students or apprentices but only selected individuals had the privilege of gaining such a position. Prior to his apprenticeship Juran had lived high in the hills near the source of the Elkwind River amid the Elvin lands. His mother was said to be a witch, although she, being an Elf, preferred the term 'enchantress'; but her tinkering with the black arts, which was frowned upon by the Elf nations, gained her the label of witch. Hence they lived isolated in the hills and rarely ventured into the towns or cities of Elkwind. His mother had taught him various magic tricks and incantations during his adolescence, and he quickly learnt to apply all he was taught, showing a certain amount of flare and innovation, trying his own slants on the magic he was shown.

A sorcerer of the order of the Pristine Priests named Mussrife had, whilst dabbling with an energy field spell on Umkush, sensed a power far off that was in its infancy but had all the indications of becoming a powerful force. He noted its location and despatched the Red Dragon, Umkellier, complete with Jiwan his servant, to the source of the energy. Jiwan had been instructed to offer the boy an apprenticeship on Umkush Island and not to take no for an answer, and to do anything necessary to achieve his aim. There was a slight problem with Juran's mother, who did not wish her son to be taken from her; so Jiwan brought both of them to Umkush and there they remained.

Juran studied long and hard, showing dedication along with his natural ability. Mussrife was a wise old man and no better teacher could he have had. His Order, the Pristine Priests, were of ancient origin and probably amongst the first sorcerers to walk the Earth. They had two seats of power: Glade East, which dealt with Earth Magic such as tremors and landslides; and Pool West, who specialised in elemental magic such as lightning strikes and the creation of tsunamis. Juran studied in both of these seats and was also taught the hidden magic of Belaphorus, the Sky God and deliverer of light. After twenty-five years, Mussrife told Juran he was ready to work alone as an Elvin Mage and so sent him to Elkwind to further his experiences and knowledge, before the expedition into Markesh. Mussrife summoned Juran to Umkush, and for the second time in his life he was plucked from Elkwind by Umkellier. Mussrife had read the runes and they had indicated that Juran had to go to Markesh, though for what reason Mussrife was uncertain, so he thought it best to hide the mage's identity until inside the continent. His unknown powers were undoubtedly at work.

So Juran was taken to the Green River ports under the guise of an Elvin traveller, and the rest we already know. Mussrife, however, had reservations, for he knew Juran still had much to learn; but alas, he could not teach Juran the experiences gained in conflict and discovery. He did however give Juran something that would boost his power; the silver crest of Siselmere. He told him the charm would amplify his energy and give him an extra edge to his blade, thus far Juran felt it had not performed these functions too well, but he had faith; and Mussrife, after all, would not let him down.

Chloe returned to the library as predicted just before the arrival of the new hour. She was a slim, dainty Elf, with large, (as is the norm for an Elf), hazel eyes. She had short dark hair, which was cut in a casual manner that would merely require fingers running through it to prepare it for the new day, though it was still attractive. Her clothes were practical, loose and elegant, but did little to hide her feminine figure.

As Juran approached her she gave a friendly smile and said, 'I hear you wish to consult with Soothsayer? He knows much that is meant to be known, and some of what should not be known, so please – at your pleasure.' She smiled again as she finished speaking.

'Thank you. Well, where to start? Indeed, where to start?' said Juran, thinking deeply before he poised his first question. 'What can be told of the forefathers of the Ajya-Na-Ku?'

Chloe spoke with Soothsayer at length, and the old bird seemed quite agitated at times as he told her what he could tell. Chloe then spoke to Juran, translating all that had been said.

'The forefathers were a group called the Coeur-Vu-Do, dabblers in the black arts and powerful sorcerers. They once controlled the entire world, or so it is believed. Their influence was felt in the farthest reaches of the globe and none could escape their clutches. The Dawn of Time was their mother, and the Wind of Life their father. They were the first, and it is said they shall be the last. Hold them you can, but time has a way of forgetting, and to forget is to admit ignorance, and ignorance gives way to blindness, and their return shall not seen before it is too late.' Chloe finished her translation and said, 'He speaks in riddles sometimes, and I'm never too certain it comes out right in translation, but he knows much and often sees what is yet to be.'

'So, the Coeur-Vu-Do, did not die?' asked Juran, intrigued by the Owl's words.

Chloe and Soothsayer spoke at length again before she replied, 'He says they cannot die, but they die as would you or I.' She paused, raising her hand to her mouth as if in thought, and said, 'Riddles, see... he's like this at times, but I suppose he knows what he means. But I think he's talking about them becoming Spirits or something.'

'Fine, I think I know what he's getting at. So what of the Ajya-Na-Ku – what do they desire?' replied Juran leading straight into another question.

Again there was an exchange between the bird and his translator before she turned to Juran and said, 'He doesn't know. He thinks they are plotting an advance on Green River, but feels this may be a diversion from something else, but he says the powers at work here are skilled in screening their actions.'

'Thank you,' said Juran, and then asked, 'are there any sorcerers, Mages or wizards nearby who might aid me in my quest for knowledge?'

The Owl answered, through Chloe. 'Three days' ride from here to the south of Falcon's Nest, there is a small settlement known as Kumbran. Only a couple of dwelling places are there, but there is an old wizard of human origin, called Glider, he may help you, but then again he may not. He tends the cathedral there.'

'A wizard attending a cathedral... how strange!' commented Juran.

'This cathedral isn't a church, it's a hill. It's said to resemble a church, it even has a tower-like feature. Why he tends it is not known,' added Chloe. Chloe then stopped as the bird spoke to her; then she said, 'He wishes to ask you a question.'

Juran seemed a little surprised, but having travelled with Winger, Singer and Stinger he knew that birds were sharp, 'Fire away, I'll answer as best I can,' he said.

'He wants to know how long you have carried the venom stick?' asked Chloe.

'Venom stick? Ah – the baton! I was given it by a courier in Kondama, he said it was a gift from the Willow Tribe, and they said it would aid me on my journey,' came Juran's answer.

There was a swift discussion between Chloe and Soothsayer, before she responded with the translation of the Owl's reply.

'It did not come from Willow; impossible. No, it's is a wolf in sheep's clothing... The stick is powerful, be careful in its use, and suspicious of its provider, for if their design is evil the stick may turn on you. Yet fear not if their design is pure, for it will become a mighty ally.'

'So, how do I discover the provider's intent?' asked Juran, fearful of the strange gift.

'Time, time, my dear fellow! It reveals all, and the outcome is written by the fates and is not easy to change. Keep it you should; just be watchful of its jewel. If it begins to turn red, discard it immediately; any colour is fine, but red,' said the Owl, and Chloe translated this message for Juran.

'Good, it is sound advice and I shall heed his warnings. Please thank him for me,' said Juran, noting well the information on the baton. Then he said, 'One final question: magical items, potions, lotions, spells and the like – is there anywhere in Matrosse I can obtain such things?'

'That's simple,' said Chloe, without having to consult the old bird, 'Madame Phoebe's... it's a shop set deep in the south side of the city; it's a little strange for my liking, but I'm certain she will be of some help to you.'

'Excellent, so how do I find it?' asked Juran.

'I thought you were a Mage! And that question, is it in addition to your final question?' replied Chloe, smirking. She then said, 'If you're in no rush I'll take you there, but I have to stay here for the next hour – work calls.'

'Even better,' answered Juran, rather pleased with her offer. 'I'll just carry on browsing here; just give me the nod when you're ready. And thank you, sir,' he added, bowing to the Owl.

Madame Phoebe was an elder Dwarf, who had often practised the white arts; she was also a reputable healer, and a kindly woman. Her shop was at the end of a very intricate series of tunnels, and without Chloe's help Juran would probably have spent days looking for it, if he hadn't been tempted to use magic to illuminate the way first. The interior of the shop was like some museum dedicated to all things magic, and as would be expected of such a place it was covered in dust, with cobwebs strung in every gap. The floor was damp and the ceiling dripped, which made the odd croaking toad or frog that hopped around the place in pursuit of insects feel most at home. Shelves covered the walls and a variety of books bound in all manner of fabrics and hides littered the shelves. Half-burnt candles illuminated the room, flickering light over some rather strange items, such as a stuffed gorilla in one corner, a stuffed eagle in another and a seemingly shrunken head mounted on the back of an old wooden chair. The creaky door and wooden floor meant none could pass without drawing attention to themselves.

'Who's there?' said a rasping voice, whose owner cleared her throat with a couple of coughs and a splutter.

'Hello? I'm sorry, I thought you were open,' said Chloe, in answer to the question.

'Oh! Customers, is it? Don't get too many of them nowadays,' said the little woman, appearing from behind a bookshelf. 'Anything in particular you need, or is the visit more out of curiosity, like most folk.'

'No, Madame, I was actually looking for any and all who may deal or practice in the arts, and where better to look?' stated Juran, though his question was rhetorical.

'And why would you be looking for such people, supposing they were around?' asked the small woman, now standing fairly close to them, with the candlelight making her eyes look like deep shadows, thus giving her a serious and somewhat sinister appearance.

'An alliance, a Sorcerers' Guild, to fight the Ajya-Na-Ku – what say you? You know of any who might be interested?' answered Juran, trying to tempt the woman with his offer.

'Maybe, maybe not... who asks?' came her reply, adding caution to this meet.

'I am Juran Garrand, born of the two ashes of Glade East and Pool West on the Island of Umkush, created long before the time of men. I was frozen as one with the craft of the Pristine Priests of old, I am knowledgeable in the incantations and charms of Belaphorus and am the keeper of the silver crest of Siselmere here, in hope of help against the impending evil that is upon us.' Juran used a similar introduction to the one he had uttered when revealing himself to the other expedition members.

'Sounds impressive! Silver crest of Siselmere, eh! Never heard of it,' said the woman.

'So what have you heard?' asked Juran, challenging her disparaging remark.

'I've heard a lot of bullshit in my time, young man, and Siselmere... well, it's an ancient term for folly, so don't try and trick me with that one,' said the old woman, laughing at him.

'But I was given it by my master, Mussrife. He said it would amplify my powers,' said a rather disgruntled Juran.

'Ha! Mussrife, eh! Well, I've heard of him, so I take it you were his apprentice – and not too bright a one, I'd wager,' said the chortling old lady. 'It's an old trick, to boost confidence in those who need it,' continued the woman.

'So you're saying it's quite useless?' asked a dejected Juran.

'Most probably, but if you've come this far, you don't need its false promises,' answered the woman. She continued, 'Well son, a guild... It may work, but you need a better salesman, I'd suggest Glider.'

'That's what Soothsayer said to him,' added Chloe.

'Well, that bird's normally right. Speak with Glider, he may help, but he's wrapped up in other issues at Kumbran – witches or something,' said the woman. Before continuing she lit a larger lamp that was on a table near the gorilla.

'Phoebe's the name. Go to see Glider, but go alone, without human help. If he sides with you, I'll know and will start to make arrangements here; if he does not, then I offer only what is on sale and no more.' She turned to the eagle and tapped its wing, 'Henry,' she said, 'keep an eye on this chap, will you?'

At this the eagle nodded and beat his wings a couple of times, which made Chloe and Juran jump as they had thought he was one of the stuffed animals.

'He'll see you right, and Glider will know I sent you if Henry's with you,' said Phoebe.

Juran left a note at the Drop Inn, and, taking Yew and Strongfoot, rode off towards Kumbran with Henry as his guide. Fortunately the weather remained fine and the anticipated three-day ride was in fact done in two. En route the Dwarves' alliance build-up was evident, as many dragon riders flew on their mighty steeds above Juran on their way to Matrosse; an impressive sight, he thought, as he moved southwest to meet with Glider.

Glider was warned of their impending arrival by Henry, who flew ahead to greet the old wizard, for very old he was. He had lived in Kumbran for centuries and knew tales of when it had been a city, not the few buildings it had now become. He was a simple man, who wore robust grey hooded robes and a round fur cap, also in grey. His face told of the passing of ages, and difficult times they were shown to be. He had a small, thin white moustache that stopped at his chin and a few tufts of hair around his ears. He was a tall man, towering above Juran, and despite his age still seemed dominating.

'So, you come,' said Glider. 'I know of the danger that presents itself, it is long in the making, and must be halted before it grows beyond control.'

'I sense it too, but am at a loss, I know not what is afoot, which is why I seek aid, aid from any who would ally themselves with me to stop the Ajya-Na-Ku,' said Juran in reply to the wizard's words.

'Ajya-Na-Ku eh! My friend, they are the least of our worries! A far greater problem is awakened, but to understand you must first know the significance of Kumbran and what has preceded this day,' said Glider, offering Juran a seat, for his tale would be a long one.

'Kumbran was in fact an ancient settlement, and the few buildings that now make up the place are sited on the ruins of a once magnificent city of some historical importance. It was believed that Kumbran had been Markesh's western islands' capital city, then home to the Rydren Empire. This Empire controlled most of the western states, including Elkwind, Proteous and Broderland, before the rising of the great rocks. The eastern part of the world was controlled by the oldest civilisation, the Coeuran, of whom the Coeur-Vu-Do, a sect of sorcerers, was the governing body. The Rydren Emperor, Nathaniel the Third, had many kings governing his provinces; his favourite and most trustworthy was Blastair, who was King of Pkush and the holder of Cleaver, a weapon of the Storm God. Pkush was the key strategic island of the Rydren Empire; for as long as it was under the Empire's control, they controlled the seas, and thus access to the western world. The sorcerer Shukran, head of the Coeur-Vu-Do engaged in a campaign to capture Pkush, and Blastair, despite a valiant defence, was pushed from his kingdom and sought refuge in Kumbran.

'The Emperor massed his armies along the mountain ranges of the Dragon Mountains and Falcon's Nest in anticipation of impending assault, but no assault came. Years passed before the Coeur-Vu-Do made their next move, for they had massed a new army – an army of creatures – some men, some ethereal, some of denominations unknown. They called them the Ajya-Na-Ku, and with them came an airborne menace, the dragons.

'The assault came in force, and much of the west was quickly overrun. Kumbran held strong, as did Falcon's Nest. The assault was quashed in the Great Forest by the scorching of Sycamore by the witches of the woods, who were allied by Basterdor a sorcerer supreme. Even with these small successes, ground was being lost quicker than it could possibly be regained, so an evacuation plan was made, and the western island of Markesh would be abandoned. Basterdor had, unbeknown to the Coeur-Vu-Do, links to a small race in the east. This race lived beyond the Coeur-Vu-Do's home at the end of the Myrkdalen valley, and was a magical race, full of wizards, witches and warlocks. So whilst besieged the defenders plotted and planned, drawing the sorcerers of the Coeur-Vu-Do ever closer. The war had raged for years and all the time the wizards of the east were planning their intervention.

'Once the evacuation was complete, the plan was to make Markesh a huge battleground, a battleground unlike anyone had ever witnessed, a battleground of wizards and sorcerers, necromancers clashing with unearthly power until the Coeur-Vu-Do were defeated. The Trinity – three of the strongest wizards from the east – conjured up a mighty earthquake, tearing rock from the depths of the earth to form a barrier, cutting off Markesh from the rest of the world, thus protecting all who had evacuated. Kumbran was sacrificed to make the Coeur-Vu-Do overconfident, and as it was razed to the ground. A trap was sprung that entombed the Coeur-Vu-Do for eternity in a mighty slab of granite, called the Coeur Rock but more often the Cathedral. Only the more powerful sorcerers, the governing body, escaped; but their snare would soon be set, as they had lost their control over the dragons, due to Dagtorn, the sorcerer who had enchanted them falling at the Coeur Rock. The dragons turned on the Ajya-Na-Ku, because of the cruelty they had suffered as their slaves; and thus the hatred between them was born.

Six sorcerers were left in the Coeur-Vu-Do: Mazon, Idrel, Coettee, Vinnittor, Eskabar and Shukran, their leader. These sorcerers were pressured by a new alliance between the dragons and the Rydren Empire, and forced to a final battle at Falcon's peak. Here the Trinity entombed five of the sorcerers in ice and their leader, Shukran, fled. The Trinity fought hard to achieve their goal, and though successful it cost them their lives. With them destroyed there was no one to reverse the spell that held the great rock barrier in place; so there it has remained and only time has managed to breach its walls. With Shukran a great concern to all, a mighty soldier called Kamble was given the sword, Charlock, forged in the dragon's breath to pursue Shukran and destroy him. After many months Kamble returned, confirming that, wielding Charlock, he had killed Shukran.

'However, with the majority of people evacuated to the west, and many of the key members of the Empire dead, chaos reigned.

Old arguments surfaced and families split; brother fought brother, and soon the alliances that had allowed the Coeur-Vu-Do to be defeated were broken. The Ajya-Na-Ku, without their masters, had time to regroup and form a new hierarchy; soon they were the most unified force and controlled much of Markesh, and have done so ever since.' The wizard finished his tale and picked up a long bone pipe. Lighting the end, he took a few puffs before Juran spoke.

'So what has this to do with the Ajya-Na-Kops today? Why is this history so important?' he asked Glider.

'Did you not see? The sorcerers were freed,' said Glider, with a surprised expression.

'Idron!' said Juran. 'By the gods, he released them – but why?'

'*Why* is not the question; your friend was merely a vessel. The Ajya-Na-Ku, now they're the ones who released the sorcerers – the five, Mazon, Idrel, Coettee, Vinnittor and Eskabar. I can sense them,' answered Glider, taking another puff on his pipe before continuing. 'They come here next.'

'How do you know?' asked Juran, still not understanding the significance of the story Glider had told him.

'The Coeur Rock... were you not listening? It holds the remainder of the Coeur-Vu-Do. It is quite clear, the Ajya-Na-Ku plan to bring back their gods, the Mountain gods,' said Glider, pointing his pipe at the hills behind him. Then he said, 'This is why I remain here, like Cedric on Falcon's Peak, though he was careless. I watch over the sleeping rock, in the hope that it will remain that way, at least during my watch. The Ajya-Na-Ku are coming, and should this rock fall the dragons will also turn, and this time the mighty Rydren Empire won't be here to stop them.'

'So, it is graver than I suspected. What should we do?' asked Juran, wishing now he had far more experience in the art of sorcery.

'Your plans are fine. Alliances must be sought. The Dwarves are on the move, it's a start, you may hold the enemy long enough at Matrosse Pass, but in the meantime send word to the west. Let the armies of the lost lands [the Markesh term for Proteus, Broderland and Elkwind] come forth. Ally the Forest tribes; tell Basterdor to keep them in check, tell all that are willing, and those who are not, to allow free passage to those who will come. They will struggle to reach here and will have to fight the Ajya-Na-Ku along the way, no doubt; but this battle cannot be lost,' said an only too serious Glider.

'So it will be. I move soon and will ride hard, Henry will fly ahead with word; it seems there is no time to waste,' said Juran, wanting to jump straight into the solution.

'My dear boy, they are coming – but not tonight, or tomorrow; and the Pass is strong. Send word to the dragons of Dragon Mountain, they will more than likely join with us and speed the influx of troops; but in the interim a company of Dwarf riders and their mounts from the Dragon Clan should be enough to help me here,' Glider said trying to steady Juran's young mind.

'Fate will take its course, my young Mage. Let's hope it lies with the righteous; an army requires a general, and I see you have one in your party. Use him well, he may swing the coming battle. Now ride on with good speed, and may the sun light your way,' added the wizard.

At his words Juran mounted Yew, and leading Hardfoot, rode back toward Matrosse Pass.

None Shall Pass

'An army!' said Benjamin. 'They're putting together an army.' He was speaking to the other members of the expedition, though Juran was still abroad. 'And they want us to aid them,' he continued, pointing at those present. 'I told them we have a Protalien officer with us, and explained all about your race's warrior culture; they seemed most interested.'

He spoke with excitement as the thought of being part of a Dwarf army once again pleased him more than anyone could imagine. It was as though his suppressed inner wishes had been granted. 'So what do you think?' he asked Tyler.

Tyler paused before answering, as images of the Academy flickered across his mind. In his head he pictured Meme and his brother, then he said, 'Why ever not? If we are not yet to move on, then at least the pace of time will quicken, and it will feel good to mould a new army.'

'Good – cause we start tomorrow,' said Benjamin, and a smile broke the frown he was using to portray the serious nature of the idea he was trying to sell, though now it seemed had already agreed to start training.

'Ha!' said Tyler, grinning at Benjamin, 'you're a sly old fool! So tomorrow it is.'

'And the remainder of us?' inquired Erin, keen to get in on the act.

'Advisers, Erin. You'll join Tyler and me, Chantelle and Torres, you'll work together with the dragon riders, it seems they've never actually spoken to the dragons, so you may add a new twist to their operational procedures. Chevon and Elsbeth, we suggested you work on the casualty collection and treatment plan,' said Benjamin laying down the general plans that he and Elsbeth had worked on with the Chieftains of the Cave Clan. They had been working on these matters the previous day, whilst the others had been to the Victory Vault.

'Great,' said Erin, somewhat cynically, 'but can you tell me what the three of us will be working on? Or is the secret so secret that you'd have to kill me after you told me?'

'Sorry, it slipped my mind. We'll concentrate on combat techniques and strategy,' answered Benjamin, still beaming with enthusiasm.

'What of Juran?' asked Chantelle, 'where will he fit in?'

'Well, I had hoped he could help enhance our weaponry, but with three days' ride to get where he's going, and the gods only know how long he'll spend there. Then the journey back... well, you see my point, he'll just have to stay out of the equation for the moment. But here will no doubt time when he does return. It's not as if the Ajya-Na-Ku are planning to attack tomorrow,' said Benjamin.

The Alliance's army was merely undergoing its formation because the mountains were no longer a no-go area for the Ajya-Na-Ku. It was in fact a token effort, a precautionary measure; the plan being to have a reaction force, whose components, once trained in working together, would stay within their respective clans' own territories. Any attack on one sector could then be reinforced by elements of the other components or the whole force if it was needed.

'Any timings – or do we just turn up when we want?' asked Chevon, not overly happy that she had been picked as a medical orderly.

'Yes, well, they want us to meet with the Elvin Ambassador before we meet the units, and he plans to meet us at ten. The embassy's just down the next street, so it'll take only five minutes or so to get there,' Benjamin said, guessing Chevon's disappointment in her task from her attitude. 'But don't worry, the casualty thing involves battle, not sat back in some hospice, so it shouldn't be that bad.'

At ten sharp the next morning, all seven were stood in line in front of a podium of marble in a fairly small but adequate hall in the Elvin Embassy in Matrosse. Being Elves, there were no guards to oversee them and they were left to their own devices until the arrival of the Ambassador. They did not have to wait long, as the curtain of laced red flowers at the podium's head parted and an elegant Elvin gentleman came forth. He wore a finely woven blue and white robe that cascaded over his body like shimmering water, its quality underlining his importance. With open arms he greeted them in the Elvin tongue, whilst bowing his head, and said:

'*Tanwar arum uvan supra teh uprum sun Samakar pum orik savoid uvan Nabrudor anie Gador.*'

Which translated means, 'Welcome are you under the roof of Samakar, may fate grant you deliverance and life.'

Chantelle replied whilst Torres translated what was said to those not of Elvin origin.

'*Anor teh Dimnakor,*' she said, 'before the Lord.' This being the traditional and correct reply under Elvin custom when one has been welcomed into someone's residence. Once these greetings were made, the Ambassador relaxed his arms and, looking upward, spoke in a dialect that all present could understand.

'Many times I've gazed along the open road that leads to Pkush, and felt great relief that those who dwell there dare not enter these mountains. Yet the sands of time flow through open hands, and try as one might its grains cannot be held. The circle of life will roll on long after the likes of us have gone from this world. An army is only as mighty as its will, and victory will only reward those who see no other way of achieving their goals. A storm rides on the winds of change; how it changes that which we have today is known only by the Fates; let us hope they look kindly upon us. The enemy will come, that much is certain; but I have heard that this time they will come with purpose, and not just to enforce their authority. No, greater goals are afoot, though as of yet I do not know their aim,' said Samakar the Ambassador.

He walked down from the podium and gestured for them to follow him. He stopped at the left-hand wall of the chamber where a large map of Markesh was mounted on the wall. Skilled cartographers had drawn it and its relief features were raised from the parchment. The map showed far more detail than the one Idron had made under Cedric's guidance and covered most of the wall. The Ambassador pointed out their location and the location of Pkush, then he pointed to the islands to the north, north-east of Pkush, and said, 'Here is Selkuna, the Elvin homeland; it was from here the Elvin exodus set off, many centuries ago, heading to the West and never to be seen again. It is thought the rising of the Great Rocks prevented their return – that is, till now. I heard of your arrival some weeks ago and have been eager to meet with you. Is it true that you come from beyond the Great Rocks?' he asked the party.

'We do, one and all,' said Chevon, 'and an exodus is made mention of in our teachings too; though our tale tells of the homeland, Sekounya, being destroyed shortly after the exodus was made.'

'Twists in the telling, but undoubtedly the same tale, though time appears to have played its tricks on its verification. But be in no doubt, we are of the same family, our language and customs appear intact; but I notice an accent may have crept in somewhere down the line,' said Samakar. 'This meet comes to me as an honour I shall not forget, and again I welcome you.'

'We are pleased to accept your hospitality,' said Benjamin, 'but the talk of a goal, and a coming storm... what do you feel deep down, what is it you feel they plan?'

'I know not, as I have indicated, but I'd wager it has to do with the tip of Falcon's Peak and the area of Kumbran, sacred places to the Ajya-Na-Ku. They believe their gods are imprisoned there. Some curse or spell has kept them away for centuries, but the assault on your party at the Falcon's Peak cabins marks a turn of events. What kept them back can no longer be regarded as an ally; so as I have said, they will come,' came Samakar's reply – a reply that showed the extent of his concern, as he suddenly seemed downcast, as though the executioner's song had called him.

'The Elves of Selkuna, will they join with us?' asked Tyler, trying to assess what forces he might be able to count on when the time came.

'An army is ready, but will not join us here; they have their own borders to defend. But the third fleet are upon the Sea of Hope, and may offer some assistance; however this too will be limited, so we are alone, which is why we requested your assistance. The Dwarves' governments have secured the alliances of the clans, and each sends a battle group to Matrosse as we speak. Once contingency plans are formulated and rehearsed; they should be strong enough to secure the mountains, though I suggest an emphasis on the defence of Falcon's Peak and Kumbran, if my predictions are to be correct. Yet without any confirmation of their goals we cannot leave other areas unguarded. The commanders of each battle group will be in the Chambers of the Council of Conflict within the hour, I will lead you there when the call comes and we can discuss whatever courses of action arise. Until then, make yourselves comfortable; there are refreshments on the table at the rear of the hall, I will return when the time comes. Again, it is an honour to meet with you, and your help is most appreciated.' Samakar ended the meeting leaving little room for more questions and disappeared through the laced flowers.

The Chamber of the Council of Conflict was set high in the northern side of the Pass, as this had the higher ridge of the two sides. It was reached after a long trek through the tunnelled streets a climb up endless twisting stairs that would make an assault on the chambers a hellish upward struggle. The chamber was cut below the overhanging ridge of the mountain making assault from above near impossible. A large viewing gallery was constructed at its forward edge, giving fantastic views of the Pass and all approaches, apart from the rear, which would mean an approach from the mountains that remained under the Dwarves' control.

The chamber's interior was fairly basic, yet practical. A planning table and chairs were set back from the gallery. To the left flank of the gallery was a pigeon coop, no doubt for the delivery of messages. Seated at the table on the left was Heyador, a lean dwarf with a greying bushy moustache and squashed red nose that filled his face. He was the battle group commander of the Hill Clan. To his right stood Syvon, whose strong bulging thighs seemed out of place below his slight upper body. He was clean-shaven and years of walking in the mountains had kept him in peak condition. He was the commander from the Mountain Clan. Borlock, the leader from the Cave Clan, whose city they were now in sat at the head of the table. He looked finer than the others and was obviously not a fighter; to his right was his battle group commander, Driller, who was scarred badly across his left cheek, and sported a short scraggy white beard. He looked mean and his hands were like shovels. Next to him sat a Dwarf in silver armour that shone like some warning beacon, its brightness contrasting drastically with everything else in the room. He wore no helmet, was clean-shaven, and his black hair, plaited in dreadlocks, fell about his shoulders. His name was Scyther, and he was the chieftain and leader of the Dragon Clan's battle group.

Each Battle group brought with it its own speciality, The Hill Clan were cavalry soldiers, mounted on strong hill ponies that were surprisingly fast and robust. The Mountain Clan were skilled in siege warfare and had the hardiest foot soldiers of all of the Dwarves, and had skilled archers at their disposal. The Cave Clan were masters in close-quarter fighting and also had many projectile weapons, such as giant catapults, spear launchers and battering rams. The Dragon Clan were skilled assault troops, mounted on the most formidable of beasts that brought talon, strength, fire and fear to the battlefield.

Together they had the potential to form a flexible and unpredictable army that would have some hope of holding their lands from the Ajya-Na-Ku. They sat down together for the first time and made a pact.

'Together as one, we end past grievances. Forward in unity we must travel, and we pledge to one another that wherever the enemy strikes our band will join in his defeat, and not one foot of the mountain will we allow to fall so long as we breath. So say we all this day, with blood, spit and soil binding our words.'

They said this in unison. Then, each taking a dagger, drew blood from the palm of the man on their left, then spat on their own hand, sprinkled soil on the blood and spit then raised their hands together pointing inwards forming a pyramid shape above the table.

They then shouted, 'So say we all!' and slapped their hands together. This was followed by handshakes all around, and a great feeling of euphoria until all had shaken each other's hands. They then sat down and were introduced to the seven members of the expedition before business began in earnest.

Tactics were the key issue, and proved a difficult one, as in a discussion many scenarios can be presented, and there are of course many, many ways to achieve a goal. Alas, only in battle when the chips are down will good and bad ideas reveal themselves. Add to this the issue that not every battle is the same and then reason that just because it worked in the last fight by no means proves it will work in this one. Such dilemmas help give an idea of the sort of discussions that went on this day. Heated at times, yes; frustrating, absolutely; but necessary – unquestionably. These clans had never worked militarily together, so there would be many problems to iron out and no doubt mistakes would be made along the way. Their biggest problem was the fact that they had no way of knowing exactly where the Ajya-Na-Ku would strike, and hence did not know which terrain would become their battleground: the pass? The foothills? The mountains? The caverns and tunnels? Or of course combinations of all these places; or even all at once? Thus the day was long, and during it there was much self-praise whenever a leader felt his troops could achieve a task another clan could not. This was of course one-upmanship at its best or worst, depending on your views.

The following day was spent with the troops, practising procedures and cross training went on between the various units of each clan. Many friendships were made this day, and Tyler noted the one winning factor they all had was their enthusiasm and pride. They wanted to hurt the Ajya-Na-Ku, and hurt them bad. They had lived free of their talons for so long they had no intention of lying down and letting these fiends roll in and take whatever they desired. The attack on the cabins on Falcon's Peak had sent shock waves across the entire mountain range and the Dwarf Clans. Determined to defend the territories they loved they were more than willing to brush aside old feuds and take up arms together against the common enemy.

The dragons were just amazing, and Chantelle and Torres thoroughly enjoyed their day. They had never spoken to dragons before, as they were beasts of terror and to be avoided at all costs. They were also quite rare in the western world, so this made meeting such mythical creatures even more exciting. A basic formation in the Dragon Clan consisted of a flight of six dragons, and the battle group had six flights totalling thirty-six dragons, an impressive and rather intimidating sight. The dragons varied in size, shape and colour, but all had enormous talons that protruded from their fingers like giant sickles. Their skin was as tough as diamonds and coarse to the touch, as though they wore a coat of granite. Given the size and shape of these beasts, it was a sheer wonderment they could fly at all. The flights were all named, with lead flight being the command and control element of the formation. There were three assault flights, Clout, Clobber and Wallop flights. The two remaining flights were supporting flights, mounted on the biggest of the dragons, the ones who were able to produce the biggest and nastiest fireballs and spew the hugest volume of flames. These were Scorch and Sear flights.

Chantelle spent her time with the lead and support flights, and Torres with the assault flights. The dragons were in fact very pleasant and polite; they only wished to destroy what they felt needed to be destroyed, and the Ajya-Na-Ku was on the top of their list. They liked the Dwarves, they had proved fine companions over the years and treated the dragons with the greatest respect; and although they could not communicate with one another there was an inexplicable bond that allowed them to understand what each party desired of the relationship, and this led to an affable link between the two species. Thus the two Elvin speakers had few discrepancies to resolve and the day became quite jovial as dragons and Dwarves were able, through the two linguists, to say exactly what they wished to each other for the first time.

Chevon and Elsbeth worked with representatives from each battle group and discussed herbal medicines and improvised medical procedures that could save lives in the midst of battle. This, as Benjamin had commented, had not been such a bad subject to discuss and Chevon did enjoy the day; and from the response she had from the troops she felt a great sense of achievement. She returned to the Drop Inn with a positive outlook on the Dwarves' Alliance.

Tyler, Erin and Benjamin watched the assault troops train, adding a few tips or ideas wherever they deemed necessary. They discussed tactics with sub-unit commanders, and they too saw a promising army resulting from this alliance.

The following two days brought more preparations and a series of mock battles, testing different ideas and courses of action that could be played out in the event of a real assault by their enemy.

Stinger, Winger and Singer patrolled the sky through the training days, and on the second day spotted flights of Black Owls closing on the pass. This was immediately conveyed to Tyler, who in turn spoke with Scyther, the Dragon Clan commander, who immediately despatched Clobber flight to intercept these spies. This was done in next to no time, but it confirmed the Ajya-Na-Ku were indeed targeting the pass.

With the third day came Henry the eagle, bringing Juran's message to Phoebe. She informed Chloe, who in turn sought out the remainder of the expedition. The news and recommendations passed to them brought a lull in the training and an immediate conference was called. Tyler spoke with the commanders from each Clan, along with Samakar and Borlock.

'The message is clear, we must build an army far mightier than the one we currently undertake,' said Tyler to his audience of military commanders; but he spoke with confidence and conviction, showing he was a natural leader. 'We must send message to all who may help, to march forth and join us. It seems your predictions were spot on, Samakar. Yet it is worse than we thought; the Peak has fallen, whatever they needed there has been stolen from under our very noses. Kumbran is their next goal and it is with urgency that we must send troops to protect it. A company of Dragons is requested, Scyther, can you manage this?'

'Aye, and some, I'll despatch Wallop and Sear flights, that should be more than enough,' replied Scyther.

'Good, but I'm still uncertain that this will be enough, I'd prefer it if a troop from Hill, Mountain and Cave accompany you, this will cover all avenues; besides, lest we forget what we have practised here these past days. Any objections to a troop each?' asked Tyler, peering at the other leaders, who all endorsed his decision without hesitation.

'Fine. We need message couriers to seek alliances in all of Markesh, and I fear the distances are too far for the birds to be speedy enough. Any suggestions?' Tyler asked of his audience.

'We can cover this too,' said Scyther, 'I'll split Clout into three pairs, the dragons are the swiftest creatures present and they will return in less than two days. However, the message delivery will be quick enough – but will their coming?'

'Let's hope and pray they sense the urgency and have the gall to face the common enemy! And the western lands – can the dragons reach there?' replied Tyler, still eager to gain as many allies as possible.

'They have never crossed the Great Rocks, Green Port is their limit, but I fear an approach by them may draw fire and confrontation from the defenders there,' answered Scyther, with honesty and concern for his troops but mostly for the dragons.

'Let me go with them,' said Chevon, 'they can set me down short of the perimeter, the rest I can do on foot, Singer can accompany me and pave the way for my entry to the port.'

'But what if no linguist can be found?' asked Tyler, concerned for his own party's safety.

'Don't be silly! There's always a contingent of Elf sailors in each of the ports. How do you suppose they send messages?' said Chevon, making refusal of this idea nigh impossible.

'Okay, then have it your way, but be careful, I don't want some dumb-assed sentry drilling you full of arrows!' said Tyler. He made light of the decision, but still worried his words could become reality, for he thought little of the professionalism of the troops guarding the ports; none of them were Protalien, after all.

'Then we make haste,' said Driller, trying to add his bit of authority on the proceedings, not completely happy now Tyler had grasped the reins.

'Indeed,' said Tyler, 'but only to prepare the immediate deployments – the message carriers and the reinforcements for Kumbran. The rest of us meet back here in one hour, there is still much we can do.'

With this, the meeting ended and the battle group leaders all departed after which Tyler turned to Chevon and said, 'Be safe, and take no unnecessary risks. We need you with us, now more than ever.'

'Not to worry, I'm a healer, remember, and I don't like

healing myself! Blood's fine unless it's my own. Besides Singer won't let me down, and I've always wanted to ride a dragon... cool, eh?' came Chevon's reply, after which she too left the room, en route to Clout flight's location.

'Now what?' asked Erin. 'We just sit here and wait for an army to come together... great plan!' She was as cynical as ever, but nonetheless had a valid point.

'What else can we do? Attack the Ajya-Na-Ku? I don't think so,' said Chantelle in response to Erin's comments.

'No, that would be a foolish action,' added Elsbeth, seeing no other options. 'We're better off here amongst the Dwarven Clans. After all, the city – well, it's a fortress.'

'Quite right,' added Benjamin, backing up any comment that sided with the Dwarves. 'A fine city it is, and the company is grand, they'll never take these walls.'

Torres also agreed. 'We have to wait, but it may take a great deal of time before an army is ready, so I suggest we make the most we can of Matrosse. The gods only know what we will meet with once we leave this place, and I'm in no hurry to find out.'

'What say you, Tyler?' asked Benjamin. 'You've said naught since Chevon departed... are you so worried for her?'

'I say nothing because I hear all your words. You all say a good deal of time is needed before an army is ready, and that we must stay in the safety of the city,' Tyler replied in a rather intense voice. 'That is, if an army comes, and until the city is overrun. Time may be our undoing.'

He said no more but walked over to the window and gazed across the pass in silence.

The hour passed slowly after these words and the room remained silent, with everyone caught up in their own thoughts, ideals and concerns. The commanders returned, confirming the troops had been readied and would depart shortly. After they had all sat down the silence that had greeted their arrival returned. They looked at each other in wonderment but said nothing. Then Tyler broke the hush. Leaning over the table at which they sat he said, 'I told you we had much to discuss, and I have thought long and hard about that which troubles us. We can never anticipate their moves; we never know their numbers or how they will arrive. We remain cornered like some outwitted fox waiting for the hounds. Enough! We can never win if we continue to take this approach.'

He paused, then stood up and paced the floor, while his companions anticipated and feared the coming of his words; they now knew his intentions and were suddenly reminded of his suicidal charge at the Great Hall of the Ten Tribes.

'So what do you suggest then?' inquired Heyador, wishing Tyler would cut to the chase.

'We cannot sit and wait for them to come to us! We should go to them, we must strike the Ajya-Na-Ku in an offensive action. We leave an adequate force to hold the pass, then we advance toward the sea, striking any and all we see on the way. They will never expect it and we'd catch them at their weakest. If we are in error, we draw them back to the Pass and into the sights of the defenders there.' Tyler spoke with such dominance that no one dared question his idea; this bold officer from the warrior race transfixed them.

'Prepare tonight – tomorrow we strike!'

War Cry

Council continued well into the night as plans were drawn for a quick offensive. Tyler knew the four battle groups were way too small for a prolonged attack. A bloody nose was all he could hope to present the Ajya-Na-Ku, for nothing was known about their true strength or dispositions, but he felt sitting back and just allowing them to dictate the course of events were the actions of the incompetent. The plans he made revolved around the strength and weakness of each battle group.

The strongest and most feared where the Dragon Clan. Their thirty-six dragons were an awesome sight, but they also had a strong complement of troops who were considered the best Dwarf soldiers in the world. The three assault fights of six dragons were structured in a similar manner, with each flight consisting of two light dragons, not much bigger than River Snappers; they each held one Dwarf fighter, were swift and deadly and took on the role of close support. They were thus able to hit hard and fast with insurmountable manoeuvrability. The other four dragons in the flight were bigger, and each carried seven dwarves, of which six were assault troops and one the rider. These six soldiers could be landed rapidly where the situation decreed, giving each flight twenty-four ground troops. The supporting dragons had two riders each.

Their weaknesses were firstly the size of the dragons, as they were quite easy to see from a distance, so surprise could normally only be gained by using the close support dragons. Secondly, the logistical implications of such large animals, this meant each dragon also had four, six or even eight dwarves assigned to it purely for food and water collection; a monumental task, but much needed to prevent the dragons from deciding they needed to break the Alliance and forage for themselves. This meant that herds of cattle were constantly required to accompany any expeditionary force, so expeditionary warfare was normally avoided at all costs, and the Dragon Clan had only really ever mounted quick raids onto the neighbouring clans and tribes.

For this offensive Tyler made radical changes. He wanted the six close-quarter dragons, two from each flight, to initiate a quick attack on the Ajya-Na-Ku, once they had been found by Stinger and Winger. There would be four dragons left from the assault flights. These would shuttle in three lifts the ground troops, the extra troops would come from the Mountain Clan, making a total of seventy-two fighters that would be dropped off behind the Ajya-Na-Ku. This would then cut them off if they withdrew, trapping them in an ambush. Only four dragons and a troop each from the other clans would now stay at Kumbran, and the other four assault dragons would be busy delivering the news of the Army's build-up to neighbouring lands. These changes were delivered to the Dragon Clan's commanders with such conviction they found it difficult to disagree, but it was felt the offensive was such a pressing matter they were willing to try Tyler's suggestions. The balance of the battle group lay in the support. Flight one would still go to Kumbran the other would remain in reserve.

The Hill Clan's mounted battle group were organised into six troops of twenty-eight horses and riders. They were also swift in battle and were able to manoeuvre quickly. Each troop was divided into four teams of seven riders, with two teams in each troop having the distinction of being formidable mounted archers, who whilst riding at speed could draw, fire and hit their mark with incredible accuracy. One team was armed with light sabres and scimitars for close-order battle, whilst the fourth team were lancers. With one troop at Kumbran, this left five troops for the offensive. Three troops would hit the Ajya-Na-Ku full on in an attempt to push them into the waiting ambush, whilst the other two troops would remain in reserve. Like the Dragon Clan, they also had logistical problems in sustaining this mounted army, but on a far lesser scale. They also encountered difficulties when an enemy placed obstacles in their path, as the horse could become spooked or be unable to clear the fence, so to speak.

The Mountain Clan had a huge contingent of ground troops

totalling some 1,440 foot soldiers. They were formed into twelve companies of four troops, with each troop having three sections of ten men. Within each troop were a section of pikemen, a section of crossbow men and a section of musket men. The biggest weakness they had was that it took them time to get where they were going, but their incredible stamina meant they could still put up a terrific fight when they got there. Added to this figure were 560 supporting or logistical troops with donkeys and carts, bringing the force to around two thousand in strength. Tyler had already employed some of these troops with the ambush. Three troops would stay in reserve, and three would block the far end of the pass at Matrosse. The remainder would push behind the cavalry of the Hill Clan taking the fight to the Ajya-Na-Ku.

The Cave Clan were good at defensive and close-quarter battle, so Tyler left them defending Matrosse, something they were familiar with. Then, in the event the Ajya-Na-Ku managed to reach the pass, they would be caught in the natural ambush it provided and any who survived this passage would encounter the blocking force provided by the mountain Dwarves. This seemed the best option as the Cave Clan were quite vulnerable on open ground and not at all suited to long-range attack. Space on the battlefield for them would normally result in death and defeat.

Not all of the expedition would ride out, Juran of course was still headed back from Kumbran, though he was expected at any time and could lend his skill to the battle on arrival. Benjamin, Chantelle and Elsbeth would remain in Matrosse, as would the mules and their own steeds. Erin, Torres and Tyler would accompany the ground troops as they swept forward searching for the Ajya-Na-Ku. There was a good deal of land between the mountains and the sea, and the sea lay to the north, east and south. However, given the prospect of Elvin ships they decided to move east and cross Spruce, an estuary of Green River, north, then head north toward the sea of hope and with luck they would secure a route to one of the two bays, making a Dwarf-Elvin alliance a reality.

'Ride on, my fine friends,' said Tyler, addressing the army before him. 'We shall write a new history after this day, a day the world changed, the beginning of the demise of the dreaded and the rise of the virtuous. To victory with honour we must go. Show them the clemency of our kind, but expect no compassion from their people, at least we know we did not demean ourselves with the standards of this cruel foe. For Matrosse, the mountains and Markesh, we go forth this day. Let us serve them true, and release this darkened continent from the evil clutches of the Ajya-Na-Ku!' Tyler spoke with a voice of fire, scorching his message in the minds of the audience, and none would forget what he called them to do. It was evident that without Juran's influence he had become the general Glider had spoken of.

The birds, Winger and Stinger, were the first to leave, climbing high to gain a better view, their keen eyes letting nothing escape note. Brave birds they were, for they knew the Black Owls far outnumbered them; but their mission was vital to the success of Tyler's plan and they would not let him down. Gee, Que and Vee were more than happy to venture out of Matrosse. They had been treated well, although pampered would be a better description, but the short hacks they had endured were not what they had been used to, growing up in the Protalien service. There they were tested to the limit, and only the finest horses could hope to make the grade and these three had without argument proved themselves many times. The short, closely grazed grass below the pass was magic to their hooves as they trotted along, tall and proud amid the mountain ponies of the Dwarven cavalry; and magnificent they looked, too, Vee's dapple grey in stark contrast to the glistening reddish tones of the two freshly clipped and groomed chestnuts, Que and Gee. The horses felt strong and proud and more than ready to carry their riders into the thick of battle.

The first day's ride brought a quick encounter with a small group of Ajya-Na-Ku bandits. They were ransacking a small hamlet just short of the spruce. The hamlet was the home of a group of human trappers who regularly moved up and down the river hunting and trapping for the furs they used to trade with and meat for their table. They were a non-threatening group who were well known to the Dwarf Clans and traded with them often.

Winger reported back to Tyler via Torres what had been spotted and due to the small number of enemy it was decided to leave the plan for the meantime and mount a quick attack using cavalry and infantry units.

The settlement was in a small dell set on the banks of the Spruce. The ground leading to it was well covered, so an approach was made in single file using the concealment it offered until the last safe moment. Lurching over the crest of the cover, Gee hurtled forth, churning up tufts of grass and soil as she stomped forward, spitting and snorting in a concerted effort to close a rapidly as possible with this foul enemy. Close behind followed a troop of cavalry, desperately trying to stay with Gee's lead, hooves drowned the dell with their thunderous song, and the enemy was caught unawares.

Tyler was the first to clash with them. He met with a large foe who sprang from the doorway of a nearby house; his claws scraped Tyler's thigh but did little real damage – unlike the response brought to bear in Cleavers windy blade! One quick stroke sent the fiend's head sailing through the air as though a signal had been made that the war had begun.

Their numbers were few, around fifteen, and they all seemed of human origin. So they were probably doing what they did best – stealing, tormenting and terrorising the local populace. Actions such as these were encouraged by the Ajya-Na-Ku; it kept their presence known and tightened their grasp on the land. Resistance, however, would bring dire consequences. Not only would any rebellious acts be met with these basic Ajya-Na-Ku lackeys, but the unearthly members of the organisation would also pay a visit and they were far harder to defeat. The short skirmish continued as a dark cloud blotted the sun from view; its shadow fell over the dell as though a cloak had been strewn over the land.

It was a mighty swarm of the dreaded Black Owls. Swooping down, they passed through the hamlet like fire through ice. Destruction flowed with their flight path as ponies staggered and fell, Dwarves let out shrieks of fear and agony and the battle raged anew. Fighters formed before their very eyes – fiendish, spectral fighters composed of Owl, cloud and necromancy. They were difficult to fight; normal blades merely parted the birds that constituted the figures of these creatures. This meant the fight quickly wore down the Dwarves, for each time they struck – and they struck often – the enemy broke off and reassembled in another position. For their part, the enemy lashed out with talons of deadly force, cutting down many valiant fighters and their steeds.

Tyler brandished Cleaver using its elemental edge to the full, its blade sliced through every fiend it came into contact with, its stormy swing was faster than they and delivered decisive blows from which the Ajya-Na-Ku could not escape. Nearby Quicksilver, manipulated by Erin, was wreaking similar carnage, though some Owls did escape from its lightning slashes and thrusts. Torres stood off observing from a distance and could see things were taking a turn for the worst. She spoke with Scyther and they decided to send the support dragons of Scorch flight to aid Tyler's group.

The mighty dragons with their giant bat-like wings created a turbulent wind as they took to the air. Their powerful frames sprung into action, closing the gap between them and the enemy in next to no time. They encircled the hamlet, sending a downwash that blew damaged roofs from the houses and uplifted debris and masonry, making the whole area a treacherous place to be. The dragons belched fireballs that hurtled through clouds of Owls, roasting their hides and scorching their wings; hordes of them fell lifeless to the fields below. A huge red dragon whose continuous jet of flame chased fleeing Ajya-Na-Ku from the hamlet was unaware of a small flight of Owls that had crept underneath his flight path. They flew in a deadly arrowhead formation, and making a sharp inclination in their flight, forced their unearthly bodies through the armoured hide of the dragon.

Burning red rain fell on the land, torching trees and grass as the dragon erupted from the effects of the supernatural bolt that passed through him. The mass of his carcass plummeted to the earth with such speed that his riders were unable to bail out. There was a terrible quake as the body punched the earth; momentum carried the carcass forward, carving a deep channel in the land that sent soil, rock and stone flying up as it tried to escape the force of this impacting beast. The tragic loss marked the end of this fight as the remnants of the Ajya-Na-Ku made off to the east. The hamlet was destroyed, and none of the occupants had survived the onslaught. A troop of Dwarves and their ponies had been decimated and the few survivors were unable to muster a full section. A dragon had been downed, and this was a sad blow; but they had won. The plan still stood, and they were now more determined to see it through; but for now they would make camp, bury their dead and lick their wounds. Tomorrow they would continue the advance.

Juran arrived back at Matrosse as the battle near Spruce was drawing to a close. He was surprised by the turn of events since his departure, and had fully expected couriers to go forth, but had not anticipated Tyler mounting immediate operations against the Ajya-Na-Ku. He spoke with Benjamin, who explained Tyler's plan in full, and though he did not like the idea, Glider's words regarding a general in his company suppressed any thoughts he had of intervening. Instead he again visited the library and spoke with Chloe and Soothsayer; he was concerned that armies from the west might not come to their aid. He knew that fear of the Ajya-Na-Ku among all the peoples of the world was severe, and had little hope in their taking a leap of faith and backing some distant conflict. After his consultation he decided to remain with Benjamin, Elsbeth and Chantelle, and wait and see what consequences unfolded from Tyler's bold actions. He hoped and prayed that Tyler had enough vision to choose the right path, and that it would not lead him down the road to ruin.

Tyler's second day brought news of stirrings to the east; the Hawks had spotted a huge column of Ajya-Na-Ku heading west. The most disturbing information about this group was the semblance of order they had about them. The Ajya-Na-Ku were normally a rabble, their harsh cruel disorder was part of the terror they brought, so to see a disciplined army heading to the west meant Tyler's force was about to face an unknown entity. Just how they would react in battle was anyone's guess. The only way to find out for certain would be to clash with them and discover their strengths and weaknesses. They would follow the original plan, so troops from the Dragon Clan were readied and lookouts from the Hill Clan were posted on the ridges of the valley.

The tension was electric amongst the Dwarf army, a mixture of dread and hatred and anticipation of the coming battle. They had all seen a mighty Dragon downed by a relatively small number of the enemy, but all indications showed the coming force to be far greater than anything they had expected to encounter. Some felt the plans should be abandoned and sanctuary sought in Matrosse, where they stood a much better chance of hurting the enemy. Suddenly many of the Dwarves present wished they were part of the Cave Clan. Their wait lasted long. Tyler wanted the enemy to walk as far as possible, and for them to be the ones who joined the battle with fatigue embedded in their souls. The Hawks were a fantastic asset, and relayed much information throughout the long, boring yet nervous wait; but as the enemy drew closer their task became increasingly perilous as the telltale black clouds above the advancing column came closer. Soon the messengers had to withdraw to the rear of Tyler's force and keep out of sight.

With the enemy almost thirty minutes' walking distance from the lead troops of the Hill Clan's cavalry, Tyler ordered the initial lifts of the Dragon Clan to insert the blocking force. The dragons flew low and fast, manoeuvring between hill and mountain, always ensuring they were out of sight of the Ajya-Na-Ku and their spies. This meant long detours and hence more time; with the enemy now only ten minutes away only the first lift had been positioned. As the second lift took off, Tyler signalled for the six close support Dragons to hit the enemy column.

Instantly six snarling ungainly beasts sprung up, like six giant hornets departing with amazing speed, their wings humming as they caught the air; and no sooner had the order been given they disappeared from view. Swooping down from the head of the column, two of the dragons spewed out a long stream of fire that singed the advancing enemy. Some, catching the full brunt of the heat, burst into flame, the stench from their burning flesh adding an instant repugnant smell to the area. Plumes of black smoke rose like distress beacons from the head of the column, signalling that a battle had begun. The remaining four dragons flew down the side of the column, two on either side. The lead dragon of each pair breathed deadly fire into the waiting army, whilst the second drew along them with talons slicing through their sides. The Ajya-Na-Ku was certainly surprised by this sudden encounter, and many fell in the initial onslaught. The speed of these light dragons was amazing and did much to stop them from becoming instant casualties.

As the carnage was delivered to the column from the strafing flights of the six dragons, Tyler sent forth the cavalry troops. The mighty rumble of their equine charge drowned the valley in echoes so thunderous they could be heard in Matrosse. The assault was made down a short and even incline, ideal for a mounted attack, and in no time the hooves of these brave little animals were stomping and leaping over flesh and bone as their riders frantically swung mace, axe and sword into the survivors of the dragon strikes. All seemed well; the plan was working, and pressure from the foot soldiers was applied. They ran close behind the cavalry and mopped up the bloodbath they marched over. They had been told to show compassion, but in the heat of battle this was a hard order to follow. The enemy, even when mortally wounded, did not give up and often wounded archers continued to deliver accurate fire into the advancing Dwarves. Such stubborn determination slowed the advance of the Mountain Clan's foot soldiers, and soon the gap between them and the cavalry began to grow dangerously large. This in turn allowed bypassed or wounded enemy soldiers to target the cavalry's rear. Confusion reigned and the opposition grew stronger and more tenacious. Soon the shear number of Ajya-Na-Ku began to influence the progress the Dwarves were able to make. The dragons had continued to strafe the enemy's ranks, but now they too were receiving blows they were unable to counter. Sharp bolts smashed into their sides, the force of each dislodged scales, and soon the dragons had many vulnerable, exposed spots where their armour had been simply knocked off. The enemy troops responsible for such a turn of events were larger than the average Ajya-Na-Ku soldier, and on closer inspection it became evident they were not men. The belonged to a race long believed to have passed into extinction: Hobgoblins.

Stronger than humans, Elves, Protaliens or Dwarves, they could draw more powerful bows, delivering a much greater impact at the target end. Added to this was a unique arrowhead that exploded on impact, a previously unseen weapon now being used to great effect. Specially trained and skilled members of the Ajya-Na-Ku were employed to finish off the Hobgoblins' handiwork, using arrows that bore toxins from the Parver root, a rare plant that was only prevalent in the swamps of Markesh. They were tasked with piercing the dragons' exposed skin, thus injecting this fatal poison. Before long the close-support dragons were falling from the sky – one, then two, three and four followed shortly after; and the surviving pair, seeing little hope soared high into the sky and retreated. Their retreat was short-lived as they ran into flights of Black Owls and met with the same fate as the first dragon killed during the previous day's encounter. Tyler looked on in disbelief. His ace card had already been dealt; the mighty dragons were the most formidable of his forces and now six lay dead. Four were still shuttling troops to the blocking position and only the supporting flight, with five dragons, remained. He was loath to commit them, and suddenly all seemed dreadfully wrong.

The Ajya-Na-Ku's strength was growing and their troops kept coming. Now there appeared to be little hope of pushing them into the ambush. Tyler decided to send two of the dragons from the support group with a message to the ambush; they were to advance back down the valley and hit the Ajya-Na-Ku with all they had. He also warned the dragons of the new tactic the enemy had employed in the destruction of their fellow dragons. He ordered them to ensure the dragons were protected as much as possible and that as soon as any began losing scales they were to withdraw to safety.

Amid the chaos that unfolded before him he could see the Dwarves were beginning to loose ground. They no longer had the effective support of the dragons, and the Ajya-Na-Ku they faced worked as one. They were certainly different from the foes they had previously encountered; they banded together, supported one another and operated under an effective command and control structure. They now also brought heavy weapons forward.

Catapults delivered huge volleys of hardened rock that came smashing down into the eye of the battle, and unlike most armies they cared not for the safety of their own troops; all of their soldiers were expendable, and could easily be replaced. It seemed their only goal, aim, or concern was victory – at any cost. The Dwarves were brave, no doubt, but they unlike their foe cared for the life they had. In this they suddenly proved much weaker than the enemy they faced and their dreams of a glorious campaign were shattered.

However, Tyler had no intentions of folding and hoped the fresh attack from the enemy's rear might swing the advantage back in his favour. While he waited he committed some of his reserve troops in order to apply pressure to the enemy's flanks.

A troop of cavalry, backed by a troop of foot soldiers, was ordered to the right flank and immediately met trouble. A barrage of rocks and balls of flaming fire rained down on them, making their advance falter. A hail of powerful arrows now turned against them as the Hobgoblin archers, content they had deterred the dragons, decided to concentrate their fire on the new threat.

The enemy pushed more and more troops forward to deal with these fresh troops, so Tyler then committed a further troop of cavalry and two troops of foot soldiers to the left flank. The action on the right allowed these troops to move unchecked, and soon they were in a position to assault. Tyler and Erin accompanied this new force, and now came the decisive moment of the battle; there were no more reserves, and if they could not hold them here they would have to beat a swift retreat to Matrosse and hope the pass's natural defences would be enough to defeat this mighty army.

'*Charge! Charge! Charge!*' screamed Tyler, forcing Gee into a swift gallop. Erin on Vee was at his side and the two leading the assault quickly closed with the enemy hordes. Cleaver once again showed its might and made light work of the challengers, who bounded forward like rabid dogs eager to destroy their quarry. Gee trotted round and round in circles as wave after wave of the unfaltering Ajya-Na-Ku purged forward, only to fall to the blustering blade that Tyler wielded. To his right Quicksilver worked its wonder, slicing through the armoured exterior of the enemy forces as though their plate armour was composed of rice paper. Erin merely had to consider her move for Quicksilver to strike out in the manner or direction she thought of; such an enhanced reaction time meant she constantly managed to stay one step ahead of the determined advances of the never ending queue of fighters who lined themselves up to break her attack.

Pressure now came on the Ajya-Na-Ku's rear as dragon fire once again scalded their hides. Well-drilled Dwarves pressed home their attack, fresh and keen to quell this terrible army, whose intent was the destruction and dominance of their homeland. Once more the Ajya-Na-Ku was on the back foot; they were surrounded and fighting on every flank. The heavy weapons they had employed so effectively were quickly overrun and turned to cinder with lungfuls of dragon fire. At last it seemed the battle would be won; the encircled Ajya-Na-Ku now began to fall in droves. The Dwarves had suffered many, many casualties of their own and their impending victory had not come a moment too soon.

Crushed in a vice, the enemy fought to the last breath and none surrendered, but as the Dwarves cautiously scoured the carnage that lay at their feet a new menace was sighted to the east. The Hawks with Torres had sat off at a distance, waiting to send any message or signal as or when required. Now as the battle drew to a close, Torres once more despatched the Hawks skywards to gain a better idea of the events as they unfolded. However, once airborne they saw a second column, easily as mighty as the first, heading in the direction of the battlefield. There was no way Tyler's force could lock with another army; they had barely defeated this first one and the cost had been massive. Most of the dragons were gone, and the land units were reduced by over two-thirds. At their current rate of advance the second column would be upon them in less than thirty minutes.

Time was short and the Dwarf army had to tend as many of its wounded as possible, then beat a hasty retreat. Tyler decided he and the troop of cavalry he had fought alongside would conduct a rearguard action. Their intent was not to engage the enemy but protect the rear of the retreating forces; but if battle was brought to them they would react. However, they knew their efforts would only buy their comrades time, and had no chance of halting the enemy advance. It had taken a day and a half to get to the current position, but the advance had been cautious and two battles had been fought, so it was estimated they could reach Matrosse in less than half a day. Reaching and crossing the bridge at Spruce was the first priority, for once over they could destroy the bridge and dragons could be despatched to destroy all the other crossing points. This would hopefully buy them much needed time by delaying the column's advance.

A renewed fear spread like some malignant cancer through the ranks of the Dwarf army, and their retreat quickly turned to chaos. They had become the prey of an efficient predator that was able to root them out and crush them as and when it pleased. Order turned to panic as they scrambled to escape the pursuing peril.

They had been on the move for just under two hours when Tyler's troop was hit by a volley of explosive arrows. The explosions rocked the ground; splintered fragments zipped through the calm air, transforming it to an excited turbulence that became hazardous to move in. Blood decorated the rocks and stained the grass below as shrapnel passed through unprotected Dwarves. The air became electric, and none dared move for fear of being cut down. Fear held them in place; they had never faced such weaponry and were in awe of its terrifying efficiency. The enemy drew closer and Tyler could see that something had to be done to encourage those around him or all would be lost.

Springing to his feet amid the hail of fragments he rushed forward towards the closing enemy. Cleaver's flashing blade glowed as it sang through the air. Its blade was mesmerising and was so magnificent it took all thoughts away from the invisible fragments that tormented the space around them. Screaming as he moved forward, Tyler inspired the cowering Dwarves into joining his assault. They lost all thought of self-preservation and again clashed with their mortal enemy. The ferocity of this action was just enough to cause the advancing Hobgoblins to pause and regroup. This in turn allowed Tyler's troops to remount their steeds and break clean from the fray. They spared little time and rode has hard as they could, for they knew they would be unable to survive many more encounters such as this.

As they reached the bridge they were relieved to see Erin had secured and prepared it for destruction, and no sooner had the last pony found the sanctuary of the home bank than an explosive ball of dragon fire ignited the oil that had been liberally applied to the bridge's wooden structure. The flames grew higher and more ferocious as the first of the Goblins attempted to push over its expanse; the few who managed to beat the flames were quickly despatched by arrows from the quiver that supplied Mankil's powerful bow. With the Ajya-Na-Ku delayed, the remnants of the Dwarf army were able to escape to the safety of Matrosse; but all knew the secure area would soon meet with a violent onslaught.

The Battle for Matrosse

Tyler's expeditionary force had been in Matrosse only a short time. They warned of the rapidly approaching army and soon the city was on full alert. Benjamin had worked alongside Borlock in preparing the defences, and most of the internal caverns were now sealed in case the enemy managed to breach the city. Lookouts kept a keen watch along the pass, and heavy weapons had been positioned to hit the enemy as early as possible. Troops rested behind the parapets ready to take position in an instant. The boiling cauldrons had been lit and were ready to rain down on hostile intruders. Evacuation routes were cleared and reserves were positioned to respond to any threat.

Tyler spoke with Juran about his actions, and though they had differing opinions they both believed in the fates and accepted that the action taken was the only option then available. Juran advised Tyler to take some rest, for he had been in almost constant action for two days. The advice was welcome, as it was difficult to tell when they would once again meet with battle. Tyler retired to his room at the Drop Inn. The remainder of his company also rested, and the many casualties were tended under the supervision of Chantelle and Elsbeth. Erin had proved as hardy a fighter as Tyler, and also had a head for tactics. Though tired, she had other plans she wished to pursue.

'Benjamin, the Cave Clan are a mining community... do they ever use explosives for the excavations?' asked Erin.

'I suspect so, not that I've asked, mind you. Why?' replied Benjamin, wondering what the woman had in mind.

'Just contingency plans, nothing more,' she replied. Then a nearby Dwarf butted in, he had overheard the conversation and was from the Cave Clan himself.

'Sorry, but I couldn't help but overhear. We occasionally blast using explosive, though we don't have great quantities, and it's fairly low grade stuff.'

'Great – it's better than nought! Where is it kept? Can you show me?' said Erin, eager to follow her plans through.

'It's down in the south side, at the headquarters of the clan prospecting corporation; I'll take you,' said the Dwarf, gesturing for her to follow.

'Benjamin, if I can I'll get some sectors of the city rigged up to blow, just in case they manage to breech the defences. Warn your people that if they see me running towards them during the coming battle they're to seek cover immediately!' Erin shouted back, as she began to follow her guide.

'Fine, I'll spread the word. As luck would have it, you are the only human woman here, so that'll save confusion. Good luck!' he called, as she disappeared from view.

Juran returned to Madame Phoebe's shop to thank her for Henry's aid and see if she had any news on the formation of a Sorcerer's Guild. Entering her shop he saw the familiar face of Henry perched on the counter and was immediately acknowledge by Madame Phoebe, 'You took your time! You've been back in the city for some time now; I expected a call.'

'Sorry, other issues seemed more pressing and are being dealt with as we speak,' said Juran, turning to see the small frame of the elderly Dwarf woman standing between two bookshelves.

Pulling her knitted shawl around her shoulders she came towards him. As she peered up, her long grey straw-like hair fell about her shoulders and her aged eyes met with Juran's.

'Nothing is more pressing than the Coeur-Vu-Do, my boy!' she snapped shaking her knurled wooden stick at him. 'They come for their kind in force, but they have time, and do not need to rush,' she said, her voice taking on a friendlier tone.

'Come, let us sit,' she went on, leading Juran into the store's back room. Pulling a stool from beneath a dusty old table she motioned him to sit.

'Now, let's see, you mentioned a Sorcerer's Guild, and Glider agreed it was a sound idea. He sent note with Henry. The only problem is time. The Coeur-Vu-Do has plenty, but we do not. There are few in this area gifted enough in the arts to aid our cause. I myself only dabble with medicinal magic, and there are no others in Matrosse who have the skills. I did however manage to speak with a merchant who was headed west. He's a reliable sort and can be trusted. With him I sent word of the Guild and the threat that lingers over this place. I know he will do his best to spread the word, but all we can do is sit and wait in the hope that others such as Basterdor answer our call.' She paused and then enquired, 'Drink?' pointing at the pot on the table.

'Thanks, I'd love one,' Juran said, welcoming the hospitality. He'd had a long couple of days and had not take a warm drink since leaving Matrosse for Kumbran.

She poured some hot golden liquid into a small cup and handed it to Juran. 'There you go, this will pick you up. We must nourish our souls whenever the chance is there. Soon there will be little time for refreshment.' She took a sip from her own cup and then said, 'You must leave Matrosse.'

Juran looked up, most shocked at her sudden comment, but before he could speak she continued. 'Matrosse is of little importance in the scheme of things, Kumbran is the key – more importantly, the cathedral. The feature has a central chamber and many catacombs. All are sealed to prevent those imprisoned there from escaping. Glider oversees the magic that holds them there; he is a Keeper, a guardian of the ancients – their prison guard, if you will. The Ajya-Na-Ku will indeed descend on Matrosse, but they need Kumbran and will do everything in their power to take it. Let your companions deal with Matrosse; they're capable enough without you. However, should they fail, the hordes will flow through the pass and Kumbran will be next. Maybe with your aid Glider will be able to prepare Kumbran and prevent it falling into enemy hands. Take a companion – a healer – with you, and as many men as can be spared. Remember, no matter what occurs the cathedral must not fall.' She ended her words of warning and Juran thanked her for her counsel. He was just about to leave when Phoebe said to him, 'You have a Dwarf woman with you. I need to see her regarding a matter that is of grave importance… could you ask her to come along as soon as she can?'

Juran seemed a little surprised by this last remark and wondered what Elsbeth's dealings with Phoebe were. He however asked no questions and merely agreed to send her along as soon as he could. Walking back to the Drop Inn he decided he would ask Chantelle to accompany him to Kumbran and they would leave as soon as possible.

Benjamin stood on the ramparts of the northern side of the city looking eastward. He could see the billowing smoke rising from a distant signal fire. The enemy were coming; the fire indicated the Ajya-Na-Ku had crossed the river and would by nightfall reach Matrosse. The atmosphere was tense as the city awaited the assault everyone knew would come. People were restless, pacing up and down; fear replaced logic and most just wanted this business over and done. Minutes seemed like hours and hours an eternity; weapons were checked and rechecked; defence plans were questioned and reassessed, but only time would tell the final outcome of this dreaded battle.

Two hours prior to last light, Juran departed Matrosse with Chantelle in tow. She had agreed to accompany him and was grateful to be escaping the tunnelled city. They rode at a brisk pace, and no sooner had they disappeared from Benjamin's gaze than three riders were spotted approaching from the east. These three were riding hard and were the remaining troops from a scout platoon that had been observing the Spruce River. One bled badly from his right thigh and congealed blood caked his breeches. They reached the ramparts on the northern side and broke into a canter as they climbed the gradient.

Halting in front of Heyador, Benjamin and Borlock, the lead rider began to speak. 'Sire, they come,' he said, breathing hard, a sound of sheer panic tainting his voice.

'So it is then,' said Heyador. 'How many? And how long?' he inquired, gazing at the soldier before him.

'I– I don't really know. There were so many, they stretched back as far as the eye could see, a sea of black bodies, marching forward.' He spoke with a growing sense of urgency.

'It's okay, lad. Try to calm yourself, you've done well,' said Heyador, trying to slow the anxious soldier's pace. Then the wounded rider suddenly fell from his mount. Exhausted he hit the floor with a low thud!

'Quick someone, tend to this poor fellow!' shouted Heyador, and immediately three soldiers rushed to aid the fallen rider.

Heyador continued to speak with the lead rider. 'Now, son, how long till they arrive, by your estimation?'

'Probably just after dark. They have no horses and march slowly, but seem deliberate and without fear,' he replied. Cold sweat began to bead on his brow as his body began to calm. 'But I cannot tell or guess when the Owls will arrive, for there seemed a dense cloud above the enemy vanguard.'

'Well done, son. Now get yourself and your friend here something to eat and drink, and be careful to rest as much as you can. Before the end of the next hour we may need you to serve this city once more,' said Heyador, knowing the coming battle would probably require the whole populace of Matrosse to bear arms.

Turning to Borlock and Benjamin, a grave look on his face revealed his own consternations as he addressed his friends. 'Prepare for the worst, and let us pray we can hold them.'

'Hold them we shall,' said Benjamin, 'I'll not die this day and neither will you. Remember the old saying: *Fearless and Foolish often go hand in hand*. It is good that we are anxious – it shows we have heart, the enemy do not and this shall be their undoing.'

'Well said, my fine friend,' said Borlock. 'They should hit the lookout towers within the hour, then we unleash the heavy weaponry. Let's see how solid they stand.'

Elsbeth arrived at Madame Phoebe's shop under the direction of Chloe. She had been informed by Juran of the Madame's urgent request to see her, though she knew not why. It was now half an hour before sundown and the Ajya-Na-Ku were expected to arrive at any time. Elsbeth was anxious to get this meet over with so she could return to her duties caring for the injured in the aid post. She felt uncomfortable about the present encounter for it had an unknown sense of dread hanging over it. The dim interior of the shop did little to calm her nerves, and its musty fittings left an unpleasant staleness lingering in the air. The flickering candle half illuminated the old woman who was seated on a small stool in the shop's back room. Chloe announced their arrival and they moved directly to the old woman's side.

'Ah! Elsbeth, is it?' said Phoebe, knowing that is was. She continued, 'You bring trouble with you, I sense it and it concerns me.' She commanded the room with her words, and the frail figure before them proved to be far more capable than her appearance suggested. She paused, leaving room for Elsbeth to speak. The pause lasted longer than anticipated, for Elsbeth knew nothing of what she spoke; a raised eyebrow from Phoebe sparked a simple response. 'I don't understand,' said Elsbeth finally.

'So you are unaware,' said Phoebe. She looked surprised by Elsbeth's response, and stared deep into her eyes. 'It seems you speak the truth. Perhaps you were tricked; they can be sly and quite cunning creatures.'

Still puzzled Elsbeth blurted out, 'Creatures? I've had few dealing with creatures, unless you speak of the animals that accompany our expedition. Though surely, I am not the one who chose them.'

'My dear, I speak not of natural beasts but spectral ones,' said Phoebe. 'Sit,' she ordered, 'this may take longer than I thought. No, I sense a parasite at work here. It feeds on your spirit, playing on your emotions and your compassion. It keeps tabs on your progress and was most probably brought into your service without your being aware.'

She uncovered a cup, saucer and pot and poured a cup for Elsbeth, Chloe and then herself.

'Tea – herbal; a hint of tannin and a dash of mint. Drink quickly and do not drink it all. Leave a drop in the base along with the leaves.'

Elsbeth and Chloe began to drink, the tea was quite palatable and just warm enough to enjoy. They both drank quickly, though Phoebe motioned to Chloe with a wiggle of her finger that she need not rush. Once Elsbeth was done Phoebe took her cup and placed it upside down on a saucer. She had Elsbeth twist the upturned cup three times, then tap its base three times with her right forefinger. Lifting the cup and placing it to one side, she gazed upon the tea leaves, studying their pattern closely.

'There seems to be a link one from some years past involving a child. Do any children spring to mind?' asked Phoebe.

'My son... he died twelve years ago. Then there are all the

orphans I cared for. I've had links with many children.' Elsbeth knew her words did little to aid the reading.

'No matter, you have picked up a parasite none the less. Either a silver or gold parasite, I would guess. Has anyone offered you a service of late?' asked Phoebe, growing increasingly intrigued by the reading.

Elsbeth thought, then said, 'Maybe.' She paused, considering her words, and added, 'No.'

Madame Phoebe's ears pricked up. 'Then who, may I ask, is responsible for the maybe?'

'No – it can't be him. He's not a parasite, he's brought nothing but luck and guidance,' said Elsbeth, defending her answer.

'Like I said, they are sly and most cunning. Often they are positive, initially anyway; but before you realise they begin to drain you and you begin to slip by the wayside, guided only to disaster. So who brings this luck?' Phoebe now felt she had found the cause for her concerns.

'"Sticks" is all he calls himself. He's a poor crippled lad and asks nothing of me, and has thus far been only our saviour.' Elsbeth now seemed quite agitated and felt as though she had betrayed his good intentions.

'Have you ever crossed this lads palm with coin?' asked Phoebe.

'No,' Elsbeth said, after which she paused in thought and then said, 'I did give him two gold coins – but that was for helping me when first we met.'

'After which he probably said, "Call if you need me" – am I right?' pressed Phoebe, guessing this was the chap she sought.

'Well, yes, something like that. So you're telling me he is evil?' asked a disappointed and somewhat unconvinced Elsbeth.

'Evil, no, but he may be controlled by one that is. So shake him you must. You need to break the bond that you paid for; this can only be done by getting back half of what you gave. This will free you of his burden, but getting payment back can be difficult. He will be reluctant to pass money back to you. They're often referred to as mineral parasites, and are believed by many to be servants of ancient sorcerers; others say they are demons, whilst some say they are controlled by the fates. They offer services for payment of gold, silver, diamonds, rubies, sapphires and the like.

Who or whatever they are, they are not good and should be avoided at all costs. Now you must—'

She was interrupted by a thunderous boom, followed by the cascading sound of the city's warning horns.

'The enemy are here... it begins,' said Phoebe. 'Go now, we can end this discussion at a later date, if indeed we survive; but heed my advice, and be careful of his words – they will lead to trouble!'

The two women hastily departed the shop. The situation had changed and their focus was needed elsewhere. Elsbeth felt shocked by Phoebe's revelations, and was still finding her words difficult to believe; she ran towards the aid post with a troubled mind, and wondered what demise Sticks had intended for her.

The darkened entrance to the pass erupted as a hail of projectiles burst around the advancing column of the Ajya-Na-Ku. Still some seven hundred paces or so from the eastern entrance of Matrosse, they were engaged by the heavy weaponry of the Cave Clan. Trebuchets, mangonels and giant crossbows sent their devastating payloads into the heart of the enemy advance. The firing was continuous and the crews that served these weapons worked overtime to feed these prestigious tools of warfare. Forward observers, hidden from view, reported the effects of the barrage using channelled flashes of lights – red to indicate hits and green to indicate a miss. They were unable to direct the fire precisely but the weapons' ranges were well known, and they were all sighted in on their intended target areas. A white light was used to indicate a required ceasefire, in the event the enemy had left the area, and a blue light was used to signal a need to fire. During daylight the weapons could be controlled by their crews, as lines of sight from weapon to target was possible. After twenty minutes of continuing fire a series of white lights were seen, thus pausing the firing. The crews were grateful of the lull, as were the labourers ferrying the rocks, trunks and bales used as projectiles. The rocks were in plentiful supply and hundreds of miners cut further into the mountain throughout the battle to maintain the stockpiles already available. The bales were weighted with rocks and covered in tar and oil, and once in position on the weapon of choice, they were lit then fired, raining deadly balls of fire on the enemy. The giant bolts used in the crossbows were made from tree trunks and so were in a short supply; hence the trebuchets and mangonels were the weapons of choice.

'A good start,' said Heyador, encouraging the Dwarves around him.

'Keep an eye on the heavens,' warned Benjamin. 'The Owls are of grave concern.'

'The lull seems too long,' added Tyler, now joining the Dwarves. 'They pushed without care for loss of life when we fought them, why would they falter so?'

'Our weapons are formidable! None have ever entered the pass who come with ill intent,' said Borlock, proud of his soldiers and the display of his mighty weaponry.

'Let's hope your boast is well founded, though I fear it is not your weapons that hold them,' added Tyler, concerned by the short exchange.

The night drew on, and it seemed darker than most as none of the moons could be seen in the sky; each was blotted out by thick cloud. Visibility was difficult, making the defenders strain to keep an eye on the pass. Many of the troops relaxed, their tension subdued as they had checked the enemy's initial advance. The slight feeling of elation did however not last long. Suddenly, almost two hours after the initial skirmish a series of explosions hit the walls of the southern city, causing the valley to tremble as the destructive blasts echoed into the mountains. The volley was repeated and then suddenly died.

'What the blazes was that?' said a terrified Borlock, 'Magic?'

'I think not,' said Tyler, 'I've seen such weapons before, though not ones that deliver such a blow. They are similar to the muskets the Mountain Clan use, and fire a solid round projectile. I doubt their fire is sustainable, but maybe in a few years they will change the battlefield.'

No sooner had he ended his words when a clatter could be heard below. It rippled along the length of the northern wall of the city. Dawning upon Tyler, the noises' origin was revealed. '*Ladders!*' he screamed. 'They've broken through – prepare to defend the ramparts!'

'How? The observers sent no signal – how did they pass?' shouted Borlock, not believing they had bypassed his troops and avoided his weapons.

'It matters not, they're here – though I suspect your observers were overrun and the Ajya-Na-Ku signalled the ceasefire,' added Benjamin, quite certain the Dwarves forward would undoubtedly have seen the approaching enemy had they still been alive.

'Borlock!' shouted Tyler. 'Have your men fire the heavy weapons. If your scouts were correct there are thousands en route. We can't see them, but perhaps we can lessen their number.'

Turning toward the rampart's edge, Tyler met with a huge Hobgoblin who was the first to lunge over the battlements. The Goblin was still scrambling over the parapet and a glancing blow from Cleaver sent him back into the depths of the gorge. Now, all along the wall, Ajya-Na-Ku fighters began to appear in a desperate attempt to gain a foothold in the city. Dwarf fighters held their positions and a struggle for the battlements began.

'Oil?' shouted Borlock.

'No, not yet!' screamed Tyler. 'We can hold them back, we may need oil when the situation becomes untenable, but not yet!'

He was right; this was merely the beginning, and Borlock's call had been instinctive, not tactical. After all, he was the city's head, not its general, and as such should have left the battle decisions to Driller, his battle group commander.

Many ladders were pushed back into the valley floor, crashing down on the enemy troops below. Some of the shorter ladders, however, could not be reached by the defenders, and proved the hardest to deny ascent. Close to the eastern edge of the city's northern wall a number of these shorter ladders had been positioned and an enemy foothold soon appeared. Streams of enemy fighters began to flow into the city, the Dwarves having great difficulty holding them back. A rallying call was sounded in an attempt to push back the sudden enemy surge. Reserves from the inner caverns moved forward in the well-drilled manner they had practised many times in preparation for the inevitable arrival of the Ajya-Na-Ku. Pikes prodded forward making it difficult for the enemy assault to press home. The pikemen held fast after thirty paces; anchoring their pikes to the floor, they knelt, pikes now at a forty-five degree angle.

The order was called, 'Stand by, stand by,' by the formation commander, then he screamed, 'Go, go, go!'

The Dwarves locked with the enemy and pushed to the sides, dropping lower and allowing their foes to tower above them more than they already did. Then a sudden deafening crack followed by instantaneous billowing grey/white smoke filled the air as the line of muskets were fired over the heads of the pikemen. The volley cut into the assaulting enemy, quashing their build-up almost immediately and the void they left was rapidly refilled by Dwarf fighters.

The ladders were still a problem, and new ones were appearing constantly. Tyler, seeing that the threat was only just being held, ordered a company of Dwarf archers to follow him. He led them to one of the many walkways that straddled the gap between Matrosse north and Matrosse south.

'Concentrate your arrows at the base of the walls, keep firing until there are no arrows left in the city!' Tyler ordered them with brisk authority; he then turned to move back to the battlements. Passing a group of citizens who were aiding the Dwarf army, he ordered, 'You people, collect as many arrows as possible, keep those fellows on the walkway supplied; it is imperative to our success.'

He ran past them, not waiting for acknowledgement, and returned to Benjamin's side.

Erin remained on the southern side of the city and was directing the archers on her side to train their weapons on the base of the northern wall. Leaving them to continue their task, she fell back to speak with one of the three miners who appeared to her rear.

''Tis done, lady, but it weren't easy,' said the miner at the front of the three.

'Good, did you manage to do both sides as I suggested?' said Erin with half a smile on her face.

'We did, had to cut a bit here 'n' there, but they should work a treat if they're needed, and lets hope they isn't,' he answered, grinning from ear to ear, most proud with the work he had done.

'Are your men in position?' asked Erin, just confirming the plan was in place, though she suspected it was. 'And do they know when to trigger the explosives?'

'Yep! All briefed up and ready to blow,' answered the miner with a chuckle.

'Now we wait, and let's pray we have to dismantle them once victory is ours.' She smiled and turned to check on the progress of the archers.

With the break of day came a much needed respite. The enemy held off and looked to be regrouping and saying prayers to their gods. The floor of the pass was littered with thousands of bodies floating in a sea of blood; fortunately, most belonged to the Ajya-Na-Ku.

'Now what?' Borlock asked of Tyler.

'We wait – or we attack,' said Tyler, drawing astounded looks from those within earshot.

'You can't seriously be considering an assault! We've held well with minimum casualties thanks to the city's defences,' Borlock almost squealed his reply, not believing his ears.

'No,' said Tyler, a wide grin breaking his serious expression, 'It would be suicide! We hold fast; let them come to us. Let your men rest now, they'll need all the strength they can muster when the battle is rejoined. Keep a vigilant watch over the pass. The gods only know when they will come again.'

Scyther appeared to Tyler's rear. He had spent the night in the Council Chambers observing the battle. He was chafing at the bit, and wished to meet the enemy full on. He had already lost some fine dragons to these dreadful foes, and wanted to pain them.

'Tyler, let us pester them a little while they regroup, it may delay their next assault.'

'Aye, and it may quicken it! Let's leave them, the men here need rest and to tempt the fates may deny us,' answered Tyler, showing he was beginning to pace his actions and weigh the pros and cons of all his decisions. He was becoming a more balanced leader; gone was the desire to charge recklessly into the enemy and hope for the best.

'Fine, have it your way, but you can't hold us back forever!'

snapped Scyther, facing up to Tyler but not too willing to go against his orders. After all, he was a huge man and a formidable warrior, and had a remarkable air of authority about him.

Shortly after Scyther's appearance the blocking force from the Mountain Clan who covered the western exit of the pass opened fire on a contingent of Ajya-Na-Ku troops. The enemy had, using the darkness and the cover of the battle, slipped through the pass. The three troops of Dwarves fired arrow and musket into the enemy as soon as they came into range. The pikemen stood their ground in front of the archers and musket men waiting for the enemy to come to them. The sudden crack of the muskets alerted those on the battlements to the skirmish now being engaged by the blocking force. Tyler turned to Scyther with purpose.

'Look, the fates do wish you to fight – though not where you thought! Go now, aid the blocking force, I think they may need backup.'

Scyther turned and ran, shouting for all to pass the message to his men to prepare to move immediately.

Soon five dragons from a support flight were in the air, closely followed by a vivacious red dragon from Lead flight ridden by Scyther. The dragons closed with the enemy in next to no time and their mighty flames made light work of the opposition. Shortly after the arrival of the support flight four dragons from an assault flight took off from Matrosse carrying more Dwarf foot soldiers to bolster the blocking force. Almost as quickly as it had started the blocking forces battle was over.

The remainder of the morning was quiet, allowing stockpiles of ammunition to be redistributed and the wounded to be catered for. Elsbeth was drenched in the blood of the many casualties she had aided throughout the night. She was exhausted, and in great need of cheering. Sitting down for the first time she began to drift into much needed slumber when she felt a tug at her dress. Jumping upright with a start, she saw Sticks standing before her.

'Elsbeth, stay here! Do not venture into the caverns of the city, and do not allow your friends there, either,' pleaded Sticks, trying to hand her still more advice.

'*You!*' Elsbeth screamed, 'can't you see there's work to be done here? You turn up with your riddles, coming out of nowhere… Can't you just leave me be?' She had lost all faith in this fellow, following her discussion with Phoebe, and was in no mood to pander to his parasitic advances.

'No, you don't understand. You must listen to me, I'm here to help,' Sticks cried out to her, anxiety in his voice.

'Stop – now!' squealed Elsbeth, pushing at his shoulder and causing him to fall back to the floor. Instant guilt rushed through her body but she restrained herself, remembering it was all some evil charade. 'Kindly give me my money and push off.'

'Money, what money?' said Sticks, appearing confused. Before they had time to continue their squabble a commotion could be heard coming from the inner caverns of the city. Shouting filled the air.

'Medic, we need a medic, quickly!' a man called.

Elsbeth grabbed her things along with two other aids and rushed passed Sticks en route to the troubled area. Sticks, still sprawled on the floor, pleaded, 'No don't, don't go!'

His plea turned to a whisper as Elsbeth disappeared from view.

A new battle had begun. Inside the northern part of the city, Ajya-Na-Ku fighters appeared. These were the deadlier spectral foes, those formed from the dreaded Black Owls. They had forced an entry via one of the many grilles that ventilated the city; grilles no man could pass through, though no obstacle for birds. The initial onslaught cut through unsuspecting civilians who had taken refuge from the battle in the safety of the cavern houses. Now the enemy were reaching out and attempting to capture the northern end of the city. Tyler, Torres, Heyador and Driller led a counter-attack through the dim tunnelled streets, and the Cave Clans' skill in close quarter fighting was now tested to the full. The Dwarves struggled to impose their will on an enemy that could disperse its own body when struck and fly off in the form of an Owl. Tyler managed to cause the most damage using the magical Cleaver to full advantage. They battled for some time and eventually managed to contain the threat that had developed deep in the city. However, many casualties had been sustained, and a cry for medical attention was sent forth. Torres worked frantically to patch those she could and soon she was aided by three medics who had answered the call. Elsbeth was glad to see her friends were okay, but her motherly nature soon saw her tending to fallen Dwarves.

Out of the corner of his eye Tyler saw a flashing blade far back in the tunnel. It was Charlock. 'Torres, did you see that? Charlock!' said Tyler, pointing down the tunnel, 'I swear!'

'I too thought for a moment but cannot be certain,' answered Torres, looking a little shaken.

'With me!' shouted Tyler, as he rushed down the tunnel.

Torres followed, as did Heyador. They began to clear each house en route, kicking down doors in search of their quarry. The third house was teeming with Ajya-Na-Ku, who, startled by the sudden intrusion, leaped forward to meet the assailants. Their charge was short lived as a spinning cyclone cut through their ranks, delivered by a newly mastered Cleaver.

The group continued down the street then disappeared from view as they entered the fifth house. 'Elsbeth, quickly!' came the cry.

Elsbeth recognised Torres' voice and rushed down the street to her friend's aid. She was taken back by the vision that met her on entering the house. The room was lit by a subdued red light and she could make out the bodies of her friends laid upon the floor. In the centre of the room sat a painfully underfed boy. He sat on a small wooden stool, resting his weight on its two front legs. He rocked back and forth, laughing in a low evil drone that sent shivers along Elsbeth's spine. His eyes were deep and wide, he seemed in the grip of lunacy, and slung from his right side, scraping along the floor with sparks and flames escaping its blade was Charlock, the spirit of fire, Idron's blade. There was a blinding flash followed by darkness, and Elsbeth was gone.

Erin knew the northern part of the city was about to fall. She had not seen Tyler for some time, and Benjamin was desperately trying to command the defence of the battlements as wave upon wave of the spectral Ajya-Na-Ku poured out of the caverns.

Rushing across one of the walkways, Erin reached Benjamin's side. 'Sound the evacuation! It's too late, the city's about to fall,' Erin demanded upon reaching her friend.

'No, we're not giving up. If this side falls the other side will follow,' argued Benjamin.

'Ben, we must evacuate, there are plans in motion. I don't have time to explain, but we must save who we can.' Erin was adamant and Benjamin trusted her judgement. She was a fine woman and had proved a powerful ally.

'Okay, I'll order the signal, but I pray you're right,' he said, turning to speak to one of the soldiers next to him, 'Send a message, sound the retreat.'

'Are the animals dealt with?' asked Erin, concerned over the expedition's irreplaceable stock.

'Yes, Chloe controls the stable hands; their route is clear, they should be the first to escape,' answered Benjamin, as the first bugle call rang out.

Soon the walkways were full as a sudden exodus of Dwarves made their way along pre-planned evacuation routes to the sanctuary of the city's southern side.

Only soldiers remained covering the escape, trying to fight off the spectral enemy for all their worth. The evacuation complete, a second bugle call was sounded, indicating the troop extraction. A collapsing pocket began to clear the walkways, the last men cutting the bridges' supports to prevent the enemy's passage. The pursuing Ajya-Na-Ku broke into flights of Owls as the bridges fell, taking to the air to make good their escape; they were met by volleys of arrows and musket shot as Dwarves all along the southern city walls picked off the dreaded birds.

Erin and Benjamin's walkway was the last to remain intact; as they started to cross Erin shouted to Benjamin, 'Ben, you go, hold the far end, I'll return shortly. Give me as much time as you can but if needs must then cut the bridge.'

She ran off with the three Dwarf miners by her side. Benjamin was perturbed by his friend's sudden action, but knowing Erin's character saw little point in trying to change her mind. He was furious that he had not guessed she was up to something, and had he known would have rendered her unable to continue, even if it had meant knocking her unconscious; he thought this would be the last he saw of her.

He held the bridging walkway as requested, and a tenacious

enemy made this task harder than ever. Just when he felt he could hold out no longer he spied Quicksilver slashing through the dark figures of the enemy.

'Hold the bridge, hold the bridge!' shouted Erin as she ran towards the walkway; only one of the Dwarf miners accompanied her. Cutting through foe upon foe Erin made good her escape her Dwarf ally close behind. Suddenly there was a mighty *boom*! A sudden searing heat was felt upon the faces of all who stood on the city's southern wall. Belching forth from the caves and caverns of the northern portion of the city came a crescendo of fireballs engulfing all in their path. None could escape such heat, not even the dark Owls of the Ajya-Na-Ku.

Cutting the final walkway, Erin turned to Benjamin, placing a hand on his shoulder. 'You were right, we have lost the northern part of the city, which means this side will undoubtedly receive their full attention from now on. I don't see what else could've been done, and at the very least we've lessened their numbers. Now we must prepare to fight for our lives.'

She looked sombre; hoards of Ajya-Na-Ku fighters could still be seen beyond the pass and they looked as though they had little intention of returning to Pkush.

'No worry, girl, you were right. We could not have held. At least this way we took plenty of them with us. I don't suppose this side's rigged as well?' Benjamin looked up a smile cheering his face.

'You bet ya!' answered a gleeful Erin, 'but by the gods, please don't let us use it!' Her smile escaped her face as thoughts crossed her mind. 'What news of Tyler?'

'None, I'm afraid, and there's no sign of Torres or Elsbeth, and some of the Dwarf leaders are missing also. I fear they may be lost... seems we're the only two left. I'm so sorry.'

Benjamin looked choked as he spoke. Erin suddenly looked older; she gasped, placing her hand over her open mouth and then began to weep. They had come so far – and for what? Fighting back her emotions she spoke. 'Let us hope Chantelle, Juran and Chevon are safe. At least they are free of this nightmare. Oh, Ben, whatever will we do? There's so many of them!'

'We'll do all we can, lass, all we can,' Benjamin answered in low tones as he gazed east upon the masses of enemy waiting to assault Matrosse.

The day brought only small skirmishes, with the Ajya-Na-Ku seeming content merely to remind those besieged that they had not given up their desired conquest of Matrosse. This allowed defences to be strengthened and new orders to be disseminated throughout the city. As darkness came the enemy assault again began in earnest. Once more the push was initiated by volleys of thunderous cannonballs, fired from crude angled tubes that were anchored to the ground. Designed to be used only once, these basic weapons had a tendency to explode on firing; the shot was hard to direct and thus indiscriminate, so time and skill was needed to position these once only weapons in order to hit the mark. Of the twenty fired this night fifteen hit their mark. The mighty rock walls of the southern part of Matrosse rumbled and shook against the impact of these solid metal spheres. Rubble fell in the form of large slabs into the base of the pass. On the eastern end of the wall, the dragon's teeth battlements crumbled, along with the troops standing there in its defence. This left a gap in the flank, a gap that could be exploited by a determined enemy. Soon after the volley had ended, ladders again allowed the Ajya-Na-Ku to scale the walls. This night, however, Tyler was not there and none on the battlements wished to spend hours holding back the assaulting enemy. Borlock ordered an immediate use of the boiling cauldrons.

The order caused all along the wall to retreat into the nearest cover. The oil then began to flow. Its thick molten fluid initially dripped from above as citizens struggled to turn the infrequently used wheels that turned the chains controlling the tipping mechanisms of the pots. Droplets of fiery pain sprayed the enemy hordes as they clambered up the ladders. Hot embers and splashes burnt through flesh, causing many climbers to lose their grasp. Some of the uppermost troops managed to escape over the parapet and rushed forward to bring the battle to the Dwarves. Clashes broke out all along the battlements as the mixture of oil and lava started to flow without interruption. The torrent of heat prevented others from managing the ladders' ends. Indeed, the ladders were also destroyed, collapsing into the sea of fire that now covered the floor of the pass. Benjamin worked his axe like the professional he was, hacking through limb after limb of those foes who lunged toward him as he cleared along the frontage of the battlements, encouraging the soldiers to hold their ground and rid the city of these terrible invaders. Erin moved by his side, brandishing quicksilver with the unearthly speed it allowed. The sight of this fine woman fearlessly taking the battle to the enemy was an inspiration to all.

On top of the city Black Owls once more sought to infiltrate the city as they had the previous night. This time they only discovered another fiery end. As the huge flights landed they were caught in streaming jets of intense fire spewed from the jaws of the dragons who lay in wait – dragons under Scyther's command.

Back in the pass the molten lava and oil lingered for some time, making further advances by the enemy near impossible. Many, many Black Owls had been destroyed these past few nights, more than the Ajya-Na-Ku believed possible. The ranks of these elite enemy forces had been significantly reduced, and it would be some time, perhaps years, before their numbers could be re-established. Their demise left only normal troops to carry out the bidding of their masters, and these were far easier to fight than those from the spectral realms. These foiled assaults were the only ones that came this night; a short sharp battle that kept Matrosse south in Dwarf hands. A vigil was maintained throughout the siege; the enemy were resourceful and one could not relax one's guard so long as they were near.

The next day the enemy remained distant but could be seen scurrying around frantically. Just what they were doing was unknown but the sight of their industrious behaviour concerned everyone. They worked all day without end, chains of enemy passing the gods only knew what between them. With the night came the product of their labour. Now, volley upon volley of iron balls came crashing down along the city walls. This was not the token effort of the previous nights but a barrage like nothing anyone had ever experienced. The noise alone was deafening, but it was joined by clouds of fine rock dust that made breathing difficult. Shards of rock fell all around making the battlements untenable. The troops had no option but to fall back into the relative safety of the cavernous houses of the city. Eyes were irritable, filled with dust; minor cuts and abrasions affected everyone, and all felt as though the struggle was almost over. How could they counter such weapons and emerge victorious? The barrage lasted the best part of an hour. Scouts were sent out to assess the damage. They returned with the surprising news that the battlements still stood. There was a fair amount of damage, yes, but most was superficial and if anything the rubble that now littered the gorge would most probably make it harder for the enemy to approach. It seemed as though the mighty weapons had worked in the defenders' favour...

As the dust settled soldiers once more took their posts and shortly afterwards an assault came. This time the enemy concentrated their efforts on the large ramped walkways that led up to the main gates of the city. With them they brought battering rams and shields to protect those troops who controlled the rams. The Dwarves answered this fresh assault with the release of netted rocks. The heavy boulders, gaining momentum as they fell, smashed hard into the tortoise-like formations that manoeuvred towards the gates. Archers and musket men showered the advancing enemy making their movement treacherous. Explosive bolts were fired in return from the protective battlements of the city's northern wall. Hobgoblins had moved to vantage positions in the ruined part of the city where many fires still smouldered. They now presented another thorn in the brave Dwarf defenders' side. The weapons these Goblins used were the ones that had brought down the dragons so using Scyther's troops to flush them out from the air was not an option. Erin turned to Borlock with purpose in her eyes.

'Are there any other entrances to the north? We have to stop those bastards.'

'The chancellors' tunnels,' said the Chieftain, 'they're sealed by Elf magic – only a few can open them.'

'Like who?' pressed Erin.

'The Elf Ambassador, the chancellors and some of the Chieftains,' replied Borlock.

'Are any of them at hand?' asked Erin, eager to do something.

'Why, yes, Driller can open them – take Driller,' said Borlock, in astonishingly subdued tones.

'Fine!' shouted Erin as she rushed over to Driller's position. On reaching him she said, 'Driller, come with me and bring all the reserves you can muster. I believe you are able to unlock the chancellors' tunnels?' said Erin.

'Who told you that?' inquired Driller.

'Borlock, are you able or not?' answered Erin, thinking she had somehow been led astray.

'Sure I can, but you would have thought the head of the chancellors would have taken you himself,' said Driller shrugging his shoulders. 'That Borlock's a coward, I'd always thought so! Come, let's go.'

Once the reserves were mustered, almost five companies of them, mainly from the Mountain and Cave Clans, they picked their way through the lower tunnels of the city until they came to a plain brown door. It looked nothing special, which probably aided its concealment, but it was sealed using Elf magic. Driller stood before the door and rapped it three times with his sword's hilt. He then uttered the word '*Aquashorn*' which was Elvin for 'aside'. Immediately the door disappeared revealing a dark narrow passage. 'This is it,' said Driller, 'it's not far, stay close.'

They column of troops trundled through the passageway, making as little noise as possible. Once on the other side, Driller opened the second door in the same manner he had opened the first. They now entered the scorched remnants of the northern city. The stench of burnt flesh, like rotten pork, made their move disconcerting, and they had to clamber over many of the charred remains of copses of both their enemies and their beloved companions. They moved through the ashen tunnels, fighting the effects of the fumes that were still held in the air. Their march was a difficult one, something none wished to ever repeat.

After what seemed an age they came close to the entrances of the battlements of the northern city. The troops fanned out in the many tunnels in order to mount simultaneous assaults on the unsuspecting Hobgoblins. Shortly after their dispersal the group controlled by Driller fired the first volley of shots to initiate the attack. The Goblins were caught unawares and the few that held these battlements were quickly overrun by sheer weight of numbers. The northern battlements being now secure allowed a squadron of the waiting support flight from the Dragon Clan to strafe the length of the pass. The pass lit up quickly, turning once more to the inferno it had been the previous night. The pools of oil that had finally been extinguished were now reignited, forcing the Ajya-Na-Ku to again withdraw. Only the enemy on the ramps leading to the gates now remained. Trapped between wall and fire, they were easy pickings for the dragons' anger, and soon the night was calm.

The Ajya-Na-Ku's numbers were falling; only a thousand or so now remained, but it was not known if reinforcements would follow. None knew the strength of their armies; in fact little at all was still known of them. So the siege continued.

The next day remained quiet in both quarters; even the Ajya-Na-Ku appeared to rest. Erin spent the day clearing through the northern part of the city along with Dwarf work parties. Surprisingly, some survivors were discovered, including Heyador. He had been sealed up in a cave deep in the city, as were many Dwarfs. He told them of Tyler's demise, but noted that one minute they were there the next they were not; just how they had died he was uncertain. Bad news, but at least they knew how their friends had been killed, fighting to the last.

Late that afternoon relief arrived in the form of a mighty army. Dwarf battle groups two from each clan arrived at the western edge of the pass. The blocking force were the first troops to meet them, and they quickly embraced their arrival. Cheers echoed through the pass at the sight of this mighty force. Hope returned to the Dwarves, now Matrosse would hold.

The arrival of this vast army saw the remaining Ajya-Na-Ku troops collapse their camp and return eastward en route to Pkush. The battle was over, or so everyone thought. Unbeknown to those defending Matrosse, the block force's skirmish on the first night of the siege had been used merely as a diversion. This diversion had allowed a stronger force to push on beyond the pass and towards Kumbran.

Kumbran Cathedral

Kumbran remained silent. Glider paced up and down thinking thoughts far deeper than most were capable of. He was one of the ancients and had lived an eternity. His task as Keeper had lasted for centuries, and he held his house in order. The lax manner in which the mountains peak at Falcon's Nest had been guarded troubled him. The Coeur-Vu-Do had been a fearsome foe, evil to the core, and it had taken an age to defeat them. They who cannot be killed cannot be guarded lightly, and the very thought of others charged with the security of their tombs neglecting their responsibilities worried him immensely. Members of this powerful sect had indeed been freed, and this would undoubtedly bring a catastrophic shock wave that would touch every part of the planet. Kumbran could not and would not fall, as long as Glider held the responsibility for its keeping. He was grateful of Juran's arrival; he needed someone to confide in for he had had few companions skilled in the arts during his many years in Kumbran. A companion with magical knowledge had been something which he had missed the most in his solitary post. He was also charmed by the beauty of Chantelle, her beauty in both appearance and manner.

'You are troubled?' whispered Chantelle, as she approached the wizard.

Returning from the recesses of his mind, Glider looked up raising a brow. 'Yes, my dear, deeply. It seems people have forgotten the importance of what is done here and other similar places. This ignorance has far-reaching implications and I fear it may soon be too late. There a rumblings everywhere, even in the western lands. Your mission, for instance; it was not undertaken merely for exploration.'

'I don't follow,' said Chantelle, a puzzled expression showing on her pretty face. Juran's ears also picked up, wondering what the wizard knew.

'Not all in the west are ignorant. After all, your origins lie here. Some in your lands will know the true history of the world. Your expedition delivered the catalyst for the escape of those held in the Falcon's Nest. Such things don't happen by chance. No someone knew who to send and when. Someone in your world is a servant of the Coeur-Vu-Do and does their bidding. This is not the first time such a so-called "expedition" has passed this way.' The wizard was sincere; he had seen many things during his long life. 'Fortunately, others have failed where yours has not.'

'*Others*? This cannot be! No one has ever ventured beyond the Green Ports,' answered a shocked Chantelle.

'So they would have you believe. How else can they justify their voyage of discovery? Second and third attempts are not as appealing to the masses. No, volunteers are needed, people like yourselves: ambitious, resourceful people who are able to pass the perilous lands before one reaches the tombs of the Coeur-Vu-Do. Plant a few people in the group who were trained to do your bidding, and the task is complete.'

The wizard paused as his mind began to drift, and Juran interrupted his wandering thoughts. 'Are you saying Idron knew from the start what he was to do at Falcon's Nest?'

'Probably not; he would have been conditioned from an early age – a sleeper, so to speak. He just needed awakening to carry out the bidding of his masters,' said Glider, looking up.

He strolled towards them, a worried expression showing on his aged face. 'This is why other mechanisms were put in place, to stop such sleepers from reaching their goal. The Spirits of Sycamore, for instance. This one must be strong, well chosen, with maybe genetic input; I am uncertain, but definitely stronger than those who tried before.'

'And what of these others, what became of them?' asked Chantelle, fearful of the answer, for if negative they would surely meet the same fate.

'A few survived… most died or were taken into the ranks of the Ajya-Na-Ku. One works closely with me – Wade, a good man; he's been with me for… let's see… it must be close on ten years now… erm! Time does run away with itself doesn't it?'

'I should quite like to meet this fellow, Wade. Where is he?'

inquired Juran, curious about who had commissioned the other expeditions.

'Who knows? I said he works closely *with* me, not *for* me. He will be around, he keeps an eye on most things; he's very sharp, you know. No doubt he'll surface at some stage,' answered the wizard, who still paced about like a hyperactive child.

'Now then,' he said, standing still only to address them, 'come with me, time presses on, there's much to do… so much.' He half mumbled to himself and in many ways seemed a tad eccentric.

He led them from the small one-roomed shack they had been sitting in and along a winding track that led toward the Coeur Rock. The Rock, or Cathedral as it was known, towered above them and although structured in rock it did not seem natural, though it surely was a hill. Wild grasses, weeds and small shrubs grew over its spine and one could walk from its base to its summit. The ridge of the summit ended sharply and a small expanse lay between it and the single column of rock that stood on the hill's northern side. The column looked like a huge tower though it had none of the hallmarks of a man-made tower. The overall appearance of the hill did indeed resemble that of a church. At the tower end of the feature the wizard waved his left hand, palm forward in a sweeping motion across his body. There was a faint humming followed by a low grating of rock. Then the rock face before them began to change colour until it became a translucent grey. The wizard gestured for them to follow, but said nothing and stepped forward, passing through the translucent doorway; the others followed. Inside they found themselves in a huge chamber that was brightly lit. The illumination however did not come from lights but a monumental dome of dancing blue energy in the centre of the chamber.

'This is my reason for being here,' announced Glider, pointing at the energy dome. 'This field of energy is the second barrier. The first is the rock of the Cathedral. I protect the Cathedral – only my hand is able to unlock its entrance. This second barrier will remain for eternity, so long as none interfere with the magic that binds it. If they should, then I must maintain the barrier's integrity. If you look beyond the barrier you should just see a second dome, a dome of solid amber, the first barrier. Entombed within are the sorcerers of the Coeur-Vu-Do, the forefathers. Should the second barrier fail they will be able to influence any who are in or around the chamber. I suspect the barriers at Falcon's Nest had been neglected. The Dwarves may not have employed a magician as their Keeper. This may be why they placed the peak out of bounds, so to speak, to prevent any from coming within range of those bound within.'

Juran and Chantelle looked beyond the energy field and could see obscured figures set deep within the amber core of the first barrier. The figures were lithe, unnaturally tall with unearthly long faces and eyes that seemed alive. Their glance alone made Chantelle shudder and avert her eye.

'One thing puzzles me,' said Juran, intrigued by the whole affair, 'we saw no sign of these creatures on Falcon's Nest. How can we be certain they escaped?'

'Ah! The bodies you see are quite alive, that is true, Gilder answered. But should the amber be broken the shells you see before you would turn to dust. No, they only need vessels to carry their essence. Idron would have been enough of a shell to carry them all. Most probably they will all remain with him, for their means of conveyance matters not to them. But this makes Idron a frightful power, and 'tis worth remembering should your paths cross again.' Glider guided them around the chamber as he spoke, pointing to this and that.

'If their bodies would crumble, should the amber be destroyed, why don't we just destroy the amber? ...From a safe distance, of course,' asked Chantelle, finding a blindingly simple solution to the problem.

'Remember the Coeur-Vu-Do cannot die. Yes, their bodies would be no more, but they a beings of energy, and energy does not die, it merely changes form. Should the amber crumble their energy would be released and the effect would be the same as someone destroying the second barrier and staying within their reach.' Glider spoke with a slight smirk, for he felt the question came from the logic of a child – and given his years, she still was a child to him, even if she had lived hundreds of Elvin years.

'Now, the reason I bring you here is to signal the importance of my task. Should the Ajya-Na-Ku come I must remain within this chamber. My efforts must be to prevent the breaching of the barriers. You, my friends, will do me great service by preventing the battle from reaching this far. Should you fail it will be left with me, and given that some of the Coeur-Vu-Do are already free I may not be able to hold. The Dwarves must be told of the importance of their mission; they will fight harder for a just cause.'

They completed the circle of the barriers and once more passed through the translucent door of the Cathedral. Once outside, a man of human origin approached them. He had a rugged appearance, and a somewhat military manner. His wild green eyes were set below loose-cut locks of brown hair that fell to meet his brow and shoulders respectively. A short well-kept beard streaked with grey framed a half-smirked smile that revealed a chipped front tooth. He paced toward them in light bouncing strides that suggested a man nimble of foot. Standing before them, his weathered brown leather jerkin and thick woollen trousers showed a certain practicality. Soft leather boots had made his footfalls almost silent in his approach and given him the sort of movement could undoubtedly make him a deadly foe. He nodded his head towards Juran and his face broke into a pleasant smile when his eyes met with Chantelle.

'Ah! Wade, I told them you'd turn up before long. This is Juran, the Elvin Mage,' said Glider smiling towards his old friend, 'and this is Chantelle, an Elvin animal friend, they've come to aid our cause.'

'Delighted,' said Wade, looking at Chantelle as he spoke, catching her eyes in a mutual attraction. 'We have little time, so I'll be blunt; the Dwarves at Matrosse appear to have failed. They come maybe half a day, perhaps a little more, but they do come. I spotted the forward edge of their column last night, though it seemed only the vanguard. Maybe a thousand or so, I'd guess, and probably the same number of Owls above them.'

'So the pass fell... most unfortunate,' said Glider, brushing this disastrous news aside.

Juran and Chantelle gazed at each other, their greatest fears evident, 'Oh! My... all those... friends,' whispered Chantelle, slumping to the ground. Juran placed his hand upon her shoulder and bowed his head, a tear forming in his eye.

Wade dropped to a squat before Chantelle, 'Worry not, my fair maiden, once the battle here is done we will find your friends, this I promise.'

The Dwarf companies were briefed on the approaching threat and set up a perimeter surrounding the Cathedral. Glider took his position within and Juran remained outside, Chantelle by his side. Wade worked with his band of hunters and woodsmen, moving forward and acting as scouts. At around midday Wade's party again spied the forward edge of the enemy forces. He silently signalled for two of his best to work their way around the enemy, then lie in wait to act as spotters, an early warning for the enemy's main body.

After a quick discussion with the remainder of his party they departed company. Each moved to positions flanking the column. The first group loosed a flurry of arrows that struck the centre of the column. This caused the Ajya-Na-Ku to pause for a moment, then a number of troops were despatched from the ranks to close with their attackers. Wade's archers turned and fled and six Ajya-Na-Ku followed in hot pursuit. Suddenly the pursuers were hit from the side by other concealed archers from Wade's crew. This tactic was repeated simultaneously along the length of the column and although it whittled down the number of troops, albeit slightly, it did not halt the advance. Wade had taken a gamble, trying to buy the defenders at the Cathedral time, but so far his plan had failed. He hightailed back towards the Cathedral, sounding his horn as he moved. His woodsmen responded to his call and those who had survived the skirmish rallied at the preordained point.

Thinking quickly, Wade gave new orders. They were to continue to harass the advancing column only this time they were to locate and target only the Hobgoblins. They carried the strength to down the mighty dragons, so to kill these would aid the coming fight. Leaving his trusted men to continue their task, Wade returned to the Cathedral to find the Dwarf leaders.

Winger flew toward Matrosse; he had been dispatched shortly after Wade had broken the news of the city's collapse. Chantelle had asked the bird to scour the remains of the city and try to discover if any sign of their companions could be found. Despite the message she had heard, she still had a feeling of hope. She had dreamt that Torres had called out to her a few nights earlier, and now she wondered if this had been another example of Torres' remote messaging manifesting itself. Winger flew east and then north, ensuring the Ajya-Na-Ku column was given as wide a berth as possible. He travelled cautiously, alone on his path, wondering what had become of his friends, Singer and Stinger. It would be another day before he reached Matrosse, by which time the battle for Kumbran would be well under way.

The beastly Black Owls were the first to descend on Kumbran. They appeared in the centre of the Dwarf defences causing turmoil and confusion. The Dwarves struggled to despatch these near-spectral figures and soon the Dwarven hopelessness bred despair amongst their ranks. Juran cast a spell that slowed the actions of the Owls, making the following of their swift actions easier; even so they were still fast, and only the more skilled marksmen among the archers and musket men were able to hit their mark. There seemed to be a distinct difference between the Owls encountered here and the ones they had met before. They were much, much faster – even with the spell in action – and they also seemed slightly larger. Unlike the Owls already encountered, they showed no effort to join and remained aloft, swooping past the Dwarves and lashing out with razor talons. Dwarves were felled by the deeper cuts, and it seemed some slow-acting poison or magic curse had been delivered with their blows. The dragons from Wallop flight now engaged the Owls at close quarters. Their dragon hides were too thick for the birds to penetrate making efforts to retaliate futile. The scorching flames delivered saw the Owls beat a hasty retreat. No sooner had the Owls pulled back then the land element appeared in a sudden rush at the eastern flank of the Dwarf defences. Now Dwarf and Ajya-Na-Ku fighters clashed for dominance of the fields surrounding the towering Cathedral.

Juran joined the fray, bringing fire and ice to bear on the assaulting enemy. The struggle was short and before long the Ajya-Na-Ku pulled back to regroup and rethink their plan of attack. A stand-off began, with each side pondering at the other's next move. This continued long into the night. Wade took advantage of the lull. Sneaking past the enemy positions, he made for his forward scouts, seeking news of Ajya-Na-Ku reinforcements. He suspected the enemy stand-off was an indication of their waiting the arrival of the main force.

Reaching his two men, he was surprised by their report that no hint of other enemy advances had been found. This was not what he had expected, and he considered whether the initial reports of Matrosse's collapse had been exaggerated. If so, then in all probability the forces they now engaged were their only concern.

As night drew in the stand-off continued, neither side making any move on the other. An hour before dawn there was a blinding flash at the base of the Cathedral tower; someone had breeched the defences of the outer barrier. Juran leapt up from his slumber, a look of sheer panic on his face; the unthinkable had occurred.

Turning the corner at the base of the rock Juran observed a new barrier, though not one conjured by Glider. Rushing forward he attempted to propel himself into the chamber, but the shimmering violet aura across the door merely acted as a counter-thrust and he found himself hitting the dirt in an ungainly manner. Regaining his posture, he began a series of incantations in an effort to collapse the obstacle which stood between him and the inner chambers. Chantelle remained close by, feeling powerless; her limited knowledge in the arts left her awestruck amid the flashes of blues, whites and reds as surges of energy struggled against one another.

Wade was still outside the perimeter of his own forces. On seeing the vibrant activity at the Cathedral's base he issued quick orders to his men to watch for Ajya-Na-Ku movement and do whatever they could to stop it. He then moved at best speed to aid the commotion at the Cathedral.

Within the chamber, Glider faced a new foe. Stood before him was a mighty warrior of unearthly proportions. Formed from as many as thirty of these larger Black Owls this mighty brute pounded heavy fists upon the aged wizard. Glider protected himself with hand gestures that wielded some invisible field which managed to cushion and deflect the blows. He fended off the assault with ease, but if it were to be sustained he would begin to feel the strain; then he would weaken and any slight lapse in concentration would make him vulnerable.

To the rear of the spectral brute stood an impish creature that had been formed from a single Owl. This imp was responsible for the barrier at the Cathedral's door that Juran struggled to break. The strike and counter-strike continued for hours, with neither side gaining ground; then the break the enemy desired was presented. Glider, fatigued from the battle, slipped, though only for a moment; but it was enough for the brute to strike a glancing blow that sent the wizard careering into the energy barrier. The barrier sapped the wizard's strength and at the same time flickered. Then, in the blink of an eye, the wizard regained his composure, and he and the barrier became as one. Spreadeagled, the wizard drew on the energy field's strength; the field began to pulsate and grew steadily in size.

The flicker however had been enough for the imp to pass between the second barrier and the amber wall of the first. Out of the wizard's view the imp now began to work on the amber, making his tiny body a vessel for the Coeur-Vu-Do trapped within.

With the imp clear of the door, Juran, Chantelle and now Wade rushed into the hall.

The brutish creature saw these intruders and charged towards them with flailing arms.

Fortunately he did not get far, Juran using his short staff as a spear, hurled it at the beast's centre mass. Before the staff struck it began to glow an icy bluish white, a beam of frozen energy formed into a deadly tip similar to the forged point of a blade. The tip hit the beast full on, and immediately the creature broke up into multiples of Owls in an attempt to escape the weapon's power. Wings struggled to gain height, but all were trapped in the rapidly expanding branches of freezing air. The creature now stood frozen like some surreal oak upon a frozen waste.

Turning to Glider, Juran could see the wizard was trapped within the barrier but still able to manipulate its power.

'Lower the barrier! A second or so will free you, then I can erect a temporary field to hold the amber!' shouted Juran, unaware of the imp's presence.

'No, I cannot, the barrier is all that holds. I must remain, for one is free,' squealed Glider, obviously pained by the fusing with the energy field.

Turning, Juran could see the small creature beyond the barrier; it paced back and forth, clawing at the obstacle. Its eyes had the same evil look observed in the alien creatures held within the amber, confirming the presence of the Coeur-Vu-Do. Words began to erupt from the imp's mouth, words that had not been spoken for centuries, words spoken in some ancient tongue, words filled with hatred, words of evil. The only word uttered that they understood was *Dagtorn*, the sorcerer Glider had said controlled the dragons.

Outside, the Ajya-Na-Ku continued their wait, though they grew impatient. The main force was meant to be only hours behind them, yet still they did not show. They knew their allies, the Black Owls, had penetrated the Cathedral, and felt no matter what their gods would soon all be free and the dragons they faced would soon be under their control; when this happened the Dwarves' resistance should easily be broken. Wade, however, seeing the problem brewing within the chamber, decided the only option remaining was to fight the enemy surrounding the Kumbran perimeter as soon as possible; for should they wait they might have to face both the black army and the demons escaping the Cathedral. He spoke to the leaders of the Dwarf companies and they agreed it was better to take action now than wait for the enemy reinforcements to arrive.

Leaving the meeting, Wade sounded his horn, indicating to his men that the fight was about to begin. His men responded quickly, hitting the enemy encampment from all angles with more long-range harassing arrow fire, the type only the longbow can deliver. Again, these skilled archers targeted the few Hobgoblins who remained, preventing them from mounting an effective deployment.

The Dragon companies took to the sky. Circling the enemy, they moved rapidly, striking with fire, tail and talon at the heart of the enemy force. Troops from the Mountain Clan advanced tactically, musket men firing to cover the archers as they ran forward. Once their advance was completed the archers poured shafts of death into the enemy as the musket men closed the gap. Both groups were followed by a contingent of pikemen who protected the firers when static.

The Hill Clan's cavalry pressed forward at right angles to the Mountain Clan troops. They prodded with sharp lances, then drew closer with sabres, bringing to the battle a new ferocity. These cavalry were complimented by the finest close-quarter fighters in the domain of the Markesh Dwarves, soldiers of the Cave Clan. This coordinated assault delivered with an aggressive spirit under courageous leadership soon saw the Dwarves gaining the upper hand; in less than an hour the battle was over and the Ajya-Na-Ku soldiers lay dead on the fields of Kumbran. Wade again linked up with his forward scouts, but still there was no sign of any approaching enemy. For now, the Dwarves could relax and tend to their wounded. All attention was focused on the struggle within the Cathedral; most prayed the gods would favour their cause and that this day the Coeur-Vu-Do would not escape.

In the chamber the imp now attempted to break the energy barrier and emitted his own energy field from bony fingertips. His trail of pulsating red energy collided with the blue barrier, causing a multitude of coloured sparks to fly. Glider fed from the barrier that held him, making him far more powerful than Juran could've imagined, this ancient wizard knew what he faced and would do anything and everything to prevent an escape. Juran wondered if Glider had faced the Coeur-Vu-Do before in an age long since passed. After what seemed hours, the imp saw his power was doing little to make good an escape and lowered his arms; once more he paced about the foot of the amber.

Glider took advantage of the lull to speak with his new companions, 'Juran, the battle in which I am engaged may last minutes, days, weeks... most probably months and years. Then again... new centuries may dawn before we are through. The barrier will sustain me for as long as it takes; drop it I cannot, for he would escape. You must leave this place... the chamber, that is.

Build a city... a garrison... nay, a *fortress* about this feature! Make Kumbran again the mighty city it once was. But set you the defences inward, towards this chamber. Vigilance is needed, and should any but I emerge from this doorway, hold them back! The Guild of Sorcerers you spoke of, sow its seeds on the fields of death that surround this place, their purpose to defeat the Coeur-Vu-Do and those who serve them – the Ajya-Na-Ku.

'Prepare for the time when those who have been set free return for their brothers. Time passes quick for them, our centuries may seem as seconds; so time should be on your side. Use it well. Now leave the chamber and seal its door; my fight is eternal, yours is not. Take this gift, both of you, it will serve you well and will also ensure only you are able to enter this chamber.'

An orb of energy broke from the barrier and floated gently towards the two travellers. It stopped spinning in mid air, then popped like a water bubble. A fine blue mist replaced the orb and wove around the two bodies before it. The mist entered through Juran and Chantelle's nostrils, then disappeared. A feeling of euphoria surged through their bodies with a sudden judder. They looked at each other and smiled, forgetting for an instant the seriousness of their surrounds. Then Glider urged them to leave. They heard an alien tongue babbling on in the background as they departed the chamber and sealed the door.

Aftermath

A month had passed since the battles of Matrosse and Kumbran. Very little had been seen of the Ajya-Na-Ku since their defeat. Only the occasional Black Owl was observed, and they had been alone and not in the droves that one had become accustomed to seeing. All indications pointed to a sudden decline in the enemy numbers, making it apparent they had not expected to be beaten so badly. No one in Markesh had dared challenge their ranks for centuries, and their withdrawal to Pkush would most probably bring about a rethink in the way they operated. With the nucleus of the Coeur-Vu-Do now free of their bindings, the only certainty was that conflict would doubtless follow – but when?

The Dwarves laboured hard to renovate the damage Matrosse had suffered during the siege. Work progressed well and before the year's close some three months later the city would be close to its former glory. A series of watchtowers and keeps were planned, and work was soon to be commenced erecting them between Matrosse and the Spruce River. A draft document had been approved for the construction of a fortress at Kumbran, and the New Year would see its foundations set. Dwarf armies flooded in from the mountain ranges setting up encampments around the Kumbran settlement.

The doors to the Cathedral remained sealed and the monumental struggle between Glider and Dagtorn continued. Juran returned to Matrosse along with Chantelle, leaving Kumbran under Wade's charge. Plans for the Guild of Sorcerers would take time, as willing contributors were needed to make it work, and thus far none had been forthcoming. Juran planned to boost efforts with the aid of Phoebe and Chloe in an attempt to spread the word of the Guild's formation and purpose.

Que, Stinger, Surefoot and the other animals were well looked after and often travelled between Matrosse and Kumbran, allowing them the exercise they required, though the journeys did lack the excitement they had become accustomed to during the expedition.

Erin took position with Benjamin as honorary generals in the Dwarf army and spent their days working on the defensive plans for both Matrosse and Kumbran. They had arranged the influx of troops around the Cathedral and also suggested the construction of the watchtowers. Their days were full, and this helped focus their minds; both revelled in the renewed purpose their positions gave them, and this prevented them from thinking of their losses too much.

Chantelle was probably the worst effected. Torres was gone, and Chevon had departed over a month before. She had lost her sisters and now worked both her own and Torres' birds, though they needed little in the way of training. She spoke with the animals often, and this too made her miss those that had fallen all the more. However, as the month drew to a close, news arrived from two sources, news that gave a little hope and brought about plans for the future.

Chantelle was sitting in the foyer of the inn drifting into sleep in one of the plush chairs when she felt a soft hand touch her shoulder. She turned slowly still very relaxed to see the small silhouetted outline that had brushed against her.

'Sorry to trouble you, but I've needed to speak with one of your party since the siege, yet I have found it awkward. I do not wish to intrude,' said the soft yet captivating voice that emanated from the silhouette. The figure scurried around the chair, coming to rest at the base now, with the light illuminating its previously darkened form.

'Sticks!' exclaimed Chantelle, surprised to see the odd chap. 'I thought you'd surely fallen! Though quite why you feel the need to shy away from us, I do not know!'

'It's Elsbeth – I have finally discovered why she ignored my advice. She thought me to be a parasite… Madame Phoebe only advised what she felt to be true, but she was mistaken. Oh, my! And poor, poor Elsbeth, now she is gone. We have to get her back,' said Sticks in an obviously frustrated voice, for he felt he had let Elsbeth down.

'Get her back? I don't follow. She fell during the battle, she is gone forever... I'm sorry, I know it's hard.' Chantelle spoke with compassion and her emotions began to surface at the memory of lost friends.

'No, no! Did you see the body? She did not die, they were taken,' said Sticks convincingly.

'Taken? Where? And by whom?' asked Chantelle, certain her friends had died.

'Master Idron, he tricked them... has them, he does, but to what end I cannot say,' answered Sticks, 'Pkush maybe or even Myrkdalen, perhaps further; as of yet I am uncertain, but has them he most certainly does. I found this in the room they were trapped.' He then presented Cleaver to Chantelle, 'He could not take this, the spirit is too strong.'

'What do mean, spirit?' enquired Chantelle, becoming confused by Sticks' words.

'The weapon holds a spirit, the spirit is as much a part of the journey as are you. Cleaver is the spirit of the storm, though some say it is the spirit of death. It was created using ancient necromancy; it completes the wheel. Forever turning, the struggle is eternal,' Sticks explained, though Chantelle merely caught a small part of the meaning, it all seemed very confusing.

'Spirits... journey... eternal struggle – I'm not certain I get you, but are you trying to say these events were preordained?' asked Chantelle. She looked baffled; she believed in the fates, but did not believe they were so specific.

'As with everything, the spirits involved have met many times before and always side with either good or evil. Charlock, for instance, the spirit of fire, it always leads to betrayal. Things do not happen by chance and such weapons do not fall to anyone's hands. The ways of the ancients are complex, but enough of this. Like I have said, we... you must find your companions. Speak with the others. Plan well and do not rush, they may be anywhere. I shall keep my ear to the ground; if I learn more I will find you.' He spoke slow and gently – almost a whisper – and Chantelle faded into deep slumber.

On awakening she wondered if her meet had been a dream, but the presence of Cleaver confirmed Sticks had indeed reappeared.

Elvin travellers also arrived at Matrosse bearing a message of friendship from Selkuna the Elvin homeland. The head of the travellers spent some time with the Elf Ambassador to Matrosse, behind closed doors. On concluding the meeting, the Ambassador arranged a conference to be held in his chambers. All the heads of the Dwarf Clans were present, as were Benjamin, Juran, Chantelle and Erin. The chamber had been prepared in typically relaxed Elf fashion. A large low circular table was set in the centre of the room, about which were an abundance of scatter cushions. All present would sit comfortably at floor level for the duration of the conference. The Elves found this manner allowed for the varying heights of the different races, disadvantaging none. Set on the table were many jugs and goblets to cater for the Lannure, a type of wine produced exclusively on Selkuna. All guests were seated prior to the Ambassador's arrival, and the servants rushed amongst them ensuring all had adequate refreshments.

A series of chimes as sweet as birdsong interrupted the casual chatter that enlivened the room. All eyes fell on the entrance to the chamber as the heavy maroon curtains that formed the doorway were brushed to one side. The Ambassador led the way through, followed closely by a tall lean-looking Elf with a strikingly chiselled appearance. His face seemed almost expressionless but was most angular. Cut into this cheeks were two deep furrowed scars; three similar evenly spaced scars were carved into his forehead. His hair was a mixture of browns with a hint of gold running through his shaggy locks. The pointed tips of his ears were only just visible. He stepped forward coming to a halt to the Ambassador's side amid the gapped area left in the table's circumference. His soft green three-quarter-length coat gathered around his feet as he sat before his audience.

'Greetings and good health to you all. I am Aronsol, messenger of Selkuna and servant of its king. I offer peace, fortitude and friendship in our struggle against the servants of evil.' He raised his arms slightly palms turned upward and nodded his head to the left in a slight bow on completion of his formal introduction.

'Passage between our nations remains difficult. The seas are unforgiving and the enemy patrol frequently. We in Selkuna have had fewer incursions into our territories of late, for it seems the desires of the Ajya-Na-Ku have led them westward. Your struggle with them sends repercussions throughout the east. Pkush has been a hive of activity of late; many, many slaves have been taken into its ports. We fear these slaves will form the majority of the legions we believe they plan to rebuild. Some undesirable practices will no doubt transform many into Black Owls, for the decimation of their ranks will no doubt be felt the most.

'Our army prepares but we cannot mount an assault on Pkush alone. We look to you and others to the west to join us and crush the scourge that plagues our land. Time is needed to prepare, but time is ever short. The longer it takes for us to make our move the harder it will be. They will strengthen. We pray for a summer offensive which allows eight months for the build-up, but they too have this time and we are uncertain what they are able to achieve during this interval, especially since the return of the ancient ones. My king offers this pact in good faith and we pray you will accept, for the sake of all that is right in this world.'

Aronsol finished his address with the same slight bow he had made following his introduction. He then lifted a goblet and took a sip, still no expression was visible and his features remained impassive.

'Your concerns are well met, good Elf. Your king's offer is welcomed, though we had hoped for earlier intervention during the siege we endured. You may return to His Majesty with the seal of the Cave Clan, for any ally in these troubled times is most welcome.' Borlock accepted the pact without hesitation; he still feared retaliation for the defeat of his enemies and did not think his people's fortune would hold a second time.

'I speak for the other clans present here this day,' said Heyador standing to address the audience. 'We cannot say aye at this time. We are but generals not the voice of our clans. We do the clans' bidding, yes. But we do not decide their policies. We will send couriers with your proposals. This will take some days though I believe most would accept your alliance.'

'Your point is understood and protocol decrees your councils should be the ones who consider this offer. I shall await their answer before I return to the King,' said Aronsol, still without emotive expression – a point Chantelle found most intriguing; she had never seen so blank a canvas on any living being.

'If I may,' announced Scyther, 'I, unlike these other generals sit on the council of my people, for it is and shall forever be a war council. It is the way of my kind. I speak for my nation, as is my right. We also shall accept this alliance it would be foolish not to, or to let protocol delay the ticking clock,' he said, looking upon the other generals with utter contempt. 'We will send messages and place our footfalls forward. Build-up shall begin at once. By spring we shall have an army larger than you could imagine. I ask only that you are able to aid with provisions and cattle, for dragons have a mighty appetite – though it strengthens a mighty ally, so we endure its burden.'

'We shall do what we are able, only the waters will stop our aid, so pray for calmer weather. Your forward manner is appreciated, General, as are the concerns the others have for protocol.' Aronsol spoke with clarity and diplomacy, already attempting to quash the build of friction between the Dwarf Clans.

The meeting's tone changed as more Lannure was consumed, and the talk became more jovial. Soon the mood was almost akin to celebration, and the doors of the chamber did not open until early the next morning. Throughout, Aronsol's expression did not change.

It was a week before the Dwarf Clans had all finally accepted the alliance and Aronsol departed Matrosse. He had been seen often in the city during that time, though more often than not with the Elvin Ambassador. Chantelle spoke with the others about Aronsol's strange expressionless features and none could figure how a man was able to remain so unreadable. Erin commented that he might be some product of the necromancer and perhaps not a living creature at all. Juran dismissed her remark, saying the Elf's aura was present and he seemed very much alive. Whatever the reason, his departure made their enquiries less likely to be answered.

Two days following Aronsol's departure, an old friend flew into Matrosse. Singer announced the imminent arrival of his companion, Chevon. Warm welcomes were extended, with everyone happy to see Chevon safe and sound, especially Chantelle.

Once the reunion had died down Chevon spoke of her journey. She had indeed caused some panic when approaching the Green River ports. The dragon she had ridden was spotted some way out by one of the sharper lookouts. The whole port was placed on alert, making it difficult to approach as tense soldiers peered out in anticipation of the suspected attack. Singer had to fly the gauntlet of itchy bowmen who fired at anything that flew. Eventually Singer managed to locate an Elvin animal friend who was able to finally convince the authorities that the dragons posed no threat. When the message had been conveyed and it was deemed safe, the dragons flew into the centre of Green Port, east. The beasts drew initially timid crowds, for they had never seen such creatures before and thought them mere legends.

From the Green Ports, passage was granted and two dragons passed through the Great Rocks – the first ever to do so. Chevon headed for Caratush on Cornhill Island, for this had been the expedition's staging post where Bramley had worked the animals prior to departure to Markesh. Seeking counsel with the Protalien Embassy, she highlighted the concerns of those at Matrosse and Kumbran. The call for armies had been sent to all the nations of the west, and many weeks of discussions followed. Chevon found herself subjected to lengthy questioning throughout the period.

Just as it seemed the army would become a reality, Izacon III, the expedition's founder, blankly refused Protalien intervention in the Markesh matter. Furthermore, he vetoed any actions by nations of the west, arguing that to send forces into Markesh would openly be interpreted as invasion and thus bring the full wrath of the Ajya-Na-Ku down on the western nations. Without Protalien backing, the other nations shelved their plans for sending aid. The matters of Markesh were truly an internal affair, and would be left as such. Devastated by the decisions of those far removed from the reality of the coming war, Chevon returned to Markesh following wasted months of negotiations.

News of the Ajya-Na-Ku's failure to take Matrosse and Kumbran travelled quickly, and even the ports of Green River were full of whispered rumours. These rumours cheered Chevon somewhat, and she felt that the survival of these places at least gave some hope. So it was that she set off to find her friends and deliver the disappointing news from the west.

Of the original expedition team, Idron had been absorbed into the enemy ranks. Bramley, Meme, Jethro, Cee and Eee had been killed. Tyler, Torres and Elsbeth were either dead or prisoners of the Ajya-Na-Ku. One human, three Elves and a Dwarf remained, along with six horses, four mules and three Hawks. The journey thus far had been an uphill struggle. They had discovered their expedition was not the first, and that it had been a mere ruse to fulfil the designs of an ancient race that would not die. All were now heavily entwined in the war that lay ahead. The Mapping of Markesh had been a folly. A war loomed on the horizon and with any luck they would be the ones to deliver the battle to the Ajya-Na-Ku. But even if they were victorious, the ancient ones – the Coeur-Vu-Do – would still pose a greater threat. It looked as though years would pass before the final outcome would be met.

All thoughts of returning home following an adventurous mapping expedition were dead. All that filled their minds now was how not to join the ranks of the dead. They settled in for a long winter, one that would see them plan over and over; one that would give them time to think, to brood over their next move: the battle for Pkush.